Praise for Katie

'With an abundance of sex, scandal [...] ing glamorous setting, this is defini[...]

'The perfect beach read' *STAR magazine*

'For escapism slathered with lashings of sultry glamour . . . the ideal way to while away an afternoon . . . Set against the decadent backdrop of Monaco, Agnew's pitch-perfect eye for detail will keep you captivated page after page' *Sunday Herald*

'A scorching bonkbuster' *Daily Express*

'They don't come much bigger or better than this . . . Throw plenty of scandal and sex into the mix too, and you've found the perfect beach fodder. Just don't forget your SPF, because you won't be shifting from that sunlounger all day. 5*' *Heat*

'Expect to see this tale of sex and scandal entertaining women on beaches and beside pools all summer long' *Daily Record*

'A delectable tale of husbands, lovers and how far a woman will go to find happiness' *Express*

'A grown-up novel that excites from the off: Agnew has a keen eye on the dark side of the high life as well as its shallowness, and her writing is as lively as her plotting' *Metro*

Katie Agnew was born in Edinburgh and spent her childhood in Scotland. She worked as a journalist for many years, writing for *Marie Claire*, *Cosmopolitan*, *Red* and the *Daily Mail* amongst other publications. Katie now lives in Bath with her family.

By Katie Agnew

Drop Dead Gorgeous
Before We Were Thirty
Wives v Girlfriends
Saints v Sinners
Too Hot to Handle

Too Hot to Handle

KATIE AGNEW

The Orion Publishing Group's policy is to use papers
that are natural, renewable and recyclable products and
made from wood grown in sustainable forests. The logging
and manufacturing processes are expected to conform to
the environmental regulations of the country of origin.

An Orion paperback

First published in Great Britain in 2012
by Orion
This paperback edition published in 2013
by Orion Books,
an imprint of The Orion Publishing Group Ltd,
Orion House, 5 Upper St Martin's Lane
London WC2H 9EA

An Hachette UK company

1 3 5 7 9 10 8 6 4 2

A CIP catalogue record for this book
is available from the British Library.

ISBN 978-1-4091-2159-6

Typeset by Deltatype Ltd, Birkenhead, Merseyside

Printed and bound in Great Britain
by Clays Ltd, St Ives plc

For Dad

Prologue

'Don't look so sad,' he said. 'Who knows the future, eh?'

He hesitated at the door and looked back at the young woman with what she hoped was affection, but could easily have been guilt or discomfort. Her stomach lurched with love and desire, and her heart reached out desperately for the tail end of hope. For a moment she thought he was going to say something more, something that she could cling onto for dear life once he was gone, but all he said was, 'You are very, very beautiful. Extraordinarily beautiful. You do know that, don't you?'

Then he looked away again, raised his hand in a casual gesture of goodbye and disappeared down the dark stairwell.

'And if I call you tomorrow?' she cried out after him, hearing the desperation in her own voice. Knowing this was her last chance.

Silence.

'You won't answer? If I call? You won't answer, will you? Will you?!'

Silence.

She knew she sounded weak. Pathetic. It was all she could do not to run down the steps after him. Finally she heard the bang of the heavy door that led out to the street, the knife twisted in her heart and this time she knew he'd

1

gone. Maybe he'd be back, she tried to console herself. He'd always come back before. For three years he'd been breaking her heart, leaving, and then regretting his decision. He'd always return – eventually – telling her that he'd made a mistake and that he still loved her. But for some reason tonight felt different. The sex, which had always been so good, had felt wrong. He wouldn't look her in the eye and he'd touched her too roughly. There had been no tenderness from him, although everything she'd given had been offered with her whole heart, and now she felt used, abandoned and cheap.

The woman pulled her thin dressing gown around her shivering body and slumped to the floor. She could still feel his fingertips on her flesh and smell his aftershave on her skin. When she licked her lips they tingled from where his stubble had grazed her. Somehow the physical evidence that he really had been here, just five minutes earlier, made her loneliness all the more acute. Why had she done it again? She'd ripped that gaping, bleeding wound right back open and the pain was unbearable. Every time he called, or more often just turned up at her door at midnight, her heart would leap and she'd think, 'This time. This time he's here to stay.'

Why wouldn't she think that? Every time he left, she kept telling him not to come back unless it meant something. No, unless it meant *everything*! So, when he did return, she'd give herself to him completely and utterly – body, heart, mind, soul. Her body he took gladly, hungrily, desperately. The rest of her? Well, that he had left unclaimed.

It was the middle of the night and even London was deathly quiet. She lay there on the cold kitchen tiles, sobbing, as night turned to day, with no one to comfort her, no answers, no future and no past that made any sense. She'd given it all to him and now he wasn't there.

When she called the following day he didn't answer. Not the day after that, nor the day after that. Somewhere deep down she knew he'd never answer her calls again.

The young woman spent her days in a daze. Sometimes she'd sleep for twenty hours; sometimes she couldn't sleep at all. She barely ate. When the phone rang she jumped, ran to see who it was and then felt her heart plummet to the pit of her stomach when she saw the caller ID and realised that, of course, it wasn't him. When her family or friends rang she ignored them. When the post arrived, she'd check for a handwritten envelope in his writing. And when it wasn't there, she left the rest lying on the floor for her flatmate to deal with. She lost her job. The job she'd worked so hard to get. The one that had given her a sense of achievement and purpose. She didn't care. She felt nothing.

Her friends made an appointment for her to see a doctor. They told her she wasn't well. They talked to her; no, they talked *at* her, about depression. But she didn't let their words penetrate her brain. She knew she wasn't depressed. She was heartbroken, she'd lost her soul mate, and no pill would make that better. She didn't go to the appointment. One day her mother stood outside her flat for seven hours in the rain. She rang and rang, buzzed the buzzer, cried and waited. The young woman didn't let her in. She was too ashamed. It was enough to live in the shadow of the pain without having to see it reflected in her mother's eyes. Her mum wasn't a strong woman. The girl didn't want anyone else to get broken, so she pulled the pillow over her head and went to sleep. When she woke up it was dark and her mother had gone.

She wished for him on every stray eyelash, every crack of the pavement, every black cat that crossed her path. Her birthday came and went. He didn't call. He didn't send a card. Her savings ran out. She missed the rent. She had to sell her car.

One day she found herself walking down his street. There were removal men there, packing up a life she didn't recognise. A woman, slightly older than she was, stood on the steps, chatting happily to the men. She was tall, blonde and beautiful. What's more, she looked bubbly, bright and animated. She smiled a lot. His wife was not how he'd described her at all. 'Reasonably attractive, I suppose,' he'd said grudgingly when pushed. 'But nothing special.' God, what an idiot she'd been. What a gullible, naive fool to believe the clichés of a cheating husband! She'd felt so sorry for him when he'd explained that his wife had become cold, unfeeling and moody. That she had no sense of humour any more, that she never laughed at his jokes or appreciated any of the gifts, holidays and clothes he'd bought for her. She'd lost her looks, she had no interest in going out and sex repulsed her. Was it any wonder he'd strayed? He was a sensitive, passionate man, trapped in a dead, loveless marriage. The knowledge that his wife was such an unfeeling bitch had made the young woman try even harder to be funny, sexy, outgoing and grateful to compensate for what he was missing at home. It had been her role to make him happy. But who was looking after her happiness?

And now here was this wife – beautiful, smiley and apparently full of joie de vivre – and if she hadn't been standing in *his* doorway, wearing *his* blue cashmere sweater, the young woman would never have recognised her. The young woman couldn't drag her eyes away. She stood transfixed, on the road where he lived, watching his life unfold and move on without her. He wasn't leaving, was he? He was moving house. The weight of his lies was almost too much to bear.

His wife turned round then, to pass a box to the men,

and that's when she noticed. It hit her in the stomach like a boxer's blow. His wife was pregnant. This was the wife he didn't sleep with, the one who had a separate bedroom, who had 'trapped' him with the first child (a mistake, incidentally, that he swore he'd never make again). This was the wife whom he said he had to stay with for 'complicated financial reasons only' and she was very definitely, quite heavily pregnant. The young woman's knees buckled beneath her, her mouth opened to sob but no sound came out. A fist clamped her heart, tightened its grip until she could barely breathe from the pain. And then ... nothing. The numbness took over. Finally all hope was gone. Her fingertips let go of the rope. Sometimes, when one life begins, another ends.

Now the young woman sat cross-legged on the crumpled bed sheets and studied her reflection in the full-length mirror on the wall opposite. She was naked but for a man's white shirt. His shirt. All she had left. She remembered his last words to her: 'You are very, very beautiful. Extraordinarily beautiful.' They were the emptiest words she had ever heard. Maybe she *was* beautiful. But it was not all she was.

A fluke of nature had placed her features in such a way that at whatever angle her face was studied it was pleasing to look at. Her long, auburn hair – her 'trademark' – tumbled over her bare shoulders in glossy waves. Beneath her heavy fringe, cat's eyes, the colour of emeralds, shone out. But so what? Beauty meant nothing. Her own face held no fascination for her now. It bored her almost as much as the thoughts in her head. She knew she had done nothing to deserve her looks. She was just lucky. Or maybe she was cursed. All beauty did was stop people from looking at what was inside.

She unwound her long legs and pulled the shirt round her chilled naked skin. She ran herself a deep bath and poured herself a tumbler of neat vodka. The pills she'd taken earlier had numbed her senses and left her feeling woozy, as if she wasn't really there at all. It felt like she was watching herself in her own movie. Finally, the grief that had paralysed her for the past few months had gone. And it was such a relief. All she'd had to do was to make a decision to let it go. If only she'd realised it weeks, months, years ago she could have saved herself so much torment. All that was left of the crucifying pain was a dull ache somewhere deep below the numbness.

The water was a little too hot and she winced as she slid down under the bubbles. She downed the last of her drink and placed the glass on the edge of the bath. And then she reached for the knife.

This was not a cry for help. She had cried and cried. She had left long, desperate messages on his voicemail. But he had never come. Nor was she doing this for revenge. She didn't need him to feel her pain. He was immune to it, she realised now. This was not about anybody else. She was on her own. That was what life had taught her. No one would save her. So she was saving herself. All she wanted was for it to be over. She'd made her decision and now she would be free.

There was no hesitation as the blade slashed deep into the fragile skin on the inside of her wrist. And then she cut open the other wrist. Her head spun. The room faded to a blur. She wondered if he would come to her funeral. It was her very last thought and, of course, she gave it to him. A tear trickled down her cheek. And then it was gone, washed away with the memories, the disillusion and the disappointment, by the blood-red water that engulfed her.

In the bedroom her mobile phone was ringing. It stopped and then rang again, and again, and again. But there was no living soul to answer the call.

PART ONE
The Journey

I

Eight years later ... Temple Bar, Dublin

Molly's eyes felt gritty and sore from a combination of tired-ness and the furniture polish that she'd accidentally rubbed into them over the course of the morning. She opened the heavy, brocade curtains of Room 237 and let the hazy winter sunrise seep its half-light into the room. She sang to herself as she worked. She liked the old ones best. Songs she could really belt out. And ones where the lyrics made sense to her. Today she had a Tracy Chapman song in her head: a song about a girl whose dad drank too much and whose mother had gone. A song about a girl who had no choice but to leave school and work to feed her family. It was a song about lost dreams and dead ends and it spoke directly to her.

She sang. She stripped the sheets, the pillowcases and the bedspread and then dumped them in the laundry cart. She sang. She made the vast bed – 800-thread-count Egyptian sheets, hospital corners, pillows arranged just so – and although her back ached, and her eyes itched, and her feet throbbed, and she'd been up since 3.30 a.m., just to get here on time, she sang, sang, sang. Room 238, 239, 240 ...

People said she had a good voice but she was too shy to use it much in public, so it was here, in the big, old, grand, empty rooms of the Dublin Court Hotel that she sang. Her nan said she should go on *The X Factor* but her

9

nan was ridiculously biased and, anyway, no one would want to watch the likes of Molly Costello on their box.

She never looked in the mirror as she sang, even though the hotel rooms were full of them – huge, ornate, gilt-framed ones. She wasn't a vain girl, and didn't care much for her own reflection, although her nan, bless her, always said Molly was the prettiest of her thirteen granddaughters. Molly thought that was nonsense. *Knew* it was nonsense. Yes, she had been blessed with thick, dark hair, that when it was wet looked completely black. But hadn't they all? And Molly's was so poker-straight that it never bounced like Cheryl Cole's. Cousin Sinead was the one with the ebony curls down to her waist. And yes, Molly's eyes were the same green as her mam's had been. But it was cousin Niamh's jade eyes that could melt a man's heart from fifty metres. Molly was slim and curvy but she was also short – barely five foot two even if she pulled herself up to her absolute tallest. Molly's legs were exactly five and a half inches shorter than cousin Maggie's. They'd measured them once with Uncle Bernie's metal tape measure and laughed their heads off at the discrepancy. In fact, Maggie's legs were so long that Molly had to trot to keep up with her.

Molly had good, clear skin. But her complexion was so deathly pale that she looked like a ghost now in the winter months. She wondered if she would go properly brown if she went somewhere hot. What a colour her sister Nula had been when she'd come back from Tenerife this summer! Ach, what Molly wouldn't give for Nula's olive skin. Nula's face was always so beautifully tanned – she visited a solarium – and she was always so perfectly made-up that she reminded Molly of those gorgeous girls who worked behind the cosmetic counters at Brown Thomas department store. Sometimes Molly wanted to reach out and stroke her sister's cheek, just to check that she was real. She didn't look like the rest of them any more. She looked classy. Rich.

But Molly would never have the nerve to touch Nula. Of all the girls in the family, her eldest sister was by far the scariest. There were three years and a gulf a million miles wide between them. Nula was already married, for the love of God, and had her second baby on the way. She had a nice semi-detached house in Swords, a respectable middle-class suburb beyond the city's greenbelt. Her new-build house had three bedrooms, a neat little garden, and was full of IKEA furniture and the latest gadgets.

Nula had a handsome husband called David, who was gentle, quietly spoken and dressed in suits or golfing clothes. He was a graduate of Trinity College and he had a good job in insurance. Molly thought he seemed nice enough but he was such a grown-up that she never had the confidence to hold a proper conversation with him. David made Molly feel like a kid, which she guessed she probably was. Nula had a brand new car of her own in the drive, and so many shoes that Molly never saw her in the same pair twice any more. This was the only thing Molly was truly envious of. Oh, to own all those divine shoes! Nula's house was a far cry from where they'd grown up. But Nula didn't talk about anything as distasteful as Balymun any more. Not now she was so classy. Nor did she visit her siblings who still lived there. To be honest, Molly couldn't blame Nula for that. Who wouldn't want to escape from their family?

Molly carried on singing, glanced at her watch, realised she was running two minutes behind schedule, tutted, pushed the laundry cart out of Room 240 and carried on down the corridor.

Room 240, 241, 242 ... Finally, she was on the last room. It was ten to ten in the morning. When she finished it, she'd have until four p.m. free, when the late shift started. Well, not 'free' exactly. It took her an hour to get home, by the time she walked to the bus stop, waited for the darned thing to arrive and then walked home at the other end. When she got back to the flat, her dad would invariably be asleep on the couch in the cramped living room, either sleeping off a night shift or a hangover, depending on whether or not he was in employment that week.

As the eldest girl still living at home, it was Molly's job to tidy up the mess left from the three younger children. Shane, Joey and Caitlin had to get themselves ready for school in the morning with Molly at work, and their daddy asleep. They did well enough but the tiny kitchen was always a bombsite when Molly got back, and then there were beds to make, clothes to wash and school uniforms to be ironed. They might be poor, they might come from Traveller stock, and they might have no mammy, but Molly wasn't having anyone saying that the Costello kids were dirty. She still remembered the day at school, aged about twelve, when one of the older, popular boys had come up to her with a bar of soap. In full view and earshot of everybody, he'd handed her the soap and said, 'There, Molly Costello, I think you might want to use this. We can smell you from all the way down at the chemistry block, you stinking gippo.'

She'd been used to the insults – tinker, knacker, didicoy, pikey, gippo – but that particular incident had hurt her the most. It was so humiliating, so public! And her friends had just stood there and let it happen. Worse, they'd shrunk back into the crowd, as if they were ashamed to be associated with her. It still haunted her now. She remembered how the tears of shame had burned her cheeks, as she'd run down the corridor, with all those kids holding their noses and laughing at her as she'd passed. There was no way she was going to let her younger sister or brothers go through that, so now she made sure they always looked neat (even if their clothes were second hand). Molly smiled, briefly, as she remembered how Nula had cracked an egg over that same boy's head the very next day. Yup, Nula was scary, and completely untouchable, but she had a heart of gold hidden somewhere under all that make-up.

Their da, Francis Costello, was a Traveller. At least he had been until he met their mam and she'd persuaded him somehow to settle down in Dublin. But the fact he lived in a high-rise flat didn't make him any the less of a Pavee. He still spoke the Cant (the language of the Irish Traveller) when he was drunk, and on the rare occasions he was sober, when he did at least attempt to speak English, his accent was so thick that Molly often had to translate what he was saying to people. Molly had mixed feelings about her gypsy heritage. She felt one part proud and different, one part outsider and alien. Her da's family had disowned him when he'd married her mam. They saw it as an insult that he'd married an outsider; they thought he'd turned his back on his culture, traditions, community and family. Francis's father had publicly denounced him and over time he'd lost contact with his entire family, even his twin brother. So, as the third child born to the Costellos of Balymun, Molly had never even met her Pavee relatives. To them, she was a crossbreed. But the kids at school never let her forget her roots. It always felt like being a Costello meant not really fitting in anywhere.

It wasn't surprising really, the way her da had turned out. He was still spat at in the street sometimes. There were bars that didn't let him in. The neighbours treated him, at best, with caution and, at worst, with open disdain. He'd never really been to school so he didn't read or write well. It made getting work difficult for him. And then, when Molly's mam had died, so unexpectedly and so painfully young, he'd been left heartbroken and lost in a world he didn't really understand, with six motherless bairns to clothe and feed and love. Molly remembered that he had tried to take care of them at first but in the end his sadness, loneliness and self-pity had won. Now, her da was nothing but a useless drunk. It was a terrible thing to think about her own father but there was no denying it was true. He was more of a burden than a help these days and if it hadn't been for Nan (mammy's mammy) the Costello children would have been taken into care years ago.

As it was, the others had escaped the minute they could – Nula had moved into David's riverside flat at seventeen (that girl had known how to work her charms on the opposite sex from an early age), and Liam had left for England to work in construction a week after his sixteenth birthday. Now they were lucky if they got a phone call from him at Christmas and they never knew if he was living in Liverpool, Bristol or Dubai! Only Molly had stayed at home, knowing she couldn't leave the younger ones alone with their dad. But Shane was almost seventeen now. And he'd done so well at school, even staying on to do his exams, that he made Molly feel proud. He was almost a man, she supposed – already taller and stronger than their father. Next year Shane would go to college and then it would be down to him. But Shane was smart and level-headed so Molly had no doubt that her younger brother would succeed in life without any help from her.

The twins were the problem. Caitlin and Joey were a year younger than Shane. Caitlin was young for her age and painfully shy. She didn't have many friends and she relied heavily on Molly for support. Joey, on the other hand, had more than his fair share of confidence. Unlike his sister, he also had plenty of friends – just not the type of friends that would do him any good. Joey had got into a bad crowd lately and kept getting into trouble with the Garda. Just minor stuff – throwing stones at cars, setting litter bins on fire, smoking weed at the bus stop – but it was enough to make Molly fret about where the hell Joey was headed in life. The twins were too much for their nan. She was getting old now and she should be putting her feet up, not having to go down to the police station to collect Joey in the middle of the night.

So there was Molly Costello, twenty-one years old – a straight-A student who could have gone to any university of her choice, according to her disappointed teachers – still cleaning rooms at the Dublin Court Hotel, still living at home, being a mother to her younger siblings and a house-wife to her drunken dad. She wasn't one to feel sorry for herself, or to compare herself to others, but sometimes Molly had to wonder if life was fair, especially when she saw the girls her age who stayed at the hotel with their swishy hair, their beautiful clothes, their high-heeled shoes and nothing to do all day but go shopping on Grafton Street with their daddy's credit cards.

Molly shut the door to Room 242, wiped the sweat from her brow and took a deep breath. There, the first part of her day was done. Now it was time to get back to Balymun, tidy the flat, go to the supermarket, make lunch for her dad and sandwiches for Shane and the twins, ready for them to eat when they got home from school. Then it would be back onto the bus into the city centre ready for the late shift. She'd work until eight, get home again at nine and do more housework until she finally collapsed into the bed she shared with Caitlin at around half past ten. At three-thirty a.m.

the alarm would go off and Groundhog Day would begin all over again. Was it any wonder she was dead on her feet this morning?

In the staff locker room Molly chatted to the other girls. The maids were mainly Eastern European and their lives seemed to be as hectic and exhausting as Molly's, so there was a shared camaraderie in the locker room, despite the differences in the girls' backgrounds. Molly changed out of her uniform and back into her jeans and anorak. She let her long hair down and applied some lip balm to her chapped lips – it was the nearest she got to wearing make-up. What was the point of making an effort? Whom did Molly Costello have to impress? She called goodbye to the girls, told them she'd see them later, threw her backpack over one shoulder and let herself out the staff exit at the back of the hotel.

It was a cold, damp December morning in Dublin. Temple Bar was busy with Christmas shoppers, who wrapped their coats around their bodies against the wind and kept their faces cast down at the pavement to protect themselves as best they could from the freezing drizzle. Molly shivered in her thin anorak and wished she'd worn her good winter coat instead. She didn't know why she left it hanging on the back of her door, unworn. It just seemed too good to waste on the Number Four bus. But where else was she going to wear it? She never went out anywhere except to work and she was freezing in this stupid cast-off of Nula's.

Molly cast her own face downwards and made her way round the side of the hotel. She always crossed the road before she passed the hotel's grand front entrance. She did it instinctively, out of respect. Molly was a chambermaid and had no place walking in the path of hotel guests as they arrived in their taxis from the train station and the airport. She looked up briefly and waved to Billy, the doorman, from across the street. He was standing just outside the foyer, ever so smart in his dark green uniform, holding a large golf umbrella, bearing the hotel logo, to shield the arriving and departing guests from the rain. He nodded in recognition and smiled but couldn't wave back. They all knew their positions in the hotel hierarchy and it wouldn't be right for the doorman to be seen waving to an off-duty chambermaid, despite the fact he was her cousin, and the one who'd got her the job in the first place.

Molly started to look away from the foyer but something in the corner of her eye made her turn back round to look for a second time. An elderly gentleman stood outside the hotel, just beyond Billy. Molly was used to seeing classy-looking businessmen at the hotel but this man was different. He wore a pale linen suit, a panama hat, tan brogues and a serene smile on his tanned face. He had no overcoat and yet seemed completely oblivious to the cold and the rain. His hair, which was thick and long enough to poke out from beneath his hat, was white and fluffy and Molly could see, even from across the street, that his eyes were unusually pale. He was tall, although he stooped a little, and broad-shouldered. He had the air of someone very, very important. Molly wondered if he might be famous. There was something vaguely familiar about his warm, open face but she couldn't pinpoint exactly where she'd seen him before. Not at the hotel, she didn't think. She would have remembered him. He was so unusual that she felt sure she would never have forgotten this guest.

The man stood smiling, almost glowing, in his pale linen clothes. In the sea of grey shoppers, he stood out like some sort of angel. He looked completely at odds with his sur-roundings and yet, Molly thought, it was everybody else who looked *wrong*. Molly hesitated, mesmerised by the stranger.

She watched as he placed his brown leather briefcase on the damp pavement and took a mobile phone out of his inside jacket pocket. He looked just like the man from that advert when she was a kid. Yes, she remembered – the Man from Del Monte! Molly smiled to herself, took one last look at the fascinating elderly gentleman and hoped that maybe she'd see him again when she came back for the late shift. She dragged her eyes away a little reluctantly and started on down the street.

She'd barely taken two steps when she heard a commotion across the road. As she turned round she could hear Billy shout, 'Oi! Stop, you thieving toe-rag!' And then she saw the skinheaded youth, with a brown leather briefcase in his arms, running straight towards her. Molly didn't really have time to think. She just stretched out her leg, hooked her foot around the lad's shin, held it there for a moment so that she knew she'd got him properly, and then she watched him fall, bam, right on his stupid, ugly face, before he had a chance to put his arms up to protect himself. It was a manoeuvre she'd used plenty of times on her younger brothers and, as always, it worked a treat. The briefcase skidded across the wet pavement. As Molly ran towards it, the thief started scrambling to his feet. He had blood gushing from his nose and he was *not* happy with Molly.

'Leave that alone, you fecking little bitch,' he shouted at her. 'You touch that and I'll kill you, you hear me? I'll fecking kill you.'

Molly wasn't scared of boys like this – with their skin-heads, their scars, their tattoos and their piercings. She'd grown up surrounded by them, been to school with them, been bullied and taunted and harassed by them her whole damned life. They annoyed the hell out of her. But they certainly didn't scare her. She ignored him and grabbed for the briefcase, elbowing him in the stomach as she did so. The boy was younger than her, and skinny as a malnourished greyhound, but he was a good deal taller and stronger than Molly. He grabbed her by the hair, jerked her head right back so hard that her neck clicked. He punched her in the side of the ribs, grabbed her hands, and tried to prise her fingers off the case so hard that she thought he might break them. She could feel her nails snapping off at the quick as she desperately tried to hold onto it. Then, just as her grip began to loosen, Billy was there, laying into the lad and pulling him off Molly.

Molly found herself in the middle of a three-way street brawl. Billy and the thief were trading punches and kicks so viciously and violently that she had to put the briefcase over her head to protect herself. Still, she got caught in the middle a few times, punched and stamped on, mainly by the thief but also by an over-zealous Billy. Every time the yob got the chance, he'd try to grab the case back from Molly. She tried to get to her feet and back away but he came after her and this time he gave her one almighty punch straight to the face. After that it was a blur. Molly could hear shouting, and the hideous crunching sound of knuckles on bone, but her head was spinning and she was on the ground and people were calling out, 'Are you OK there, darlin'? Do you need an ambulance, pet?'

It took a while for the world to stop spinning and for Molly to catch her breath and open her one good eye (the other one had already swollen up so badly that she couldn't see out of it). She looked up. Above her, peering down with grave faces of concern were Billy and the man in the panama hat.

'It's OK, I'm not dead,' said Molly, trying to force a reassuring smile. 'And I think I've still got all my teeth. Did you get him? The thieving bugger?' she asked Billy hopefully.

Billy shook his head forlornly. 'The fecking scrawny little weasel managed to wriggle out of my grip,' he said through gritted teeth, obviously gutted to have let the thief get away.

Molly felt for him. He was so proud of his job and here he was now, bruised, battered and defeated with his uniform all torn.

'Ach well, not to worry.' Molly struggled to sit up. 'He'll get his comeuppance. The likes of him always do and at least I managed to hold onto this.'

She handed the now rather battered brown leather briefcase to the elderly gentleman.

'I really am quite stuck for words, young lady,' said the gentleman in the most beautifully polished, old-fashioned and campest English accent that Molly had ever heard. 'And if you knew me, you would also know that that is a most unusual occurrence.'

He doffed his hat at her and bowed. 'Gabriel Abbot,' he said. 'And I am for ever at your service, Miss …?'

'Molly,' she grinned through her pain. 'Molly Costello.'

Gabriel Abbot. Why was that name familiar?

'Well, Miss Molly Costello, how can I ever repay you? This briefcase is very, very dear to me. And the contents are quite irreplaceable. No, no, don't try to get up, my dear. There's an ambulance on its way.'

'Ach, don't go worrying about me,' Molly said. 'It's not the first time I've got myself beaten up and I'm certain it won't be the last. Mr Abbot here hasn't met my daddy, has he, Billy?'

'No, I doubt very much Mr Abbot has ever met the likes of your da,' said Billy with a grimace. Molly's dad was not popular with her mother's side of the family.

After that it all got a bit blurry again. The paramedics arrived and Molly drifted in and out of consciousness as she was put on a stretcher, into the ambulance and then taken to hospital. Hours later, still aching and mildly concussed, Molly was sitting in her hospital bed, wondering if her throbbing head could cope with watching a bit of telly. She'd had her eyebrow stitched, her fingers put in splints, X-rays done on her ribs (which were thankfully not broken, just badly bruised), and now it was over she was thinking that it had been a dramatic way of getting a few hours' rest, and avoiding the late shift.

'You've got a visitor here, Molly,' said one of the nurses, disturbing her from her thoughts.

Molly looked up, expecting to see her nan. But instead, there was Mr Gabriel Abbot, still in his pale suit, carrying the largest bunch of pink lilies Molly had ever seen. He sat on the edge of her bed for a while, poured her water, offered her posh chocolates, asked her about her job and her family. He told her that he owned a hotel on a tropical island in the Caribbean, that he'd been in Dublin on business, and that tomorrow he was heading back to the sunshine. He kept telling her how eternally grateful he would be to her and repeatedly asked her if he could give her a reward.

'Ah, get away,' she scoffed. 'I didn't do it for a reward, Mr Abbot. I did it because it was the right thing to do. Anyone would've done what I did if they'd been standing in my shoes.'

'No, Molly.' Mr Abbot shook his head. 'Unfortunately that couldn't be further from the truth.'

When he left, he handed Molly his business card and made her promise if there was ever anything he could do for her then she was to get in touch. He touched her gently on the top of her head before he left and the compassionate look in those pale blue eyes told her that he meant every word he said.

The card was green with a modern sketch of a palm tree on it. The writing said:

Paradise
Boutique Hotel
St Barthélemy, French West Indies
Mr Gabriel Abbot Esquire, Proprietor

It was three weeks later that it happened: the week between Christmas and New Year. Things had been going from bad to worse. Joey's behaviour had spiralled out of control. He'd been in a fight, he'd been caught shoplifting, the Garda had stopped him and his gang again, vandalising a graveyard this time – ach, the shame of it! – while completely plastered and out of their tiny minds on God knows what drugs. Then, finally, he'd been caught joyriding a stolen car, also while drunk and high. Joey Costello had spent Christmas on remand at St Patrick's Young Offender's Institute and Molly was going out of her mind with worry.

Meanwhile, Francis Costello dealt with his son's incarceration by losing his job – again – and rolling in paralytic after another twelve-hour drinking session. Molly had had enough.

'You can see where our Joey gets it, can't you, da?' she said as he tripped over the rug and crashed into the mantelpiece.

Molly stared, disgusted, as her father swayed unsteadily in front of her, gripping the mantelpiece for support. His clothes were stained and soiled. He stank of stale booze and cigarettes. His eyes rolled in his head and his tongue darted in and out of his open mouth as if he could neither focus nor speak. He lifted his finger up to point at Molly, obviously attempting to tell her off for her cheek, but the action made him lose his balance and he staggered, tripped over the hearth and knocked everything off the mantelpiece. Molly watched the little china bluebird wobble for a moment on the edge of the mantelpiece. She lurched forward, trying to save the bird, but it was too late. The ornament toppled and then fell, almost in slow motion, onto the stone and smashed into a thousand tiny pieces.

'No!' she shouted. 'That was Mammy's! I gave that to Mammy! She loved that little bird.'

Francis Costello got up and rubbed his elbow. He looked uninterestedly at the mess on the floor – the smashed bluebird, the dented carriage clock, the family photos in broken frames.

'Ach, it's just fecking tat, Mol,' he sneered. 'It's all fecking tat!'

The bird might have been cheap – Molly remembered clearly that her nan had given her a punt to spend on her mam that Christmas – but it was not tat. A five-year-old Molly had spent hours choosing it in Poundworld and her little heart had almost burst with pride when she'd seen her mam's face as she'd opened the present. It was one of her only really clear memories of her mother. Mammy had her long dark hair in a plait, and she was wearing a black dress with red roses on it with her best red velvet shoes with the high, high heels. Molly had been in awe of those shoes, even though, in hindsight, she realised they must have been cheap ones from the market or the charity shop. Mammy had said she adored the bluebird. She'd kissed Molly all over her face, leaving red lipstick marks on her cheeks and forehead, and she'd hugged her to her chest, and then she'd placed the bluebird proudly on the mantelpiece and said, 'There, pride of place for this little fella.' The bluebird had stayed there ever since: a permanent reminder of happy days. By the following Christmas her mam was gone.

Molly got down on her knees and started frantically picking up the fragments of china as best she could, although there was no way she could ever put the little ornament back together again, knowing that it was yet another bit of her mam that was lost for ever now. Tears of anger and loss ran down her cheeks. Years of grief and frustration flowed in those tears as she muttered, 'Bastard. Mean, lazy, selfish, useless fecking bastard,' under her breath.

She knew her da would flip at her foul language and her lack of respect but she didn't care. She really didn't care. All Molly could think about was the bird, and what it represented. She'd lost her lovely, perfect mammy when she was barely more than a baby, and she'd been left with this! This wretched, drunken father who didn't give a toss about anything any more.

She didn't see the first kick coming. She was too busy weeping on her knees, still collecting tiny bits of broken bluebird. But she felt it. Her da struck her right in the ribs, where she was still bruised. She looked up at him then and saw the rage and pain contorted on his face. 'Don't, Daddy,' she wanted to say. 'Please don't.' But her words caught in her throat. He wouldn't have listened anyway. He was too lost in his own anger. He didn't hate her. She knew that. He hated his life and he hated himself. He had no respect for anything or anyone – not even his own children. And Molly was just there, an easy target to vent all that failure and frustration on. He wouldn't even remember doing it in the morning, when he woke up on the couch with another hangover. He'd just expect his tea and toast to be made by his daughter as normal.

Her da gritted his teeth and kicked her again, stumbling

as he did so, falling over, getting up, trying to kick her again but missing her this time because he was too drunk to stay upright. Molly knew her stitches had burst open. She could feel the blood trickling down her face. Molly didn't have the energy to fight back this time. It wasn't the first time Francis Costello had beaten up his daughter and Molly knew that if she stayed in Balymun it wouldn't be the last. She kept her hands clamped tightly over her head until she heard the front door slam. Her da had finished. He'd be back in the pub in five minutes' time and no one there would have a clue what he'd just done to his own daughter.

It was Shane who found her there, hours later, in a crumpled heap on the living room floor. He took her to the hospital in a taxi, paid for with his Christmas money, and he waited while her eye was stitched back up. The nurses asked their questions: 'Was she OK at home? Was there anything she wanted to tell them? Should they get the police?' But Molly stuck to her story – she'd been attacked by a mugger outside work a few weeks ago and then she'd tripped over the rug at home and reopened her wound. Her da was a bastard, but she wasn't about to report him to the authorities. One Costello in custody was enough this New Year!

'You need to go now, Moll,' said Shane afterwards, as they huddled together in the bus shelter. There wasn't enough money for a taxi home. He brushed her hair gently out of her battered eye. 'Put yourself first this time.'

'I can't,' said Molly. 'What about you? Caitlin? Joey?'

'I'll be fine, Moll,' he reassured her. 'I can move in with Nan. Caitlin can too. We're not kids any more. We can help Nan as much as she can help us. And as for Joey ... well ... I hate to say it about my own brother, but he's a wee gobshite and he's where he deserves to be right now. You can't save us all, Molly. You've done your best but it's time to put yourself first.'

Molly frowned, shook her head. 'I can't, Shane,' she insisted. 'I can't just walk out on you all.'

'Moll, we'll all be gone soon enough. D'you think the rest of us are going to hang around to get beaten by the aul fella our whole lives?'

Molly shrugged, 'I suppose not. But anyway, even if I *did* leave, if I *could* leave, where would I go?'

'Anywhere,' said Shane as if the answer was obvious. 'Anywhere but here.'

Molly fingered the piece of card in her pocket. It had become soft and dog-eared she'd taken it out and looked at it so often over the last few weeks. One word reverberated around her head: Paradise. Could she? Would she?

'You've got one life, Molly Costello,' added Shane, suddenly, as if he could read her mind. 'Don't make it a little one.'

2

Gabriel slipped the letter into the envelope and placed it neatly on top of his other, more mundane correspondence with a flourish. There. It was done – a vanilla-coloured rectangle of the highest-quality paper, handwritten with a fountain pen in a rather elegant hand (even if he did say so himself). It had taken him years to get to this point, for the shock to sink in, the grief to permeate, the anger to settle and then finally for the plan to formulate.

The list had been longer at the start, of others who had also been partly to blame, and back then he had often turned the guilt and anger on himself too, wishing that he'd been there to do something to change destiny. But on reflection, Gabriel had realised that his role, and the roles of all the others, in the whole affair had been peripheral: mere cameo appearances, as it were. Over time his anger had solidified and he had concluded, beyond all doubt, that there had only ever been one real villain of the piece. While many people had been guilty of inaction, it was the actions of this man that had done the damage.

Gabriel fingered the envelope with satisfaction; the name was so familiar to him, the address too. Damn, even his life story was as familiar to Gabriel as his own, although he had yet to meet the man in question. This was the star of the show. Now all he needed was for that 'star' to accept Gabriel's generous invitation. Which of course he would. Gabriel had checked the man's schedule; it had been difficult to find a gap, but in two weeks' time, he knew the bastard was free. And who would turn down a luxury holiday in the Caribbean when someone else was picking up the tab? An angel would find it difficult to say no; the Devil would be packing his swimming trunks in an instant.

In his younger days, Gabriel had been hot-headed. If somebody had crossed him, or hurt him, he'd sought revenge straight away. But age had taught Gabriel to be patient. Revenge – no, not just revenge, *retribution* – was a dish best served cold. And it would be all the more delicious after all these years.

Satisfied with his work, Gabriel sat back in his creaky wicker chair, stretched his legs in front of him and took in the view. It had been twenty years since he had first escaped here – heartbroken, lonely, reeling with grief, so damaged by life and battered by death that he was barely able to limp through the days any more. This tiny speck of an island in the French West Indies had proved his salvation, and his sanctuary. It had saved his sanity and soothed his soul. And while Gabriel had never been able to truly find happiness again, he had managed to find a place where he was at peace. Paradise. His Paradise. His hotel.

He was an old man now. The face in the mirror still took him by surprise sometimes – the shock of white hair, the brown leathery face, the bushy eyebrows, the slight stoop of his frame. The bone structure that had once supported his elegant features had long since disappeared under jowls and collapsing brows. It was a tragedy, Gabriel thought, the damage that time ravaged on the human body. And the irony was that just as his mind had ceased to torment him, just as he felt comfortable in his own skin and just as he had finally, finally, 'got it' – this crazy, confusing, painful, beautiful, awe-inspiring world – his body had begun letting him down. Everything hurt, just a little. Movement was less fluid. The feeling of running free down the beach was as distant and delicious a memory as that of his last sweet kiss. He sighed at the memory and his stomach did a small, involuntary somersault. But still, it wasn't so bad, Gabriel mused. The ghosts of the past walked slowly beside him along the sand now, supporting him, helping him on his way, their invisible footprints washed away with his own by the waves. It wouldn't be long now. His work here was almost done and then he would leave Paradise for ever.

It had rained overnight and now, in the bright morning sunlight, the lush green foliage, the clear blue sky and the turquoise ocean seemed to glow as if someone had turned up the contrast on the great television set in the sky. Even beneath the wide brim of his panama hat, Gabriel had to squint to make out the figure in white, winding its way up the path from the plantation house. Eventually he realised it was Molly, the new maid, coming to clean his cottage.

'Ah, Molly! My little Warrior Princess. How are you settling in?'

Molly blushed, and rearranged the pile of towels in her arms self-consciously. She was barely five feet tall and her frame was tiny. But Gabriel knew from experience that the little Irish beauty was no weakling. She'd been at the hotel for less than a week and her skin was still deathly pale against her long black hair. Still, Gabriel noted, her alabaster hue only heightened the drama of those piercing green eyes. Those eyes reminded him so much of … no … he mustn't be a sentimental old fool … now wasn't the time.

'I'm very well, thank you, Mr Abbot,' replied young Molly,

brightly. 'I can't thank you enough for this opportunity. I'm blown away by Paradise, and by the island, I really am.'

'No need to thank me, Molly. As you well know, it is I who will for ever be indebted to you.'

He bowed theatrically to the little chambermaid. 'And for goodness' sake call me Gabriel – I insist that everybody does. Although most of the staff call me Mr Gabriel, or Monsieur Gabriel ...' He mimicked the French staff. 'But I prefer plain old Gabriel, I really do. Christian names make one feel young. And I need all the help I can get to cling onto my long-lost youth.'

Molly giggled.

'You're the boss, Mr Ab—, I mean, um, Gabriel, but I do need you to know what a huge deal this is for me. For someone like me to end up in a place like this, it's mind-blowing! I'd never have got here in my life if I hadn't met you. I doubt I'd ever have got out of Dublin. Sometimes I think you might be my Fairy Godfather.'

Molly had a mischievous twinkle in those gorgeous green eyes and that was just one of the reasons that Gabriel completely adored her. She also had a background he could relate to. He knew how difficult it was to escape poverty. His own journey had been traumatic. But he'd made it and he was sure Molly could too – with his help. Gabriel had made a habit of playing God with talented youngsters over the years and it made him proud to see how well his chosen ones had done in life. Perhaps he could have given her a more glamorous role than chambermaid but it was import-ant she started at the bottom, worked hard, proved herself and earned her status as one of his little disciples. Besides, it was the job she was doing when he found her, so it made perfect sense.

Gabriel suspected Molly would rise quickly through the

ranks at Paradise with or without him. Despite her background, she seemed well read, articulate and keen to better herself. What's more, she positively radiated goodness and joy. She was a veritable little ray of sunshine and Gabriel really enjoyed having her around. Even better, she seemed to instinctively understand the game. She'd just called him her Fairy Godfather and that was exactly what he was. It was a shame that he wouldn't be around to see her reach her full potential but he'd given her one foot on the ladder, just as someone had once done for him. The rest would be up to Molly.

Molly grinned, showing perfect, straight, little white teeth. He noticed that the wound above her right eye was healing quickly now that the sun had got to it and he hoped that it wouldn't leave too bad a scar. She really was such a striking beauty. And the most charming thing was that, unlike the conceited French mademoiselles he normally employed, Molly was completely oblivious to her looks.

'Well, there we are,' she said. 'What a lucky girl I am! Now, may I see to your room, or am I disturbing you?'

'No, no, it's fine,' said Gabriel fondly. 'Clean away, clean away. I have some letters to get in the post and I really must check on Delilah. Is there any sign of Her Majesty this morning?'

'Not that I've seen, Mr A—, um, Gabriel, but I haven't been to her room yet. I get the impression that Miss Delilah prefers a lie-in so I thought I should do her last. Am I right?' asked Molly, obviously eager to please.

'You are indeed, Molly. I knew you were a clever girl. Yes, Delilah has many charms but she is certainly not at her best in the morning. It is a wise chambermaid indeed who leaves room twelve until last. I shall look in on her anon.'

As was his habit, he doffed his panama hat at Molly,

who blushed and giggled again, and then carried on slowly, because his bones ached, towards the main house. It still made Gabriel proud to walk through his resort, smiling hello to his glamorous guests, feeling the warmth of the sun on his skin, listening to the birds and the rustle of the palms in the breeze, admiring both the breathtaking ocean views and the quaint cottages he'd had built, dodging the golf buggies the staff used to ferry the guests to and from the beach, checking that the tennis courts were pristine and that the infinity pool was picture-postcard perfect, perusing the menu outside the à la carte restaurant as he passed by to see what would be on offer that evening. Ah, perfection. Just as they had planned.

The guests would never imagine now how this piece of land had looked twenty-five years ago when he'd first stumbled across it. Or at least when Benjamin had stumbled across it. How typical of dear Benjamin to lead him off the beaten track! They'd been holidaying at Eden Rock as usual. Benjamin was addicted to St Barts, had been ever since Gabriel had first introduced him to the island ten years earlier. He adored the island's French chicness, its innate glamour, the yachts, the beaches, the cocktails, the beautiful people who both lived and holidayed here. Most of all he loved the fact that Gabriel had been coming here since the island's heyday in the 1960s. It appealed to Benjamin's boyish imagination that he was walking on the same sand as some of the Hollywood greats.

They'd been in a big party as always. Their great friends Willow and Buck Starling had been there that year, and that outrageous lesbian couple (whom nobody ever outed, come to think of it), and also some poor young actress who was pretending to be Benjamin's latest squeeze at the time. Gabriel forgot her name. There had been so many of them

32

over the years, bribed by the studio to 'act' the part. Unfortunately none of them had much talent for their chosen profession so they'd quickly be replaced by the next, and the next, and the next. Some of the silly little cows even thought they could make the sham real. They thought they were so hot they could 'turn' him and become his girlfriend in reality. But Benjamin was gay through and through, despite the public image. Of course the press had a field day with the ever-changing beauty parade of new girlfriends. They labelled poor Benjamin a womaniser and a heartbreaker because he never settled down. Oh, the irony! Poor Benjamin was faithful to Gabriel for more than fifteen years. Well, *almost* faithful …

It had been tough for both of them to keep up the charade but it had been absolutely essential for Benjamin's career. Benjamin – or Ben Houston as the world knew him – was one of the highest-earning, most lusted-after, manly, butch, all-American actors of the eighties. In private, he was one hundred per cent homosexual, but on screen he spent his time blowing up buildings, shooting baddies and bedding voluptuous blondes. Ben Houston was simply not allowed to be gay. Not when half the teenage girls in America had his poster on their wall.

And so he and Gabriel hid their relationship. This made having any private time almost impossible. Particularly since Gabriel was also in the public eye. Oh, he wasn't nearly as famous as Benjamin, of course not. Benjamin was always the star of the show and Gabriel had been happy just to bask in his glow. But at that time, he was a little ashamed to admit, Gabriel had been playing a camp butler in a rather lowbrow sitcom and, after years of relative obscurity, that had made him recognisable again. He was also publicly gay.

So, for poor Ben Houston, any association with the older actor was bad PR.

What it did mean was that it was difficult for the couple to go anywhere together in public, even when they were on holiday somewhere as tiny, as intimate and as far-flung as St Barts, just in case a paparazzo was hiding behind a palm tree with a long lens. Hence the group vacations and the fake girlfriends. Mostly, the couple spent their time at Eden Rock, or in the bars and restaurants of St Jean and Gustavia with their friends, being careful never to so much as brush hands. But every now and then they'd get some time together, just the two of them – sundowners at Shell Beach, or a day on a chartered private yacht.

One day, during this particular holiday, they'd decided to take a risk, hired a jeep and taken it off round the island to explore. Which was easy to do, since St Barts is only eight square miles in all. They'd headed north-east from St Jean, away from the crowds, following the winding coast road, past Lorient and Marigot and then as they'd approached the most easterly part of the island they'd taken a track down towards the coast, for no other reason than they'd been hungry and ready for the picnic they'd had prepared back at the hotel. The track, it turned out, got narrower and narrower and eventually disappeared. The jeep had ended up wedged between a couple of palm trees and they'd had to resort to finding the beach on foot. Benjamin, who'd been the one driving, had found this hilarious but Gabriel remembered how he'd got a bit cross and scolded his partner for scratching the jeep's paintwork.

Benjamin, playing the action hero again, had gone ahead, clearing a path through the palms and shrubs with a large stick. They'd stared in awe as a huge turtle crawled out from the undergrowth and scuttled away and then Benjamin, not playing the action hero this time, had actually let out a scream when an enormous iguana had suddenly appeared in their path. Finally, sweating and hungry, they'd fought their way through the trees and found themselves in a clearing. And then they'd seen it – the Plantation House. The white paint had peeled off almost entirely, leaving only bleached wood behind; the wooden veranda had collapsed, and the roof had obviously been blown off by many hurricane seasons. And yet the huge, grand, abandoned house was the most breathtakingly beautiful place either of them had ever seen. It sat perched on a plateau about fifty metres above the sparkling turquoise ocean, flanked by the tallest palm trees imaginable.

'It's paradise,' is all that Benjamin had said.

And it was. And it still is, thought Gabriel, wiping a stray tear from his cheek. If only his darling Benjamin could see it now.

But Benjamin never saw Paradise again. It wasn't long after they returned home from that trip that Benjamin started to get ill. The disease, when it took hold, destroyed him quickly. There was very little understanding of HIV/ Aids back then and there were no drugs to treat it. People were terrified of this 'gay epidemic' and anyone who got sick was ostracised and feared like a leper. Benjamin's agent made the world believe that Ben Houston had cancer but his friends knew the truth.

One of the most difficult parts of that horrific time for Gabriel was having to face the fact that Benjamin had not been loyal after all. He lay in his hospital bed, painfully thin, grey and weak, and sobbed as he admitted to Gabriel that there had been just one indiscretion. Some people are not allowed to make mistakes. There would have been no point in Gabriel getting angry with Benjamin (although the infidelity cut his heart in two). Benjamin was receiving the ultimate punishment for being unfaithful. The sentence far outweighed the crime – it was a death penalty. So Gabriel swallowed his anger and looked after Benjamin as best he could in those last few weeks. When Ben Houston died, he did so in Gabriel's arms, knowing he was loved and forgiven.

And then, just as Gabriel was disintegrating under the weight of his loss, all hell broke loose. The press got hold of the truth and all the secrets and lies came tumbling out. Endless column inches and television minutes were given over to the story of Ben Houston – closet homosexual, sexual predator, Aids victim, liar, cheat. Inevitably Gabriel's name was dragged through the mud too. Life in LA changed for ever. It was destroyed, buried alongside Ben Houston's body, and it could never rise again. A chapter was over.

Gabriel was middle-aged by now, Benjamin was gone, and he found himself alone and in pieces. But he was still alive. By some miracle he had been given the all-clear. Benjamin had not infected him with the disease. Gabriel had always been a fighter and although there were days when he wanted to die, there were other days when he found himself thinking, 'What now?'. Often, when he lay on his bed, staring at the ceiling, feeling empty and wretched, it was the image of the beach in St Barts that soothed his mind. Gabriel could never have his beloved Benjamin back, but he could continue their dream. He bought the land in St Barts, left California for ever, and out of pain, anger, hatred and despair, Paradise was born.

But that was all such a very, very long time ago … Gabriel took a deep breath and composed himself before entering the reception area. The air-conditioning hit him like an Arctic wind and he shivered in his thin shirt. Quite why the guests wanted it this cool inside he would never understand.

The majority were from the States, many popped over from Miami, and he guessed that for them goose bumps were a luxury. But Gabriel was British. And even though he'd left the smog of post-war London behind more than half a century ago he could still feel the chill of a damp East End slum in his bones. The journey that had taken him from Bow, to New York, to LA, and then finally to Paradise, had been a harrowing one but it had almost certainly saved his life. And he hated to be reminded of the days before the sunshine.

'For goodness' sake, it feels like a morgue in here, Serge,' announced Gabriel as he strode past the concierge desk. 'Turn it up a couple of degrees, please; I am an elderly gentleman and I do not wish to catch pneumonia, thank you.'

Serge looked stricken. He was a bright, eager Ukrainian boy. Or man, Gabriel guessed. Probably in his early thirties, but to Gabriel anyone under fifty was a boy. Anyway Serge took his job very seriously and was incredibly loyal. He understood that while the guests were of the utmost import-ance, at the end of the day it was Gabriel who ran the show. He took any criticism from his boss very personally and Gabriel lived in dread of making the poor boy cry.

'I shall do it immediately, Mr Gabriel,' said Serge, sliding on the highly polished wooden floor in his leather-soled shoes, as he rushed to turn up the thermostat.

'Thank you, Serge. Efficient as always. Now, my dear, Colette,' Gabriel spoke to one of the receptionists. Another identikit French girl, taking a year off after gaining her degree from Strasbourg University. 'I need these posted at your earliest convenience. This one is of particular import-ance.'

He placed his letters on the marble desk in front of her and tapped the handwritten envelope on top. 'In fact, it is so imperative that this does not get misplaced that I would like you to go to Gustavia yourself and personally hand it in at La Poste. Have it sent guaranteed first class and make sure it's done before lunch.'

'Of course, Monsieur Gabriel,' said Colette, nodding obediently.

'Has Delilah shown her face yet this morning, anyone?' Gabriel asked his reception staff.

They all shook their heads.

'Serge, get the kitchen to send her breakfast up to her room immediately. And for heaven's sake make sure her fresh orange juice doesn't have bits in it. You know what a fuss she makes about that.'

'Of course, Mr Gabriel,' Serge nodded obediently.

'I shall see you all anon, my dears. Until then have a marvellous day.' Gabriel doffed his hat and headed back into the warmth of the Caribbean sun.

He strolled towards room twelve, saying hello brightly to the guests who were either making their way back from breakfast, or towards the beach, depending on how early they'd started their day. Darius and Simon, the gorgeous young gay couple from Miami, who visited Paradise at least twice a year, stopped for a quick chat. Yes, their design company was going from strength to strength; yes, they'd had a wonderful Christmas with Simon's mother in Vermont; yes, the dogs were just fine thank you; yes, they were absolutely delighted to be back in St Barts; and yes, they'd just finished in the gym before another *exhausting* day reading and sunbathing on the beach.

'No rest for us wicked boys, eh?' laughed Darius as he and his boyfriend headed back to their room, no doubt to change back into those minuscule bathing shorts they both wore so well.

'Ciao, Gabriel,' they called over their bronzed shoulders, holding hands as they strolled up the hill.

It warmed Gabriel's heart to see a gay couple being able to enjoy their relationship so publicly. He guessed Darius and Simon probably took something as simple as being on holiday together for granted. And he was so glad for them that they had that chance. It was their right after all. But had they been born just a generation earlier, their lives would have been very, very different. Darling Benjamin was always on his mind.

Delilah's cottage was pink. Naturally. The path leading up to it was half-covered by a wooden, latticed archway which was heaving with plush green foliage and shocking pink blooms. A tiny hummingbird hovered above Gabriel's head as he approached. He knocked twice, gently, on the door. There was no reply. Gabriel waited, knocked again. Still no reply. He made his way round the side of the cottage, towards the back terrace, to see whether perhaps Delilah was sunbathing already. He was just turning the corner when he bumped straight into a large, rugged man tiptoeing the other way. Both men jumped and sprang back from each other. Gabriel screamed and clutched his chest.

'For goodness' sake, Mr Styles,' he spluttered, trying to regain his composure. 'You almost gave me heart failure! I do wish Miss Delilah would allow her visitors to use the front door.'

Jim Styles blushed so hard that his cheeks turned the same colour as the blooms. He pushed his sweaty hair off his face and tucked his T-shirt into his shorts. Gabriel noticed with distaste that his flies were undone.

'Um, er, good-morning, Mr Abbot,' said Jim, staring at his flip-flops. 'I was, um, I was just—'

'Doing some early-morning yoga with Delilah?' suggested

Gabriel, tactfully. 'I know you and she share an avid interest in the discipline.'

Jim smiled thankfully at Gabriel for the ready-made excuse. 'Yes! Yes! Yoga. Ashtanga. She's marvellously flexible, Delilah ...'

The younger man blushed again, realising his faux pas.

'I'm quite sure she is, Mr Styles,' replied Gabriel tartly. 'Do send my regards to your wife. I thought she looked rather lonely at breakfast.'

A shadow of concern crossed Jim's handsome face. 'I must go,' he said, clearly panic-stricken at having been caught. 'Bye, Mr Abbot.'

And with that the three-times Wimbledon champion (now retired) sprinted back through the undergrowth towards the path, and room four, where his poor wife was waiting. Gabriel shook his head and smiled dolefully. Why, oh why, did Delilah insist on playing this little game of hers? It really was most unfair on the wives. He knocked twice on the glass double doors that led from the terrace to Delilah's suite. He could see her through the glass, sitting upright at her dressing table, with a perfectly straight back like a ballerina's, brushing her long black hair. She wore a short, grey satin bathrobe and a pair of marabou-feathered high-heeled mules. Her impossibly elegant legs were tucked underneath the stool, crossed at the ankles just so.

'Do come in, Gabriel, and stop the peeping Tom act,' she called from inside. 'I'm quite decent.'

Gabriel slid open the door and walked inside. The room smelled of expensive perfume and cheap sex. He walked up behind her and kissed her on the cheek.

'You, my darling Delilah, are anything but decent,' he told her.

She laughed, a deep, throaty, filthy laugh. 'Decency is overrated, Gabe,' she replied.

'Have you had your tablets, Del?' he asked, walking to the bathroom and unlocking the cabinet.

'Nope,' she said. 'You know I can't stomach the things without my orange juice. Where is my orange juice? And it had better be smooth today. Have you reprimanded the chef, Gabe? I do hope so.'

Gabriel collected the bottles of pills from the cabinet and called through, 'Yes, he's had his hands slapped, and yes, your breakfast is on its way, complete with orange juice. The bits have been hand-picked out by fairies just for you, my dear.'

'Oh good-oh,' she called back.

Sometimes Gabriel wasn't sure whether she knew he was joking, or whether she thought there really were fairies whose only job in life was to pander to her every whim. He sighed. Was she getting better or worse? He really wasn't sure. There was a knock on the door. Gabriel answered it because he knew Delilah wouldn't.

'Thank you, Jacques,' said Gabriel, to the French boy who'd brought breakfast. 'Just lay it out on the terrace for her, please.'

'Morning sweetie,' called Delilah to Jacques, without turning round. 'How's my favourite waiter this morning?'

Gabriel watched as Jacques blushed too. He shook his head and shrugged by way of an apology to his poor staff member. If Delilah had been a man, she'd have been sued for sexual harassment years ago.

'I'm fine thank you, Madame Delilah,' replied Jacques, scuttling to the terrace as quickly as he could. He laid the breakfast out on a crisp, white tablecloth – croissants, pains-au-chocolat, fresh fruit, yogurt, preserves, a pot of strong coffee and, of course, the freshly squeezed orange juice with no bits. And then Jacques practically ran out of the cottage, mumbling his goodbyes as he went.

'He's terrified of you, that one,' Gabriel told Delilah. 'Finally, a boy who's immune to your charms, my dear. And he's not even gay! Perhaps you're losing your touch.'

Delilah threw her head back and laughed as if she'd never heard anything so funny in her life. And then finally, with her full make-up done, and her hair tied up in a turquoise silk scarf, she spun around on her stool and faced Gabriel. She stood up, slipped off her satin robe and, standing in a pose from her modelling days, revealed a blue and green printed Pucci one-piece.

'Exquisite,' said Gabriel, whose job it was to comment on Delilah's undeniable beauty each morning. 'You don't look a day over twenty-five.'

Delilah smiled, satisfied. It was a lie of course. But it was what she needed to hear. Delilah was far too fragile to take criticism, particularly about something as important as her looks. The truth was that, despite her sculptured bone structure, her statuesque body, the face-lifts, the spa treatments and the hours of yoga, Pilates and 'workouts' with young men, Delilah could not turn back the hand of time. Not completely. She was still beautiful. In her way. But there was something of the Miss Havisham about her these days. Miss Havisham in a designer swimsuit.

She put on an enormous pair of black sunglasses, took Gabriel's hand and led him out to the terrace for breakfast. Once she'd eaten half a croissant, a mouthful of yogurt and a slice of watermelon he handed her tablets to her one by one. She took them obediently and swallowed them down with her orange juice.

'And they're working?' asked Gabriel, concerned. 'This

new combination? Because the doctor said we absolutely must go back to the clinic if you start to feel worse.'

'I feel amazing, Gabe,' said Delilah, gazing across the bay. 'Really, I do. In fact, I can hardly feel a thing.'

Her voice sounded slightly muffled, as if she was talking to him over a long-distance phone call. Delilah always seemed detached. She was sitting here, right next to him, but it was as if the essence of her was floating somewhere up in the fluffy white clouds overhead. And it didn't seem to matter how many doctors they saw, how many private clinics in Miami, New York or London; Gabriel could not recapture Delilah's soul and reunite it with her body.

'Not all there ...' It was the phrase people used to use, in whispered tones, about his mother when he was a child and it was the phrase that popped back into his mind right now, as he watched Delilah stare vacantly out to sea.

3

Mal woke up slowly and noisily like a lazy dog in a basket. He stretched his legs until his knees clicked, itched the stubble on his chin, scratched his privates, yawned noisily and then farted loudly. Finally he opened his eyes. Not fully – that would be too much of a commitment to the day – but in gradual, squinting blinks that allowed flashes of the room to seep gradually into his brain.

He took in his immediate surroundings indifferently. Being an International Rock God and General Superstar of Mega Proportions (his own terms) meant that his lifestyle had been entirely nomadic for more than a decade. He liked to think of himself as a Bedouin of the Western world (and indeed often described himself as such in interviews). 'Some people like shabby chic,' he would say, amusing both the interviewer and his audience with his witty observations. 'Some prefer modern minimalism. But my favourite look is Bedouin Bling. You see, I'm never in one place for more than a week, and I spend a lot of time living on a tour bus, but wherever I find myself, it's always got a hot tub and a plasma screen!'

A combination of world tours, jetlag, hangovers, comedowns and a memory that wasn't quite what it used to be, meant that Mal often played a game of 'Where the fucking hell am I?' when he woke up in the morning, or the afternoon, or whatever hour of the day or night it might be. He did it now. Plush hotel suite? Check. Super duper bed the size of a helipad? Check. White Egyptian cotton bedclothes with a zillion thread-count? Check. Hot naked babe beside him? Check, check, checkity check! He used to play a game of 'Who the fucking hell am I in bed with?' too but Mal was extremely proud to say that those days were behind him. He was (as he'd told Jonathan Ross, David Letterman and Oprah Winfrey) now a reformed character. A proper, bona-fide, one-woman man (give or take a couple of minor indiscretions that the press had blown completely out of proportion).

Lexi Crawford had rocked Mal's world. Who knew, eh?! Who the bloody hell would have guessed in a million years that little Lexi Crawford, the all-singing, all-dancing, all-American, blue-eyed, golden-haired, dimple-cheeked, precocious, vomit-inducing child star would turn out to be 'the one' who tamed Mad Mal Riley, the Stallion of Suburbia (or Surbiton to be exact), self-professed sex addict and general man whore? Not that Lexi was much of a 'child' any more. Hell no! Mal's girl was all woman these days (much to the distress of the Disney Channel, her God-fearing parents and much of Middle America). She was Sexy Lexi now – a lippy, sassy, smart-arsed, hip-swinging, vodka-swigging, nipple-flashing, table-dancing, little minx of a madam. And Mal took full credit for the extreme makeover of his girlfriend. He couldn't have moulded her more firmly into the image of his dream woman if she'd been made of Plasticine.

But Mal had a secret. Part of him actually loved the teenager in Lexi. She looked all woman but her mind was still young and unscathed. Proper grown-up women his own age terrified him. They were so opinionated! And they often seemed to think he was stupid and immature. But Lexi? Lexi looked at him like he was the oracle of everything. She thought he was smart. And he adored that adoration. He watched her now as she slept in the half-light. Despite the tattoos, the heavy eye make-up (smudged from the night before), and the blue/black dyed hair he could still see a ghost of the innocent child star lurking beneath the sheets. It was the way her thumb hovered near her full lips. It was the translucence of her skin – totally unlined, despite the endless late nights. It was the way her naked breasts, though plump and full, were as pert and perky as a couple of puppies. It was the way she reminded him of a smooth, sweet, perfectly ripe peach. All those things reminded Mal how utterly, deliciously, perfectly fresh she was. His girlfriend was just nineteen. And he was thirty-three. What a lucky fucking bugger he was! This gorgeous, sexy, untouched, untainted (yes, she had actually been a virgin when he met her!), talented, frothy filly of a woman child was his girlfriend. He sighed, satisfied. And for a moment all was right in Mal's world.

But then the word 'girlfriend' started reverberating around his head for no apparent reason, like an echo. There was something not quite right about that word this morning. Mal could feel a memory buzzing around his brain like an irritating fly. And however hard he tried to catch it, pin it down, and take control of it, the memory, like a half-forgotten dream, kept escaping him.

He pressed the rewind button in his brain and concentrated hard. Vegas. He was in Vegas. He'd had a gig in LA a couple of days ago and Lexi was shooting a movie in the Nevada desert (as they were constantly telling the press, their very busy schedules did make it hard for the couple to spend 'quality time' together) so it had made sense to catch up here ... He glanced around the suite, took in the classy, opulent decor ... At the Bellagio, maybe, by the look of things? They'd had dinner at ... Oh, God, was it Nobu? Then a club. Pure, maybe? Or Tao? Wherever. Paris (as in Hilton) had been there was all he could remember. And then ... The memory fly buzzed annoyingly out of reach again. Then ... a limo somewhere? A strange little bloke in a white suit with a big book ... A building. A small white building with a pointy roof ... Lexi giggling. So pissed. Both so fucking pissed, tripping over each other, giggling. Was Paris there too? Or was that a dream? And ... Oh my God, what did they do last night? What the fuck did they do last night?!

Mal glanced down at his hands and realised he was wearing a ring of some sort on his left hand. It had cut into his skin and he now realised his finger was throbbing and had turned a bit blue. Wait a minute. No, not a ring. A bloody ring pull, to be exact. A feeling of panic rose in his chest and he started shaking his pretty little child star girlfriend a little bit too violently by the shoulders.

'Lexi!' he shouted, terrified. 'Lexi baby! What did we do last night? Lexi, honey bun, can you remember?! LEXIIIIIII!!!!'

Lexi opened her enormous, cornflower-blue eyes suddenly. She sat bolt upright in bed. Her full mouth formed a perfect 'O'. With her make-up mostly still in place from the night before, and her hair fluffed up in a blue/black halo around her head, she looked exactly like a life-sized doll. His living doll blinked twice, held up her left hand and showed Mal an identical ring pull on her finger.

'Holy shit, Mal,' she said, half-excitedly, half-nervously. 'I think we got hitched.'

'Oh, fucking hell, Lexi!' cried Mal, burying his head in his hands. 'What did we do that for? My mum's going to bloody kill me!'

4

'Aw look, Mal Riley and Lexi Crawford got married in Las Vegas,' said Lauren, a little whimsically, to no one in particular, as she gazed at the plasma screen on the kitchen wall, waiting for the coffee machine to heat up. 'Isn't that sweet? How romantic to just do it like that. They must be really loved up.'

'Isn't that sweet?' mocked Sebastian, her husband, from behind his paper at the table. His voice dripped with sarcasm. 'Yeah, really *sweet*. He's a druggie. She's a messed-up teenager. Love is just another word for lust – and we all know that *that* fades pretty quickly – and marriage is an archaic form of imprisonment. It's about as romantic as a car crash. Which is exactly what that is.'

Lauren jumped. Usually Sebastian ignored her comments and points of view. In fact, usually Sebastian ignored her full stop. She could generally say whatever she liked to the television, or the radio, or to the cat, or the goldfish, or the toaster if she felt the need, without her husband paying her much attention at all. That's if he was actually at home, which he rarely was these days. But very occasionally he took immediate offence to something she said and used it as an opportunity to berate and belittle her. This, it seemed, was one of those occasions. He looked up from *The Times* and pointed at the television images of Mal Riley and Lexi Crawford. He had a mixture of displeasure and self-satisfaction on his face. The only thing Sebastian Hunter loved more than his own reflection was the sound of his own voice.

'That,' he stated firmly through a mouthful of fat-free yoghurt and blueberries (Sebastian liked to keep himself trim), 'is a car crash waiting to happen. Or a divorce waiting to happen at the very least ...'

'Sebastian,' scolded Lauren, nodding her head in the direction of their daughters, Emily and Poppy, who were eating their toasted honey bagels and eyeing their father warily. She was used to her husband's cynical viewpoint, his dark moods and his even darker 'sense of humour' (as he called it, although Lauren rarely found it very funny any more), but the girls were still young and she hated him talking that way in front of them.

'What?' continued Sebastian, ignoring Lauren's wishes, as always. 'You don't want the girls to know what a sham most marriages are? Wake up and smell my soya latte, ladies.'

He turned to his daughters, aged eight and eleven, and continued unabated. 'Do not believe in fairy tales, girls,' he lectured. 'You may be pretty. Well, *you* are, Poppy. But you are not Cinderella. There is no Prince Charming waiting to whisk you to the ball. End of.'

Poppy, the younger of the two, bit her lip nervously and glanced at Lauren. Emily just rolled her eyes as if to say, 'Here we go again' and carried on munching her breakfast. She seemed unfazed by her father's opinion that Poppy was the pretty one, but then she'd heard it so many times before that perhaps the poor child had grown immune to it.

Lauren forced a bright smile and said, 'Right, girls, better get your teeth brushed before school ... And I think you're both very, *very* beautiful,' she whispered into their hair as she brushed past them, clearing the table.

But Sebastian was on a roll now. He put up his hand to indicate that he, the master of the house, was talking and that no one should dare leave the room.

'On the upside,' he said. 'Mr Rock Star there can file for a quickie celebrity divorce. And she must be worth more than he is after all those daft Disney movies she's been in, so he won't actually lose anything. Yet.' Sebastian grinned, but there was no warmth in his smile, only smugness. He stood up and pointed at the plasma screen.

'Get out now, my friend!' he advised Mal Riley, as if the rock star could hear him all the way over there in Nevada. 'Get out now before she lumbers you with children, and a holiday home in Cornwall, and school fees, and a kitchen full of Cath Kidston tat.' He swept his hand around to indicate his own kitchen.

Lauren shook her head at him and frowned. She could always sense when he was about to go too far, when vaguely funny was going to turn into downright rude. A familiar feeling of panic gripped her chest as she frantically thought of something, *anything*, to say to derail Sebastian from his monologue. She didn't want the girls to hear him talking like this. Not again.

'Come on, Sebbie,' she tried to placate him with the pet name he'd once loved her to use. 'There's no time for this now. We're all running a bit late this morning.'

But it was too late. Sebastian had smelled blood and he was going in for the kill. He glanced at his wife briefly, with a look of ... What was that? Lauren wondered. Boredom? Disgust? Actual hatred? She felt the tears prick her eyes and beat herself up inside for being so damned pathetic and weak. Why didn't she just answer him back? Or ignore him?

Why did she still care so much what he thought?

Sebastian turned back to the television. 'Escape now,' he shouted to Mal Riley. 'While she's still pretty. Leave before she starts getting fat and wrinkly. Before you know it her boobs will droop, her bum will sag and even her knees will get chubby. She'll be shopping in M&S, even though you've spent a fortune on Bond Street for her, and she'll be having her hair cut just like her mother. Run, young man, run for the hills!'

Lauren touched her newly cut hair self-consciously as the tears of shame started to trickle down her cheeks. She blinked furiously, determined that the children wouldn't notice quite how badly their father had hurt her.

'Come on, girls,' she managed to say in a falsely bright tone, which came out a bit strangled. 'Let's get you to school.'

Poppy ran to Lauren's side immediately and buried her face in the comforting cashmere of her mum's jumper but Emily sat stock-still. The look on her elder daughter's face took Lauren by surprise. It was the same cold, detached expression of disdain that Sebastian wore whenever he turned nasty. But this time the disdain was aimed directly at Sebastian. Emily stared at her father, unblinkingly. Her father stared back. Their expressions mirrored each other's exactly and Lauren felt a shiver run down her spine.

'Emily, teeth, now!' she shouted, a little desperately.

Her instinct was to get Emily out of the room and away from her father immediately. Sebastian was not a violent man. He had never raised a finger to Lauren during their twelve years together. Nor had he ever so much as smacked the girls on the back of their hands. No, Sebastian's only weapon was his vicious tongue. But, Christ, that tongue could cut as deep as the sharpest knife! Lauren had been stabbed by it too many times to underestimate its danger.

But he usually saved it for Lauren. Or for his minions at work. Yes, he would put her down in front of the girls; he would call her names. Sometimes he would swear at her, or at his staff on the phone, or at other drivers on the road, or anyone on television that he didn't agree with. But up until now he had never actually lashed out with the full force of his killer tongue on either of the children.

'Emily Hunter,' said Lauren as calmly as she could. 'Get upstairs, brush your teeth, put on your school shoes and let's go!'

But Emily just sat there, staring at her father. Sebastian stared right back. For a moment the kitchen was completely silent. And then it happened.

'I hate you,' Emily muttered, quietly at first.

The colour drained from Sebastian's tanned face. 'What did you say?' he demanded. 'What the bloody hell did you just say, young lady?'

Lauren watched Emily with a mixture of pride and horror as the eleven-year-old sat up straight and said clearly, loudly and alarmingly confidently, 'I hate you, Daddy. I think you're a rude, vile man.'

Sebastian's jaw dropped and for a moment, the Motor Mouth himself was lost for words. Emily took the opportunity to keep going.

'I wish Mummy would divorce you,' she continued, in her pure, clipped, public-school voice. 'I wish she would take all your precious money and run away with us, somewhere far away, where you could never find us. And then we wouldn't have to listen to your horrible voice or look at your stupid orange face again.'

Lauren winced. Ouch! Sebastian was vain. No, let's be honest, he was quite possibly the vainest man in London. He was always groomed to within an inch of his life. He had his eyebrows plucked and his nails manicured. He'd been a metrosexual twenty years before the term had actually been coined. And then there was the tan. To say that Sebastian Hunter was fond of sunbeds would be a bit like saying that Rod Stewart was fond of leggy blondes. And the most ridiculous part was that he would never, ever admit to it. Like a junkie hiding his habit, Sebastian's tanning sessions were his guilty little secret. At least, that's what he thought. He'd never once admitted, even to Lauren, that his tan was anything other than 'colour left over from the Maldives' or wherever they'd last been on holiday.

Lauren knew from the wives of a couple of Sebastian's friends at his club in Mayfair that his perma-tanned appearance had earned him the nickname Mr Orange – but only behind his back. There was one thing everybody knew about Sebastian Hunter: he loved nothing more than to tease, mickey-take and make other people the butts of his jokes, but heaven help anyone who tried to turn the joke on him. Sebastian could dish it out with a cherry on top, but he sure as hell couldn't take it back. And yet here was Emily, barely eleven years old, sitting at the kitchen table, bold as brass, not only telling her father that she hated him, but bringing up 'The Tan'.

Before Lauren could intervene, Sebastian had sprung forward and was leaning on the table with his face inches away from his daughter's. 'Emily Hunter,' he practically spat in her face, 'you are a spoilt, obnoxious brat.'

Emily stared back without flinching. Lauren watched in horror and awe. She always crumpled when Sebastian verbally attacked her but Emily seemed so strong. His words tore at Lauren's heart, even more now that they were aimed at Emily rather than at her, but her feet stayed glued to the spot. Part of her wanted to scoop Emily up and protect her from her dad's vitriol, but another part knew that what Emily was doing was important. She was standing up to the family bully and that was something Lauren had never had the nerve to do. Perhaps if she'd had the balls to answer Sebastian back, all those years ago, none of them would be in this position now.

'Sticks and stones will break my bones but names will never hurt me,' sing-songed Emily to her dad.

'How dare you!' Sebastian roared, losing any semblance of cool. 'I've given you everything. Look at the house you live in! The cars you get driven around in! The holidays you have! The clothes you wear! The pony clubs! The piano lessons! Ballet! The house in Rock! How many children have a life like this?'

'That's just money. Most children have a dad who's there for them,' continued Emily bravely. 'You spend all your time at the office, or the club, or wherever. Sometimes you come in at five o'clock in the morning. I hear you, Daddy!'

Lauren thought her heart would break right open. Of course she knew that sometimes Sebastian stayed out practically all night. She'd pretend to be asleep when he sneaked into bed, smelling of champagne, cigarettes and perfume. And in the morning, when he told her he'd got in at midnight, she'd pretend to believe him because it was easier than dealing with the truth. But she knew. She wasn't stupid. She was downtrodden and unloved, and maybe she was even unlovable, but Lauren Hunter was *not* stupid. She knew what her husband was. But she'd had absolutely no idea that Emily had noticed. Lauren fought back the tears of shame and stepped towards Emily with Poppy still clinging to her side.

'Emily, darling,' she said softly. 'Come on. Let's get ready for school.'

'Oh right, I see,' shouted Sebastian. 'The little madam can talk to me however the hell she pleases and it's, "Poor little Emily."' He mimicked Lauren as he so often did. Making her sound even weaker, wetter and older than she was. Then he continued, 'What about me? I'm your husband! Aren't you supposed to be on my side? Christ, is it any wonder I hate coming home when you three are so bloody ungrateful. I feel like an outsider in my own house! Well, d'you know what? I gave you all this. And you ...' he turned to Lauren. 'All you had to do to earn all this luxury that I PAID FOR was raise the children. And you can't even do that properly. All you've done is raise a couple of spoilt brats. Lazy, spoilt brats just like their mother. And fat ones at that! That's what happens when you sit on your lazy, fat backside all day instead of working for a living. You're all getting porky. Look at the three of you. Three little piggies. Oink, oink, oink!'

'What does that make you, Daddy?' retorted Emily, quick as a flash. 'The Big Bad Wolf?'

Sebastian let out a kind of strangled roar and then threw his bowl across the kitchen so that it smashed against the pristine granite worktop and splashed yogurt, blueberries and shards of china all over the Aga.

'Very mature, Sebastian,' said Lauren in as level a voice as she could muster. She was feeling so angry now that she was suddenly a little bit brave. 'You're the adult here. So go to the office, or the club, or wherever it is you spend your days – and nights. And leave me to get the girls ready for school. We'll talk about this later. Once you've calmed down and the girls are in bed.'

'Damn you,' he muttered, grabbing his Savile Row suit jacket from the back of his chair.

He flicked his head back and sniffed, before flouncing

out of the door, every inch the wounded soldier. Sebastian did that. He managed to turn everybody else into villains. Lauren had spent most of her adult life apologising to him for things she knew weren't her fault. Or at least, things that she'd thought weren't her fault at first. Often, he'd twist and turn the facts so much that she'd end up not knowing who was in the wrong. So she'd apologise. Just to get him back on side because, believe it or not, when Sebastian was on your side the world was a truly lovely place. Not that he'd been on Lauren's side much lately. In fact, she couldn't remember the last time he'd looked at her with anything other than distaste. She knew he hated the little bit of weight she'd put on, the fact that she couldn't get away with dressing like a slinky puss any more, now she was staring forty in the face. He hated her new, shorter hair, and the way she'd decorated the house and he absolutely hated that she didn't have a job.

The biggest irony was that Lauren used to work for a living. Christ, when they first met, she was the successful one – the one with the flash car, the swish pad, the confidence, the friends, the contacts, the swagger *and* the designer clothes. It had been what he'd loved about her at first. What's more, she had been the one who'd paid for the first flat they'd developed, and then she'd got the mortgage for the second, bigger flat. And she'd been the one with the idea to buy that warehouse in Shoreditch, when Shoreditch was *nowhere*, insisting that the East End was the future of cool. They'd turned that warehouse into five luxury apartments and made their first couple of million in six months. She didn't even think to complain when Sebastian set up his property business using only his name. It was his baby, after all. And the flats had only ever been a hobby for Lauren. She was a photographer by trade, and a bloody good one at that, with *Vogue, Tatler, Conde Nast Traveller* and the

Sunday Times Magazine in her book. She made good money and she was respected by art directors, editors, models, celebrities and fellow photographers alike.

For the first couple of years, Sebastian had seemed proud. But somehow, over the years, he had systematically gone about destroying everything he'd once found attractive in his wife. Wasn't he the one who'd insisted she had to stay at home with the kids? And wasn't he the one who told her she was too old, too uncool, too behind the times these days to go back to her old career once the girls had started school? Now, all she had of her former career was a house full of beautiful black-and-white photographs of a world she used to inhabit and record. No one in the business would remember her; she had no contacts left and she had no confidence left. How could she go back to work now? And it wasn't as if they needed the money. Sebastian had made plenty of that. Lauren sighed and dragged herself back to the present.

'That was stupid, Emily,' she said to her eldest daughter. 'To wind your father up like that. You know what his temper's like.'

Emily shrugged grumpily, with a glint of cold steel still in her eyes.

'It was stupid,' Lauren continued, placing her hand gently on her daughter's shoulder. 'But it was brave.'

Emily shrugged her mum's hand off her shoulder. Her eyes were still cold. 'Well,' she said flatly. 'One of us has to be brave. It's not as if you're ever going to stand up to him.'

'Emily ...' Lauren was startled by her daughter's reaction. 'Emily, come back here and apologise now.'

But Emily ignored her, just like Sebastian did, and walked out of the kitchen without a backwards glance. For some reason, Emily's words hurt even more than anything Sebastian had ever said.

5

'You're late, Clyde,' barked Ronnie. 'We said nine thirty. It's gone ten for Christ's sake. What is wrong with you that you can't even make an appointment on time, man?'

'Screw you, Berkowski, the subway was hell. You know I don't understand a damn thing about this city. I ended up halfway to the fucking Bronx,' snapped back Clyde, throwing himself onto the chair opposite and propping his dirty, battered boots up on the shiny, wooden desk. The two men didn't shake hands.

'Who the hell do you think you are, Scott?' said Ronnie impatiently, shoving the cowboy boots back on the floor. 'Crocodile fucking Dundee? What? You can't read a subway map? You can't keep your feet on the floor like a civilised human being? You're in Manhattan now, not Hicksville, Colorado. Anyway, why didn't you get a cab?'

'I can't afford a cab, you jerk,' retorted Clyde. 'That's why I'm here, remember? I'm broke!'

'Yeah, well maybe if you weren't such a lazy asshole, you'd still be making us both some money, huh?' Ronnie continued to trade insults.

'And if you were any good at your job, Berkowski, I wouldn't be in this mess,' replied Clyde, the corners of his mouth twitching.

Ronnie didn't reply this time. The false frown he'd been wearing evaporated and his broad, open face broke into a grin. Clyde felt his own features loosen too, and the smile he'd been swallowing since he walked in the office finally escaped. Jeez, the warmth he felt for this man was too immense to hide, even if the joke had been fun while it lasted.

'It's so good to see you, Clyde,' said Ronnie, leaning over the desk to hug his friend. 'It's been way too long.'

They man-hugged, shoulder to shoulder, Clyde in his checked shirt and faded jeans, Ronnie in his black cashmere suit, white shirt and gold cufflinks. They made an odd pair but there wasn't a man alive that Clyde Scott trusted more than Ronnie Berkowski.

'You look well, Ron,' Clyde grinned, sitting down again and throwing his feet back onto the desk. 'Younger than last year! Don't tell me, you've had a little nip-tuck.'

'No, but I've lost a little weight.' Ronnie twirled around to show Clyde his new, slimmer figure, although he would always be a little short and a little thick around the middle. He was just made that way. 'I've been working out, taking care of myself and trying to avoid Mrs Berkowski's famous strudel!'

'You look good, Ron. Real good,' smiled Clyde. 'How is Lena?'

'The same, you know,' said Ron, his eyes still brimming with love after twenty-five years of marriage. 'Loud, overbearing, bossy, beautiful, amazing. I was sorry to hear about Nancy, about her getting remarried. That must have been tough.'

Clyde shrugged and swallowed. The subject of his exwife — now someone else's wife — was still a little raw. 'It was for the best,' he replied, knowing it was true, but still finding the fact a little, well, final, you know? She'd actually gone and got remarried. There was no door left open there.

'Nancy's a good lady. She deserved better than the crap I gave her,' he continued, saying what he knew he should feel rather than what he actually felt. 'I was never at home. She needed love, support and stability. I never gave her that. And now I guess she's got what she wanted. He seems an OK guy, her new husband, and the kids seem to like big city life in Denver so ...' Clyde swallowed hard. The thought of his kids living with another man still felt like a kick in the teeth.

'Well, you look handsome as ever, you bastard,' said Ronnie, obviously sensing Clyde's pain and changing the subject. 'How the fuck do you do that when you live on liquor and Marlboros? I thought you were having a nervous breakdown, huh? Men who have nervous breakdowns are not supposed to turn up at my office looking like Robert frigging Redford in his prime, OK? Jeez, you're no good for my ego. I've had all the girls out there' – he indicated the vast, open-plan office floor behind his glass-panelled office – 'hiding out in the washrooms all morning. Making themselves all pretty for Mr Scott's arrival – forty-five frigging minutes late, may I repeat!'

'Yeah, sorry about that, Ron,' said Clyde, meaning it. 'You know I'm a total moron when it comes to the subway.'

'So you should have called Sylvie. She'd have gotten you a cab from the hotel.'

Sylvie was Ron's PA at Berkowski, Brewer and Jones Associates.

'I don't like charity,' Clyde muttered, staring out of the window behind Ronnie's desk, still surprised by the New York skyline, even though he'd been coming here for almost twenty years.

'It's a cab fare, Clyde,' said Ronnie softly. 'It's not charity.

This company has made millions out of you over the years. The least we can do is pay a frigging ten-dollar cab fare.'

Clyde could tell Ronnie was trying to catch his eye but he was too proud to show his friend the hurt and the failure he was feeling right now. He was six foot three and forty-two years of age. He'd made (and lost) millions of dollars. He'd had two wives, three children, several houses, a ranch and a glittering career that had seen him top the bestseller lists for most of a decade. But now he felt two inches tall. Clyde Scott was finished, washed up, over, of that he was sure. He lived alone in little more than a shack now.

'What do I do, Ron?' he asked. 'I've got nothing left. I've had to sell everything.'

'I know, I know.' Ronnie's eyes were full of genuine concern. 'And it breaks my heart to see you in this mess but it's temporary, Clyde. It's a hiccup. We'll fix it.'

'Is there any more money?' asked Clyde, trying to keep the desperation out of his voice. 'Any foreign sales we've forgotten to chase? A new film offer? Do any of the smaller publishers want me to sign for them? I don't mind. Any interview requests? Does anyone want me to do a talk, anywhere? The universities? I could inspire creative writing majors, I know I could.'

Ronnie sighed heavily, and rested his head on his hands. 'No, Clyde,' he said sadly. 'You've been quiet too long. This is a fast-moving game; you know that. Reading tastes change, new authors emerge, willing to work for practically nothing. And there's a global recession going on. No one's willing to take a gamble. Not after last time ...'

Clyde felt the shame burn his cheeks as he remembered the book that he'd never managed to finish, the one still sitting half-written on the desktop of his computer. His publishers had been patient at first. They'd moved his deadline, waited six months, and then a year. When another year passed they stopped asking when it would arrive. Of course he'd long since spent his last advance by then – thoroughbred horses are not a cheap hobby, his first ex-wife was not a cheap ex-wife and a ranch was not a cheap place to live. Had he ever finished the book, he'd have received enough money to save the day. There would have been a generous delivery advance and then the sales would have been good – he had his name and reputation to trade on. Damn, that plot was excellent. But nothing could make him write that damned novel. Not after what he'd done to get the story. So all he could do was start selling off his assets. And find comfort in the bottom of a bottle of Jack Daniel's.

Back in the day when the royalties were rolling in and the film rights were being bought, he'd treated himself to the 4,000-acre ranch, employed over a hundred staff, collected horses (the more expensive and rare the breed, the better), expanded, grown, employed more staff, more livestock, built a pool, extended the house ... Jesus, man, he'd even bought himself a seaplane to land on his lake! Then it all went horribly, agonisingly wrong. He fucked up. Not just his life, not just his family's life, but several other lives too. And one in particular that he still couldn't bring himself to think about too much. The guilt paralysed him. The writer's block kicked in, the royalties started to dry up, no new film offers emerged and, finally, his publishers gave up on him. Clyde had made hay while the sun shone, but it didn't take long for the clouds to gather overhead. That had been the beginning of the end. Now, four years later, it felt like the end of the end.

'Well, I'm screwed this time, Ron,' he said flatly. 'Totally fucking screwed.'

'There are still some modest royalties coming in from the

Poison series, but, Clyde, you wrote those a decade ago; they were huge but interest is waning. Those books are genius, but they're dated now. The thriller genre has moved on, criminal psychology has moved on, forensics has moved on, law enforcement has changed, the USA has changed, and the world has changed. And since CSI everyone's a frigging expert on crime! There were only two books after the Poison series and you haven't handed in a complete manuscript in six years now.' Ronnie was still talking. 'You have no publisher, no contract, no deal.'

'Damn, I know that, Ronnie!' Clyde yelled. 'You think I don't know that?!' He rubbed his face in his hands, screwed his eyes up and let out a deep, exasperated sigh. 'Look, I'm sorry, Ron. I have no right to get angry with you. None of this is your fault. You've been a fucking amazing agent and a great friend. You've supported me every step of the way, and I'm sorry I've let you down, but I just don't see a way out of this now. I can't write. I try. I still try. I sit there and I stare at the computer screen and I try to remember how I did it but it's gone. It's just gone. I don't remember how I ever wrote a paragraph, let alone nine books.'

Ronnie nodded, understanding. He was always so fucking understanding. Clyde knew he didn't deserve to still have an agent, let alone the best, most successful literary agent in New York.

'So let's try something new,' suggested Ronnie. 'You always wrote at the ranch; you never wanted to leave Colorado unless you had to for research or book tours, but now things have changed ...'

'They sure have,' scoffed Clyde. 'My ranch has been sliced up and sold off in chunks like a prize side of beef. When I had to get rid of the house, the stables and the last of the land they turned it into a vacation resort called Equestrian

Escapes – a summer camp for stuck-up little rich girls. The stallions and steeds have been sold and the place looks like a frigging My Little Pony convention.'

Ronnie was clearly not going to be drawn off course. He continued. 'So, now things have changed I suggest you go away somewhere for a while. Somewhere completely new, where you have no memories, or distractions. Somewhere peaceful, but not too isolated. I worry about you, in that cabin on your own, hundreds of miles from, well, anywhere! It can't be good for you. You need a change of scene, Clyde. Go away for as long as it takes. Lie on a Caribbean beach. Read Hemingway, Fitzgerald, Capote. Give yourself time to heal and then fall back in love with life and with the written word and start again. You are one of the most talented writers of your generation; I have so much faith in you. I know you can be brilliant again. The only person sabotaging you is you, Clyde.'

'The Caribbean? Do I look like the sort of guy who wants to sip piña coladas and go limbo dancing?'

'You don't have to drink a frigging cocktail, Clyde. In fact, better you don't drink at all! All you have to do is get a change of scene and a change of attitude.'

'I don't like beaches,' muttered Clyde, aware that he sounded childish. 'I don't even like the sea. I like lakes, and I don't like to leave Colorado. Besides, who the hell is going to pay for me to "go away and find myself"?' He imitated Ronnie's slight New Yoik twang. 'I've got no money, remember?'

'You don't have to worry about the money,' said Ronnie, flatly. 'I told you there are no film offers coming in but you did get an invitation.'

'An invitation?' asked Clyde, confused.

'Yup, just like in the good old days. You, my friend, have

been offered your first freebie in years. It seems the owner of some flash resort is a big fan of yours; he found out you were having trouble writing these days and offered you a writer's retreat, free of charge, in the French West Indies, for as long as you like. The words gift horse and mouth spring to mind!'

'Oh, for crying out loud. I don't want to go and hang out with some crazy fan,' said Clyde, knowing he sounded childish and spoilt. 'Besides, I can't stand being pitied. I'm not a charity case!'

'No arguments,' said Ron flatly, ignoring Clyde's temper. 'You're going. For my career as much as yours. I'm Ronald Berkowski, for fuck's sake. I don't back losers! You were my star, my Numero Uno, my golden frigging goose. Until you're back on top of that *New York Times* bestsellers list, neither of us is going to be happy. It's a matter of pride. I've already accepted on your behalf. You're going away and you're not coming home until you've got a shit-hot idea, a full synopsis and at least 35,000 words. No bullshit, no excuses, OK?'

'No, Ron,' Clyde protested. 'It's not going to work. There's not going to be a shit-hot idea. There's not going to be another book. Sending me to the Caribbean might get me a great tan but it's not going to fix what's in here.' He hit himself quite hard on the side of the head. 'Here's the problem. Right here. And unfortunately I can't go anywhere without my fucking head.'

'It's happening,' said Ronnie, ignoring Clyde. God, he was such a stubborn prick sometimes! What bit of 'washed up' didn't he understand?!

'Ron, you're my agent, not my frigging dad,' said Clyde, bristling with resentment now. He was a grown man, for Christ's sake! 'You can't send me away because I'm not

66

behaving properly. What is this? Thriller Writer Boot Camp?'

'Call it what you like, Clyde,' sighed Ronnie. 'But your way clearly hasn't worked. Just give my way a go, OK? Like you say, if it doesn't work, at least you'll get yourself a great tan. Hell, it's a five-star frigging Caribbean dream resort, full of bored bronzed babes from Miami, so you might even get yourself laid! And it won't cost you a penny. What have you got to lose, buddy? Seriously? What have you got left to lose?'

Clyde swallowed hard and met Ronnie's stare. His friend and agent was right, of course. He had absolutely nothing left to lose. He stood up and walked around to Ronnie's side of the desk. The two men hugged for a long time.

'I'll try, Ron,' said Clyde, and he meant it. 'I don't hold out much hope. I'm not promising you anything. And I still think it's a dumb-ass idea, but for you I'll try.'

'Good,' smiled Ronnie. 'I'll get Sylvie to liaise with the resort and sort out dates and flights. And stop looking so darned sorry for yourself. It's hardly the toughest assignment you've ever been on!'

Ronnie got Sylvie to arrange a private car to take him back to his hotel and then walked him to the elevator.

'And Clyde,' said Ron, finally, as the elevator doors opened. 'Lay off the booze, buddy. It's your worst enemy.'

'I will,' said Clyde, staring at his boots. 'I will.'

Clyde got the car to drop him off at a drug store a block away from the hotel. He bought two bottles of JD and walked back to the dive where he was staying. He spent the rest of the afternoon lying on the sagging bed, trying to ignore the sirens outside, watching crap daytime TV, and getting quietly smashed out of his empty, tired, broken, godforsaken mind. It was the same way he'd spent almost every afternoon for the past six years. Ronnie meant well, and the poor man still had faith in him. But he was wrong to waste his time, money and energy on trying to save Clyde. Nobody – and nowhere – could save Clyde Scott now. That was a fact. Any hare-brained idea that Ronnie had about saving his sorry ass was pure fiction. Jeez, the guy had dedicated his entire life to invented stories; he'd clearly lost touch with how the real world worked. But Clyde knew there was no such thing as a happy ending outside the pages of a book.

6

Lexi lay on the bed, back propped up on a mountain of pillows, legs crossed, tapping her foot impatiently. She took the gum she'd been chewing for the last hour out of her mouth, examined it for no particular reason, other than it was something to do, and stuck it under the bedside table. Mal frowned at her disapprovingly from the balcony, where he was anxiously smoking a cigarette, but he didn't dare open his mouth to tell her off. He had the Battleaxe, more commonly known as Irene Riley, on the phone and Lexi could tell from his ashen face, the nervous pacing and the chain-smoking that he was getting a major ear-bashing. She rolled her eyes back at him, yawned, picked up a magazine, flicked through the pictures, briefly examined her own photograph – yup, she looked hot with black hair but maybe it was time for another change – and then tossed that on the floor alongside the heap of clothes, shoes, towels and sex toys. Jeez, she was bored. 'I wanna go ring shopping!' she hollered, not for the first time that morning.

Mal frowned and nodded at her, held up his index finger to indicate 'in a minute', and then turned his attention back to Lexi's Monster-in-Law.

'Yes, yes, Mum, of course I'm listening to you. I know, I know, it was a terrible thing to do and I am so very, deeply,

69

incredibly, genuinely, profoundly sorry,' he was saying. Saying? Ass-licking more like. Jeez, if that man was any more under his mother's control, he'd still be attached to the umbilical cord!

Lexi rolled her eyes again, even more dramatically this time, and then she pretended to vomit. This made Mal smile. Just a bit. But Lexi never needed much encouragement. She licked her lips slowly, sucked her finger, looked up at her husband. God, that was sooo hilarious – Mal was her husband! Anyway, she looked up at her *husband* in that wide-eyed, moist-lipped, I-want-you-now-baby way that *always* worked on him. Mal carried on listening to his mother but his eyes were now firmly fixed on Lexi. She smiled sweetly at him and slowly slipped her T-shirt over her head. She was naked underneath except for a very tiny lace thong.

Mal shook his head at her and mouthed, 'No, not now ...'

But he didn't look too convinced. Besides, the bulge in his boxer shorts told Lexi all she needed to know. It didn't get much to get a sex-addict (reformed or otherwise) in the mood. She might be young and inexperienced but that much she knew. Lexi picked up her tanning oil from the floor, where it lay discarded with yesterday's bikini, and slowly dripped the oil over her bare breasts. The air-conditioning was on full, and despite the open balcony doors, it was a little chilly in the room. Her skin was cool and firm, and her nipples stood perfectly erect, pointing at Mal. She poured more oil onto her hands so that it trickled through her fingers and dripped onto her stomach, her thighs.

'Um ... eh ... I, I, I ... no ... I mean yes. Yes, Mum. Of course I agree with you; I've behaved terribly, awfully, yes, yes ...' Mal was struggling to concentrate on his phone call now.

The only thing Lexi liked about Mal's endless transatlantic calls to his mother was the way his voice changed. He got so English, so Hugh Grant. Gone was the Mockney cheeky chappy act and out came the proper, posh, public school boy. And Lexi was a sucker for a posh English boy!

Lexi stood up on the bed, her skin now glistening with oil, and started massaging her body in slow, teasing circles. Her stomach, her tits, her shoulders. Mal's mouth was hanging a little open and his free hand had involuntarily reached for his erection. Lexi had his full attention now. She had known from the start that Mrs Riley was her only real competition for Mal's heart but she'd quickly found a weapon that gave her the upper hand every time the old witch tried to monopolise him.

'I am listening to you, Mum. I promise ...' Mal was faltering.

Lexi massaged her hip bones, her inner thighs, and the very lowest part of her stomach, just above her thong. And then she let her oily fingers slip beneath the lace. With one hand still circling her nipples, she allowed the other to touch her clit.

'Ohhh, Jesus ...' she said breathily. 'Oh Lord, that's good.'

And it was. It was soo frigging good. Lexi had taken to sex like a shoe addict to Louboutins. She loved it. She was good at it. Her body seemed to be made for it. Her hand had now disappeared into her panties and she was rubbing herself, harder and faster, moaning and sighing as that delicious, addictive feeling built up in her groin and her pussy got wetter and wetter. And all the while she kept her eyes locked firmly on Mal.

Mal let out a slight groan. His features melted; his eyelids grew heavy. Lexi watched, fascinated, so fucking turned on by the way she turned him on, as his left hand started to stroke his cock.

'Um, yes, I'm fine, Mum. No ... of God ... um ... no, nothing's wrong, Mum ... I just think I erm ... I migh ... I might need to go in a minute ... I ... erm ... I ...' Mal stammered.

Lexi rolled her pink thong down her tanned thighs, over her knees, her calves, her ankles and then kicked it off her toe, through the open balcony doors, so that it landed at Mal's feet. He picked it up off the floor, and caressed it with his fingers and mouthed, 'Damp.'

'Oh maaaan, I'm soaking, honey,' moaned Lexi from the bed. 'I'm getting kinda desperate for that big, gorgeous cock of yours in here.'

Lexi had never seen Mal so flustered in his life – caught between a raging hard-on and a raging mother. She carried on her floor show, feeling like a porn star, playing with herself, arousing herself, bringing herself right to the brink of orgasm.

'I'm gonna come, baby. If you don't hurry up, I'm going to come all on my lonesome here ...'

Mal looked in actual, physical pain now, so desperate was he to get his mother off the phone and his hands on his nubile little wife.

'Lexi's flooded the ... um ... erm ... the eh hot tub, Mum. Yeah, that's right, the hot tub. Yea ... eah, that's all. She's, um, she's made the hotel room a bit wet. In fact, I really have to go, I ...'

The new Mrs Mal Riley was on the floor now, on all fours, crawling slowly towards her husband.

'No! No, of course I'm not trying to get rid of you, Mum. Yes, yes, I know I've broken your heart.'

Now Mal was rolling his eyes at his mother and Lexi

knew, as she crawled out onto the balcony, that she had won this battle.

'You're right, you have indeed given me everything,' Mal nodded into the phone while rubbing his cock harder and harder. 'You gave me life and I'm a complete and utter failure as a son because I didn't invite you to my wedding.'

Lexi reached Mal's bare feet. She started kissing his toes, his ankles, his shins. He groaned out loud.

'Mum, NOBODY came to the wedding.' He tried to keep it together. 'Even we didn't know we were getting married until … Um … Ah …'

Lexi's lips brushed his thighs, her fingers reached for his Calvins, started to roll them down; her tongue kissed and licked and sucked his balls. She felt his body stiffen, his cock rear up further and he had to hold the phone away from his ear. As she took the full, enormous, length of his penis in her mouth, Lexi could hear Mrs Riley's shrill voice.

'You are an absolute disgrace, Malcolm Riley. What sort of son denies his mother the chance to see her only child … ONLY CHILD! Do you hear me?! … Denies his poor, poor mother the chance to see him get married. And to someone like that, Malcolm. She is not good enough for you. How many times do I have to tell you? That girl is too young, too much trouble, and too common! She's trash, Malcolm. Mark my words, that girl is trash. She'll do nothing but drag you down!'

'Oh, I'm going down on him, Mommy Dearest, you're totally right about that,' said Lexi, lifting her head momentarily.

'Malcolm? Malcolm? MALCOLM!!!!!'

Lexi wasn't sure if it was just the phone call or if she could actually hear Mal's mother screaming from the other side of the Atlantic. She'd had enough. It was time for his mom to butt out. Lexi stood up, threw her leg over Mal's lap, and straddled him so that his dick slid slowly and deliciously into her pussy. Mal groaned again and this time he didn't even try to keep quiet. The hand that held the phone had dropped to his side. Lexi took it gently from his grasp and, as she rode her husband in smooth, deep, rhythmic movements, she spoke to her mother-in-law for the first time since the wedding.

'Mrs Riley,' she said, in her sweetest voice. 'This is Lexi. Malcolm has to help me with a little problem I have right now. I seem to have made everything all wet and he's the only one who can fix things. I really, *really* need him right now. But thank you so much for calling and offering us your congratulations. It was too kind. Bye-eee.'

She threw the phone on the floor, grabbed hold of the back of Mal's head and screwed him like she'd never screwed him before.

Mrs Lexi Riley: one. Mrs Irene Riley: nil.

7

St Barthélemy, French West Indies

It was Molly's sixth full day in Paradise and she was busy cleaning Mr Abbot's room. Or Gabriel as she was now to call him, she remembered, knowing already that she was going to find it hard to be on first-name terms with such a distinguished gentleman. Perhaps she could call him Mr Gabriel, or Monsieur Gabriel, like Jacques and Henri did. Anyway, Mr Abbot, Gabriel, Mr Gabriel, whatever she was to call him, was completely fascinating to Molly. He had been since the first moment she'd set eyes on him, back in Dublin, at the end of last year. Her Angel Gabriel, the Saint from St Barts (for he was nothing less, of that she was sure) had literally changed her life.

She stared now at the framed black-and-white photographs in his room: Gabriel with Marilyn Monroe, Cary Grant, Audrey Hepburn and, for the love of God, Elvis Presley himself! If only her nan could see that photo! Molly couldn't help but shake her head at the crazy twist of fate that had brought her here, to St Barts – a place she'd never even heard of two months ago – to a five-star hotel, where the owner was not only the kindest, warmest, most magical person alive, but a retired Hollywood star to boot! Henri had told her that in the 1960s, Mr Abbot had starred in films with Cary Grant, James Stewart, Liz Taylor and even with Marilyn Monroe. They'd only been supporting roles but, still, wasn't that insane? To work for someone with such a fascinating history? Just to know someone like that made Molly feel somehow more significant than she had back in Balymun.

Molly grinned to herself. Truth be told, she'd done little else but grin since the moment she'd stepped onto the plane in Dublin and made that long, complicated trip to the West Indies. For a girl who'd never been on a plane before, who'd been no further from home than Skibereen (to visit Great Auntie Joanie), who'd dreamt of far-away places all her life but who'd had to get her first passport specifically for the event, it had been quite a trip. A plane to Paris – oh, how she'd have loved to have stayed there a few days and seen more than the inside of Orly Airport – and then such a very long, long flight to a place called Pointe-a-Pitre, which turned out to be in a country called Guadeloupe. Whoop whoop Guadeloupe! (as Molly kept chanting in her head for no particular reason other than that it made her smile). And then that terrifying little sewing machine of a plane that had flown her the last leg to St Barts, her new home, a tiny spot of land 4,000 miles and a million light-years from the drab flat in Balymun.

The heat, when she'd stepped off the plane in Guadeloupe, had wrapped itself around her like a comfort blanket. She'd left Dublin Airport on a freezing morning at the end of January: one of those grey winter days when the weather couldn't decide whether it was raining or snowing, so it just sleeted incessantly instead. And she'd arrived in the Caribbean in the middle of a cloudless blue-sky day, in the middle of the 'dry season'. Bliss. What utter, complete, unbelievable bliss. Molly had done her research on a computer at work (they had no computer at home) and learned that the

76

temperature in St Barts had never dropped below 18 degrees (even at night), and had never risen above 35 degrees. There was no such thing as 'summer' or 'winter' there. She'd hardly dared to believe that was true but she'd taken one last leap of faith and left her red winter coat (yes, the posh red one she'd bought from M&S with her Christmas staff bonus last year) with her sister Caitlin.

She'd been met at the tiny airport in St Barts by a smiley French guy in his early twenties. His name was Jacques and he worked at Paradise too.

'I do a bit of this and a bit of that,' he'd shrugged nonchalantly when Molly had asked him about his position at the hotel. 'Whatever Monsieur Gabriel needs me to do. I am a waiter sometimes, a barman sometimes, and a chauffeur sometimes. I like to do this – the airport pick-up and drop-off. It means I am the first one to see the movie stars and models when they arrive and the last one to wave them goodbye when they leave. Hee hee.'

He'd explained cheerfully, as he drove round the winding coast road northwards, to an awestruck Molly, that, 'Oui, bien sur. We get the big stars. At Christmas it is like Beverley Hills in St Barts. And the models. Ah, the models ...' he'd sucked in his breath and shook his head. 'Sexy. Very, very sexy. Only last week we had Kate Moss here – shooting swimwear at the hotel.'

He pronounced hotel as 'otel. He smelled of expensive aftershave. His shirt was white and pristine. His dark hair was long on top and his fringe flopped over his brown eyes. Jacques was so exotic and foreign to Molly that she'd had to stop herself from staring at him in case he thought she fancied him. He was cute, but he wasn't her type – a bit too short and a bit skinny for her taste – but she liked him, she liked him a lot and she'd let herself hope that it might not be as hard to make friends in this far-flung place as she'd feared.

'Sometimes I work the beach bar with Henri – that is so much fun. He throws the best parties. Ah, you must meet Henri straight away! You will adore Henri. Everyone, they love Henri. And he will love you too. He is the bar manager. He is the, how do you say it? He is the life and soul of Paradise.' He'd glanced sideways at Molly a little shyly. 'And Henri, he will adore you too because you are pretty. He is, oh what is that word? A flit?'

'A flirt?' Molly had asked, with her cheeks burning scarlet, wriggling in her seat, half-flattered, half-mortified by the compliment.

'*Oui*, a flirt with ladies – especially ones who look like you.'

'Ah, don't be daft,' she'd scoffed. 'I'm a bleeding midget, Jacques, and compared to all those models and celebrities I hardly think any fella's going to notice me. Anyway, I'm not here looking for romance.'

'*Non?*' Jacques had raised a Gallic eyebrow. 'Well, what then? What else is there but *l'amour?*' He'd grinned, to show he was playing the part of the French lover-boy. And then asked again, more seriously, 'So what is the reason then? Everyone, they travel in search of something. What is it that you are looking for?'

'Freedom, Jacques,' Molly had answered excitedly. 'For the first time in my life I'm free!'

Jacques had glanced at her, obviously perplexed. 'And at home in … ?'

'Dublin,' Molly had replied. 'I'm from Dublin.'

'What was it that trapped you there? Why is it only now, so far away from home, that you feel free?'

What was it that had trapped her in Dublin? Molly had

thought about the question. The answers were too long, too complicated and too personal to explain to a guy she'd just met, however friendly he seemed.

'Ach, you know, family, work, money, the usual stuff.' She'd tried to sound nonchalant, like Jacques did, but, for the first time since she'd arrived in the Caribbean, Molly had felt a faint shadow fall over her heart.

She'd wondered if Joey had been sentenced yet, and if so, what he'd got. She'd wondered, with a pang of guilt, whether Caitlin had forgiven her for leaving and stopped crying yet. She'd wondered if Nan's knees were still playing her up in the cold and hoped that she'd turned the heating up, despite the shocking price of 'the electric'. She'd wondered if Shane was managing to get on with his studies now he was having to look after Caitlin, Joey and their nan. And she'd wondered what her da was doing now they'd all left him. Of course Francis Costello didn't deserve sympathy, but he was still her father, and the thought of him all alone, drinking himself into an early grave, with no friends or family, had made her sad. What a shocking waste of a life. Molly had even let herself think about her mam, briefly. She'd wondered what Mammy would have thought of her coming here. Would she have been proud of her daughter for being so adventurous? Or would she have thought that Molly had abandoned the rest of the family? She'd wished she'd had the nerve to ask Nan what her mam would have thought. She'd wanted to. The question had been on her lips so many times. But Nan never talked about Mammy. No one did. It was just the way things were.

Feeling herself welling up, Molly had shoved 'home' to the back of her mind. Now was not the time to get depressed. Not when she'd just stepped off a plane in heaven! So she'd cleared her mind, sat back in the passenger seat of the people carrier, and watched dumbstruck as mile upon mile of turquoise ocean appeared around every bend.

'This place is St Jean and here is Eden Rock.' Jacques had pointed to a gorgeous hotel that literally seemed to be perched on, and carved out of, its own rock. The rock jutted out into the sea, giving the impression of a tiny, private island. Just beyond Eden Rock was a glorious stretch of perfect sand.

'Wow,' Molly heard herself say, involuntarily.

'Yes, it is amazing, really. Beautiful, and very, how you say it? Posh! A lot of famous people have stayed here and it is where Monsieur Gabriel used to stay when he came to the island in the good old days. He likes to talk a lot about the good old days. Do not ever let him drink too much rum and then talk about these times, Molly. He will still be talking at dawn!'

Molly had giggled at his slight cheek. But Jacques was obviously very fond of his boss and the affection in his voice was genuine.

'Yes, Eden Rock is one of the most famous hotels in St Barts. Everybody from Greta Garbo, to Mick Jagger, to Fifty Cent has stayed here.' Jacques had laughed at the incongruity of the three. 'But I think it's a little noisy. You see,' he pointed at another light aircraft heading for the airport. 'It is in the flight path. And St Jean can get so busy with tourists. I think Paradise is even better. It is very isolated. Very private. And very intimate. There are only twelve guest rooms, you know?'

Molly did know. She knew everything about the hotel. She'd done nothing but study the Paradise website (at work when her shift ended and in the public library in Balymun where it was warm and where nobody could shout at her) since the day she'd got the call from Gabriel telling her that the flight was booked. There was a large plantation house, which housed the reception, the à la carte restaurant, the library bar, the spa and a boutique. There were twelve individual wooden cottages, each with a generous terrace, each painted a different candy colour and each with a sea view. There was an enormous infinity pool, with a bar in the middle and the whole boutique resort was hidden, scattered in the palm trees, on a hillside, with paths that meandered down to a perfect cove of chalk-white sand and impossibly blue sea. On the beach were dozens of wooden loungers and thatched canopies, a round wooden bar surrounded by wicker sofas with pure, white canvas cushions, a beach shop, a water-sports hut, and another less formal restaurant. A bottle of champagne at the bar cost more than Molly earned in a week. And a week at Paradise in high season? Well, that cost more than 10,000 euros per person for the cheapest room! Yes, Molly knew everything about Paradise.

'Ah, and here is Nikki Beach.' Jacques had continued his sightseeing tour as he'd pointed at a beach bar and restaurant that could have come straight out of a Bond film. 'You have heard of Nikki Beach?'

Molly had shaken her head. How the hell would she know about some super-cool bar in St Barts called Nikki Beach?

'There is a Nikki Beach in Miami, St Tropez, Marbella, Las Vegas ... You have never been to any of those places?'

Molly laughed, 'Ach, get away with you. Of course I've never been to those places.'

Jacques had looked genuinely surprised at this revelation. Then he'd shrugged and said, ' Well, it is good fun. We will go there at the weekend perhaps? The other girls who work at Paradise, they like to go there, maybe catch themselves a rich man, eh?'

'Are the other girls, erm, nice?' Molly had asked a little nervously.

Jacques had given her that little sideways glance again.

'There are some who are nice girls, but mostly, if I am honest, not so much,' he shrugged. 'I am sorry, Molly, but that is the truth. They are ...' He flicked his nose upwards with his finger. 'They are stuck up. They think they are too good for the rest of us. Except Henri, of course. They do not think they are too good for Henri. The ladies, they lurve Henri.'

'Are they all French?' Molly had probed further, butterflies rising in her stomach suddenly at the thought of the other girls.

'*Oui*,' Jacques had replied. '*Bien sûr*. We are almost all French. Except for Serge, the concierge.'

'Serge the concierge?' Molly had giggled again. 'Are you serious?'

Jacques laughed too. 'We did wonder if that is why Monsieur Gabriel gave him that job – because it rhymes so well. Anyway, Serge, he is Ukrainian, but the rest of us are from France. Bar staff, waiters, waitresses. We are students mostly; most are from Paris. I am not from Paris though. Me, I am from a little village in Brittany. I am different! Henri too, he is from Biarritz. Where we are mostly all the same is that we are taking a year off from our studies, enjoying the sun and the celebrities.'

Of course they'd be French; she'd kicked herself for being so dumb. St Barts was a French colony. She knew that. The language was French, the native population was tiny – who else was going to work at the upmarket hotels? But why was the thought of French girls so terrifying? Surely they couldn't all be as glamorous, aloof and intimidating as they looked in magazines? And students. Parisian students. Molly had left school at sixteen. She suddenly felt very scared.

'Of course the chambermaids are locals,' Jacques had added almost as an afterthought. 'From St Barts, St Martin, Guadeloupe. They seem OK. But we don't so much mix with the chambermaids.'

'But I'm going to be a chambermaid,' Molly had admitted, a little embarrassed.

'*Non*!' Jacques had stared at her as if she were an alien from another planet, rather than a young girl from Dublin, and then he'd shrugged that nonchalant shrug again and said, 'Ah well, is not important to me. I think you are nice. But you will not have to worry about the other girls. They will not even notice you if you are a chambermaid.'

Now Molly had been here almost a week and she realised Jacques was right. The other girls were mostly French, and they were mostly students, and they were mostly from Paris, and they were mostly achingly beautiful, and they were mostly a full head taller than her, and a whole lot better-educated than her and they mostly didn't acknowledge her at all. They were terrifying! Molly had already nicknamed them 'The Mean Girls' in her head. But the glamorous Gallic goddesses were the only downside to Paradise and the hotel's many charms more than made up for their presence.

'Do you know how Gabriel chooses his staff?' Jacques had asked her one day, shaking his head to show his slight disapproval.

Molly had shrugged. 'Intelligence? Breeding? Being able to speak four languages?'

'All that of course,' Jacques had said. 'But Gabriel not only checks their CVs for their education and class. He also insists that each applicant sends a photograph. Then he and Henri make their selection. They spend hours doing it at the beginning of every season. Saying that this one is quite smart but her nose is too big. Or this one's dad is a politician but she's a bit too fat for Paradise. To get a job here, it is a beauty contest. It is what the guests expect, I guess, but it is strange, *non*? To be a waitress, a receptionist, a shop assistant or a beautician here the girls must be tall, slim and gorgeous.'

'Ach, but not if you're just a lowly chambermaid, eh?' Molly had grinned. 'Which is just as well or I'd never have ended up here!'

It was true that the maids were a more down-to-earth bunch. The other chambermaids were sweet to Molly. They didn't speak much English and she didn't speak much French but they smiled at each other a lot and they were quick to cover for her if she made mistakes. She'd managed to gather that most of the West Indian women had children and they all lived away from the hotel – in Gustavia, the capital, mainly. Molly had a small but pretty room in the apartment block that housed the staff who lived on site. She could even see the ocean from her window if she strained her neck. At night, after she'd turned down the guests' beds, Molly would go back to her room, open her window and lie on her bed, listening to the waves. She was often interrupted by the squeals and giggles of the French girls, going out on the town after they'd finished their shifts. They never invited her to join them but Molly didn't mind. She was happy in her new home.

Jacques and Henri were obviously highly thought of by Gabriel because they lived in their own pad – a smaller version of the guest cottages, set up by the entrance to the resort, away from the beach and right on the main road round the island. Despite the lack of a sea view, the boys liked it up there because it meant they could smoke pot and play loud rap music without being caught by either the boss or the guests. Unlike the French girls, Jacques and Henri did invite Molly up to join them. In fact, Henri – a tall, blond, tanned, upmarket 'surf-dude' type from Biarritz – had invited Molly up to his place almost every day since she'd arrived.

Henri was undeniably good-looking and yes, if she was completely honest with herself, Molly did fancy him just a little bit. OK, she fancied him *a lot*! Who wouldn't?! He looked like an Abercrombie and Fitch model, with his long golden hair, searching hazel eyes, razor-sharp cheekbones and rippling six-pack. But she'd also seen him flirt with every other female member of staff, all the female guests, including the hot redhead (who was on her honeymoon, for crying out loud!) and the *really* old lady with the gold walking stick, who looked like Dame Barbara Cartland and carried a miniature white poodle under her arm. Molly had also spotted Henri flirting with the gorgeous gay couple who were visiting from Miami, with their matching mahogany tans, Brylcreemed black hair, gold aviators and tiny, navy Lycra trunks. Oh, and she'd watched him stroke the resort's cats too. Yup, even with felines Henri was overly attentive. Boy, he made them purr! Henri, it seemed, flirted with anything with a pulse – man, woman, cat, dog, turtle, it mattered not. So Molly wasn't about to let Henri's attention go to her head. Nor was she about to get stoned with him and Jacques. Much as she liked the boys, and appreciated their friendship, she was not about to blow this chance by misbehaving. Molly was, and always had been, a good girl. And she wasn't about to change that now.

More than anything, she would never want to let Gabriel down. She adored Gabriel. And Molly had a feeling that Gabriel was quite fond of her too. That knowledge made her feel safe here. She felt sure that if she had Gabriel on her side then nothing bad could happen to her while she was at Paradise. She carried on dusting, polishing and tidying Gabriel's cottage with the utmost care.

The other rooms (as the rest of the staff seemed to call the guest cottages) were quite alike. Not identical – room ten was the second biggest, had its own swimming pool and three separate suites, one with a huge four-poster bed. Room one was the smallest and most modest cottage. It consisted of just one room with a compact en suite and a sweet little decked area on the rocks that jutted out to the east of the resort. It was the furthest away from the action – a good five-minute walk from the Plantation House and the beach bar, but it had its own private jetty built out from the rocks. And, in Molly's opinion, from there, the lucky occupier not only had complete privacy to sunbathe, or snorkel or even to skinny dip, but they also had the very best view of the ocean on the entire island. Sometimes when she changed the towels on the loungers at the end of the jetty, Molly would pause for a moment to admire the yachts in the distance. One morning she watched a school of dolphins jump through the waves just feet from the end of the jetty and she felt so completely blessed to be in this perfect place that she shouted, 'Thank you!' to God and fate and the universe for letting her be there. Yes, she liked room one very much.

But room five was undeniably *the* best cottage at the Paradise Resort and Spa. It catered to Gabriel's richest clientele. The staff called it the Celebrity Suite. It only had two suites (each consisting of a bedroom, a lounge and a bathroom) but even the smaller bedroom was bigger than Molly's entire flat back home. The decor was super-cool and state-of-the-art. There was a remote control for everything – the sound system, the shutters, the colour-changing lighting and even for the TVs in the showers! Huge, colourful original modern artworks hung on the walls, and cowhides and sheepskins scattered the floors. It had the most enormous bed that Molly had ever had to make. She'd lain down on it just to try to work out how many Mollys would fit on it: eight, she reckoned, comfortably. Inside there was a Jacuzzi, a gym, a sauna and outside there was a private plunge pool, a larger swimming pool and also a private section of beach. The teak terrace was vast and went right down to the sand. On it was a hot tub, a four-poster day bed with muslin drapes and a fully stocked bar. Molly would never get to stay in a place like room five (this was a room that cost 20,000 euros – for one night in high season!) but sometimes, when she cleaned it, she pretended just for a moment that it was her own beachfront home. As if!

But Gabriel's room was something else. It was located at the very western tip of the resort, and set quite far apart from the others, which, Molly figured, made sense seeing as it was the proprietor's home rather than a holiday cottage. His was the only one painted white. Thick bushes and the tallest palm trees hid it from the main path and it had an uninterrupted view of the ocean from the terrace. Gabriel had a cat called Fred (Paradise was full of cats!) who was always asleep in the hammock on the veranda, and a pet tortoise called Shelley who visited every evening and ate on the terrace.

The furniture and decor in the other rooms was sleek, contemporary and modern – all crisp white sheets, chunky teak cabinets, highly polished wooden floors, shutters on the windows, huge plasma screen TVs on the wall and iPod players by the bed. But Gabriel's was grand in an altogether different way. His felt much more colonial and old-fashioned, if a little cramped, with antique furniture everywhere, some English-looking, some Caribbean, some French. He had exquisite, although slightly faded rugs on the floor and raw silk and velvet curtains on the windows. His surfaces were covered in ornaments, trinkets and silver-framed photographs. And the walls heaved under the weight of paintings and black-and-white photographs of Hollywood stars from a bygone age: one of whom Molly had already gathered was Gabriel's long-term and sadly deceased partner. There was even an Oscar on the shelf (also belonging to Gabriel's boyfriend) alongside three Emmys with Gabriel's name on them from his days as a television star. Well, she couldn't help but look, could she?

But what fascinated Molly most was the tiny, grainy photograph by Gabriel's bed, of two children – an earnest-looking boy of about ten with a tiny girl of about two on his lap. Both had dirty faces and knees, ragged clothes and the girl's feet were bare. They were sitting perched on the doorstep of a small terraced brick house on a cobbled street. They were smiling for the camera but their eyes were so sad. They looked like urchins. Beautiful, angelic, sad-eyed urchins. Something about the photograph always made Molly want to cry.

8

'I want this one,' said Lexi adamantly, twirling the enormous ruby and diamond rock on her wedding finger.

'But isn't that an engagement ring?' asked Mal, perplexed. 'We're already married, babe. It's a wedding ring we're after.'

'I want this one,' repeated Lexi, narrowing her eyes at him and chewing her gum aggressively with her perfect toothpaste-ad teeth bared, like she always did when she got stroppy.

Mal looked at the ice-maiden behind the glass counter for support but she stared back at him coldly and unblinkingly. Whether that was down to too much surgery or a personality disorder Mal wasn't sure, but he wasn't going to take any chances. Melting ice-maidens was one of Mal's particular talents but this one looked too much like hard work. Besides, Lexi was in one of her hormonal moods and flirting with a twenty-something female in front of her would not be a sensible move today. Not if he wanted to keep both his bollocks.

'OK, Mrs Riley, if that's the ring my princess wants, that's the ring she'll get ...'

Mal glanced at the tiny price tag in the space where the ring had been before Lexi had superglued it to her finger. He squinted. Nah, that couldn't be right. He squinted again. There must be an extra zero on that. Both Lexi and the ice-maiden frowned at him now. (Definitely a personality disorder then; if she'd had much Botox she wouldn't be able to frown like that.)

'What?' snapped Lexi, chewing her gum even more violently.

'I might need my eyes tested here, love,' said Mal to the ice-maiden. 'But to me it looks as if that tag says three million dollars.'

'You're correct, sir,' she replied robotically. 'This ring boasts an incredibly rare thirty-carat, pigeon blood-red Myanman ruby from Burma. The gem displays a richly saturated red colour combined with an exceptional clarity.'

'I've drunk plenty of wine that's displayed a richly saturated red colour combined with an exceptional clarity before, but it's never cost me three million fucking dollars!' Mal interrupted.

The ice-maiden tutted. Lexi stamped on his toe. Mal winced.

'The ruby is set in a twenty-four-carat band of Scottish gold—' the ice-maiden droned on.

'Scottish gold?!' Mal spluttered. 'Are you kidding me? There are coal mines in Scotland, not gold mines. Scotland's famous for bagpipes, ginger dudes, great football managers and rubbish football teams. Oh, and deep-fried Mars Bars, although my bass player Mack's Scottish and he swears they only make those for the tourists. But what I do know about Scotland is that it's not famous for fucking gold!'

'Scottish gold is the most rare and expensive gold in the world,' deadpanned the ice-maiden.

'Have you ever been to Scotland, love?' he asked the ice-maiden.

'No sir,' she replied, coldly.

'That's what I thought. You can buy a whole fucking

village in some parts of Scotland for three million dollars!' Mal explained. 'They must be pissing themselves, selling gold to you lot for that price. Christ, they saw your gullible American arses coming a mile off, didn't they? They're a canny bunch, the Scots. They must be dancing a Highland fling all the way to the RBS.'

Both Lexi and the ice-maiden glared at him.

'What's the RBS?' asked Lexi. Sometimes she looked at him as if he was from another planet rather than another country.

'It's a bank, princess,' he explained. 'And a Highland fling is a dance. See.'

Mal attempted to show her what a Highland fling was but quickly realised that he had no idea how to do one.

Lexi snorted and shook her head. He could have sworn she muttered 'asshole' under her breath but he couldn't be sure.

'If you can't afford the ring, sir,' interrupted the ice-maiden, 'perhaps the young lady would like to take it off now.'

Mal looked at Lexi nervously. She'd stopped chewing her gum. She was no longer glaring at him. She was stroking the ring on her finger lovingly and starting to cry. Not just shedding a quiet little tear – she was warming up for a major meltdown, Mal could tell. She started sobbing in great big gulps. Her shoulders began to shake and then she did it – she looked up at him with those enormous, pleading cornflower-blue eyes and wept, 'Pleeeeeeease.'

'Of course we can afford it,' Mal snapped at the ice-maiden. 'You do know who we are, don't you?'

'I'm aware of your work, sir,' sniffed the ice-maiden.

Aware of his work? Cheeky bitch. Oh well, no surprise that *she* wasn't a fan of good music.

'We'll have it,' he told her defiantly.

No stuck-up little American shop girl was going to tell him, Mal Riley, that he couldn't afford to spend three million dollars on a ring.

'Ooooh, thank you, baby,' squealed Lexi, throwing her arms around him and reaching up on her tiptoes to give him a sloppy kiss on the lips. 'I love you, I love, I love you.'

'OK, box it up,' said Mal, throwing his Platinum American Express on the desk.

'And we'll need matching wedding rings of course,' added Lexi, sweetly.

Mal looked up to the ceiling and asked God if he had any idea what was going on here because he certainly did not.

'But Lexi, my little flower, I thought this *was* your wedding ring,' he said, patiently.

'No,' she shook her head cutely. 'That's my engagement ring. Now we both need gold wedding bands to match.'

'But we didn't get engaged, Lexi,' Mal scratched his matted hair, utterly confused. 'We just got hitched when we were pissed.'

'An engagement ring shows an intention to marry someone, a promise,' said Lexi petulantly, stamping her foot. 'Are you suggesting that you never had any intention of marrying me, Malcolm?'

Why did both Lexi and his mother do that? Call him Malcolm when they were cross with him? Hmm, had he ever had any intention of marrying Lexi? He evaded the question.

'But I have married you, *Alexis*,' he replied, trying to play her at her own full-name game. 'You are now my wife. I am your husband. We are hitched. Spliced. I'm your Old Man. You're my Her Indoors. How much more do you want?'

'I want this wedding band,' she said, pointing at a dainty

gold ring. 'And I want you to have this one,' she added, pointing to a more chunky matching gold band.

'Nah, nah, nah ...' Mal shook his head and started backing away from the ring counter as if it was about to explode. 'You can have that little one if you like, babe, but I DO NOT wear rings.'

'You are so full of shit, Mal,' snapped Lexi, grabbing his right hand and waving the chunky silver skull ring he always wore in his face.

'This is not a ring,' said Mal defensively, snatching his hand away and stroking the skull as if it were a newborn kitten. 'This beauty,' he said proudly, now showing it off to the ice-maiden (still a safe distance away from the counter), 'is a piece of rock history. It belonged to none other than the legend who was, is, and always will be, Jimi Hendrix. It is more than a ring. It's a symbol of creative expression, passion, talent, free spirit ...'

Snap! Lexi blew an angry bubble in his face with her gum.

Mal tried to ignore her, warming to his monologue now. 'And I'm not going to insult it by wearing it with a poncy little sliver of gold.'

The ice-maiden sneered at Mal's favourite ring as if it offended her greatly. Lexi sneered at Mal as if he offended her greatly. Which it seemed, right now, he did.

'And that ring there,' she said, her voice dripping with anger, 'will be a symbol of love, commitment and *fidelity*.' She put particular emphasis on the last word. 'And if anyone needs a solid gold reminder that they are officially off the market it's you, Mal Riley. You're a recovering sex addict, in case you've forgotten, and you have women throwing themselves at you at every gig, every party, even on the street! Waitresses write their number on the check, porn actresses Facebook you, you get pictures of naked asses sent to your phone. I've seen them Mal, don't think I haven't snooped! So, just to remind you, and all the gold-digging, husband-stealing, smutty little sluts out there that you are now married, I insist you wear a wedding band, OK?!'

It was clearly not a question. Mal felt a bit queasy suddenly. His mouth went dry and his heart started to pound in his chest. He took another step towards the door and peered out to the Forum Shops beyond. A burly security guard blocked his way and the door to the shop had been locked when they arrived because that's what happens when you're famous – the public get kicked out and the celebs get the shop to themselves, protected from the plebs and the paparazzi.

Fight or flight? He could tackle the security guard, he reckoned. Mal was a big guy. He could unlock the door – the keys were in the lock. It wasn't as if he was stealing anything. He could run out into the mall and get lost in the crowds, disappear into Caesar's Palace, catch a cab to the airport and a plane to LA and to freedom. He could call his lawyers and get the marriage annulled – there must be a dozen witnesses to the fact that he was barely conscious when he said his vows! He could get his agent to leak a story saying he'd been drugged and didn't know what he was doing. Or better still, give a heartfelt interview telling the world that he was a failure, a fuck-up, a no-hoper who would never be good enough for a woman as amazing as Lexi Crawford, and that he'd made the ultimate sacrifice in letting her go for her own welfare. Or he could stay here and make a proper grown-up commitment to the woman he loved. Mal glanced at Lexi. She didn't look so angry suddenly, just scared. Very young, very vulnerable and very scared.

Oh bloody hell, what a pickle he'd got himself into this time. He loved Lexi. He really did, more than any other girl he'd ever met, and he was proud of the fact he'd managed to be faithful to her for the past eight months. Well, more or less ... But he'd been happy being her boyfriend. Her suspicions were right: he had had no intention of marrying her. It was all just a big mistake.

'I, um, I really don't like gold,' he muttered lamely to Lexi, glancing around at his escape route, like a fox cornered by a pack of hounds. 'Look, everything's silver.'

He indicated the studs on his black leather jacket and the buckles on his boots. Lexi was a fashionable girl; if anything could dissuade her from the gold ring idea it was the fact that Anna Wintour might not approve.

Lexi sighed, and nodded. She looked a little less scared now, as if she suddenly understood Mal's absolute terror at the thought of having to wear something as conformist as a wedding ring.

'I understand,' she said gently, as if reading his mind.

Mal let out a deep sigh and put his arms around his little Lexi. She was so cool.

'I knew you'd understand, babe,' he began waffling. 'I mean for a bohemian like me, a symbol as conservative and old-fashioned as a wedding ring is just such a challenge. I mean I'm delighted to be your husband,' he lied. 'But to be branded like that, publicly, to be owned ...'

Lexi pushed him off her, wiped her eyes with the back of her arm and then pushed her fingers through her hair in what appeared to be desperation. Eh? Why was she suddenly upset again? Despite having spent his entire life in the company of women, Mal continued to find their behaviour utterly baffling.

'I meant,' said Lexi tearfully, 'I understand that you might not want to wear gold. I was going to say, why don't you get a platinum band instead? But, d'you know what, Malcolm Riley? You can go to hell.'

Lexi pulled the ruby engagement ring off her finger and placed it on the counter. She said, 'I'm terribly sorry to waste your time, miss,' to the ice-maiden and then headed towards the door, where the security guard not only opened the door, but patted her sympathetically on the back as she departed.

Mal stood with his feet glued to the spot. He watched Lexi disappear into the Forum Shops, sobbing and tripping over her feet as she tried to escape from Mal and also from the star-hunters who were chasing her now and holding up their phones to take photos. She looked like a hunted animal and it was all his fault. Lexi never let her act slip in public. Holy shit, what had he done?

'Bollocks,' he said out loud.

The ice-maiden and the security guard were both glaring at him. Neither tried to disguise their disgust.

'What should I do?' he asked them, because there was no one else there, and he was fucked if he knew what to do now.

'Go after her, jerk,' yelled the security guard.

'Buy the rings, bastard,' spat the ice-maiden, finally losing her cool.

Mal weighed up the situation in his addled brain. He didn't want to wear a wedding ring. The thought scared the crap out of him. Neither did he particularly want to be married. But as he saw the back of Lexi's red mini-dress disappear into the crowd he felt his heart lurch. He didn't want to lose Lexi either. He really, really, really didn't want to see the back of that sexy, stroppy, warm-hearted, foul-mouthed little vixen. Five minutes earlier he'd been considering running away himself, but now that Lexi had walked out on him everything felt different.

'I'll do both,' he announced. 'You,' he pointed to the ice-maiden, 'give me that ridiculous, overpriced rock now. I'll take it as it is. It fitted her, right?'

The ice-maiden nodded.

'Come on, charge my card quickly!'

The ice-maiden swiped his card and then handed him a red velvet box with the ruby in it.

'Now box up that wedding ring she liked in her size. And then pick out the chunkiest platinum ring you've got for me ...'

'Which one?' she asked, finally melting a little.

'The one that looks the least like a wedding ring!' he told her.

'And what size?' she asked, already looking through her collection of platinum gentlemen's rings.

'I dunno,' said Mal, flustered now. He needed to run after Lexi, quick! 'Here,' he said, taking off his beloved Jimi Hendrix ring. 'That fits the same finger on my other hand. It must be the right size. Give me one the same size as that. Box that up with the others, charge my card for what I haven't paid for and then have the whole lot biked round to the Bellagio, the Grand Lakeview Suite. You know my name, right?'

The ice-maiden nodded and blushed a little. 'Of course I know your name,' she said in a much softer tone. 'I had your poster inside my locker at high school.'

'Oh, bless you,' said Mal, suddenly noticing how beautiful the ice-maiden was with her poker-straight platinum hair and slanting grey eyes.

'Oi, jerk!' shouted the security guard, who Mal guessed had not had his poster inside his locker at high school. 'Get your dumb ass in gear and get after your lady. That's Lexi Crawford you just let walk out on you. What are you? Some kind of moron? You ain't gonna get any better than that. She's a legend. Now run!'

He gave Mal a hard shove in the back and practically threw him out of the shop.

Lexi leant on the wall outside the Bellagio and pretended to be enthralled by the Dancing Fountains, like all the tourists. She leant forward with her head resting on her palms and let her hair fall over her face, trying desperately to disappear. But she wasn't a tourist, and no one would ever let her blend into the crowd.

'Hey, Lexi!' people shouted over the music that accompanied the water show.

'It is you!' they yelled. 'Love your work!'

'Congratulations on your wedding,' said some.

'Can I have a picture with you please?' asked others.

She replied 'yes' and 'thank you' and 'no pictures right now, I'm sorry' and tried to keep her bottom lip from wobbling by biting down on it hard. She was perfectly aware that all around her people were taking photographs and video footage not of the fountains, but of her back (like, how interesting could that be?!), so she leant further and further forward over the wall, trying to escape her public persona for just five minutes. She was used to the attention. Jeez, she couldn't remember it being any other way. She'd been nine when she got her first part in a kids' TV series, eleven when she landed her first movie role, fourteen when she became an official 'star' with a multi-million-dollar Disney contract. When Walmart started selling T-shirts with her face emblazoned across the front, she knew there was never going to be any such thing as 'normal' again. And, on the whole, she'd taken it in her stride. She'd been in therapy since she was ten, so she'd always had someone to talk to about her 'issues', and all of her friends were in the business too, so she'd had plenty of peers who understood the pressures of fame.

But sometimes, just sometimes, Lexi Crawford wished she was invisible. Like now: when her stupid bastard of a husband had just been such a total jerk that she wanted to curl up and die. She was a good actress and once she'd calmed down she'd managed to fight back the tears and swallow the lump in her throat. She knew that to the public she now looked composed, content even – *Hollywood actress enjoys the sights in Las Vegas!* – but inside her mind was racing and her heart was breaking and the ball of anger in the pit of her stomach had grown into a raging fireball.

She stared at the fountains and listened to the music, trying to feel calmed, knowing she should be soothed and impressed. But she'd seen the Bellagio's dancing fountains so many times before that they didn't really do much for her now. And the song playing was Celine Dion's 'My Heart Will Go On', which was not exactly Lexi's cup of tea – way too schmaltzy now she was a rock chick! Anyway, she'd seen so many fountains and fireworks, Superbowls and circus acts, film stars and musicians, gigs and premiers. Nothing really impressed her any more. How could it? She was kind of numb to 'stuff' now. Only people could make her feel, these days. And even then, to be honest, it was only really Mal who could do that. Everyone else – her parents, her brother, her so-called friends, her co-stars – they left her feeling a bit cold really. She could act out all sorts of emotions on screen but in the real world only Mal could make her truly feel.

'Fucking asshole,' she muttered to herself, thinking about him, and about his obnoxious behaviour in the jewellery store.

Why would she even want a man like that? Who'd

only married her by accident when he was drunk and who wouldn't even wear a wedding ring? The anger rose and burned in her throat. Well maybe she didn't want to be married to him either. Maybe she would just call her agent right now and have the whole problem 'sorted'. Lexi tapped her foot agitatedly while concentrating on keeping her features relaxed. The elegant swan, kicking furiously beneath the water where nobody could see.

Lexi felt the presence of a paparazzo nearby (she had a kind of radar for them now) and leant back momentarily, tossing her hair off her face and fixing her features in an enthralled smile so that they'd get the right picture – *Lexi Crawford is mesmerised by the famous Dancing Fountains!*

Mesmerised, my ass, she thought as she leant back over the wall, fuming. *Frigging homicidal, more like.*

Oh, why was Mal such hard work? Every time she felt she was finally getting settled with him, every time she relaxed in their relationship and started to feel secure, he went and did something that made her go all wobbly again. And it made her so mad! She wanted to scream and shout and throw things. She wanted to punch him in the face. She'd talked and talked with her therapist about her anger issues but it was no good. She could forgive her mom for living vicariously through her daughter's fame; she could forgive her dad for stealing half her money; she could even forgive her brother for hating her – he was jealous of her success and the attention it had brought her. But she could never forgive Mal when he didn't love her quite enough.

Why couldn't he just feel like she did about things? Keep it simple? They met. They fell in love. They realised they were soul mates. They got married. OK, they did it in an unconventional way, but they still did it. They got married. And even though the whole thing was a bit of a blur, Lexi knew it had been the right thing to do. She belonged to Mal and he belonged to her. And now she wanted them both to wear wedding bands. What was the big frigging deal with that?

She sighed, realised she was drumming her fingernails on the wall a little anxiously. She stopped herself, checked her expression, hid her feelings. She sighed again. Of course, Lexi wasn't about to call her agent. She was just angry and wanted to lash out. There was no way she was ever going to let Mal go. She desperately wanted to be Mrs Mal Riley. She wanted it more than anything else in the whole world. More than an Oscar, or a *Vogue* cover, or even an Elie Saab couture wedding gown (not that she was ever going to get that now — she'd got married in her jeans). But she was so scared that he didn't feel the same that when he'd tried to wriggle out of wearing a wedding ring, she'd lost it

Oh fuck, what if she'd blown it this time? What if Mal had had enough of her teenage tantrums? What if the press, and her mother, and his mother were right? What if she really was too young for him? What if he ran out on her this time? Not just for a couple of days, like the time she'd kicked a dent in his favourite Ferrari, and he'd gone AWOL in New York with his buddies. But for good? For ever? Lexi knew she would just die if she lost him. There was no one else to take care of her. No one else 'got her' except Mal. Lexi swallowed hard and tried to blink back the tears that were welling up in her eyes.

It took a while for Lexi to realise that there was some sort of commotion going on behind her. People were talking excitedly over the music. The crowd had turned away from the fountains, even though the show was in full swing. She fixed the winning smile back on her face, thinking that the commotion probably had something to do with her presence, and turned round. Lexi nearly fell over. There, on bended knee, with a cheap red rose from one of those street vendors between his teeth, was Mal Riley. Her Mal Riley. She grinned. Melted. Almost fainted with relief.

'What are you doing, you goofball?' she asked, giggling.

Mal took the rose out of his mouth with a flourish and handed it to her. The gathered crowd sighed. 'Awww ...'

'Alexis Matilda Crawford,' he announced ... and then he turned to the delighted crowd and said, 'Yes, folks, that's her name. I blame the parents.'

The crowd laughed.

'Alexis Matilda Crawford,' he repeated, having to shout over the music that accompanied the dancing fountain show. 'My darling, my angel, my world. Would you do me the honour of becoming my wife?'

'I'm already your wife, you dork,' she giggled, her heart bursting with joy.

'I know. But I forgot to propose and I forgot to buy a ring and, if I'm completely honest, dear Lexi, and dear citizens of America ...' he looked round, nodding at the crowds, 'when I woke up in the morning, I'd forgotten I'd got married at all.'

The crowd roared with laughter. Lexi rolled her eyes. She had big eyes. She played stroppy teenagers. It was her trademark look.

'Go on, Lexi. Say yes!' someone shouted.

And then the entire crowd started chanting, 'Yes, yes, yes, yes!' in time with the fountains that soared into the sky and the music that filled the hot, desert air. Celine had finished now (thank the Lord!) and Elton John's 'Your Song' was blasting out instead. Lexi looked at Mal, down on bended knee in his scruffy jeans and beaten-up black leather jacket. She watched his handsome, stubbly face as he smiled at her hopefully and held out the ruby ring in a red velvet box. His eyes were the colour of melted chocolate. Lexi's stomach flipped and her heart skipped and tears of joy started rolling down her cheeks.

'And you can tell everybody this is your song …' he sang in time with the music.

He thrust the box closer to Lexi, imploring her to accept.

'Will you?' he asked again, quieter this time, as if there was no one else there.

'Yes,' she choked on her tears. 'I will.'

'She said yes!' shouted Mal to the crowd, as he slipped the ring onto her finger.

And then Lexi found herself in her husband's arms, being spun around and kissed all over her face, as the amazing Dancing Fountains of the Bellagio Hotel Las Vegas leapt and soared above her head, and Elton John's voice sang their story and a crowd of thousands cheered them on. And Lexi didn't feel numb at all. She felt as if her heart would burst right open with the sheer, wonderful, amazing, pure, unadulterated joy of it all.

She could see the headlines now: *Lexi Crawford Ecstatic as Rock Star Husband Proposes – After the Wedding*! And this time she wasn't acting at all.

9

Shiloh galloped through the forest as if her life, and Clyde's life, depended on it. Twigs cracked under her hooves and branches snapped above Clyde's head as he ducked through the low-hanging trees. He felt the awesome power of her body beneath him, listened to the rhythm of her hooves, smelled her familiar, musky scent and he rode, rode, rode. Her nostrils flared and her breath turned to steam in the cold air as they fled deeper into the forest, further and further away from the roads and the towns and the people who inhabited them. Clyde had had enough of people. It was a freezing, crisp Colorado day. The sky above them was watery blue. The fresh virgin January snow flew up behind them as they galloped faster, faster, following the trails between the rows of blue spruces with the clean rocky mountain air in their lungs, adrenalin in their veins and love for each other in their hearts.

Shiloh – his beloved, beautiful, brave Shiloh – was the love of his life. Clyde just had to think of that horse and it was like a hand clamping round his heart. He tried not to think of the future or the past as he rode her, climbing now, higher and higher towards their favourite spot. He tried to lose himself in the perfection of the moment. Man and beast as one. Through all the pain and torment, the heartache and the guilt, Shiloh had been Clyde's one consistent comfort.

He'd had so many expensive, rare horses during the days on the ranch and sometimes he used to choose one of them to take out instead. Shiloh would always give him a jealous sideways glance when he did so; she'd snort, throw back her long blonde mane and trot off in disgust. She was right, of course – those horses had been fun, but riding them was never the same as riding Shiloh. It was kind of like being unfaithful when you had the perfect woman at home, he guessed. It might seem like an exciting idea at the time, to try something a little exotic and different, but the reality was never as good as true love. Unfortunately, Clyde had failed to find his perfect woman in life. And he'd pretty much given up any hope of ever finding her now. But where he had been fortunate was in finding his perfect horse. Clyde and Shiloh. Shiloh and Clyde. For eight years the pair had been inseparable.

'I think you love that darned horse more than you love me, Clyde Scott!' Nancy used to holler from the door, after they'd had an argument and he would head off to the stables to seek solace in Shiloh.

And she'd been right. Clyde had loved Nancy too, but in a fire … ? If the house had been burning and the stables had been burning … ? Clyde would have hated to ever make that judgement call because he wasn't absolutely sure which way he would have turned. He'd probably have hollered for the staff to save his family while he personally led Shiloh to safety. Such was his love for the animal. He'd had to let the rest go, some with a heavier heart than others. The rare breeds, the studs, the thoroughbreds, hell, even the foal he'd bottle-fed. Only Shiloh had come with him to the cabin when he'd left the ranch. And he'd sworn he'd never let her go.

Shiloh was a bog-standard American Quarter Horse – the

most common horse breed in the USA. Strong, fast, hard-working, adaptable, tough and loyal. They made good pets, good working horses, good ranchers, good rodeo beasts, good racers, good hunters. Some might say that Nancy had been not only Clyde's second wife, but also his trophy wife. She was a stunner, that was true, and ten years younger than him. He'd felt he'd deserved the whole package once he'd made the big time. She'd been homecoming queen in Denver in '96 and she was voted Miss Colorado in '98 and she was considered quite a catch even for a world-famous writer. The problem with trophy wives, though, is that they don't sign up for the hard times. And when Clyde's life turned to horse shit, Nancy was out of that door before she could shout 'prenup'. He guessed he couldn't really blame her. She'd married a multi-millionaire and ended up on skid row. Luckily, Shiloh was not Clyde's trophy horse. He'd had Arabians for that. No, American Quarter Horses were kind of like Fords, Clyde guessed – nothing foreign or flash, just solid, dependable, trustworthy and all-American. Yup, unlike Nancy, Shiloh had stuck by Clyde through the good times and the bad.

That wasn't to say Shiloh wasn't a looker. Man, that horse was beautiful. She never failed to take Clyde's breath away. She was a palomino and an unusually pale one at that. She was almost cream in colour with a long, fine blonde mane and tail. Her eyelashes were always a source of amusement to Clyde and to his kids. They were unnaturally long and Ethan, JJ and Clara swore Shiloh could flutter them if there was a granola bar on offer.

He pulled her up now, dismounted, patted her flank and then buried his face in her muzzle. He kissed her like a lovesick schoolboy, whispered sweet nothings in her ears, fed her a granola bar (her favourite) and tried not to cry at the thought of being parted from her. She nibbled the back of his ear, like she always did, and stared right back into his watery eyes with a look of absolute adoration.

'Love you, baby,' said Clyde, as they banged foreheads affectionately.

Why was it so easy to tell Shiloh how he felt, when it had always been so frigging hard to tell a woman those three little words? Shiloh pawed and snuffled in the shallow snow, trying to find some grass. The snow got up her nostrils and made her sneeze.

'Crazy lady!' Clyde laughed at her, sitting on a tree stump, toking on a Marlboro and taking in the perfect view. Bridal Veil Falls. Three hundred and fifty feet of the most breath-taking waterfalls in Colorado. Clyde loved this place. He'd been coming here his whole life and so had Shiloh. Most folks would think he was mad to come riding out this far in January but Clyde wasn't most folks. He knew this land like the back of his hand. He might not be able to negotiate the Manhattan subway, but the Gunnison National Forest? A piece of piss! Those spiky uptown girls in New York scared the shit out of him. But hungry black bears in winter? Pah! No problem.

He smoked another cigarette, and then another. He spoke to his horse and watched the sun get lower and lower in the sky until the light faded to a hazy grey.

'Well, my beautiful Shiloh, I guess it's time to go,' he said finally, with a heavy heart.

They took the quick way down, past the ski town of Telluride and down, down into the valley below. McNabb was waiting for him at the gate of the ranch with his Stetson pulled forward over his lined forehead and his hands pushed deep into the pockets of his North Face jacket.

'It's late, Scott,' barked his neighbour, gruffly. 'The rest of the animals are stabled now.'

He sounded pissed, but then Wally McNabb always sounded pissed. It was just his manner.

'Yeah. Well, I had to say goodbye to my old lady,' explained Clyde, making no excuses.

McNabb took Shiloh's reins from Clyde and patted her affectionately on the shoulder.

'Hey, beautiful lady,' he whispered to her. 'You gonna be a good girl for your Uncle Wally?'

Clyde relaxed a little. Even he wasn't allowed to call Wally anything other than McNabb. And he'd known the guy his whole life. McNabb had been a friend of his dad's when Clyde was still a kid and after his dad had died they'd kept in touch. When the ranch next to McNabb's came up for sale, he'd given Clyde the nod before the place was even on the market.

The fact that Shiloh at least was allowed to be on first-name terms with her new owner was a relief to Clyde. New owner. Fuck. No! How the hell did it come to this? Clyde felt tears burn his eyes and he had to screw up his face and push his nails into the palm of his hands to try to stop himself from breaking down in front of McNabb. His neighbour was a great rancher, and a famous horseman, but he was not exactly the touchy-feely type.

'Clyde,' said McNabb, placing a firm hand on his shoulder. 'I know this is tough for you. But I am gonna take such good care of your baby, OK? I know what she means to you.'

Clyde nodded but didn't trust himself to speak yet. He took a deep breath, steadied himself and placed his hand gently on Shiloh's nose. He stared right into her deep brown eyes, knowing that she understood everything.

'I'm coming back for you, Shiloh, you hear me?' he told her. 'I'm coming back. It's a promise.'

Then he turned to McNabb. 'And this is just temporary, right?'

'Sure', said McNabb. 'When you got the money, you'll be back for the horse. We shook on it. It's a deal.'

Clyde managed a weak smile. 'And thank you, McNabb,' he managed to say. 'For helping me out here.'

'I ain't doing you a favour, Clyde,' scoffed McNabb. 'This is a fine beast, I'll enjoy having her, and you're paying me back with five per cent interest when you come to collect, OK?'

Clyde nodded. He had no choice. He had debts to pay before he left. He was behind on the rent on the cabin and had to clear that before he went. He had to give Nancy money for the kids. She might be married to some hot-shot Denver lawyer now but that didn't mean Clyde was going to shirk his responsibility for his kids. He'd sold the truck, the TV, the state-of-the-art home cinema system, his camping gear. Hell, he'd even sold off his signed first editions on eBay! But still it wasn't enough. The only asset he'd had left was Shiloh. McNabb was a tough old cowboy but he was kind to his horses and Clyde hadn't known where else to turn. This way, if he got his shit together, wrote that damned book and got a new deal, he could have Shiloh back any time. If that wasn't a carrot to dangle, then Clyde didn't know what was. Because the thought of life without Shiloh was unbearable.

'So where the hell is it you're goin' anyhow?' asked McNabb.

'St Barthélemy,' replied Clyde, shaking his head at the ridiculousness of Ronnie's plan.

'Saint what?' asked McNabb, screwing up his weathered face in confusion.

'Barthélemy,' repeated Clyde. 'It's in the French West Indies, right next door to St Martin.'

'I don't have the first clue what the hell you're talking about, Clyde,' said McNabb, scratching the stubble on his chin. 'But I sure as hell hope you have a nice time, and that you get over whatever damn problems have been bothering you these past few years. You're a fine writer. And a fine horseman. You need to clean up whatever mess is in that head of yours. That's what I'm telling you and that's what your pa would have told you too. Sort your head out, Clyde, and get back to work. Then you and Shiloh here can live happily ever after, OK? Ain't that how those books of yours always end?'

For McNabb, these were warm words indeed, and Clyde felt himself well up again at the realisation that there were good people in the world, who actually cared about him, and who were on his side.

'Thanks, McNabb,' he said, placing a hand briefly on the older man's arm. 'I won't forget what you've done for me. Or for Shiloh.'

The men stared at each other in silence for a moment and then McNabb coughed and Clyde kicked the road and the embarrassment of the situation took over.

'I gotta get this lady comfortable for the night,' said McNabb, indicating Shiloh.

Clyde's heart sank to the pit of his stomach. He could barely bring himself to look at Shiloh now, knowing that he was abandoning her and that there was no guarantee that he'd ever be able to buy her back. He took her head in his hands, and rested his forehead on hers. He kissed her nose and stroked her ears, took in the smell of her one last time, wishing he could bottle that musky scent and take it with him. He told her how much he loved her and he whispered promises to her of a reunion soon. God, he hoped he could keep those promises. For both their sakes.

He walked the four miles back to the cabin. And Clyde Scott, six foot three, forty-two years old, author of nine bestselling thrillers, cried like a baby all the way home. It wasn't until he was three-quarters of the way through a bottle of Jim Beam that he started to feel a little better. That's what it took to reach comfortable numbness. That's when he stopped feeling anything at all.

10

Chiswick, West London

Sebastian had barely been home since Breakfastgate, as Lauren was now calling the unfortunate incident over the yogurt and blueberries. Emily seemed unfazed by the event and had carried on with homework, ballet and horse riding in her usual stoic fashion. Poppy had been a little more tearful and clingy since the argument but then she was a far more sensitive flower than her sister – Poppy by name, Poppy by nature. She'd taken to sneaking into Lauren's bed most nights lately, and snuggling up to her mum just so that she could fall asleep. Which only gave Sebastian an excuse to sleep in the spare room – again – on the nights he did show his face. It worried Lauren sometimes, that maybe it was her fault that Poppy was so thin-skinned. Lauren tried not to show the girls when she was feeling low, but it was hard sometimes, when her husband didn't come home from work, not to take herself off to bed and, well, just weep into the pillow for half an hour. If only she could be stronger then maybe Poppy would feel stronger too.

The weird thing was, Lauren didn't remember being tearful as a child, or even as a hormonal teenager. She'd been a pretty well-balanced, confident girl. She'd moved to London to study photography at the Royal College of Art at eighteen and she'd been quite happy making her own way in the city. She'd made friends easily, she'd been popular with a hectic social life, and when she graduated she'd thrown herself straight into quite a successful career. Lauren wasn't blowing her own trumpet – she'd been no Mario Testino – but she hadn't been half bad. It was OK to admit that, wasn't it? Not too 'up herself' (as Sebastian called it when she talked about her past successes)?

She'd always felt at ease with boyfriends before Sebastian. In fact, she was fairly sure she'd mostly had the upper hand. She wasn't one for big dramas, or histrionics. No one had ever really broken her heart, or been particularly mean to her, and in fact she'd managed to remain friends with most of them after the relationships were over. Well, until Sebastian came along and put a stop to her friendships with all men, especially those she'd previously slept with. No, Lauren didn't remember much angst at all in her childhood, or her teens, or her early twenties. It wasn't really until she met Sebastian that she'd become, well, 'unhinged' she supposed, as he liked to put it. Maybe it was having the children that did it. Perhaps she'd suffered more postnatal depression than she'd realised at the time. And having the girls had certainly been the nail in the coffin of her career. But sometimes it felt like she'd sacrificed every other part of herself in order to keep hold of Sebastian. Right from the beginning she'd had this fear of losing him and it had made her cling onto him like a limpet to a rock in stormy seas. She'd loved him passionately and completely. He'd had this way of making her see that he was the most amazing, charismatic, special man she'd ever met and would ever have the good fortune of meeting.

'You won't find this again, you do know that?' he would say, as they lay in bed together after yet another afternoon spent having mind-blowing sex. 'It happens once, Lauren. Remember that.'

And she would tell him that, yes, yes she knew that. She really, really knew that. She had no doubt that it was true. And she hadn't forgotten it to this day.

The only problem was that he wasn't very good at making her feel secure and his temper tantrums meant that he'd always been prone to storming out on her, leaving her in tears in restaurants, or foreign cities, or hotel rooms. Hmm, and even at the airport once, she remembered with a shudder. His love had always felt very conditional: if she behaved herself then he would love her, but if she misbehaved he would punish her by withdrawing affection. It made her feel as if she was always the underdog, having to beg and perform tricks to win her master's approval. She supposed it was what he was still doing now, twelve years later. It was what he did to the girls too and also to his staff. It was just his way.

Sebastian didn't come home at all for the first two nights after the argument. He muttered something about having to work late and staying at the office for the sake of convenience – which was feasible, as he had an apartment in the building for exactly that purpose, but unlikely. Lauren knew when her husband was in a huff. He came home late the next night and then the night after that he did spend at the house, but he took his dinner and locked himself in *his* living room (as he called the smaller reception room with the more expensive furnishings), watching TV and texting like a teenager. He'd kept this pattern up ever since – out, out, late, in (sort of) and then out again.

'He's having an affair,' said Lauren's best friend Kitty, as she sat at the kitchen island sipping her latte. 'I'd have chopped his bollocks off by now.'

Kitty was Lauren's only friend left from the days when she was a 'somebody'. And although the two women's lives were completely at odds, Kitty was probably Lauren's closest friend. She was a fashion stylist, who was forever flying off to Milan and Paris and New York. Kitty had never got married or had kids, but she seemed to have no regrets. She argued that her sex life was 'more than fulfilling' thank you very much, that long-term relationships just got stale and that, because she was child-free, she could not only still wear a bikini with pride but she could wear one in a size six to boot. Kitty also felt it was her role to speak frankly to Lauren because, in her words, 'those wet bitches from the school run aren't going to tell you the truth'. That's what she was doing now. Speaking frankly.

'He's not having an affair,' Lauren argued. 'I do know my husband. He's just huffing.'

Kitty raised a perfectly plucked eyebrow dubiously and twirled a lock of peroxide hair round her finger. 'You never think he's having an affair when he does his disappearing act. But from the outside looking in ...'

Lauren tried to keep her composure. She knew her marriage looked less than perfect from the outside but what did Kitty know? Really? She'd never even gone out with the same man for more than nine months. She didn't understand that marriages ebb and flow. Sometimes you need space from each other. Sebastian had explained that to her very early on but he'd also sworn on the children's lives that he would never cheat. He had his faults but he was a loyal man and everything he did, he did for his family. Lauren believed him.

'Kitty, I'm not getting into this again,' Lauren replied, firmly. 'Sebastian would never be unfaithful to me. I know that.'

'How?' demanded Kitty, ignoring Lauren's desire to drop the subject. 'How do you know that? Have you checked his phone? His pockets? His email?'

'No!' said Lauren, defensively.

'Really?' Kitty's eyebrow was practically at her hairline now. Lauren sighed. 'OK, once. I had a bit of a snoop once.'

'And?' Kitty was like a dog with a bone.

'Nothing!' said Lauren. 'His pockets were empty, I couldn't get into his email because it's security blocked – it's his business, Kitty! – and there were no messages on his phone, so ...'

'Oh God, that's awful,' said Kitty, her face full of concern.

'What d'you mean? There was nothing to find.' Lauren was confused.

'Darling,' said Kitty, placing her hand over Lauren's. 'Did you just say there were no messages on his phone? None at all? Nothing in the sent box? Nothing in the inbox?'

'That's right,' replied Lauren, snatching her hand away. She didn't like Kitty's tone.

'Lauren, darling,' Kitty persevered. 'A man only clears his boxes if he has something to hide. Haven't I taught you *anything*?!'

'Sebastian gets like fifty million texts a day. He's an important man. He has his phone set to automatically delete them so that his inbox doesn't get clogged up.'

'And that's what he tells you, is it?' Kitty shook her head, sadly.

'Yes! That's what he tells me because it's true.' Lauren found herself raising her voice now, which she hated.

'OK, so why does he look like that?' Kitty carried on regardless, pointing at the framed picture of Sebastian with Sir Alan Sugar, which took pride of place on the kitchen wall. 'What's with the tan, and the shaved chest, and the Rolex and the hair dye ...'

'He doesn't dye his hair,' Lauren defended Sebastian. 'It's naturally that dark.'

'What? At forty-four, he's the only man in London without one grey hair on his head? Whatever you say, Lauren,' Kitty said. 'But I'm telling you now, it is not normal for a married man to take that much interest in his appearance. Not unless he's still on the pull. What about down there ...?'

'Pardon?' Lauren felt emotionally exhausted by this conversation. Why did Kitty always want to talk about Sebastian? And the contents of Sebastian's boxer shorts at that!

'I bet he's got a back, sack and crack,' said Kitty. 'Hasn't he? Well ...? Hasn't he?'

Lauren's cheeks burned as the shame crept up her face. Could she admit the truth to Kitty? She'd been keeping it to herself for months but ... Maybe it was time to let it go.

'I wouldn't know,' she muttered, getting up and walking to the coffee machine to make a fresh cup.

'What d'you mean, you wouldn't know?' demanded Kitty, following her like an over-eager puppy.

Lauren sighed heavily and then turned round to face her friend. 'I wouldn't know, Kitty,' she said bravely, 'because Sebastian and I haven't had sex for over a year. In fact, Kitty, the truth is he hasn't touched me properly for years. OK? Happy now?'

Kitty stood there with her mouth flapping open for several seconds before she composed herself enough to reply.

'Lauren, sweetheart, that is not normal,' she started to say, but Lauren had dissolved into tears and was sobbing all over the coffee machine. Kitty stroked her back until the sobs calmed down enough for her to speak. Lauren turned round and faced her friend.

'Look at me, Kitty,' she pleaded. 'Why would he want to touch me? I'm old and dowdy and past it. I repulse myself. I don't blame Sebastian for not wanting me. He's a handsome man. He gets better and better with age. I'm just a bloody embarrassment to him. And d'you know what? If he did have an affair, which I honestly don't think he is doing, but if he did, I wouldn't blame him. He could do so much better than me.'

There, she'd said it. She'd let out all the fears and frustrations and now all she felt was empty, spent and wrung out. Kitty had been right though, there was no way she'd have been able to tell that to any of the women she knew from Emily and Poppy's girls' school. They only ever wanted to talk about Nigella recipes and the contents of the Boden catalogue. Thank God for Kitty. Mouthy, insensitive, tough Kitty. She was the only person in the world Lauren felt she could be totally honest with.

Kitty swallowed hard, and her face softened.

'Sit down, Lauren,' she said, kindly but firmly. 'I need to have a serious word with you. Because your head is screwed up, darling. What you just said. It's bollocks. Complete and utter bollocks. And the really scary thing is that you honestly believe that it's true, don't you?'

Lauren nodded. Yes, she did. She knew it was true.

Kitty eased Lauren back onto the barstool at the kitchen island, and placed a fresh latte in front of her. 'Right,' she said, solemnly, sitting down opposite. 'First things first. You are beautiful, Lauren. You must see that.'

Lauren shook her head, knowing that her friend was just trying to be nice.

'Babes, I spend my whole life dressing sixteen-year-old models and celebrities who've had more surgery than you've had M&S dinners. And you. You, Lauren Hunter, are still the most spectacularly beautiful woman I have ever seen. Sometimes I hate that my best friend looks like this ...'

She stroked Lauren's cheek gently.

'Honestly, babes. I get jealous. It's like walking down the street next to Elle Macpherson. But the fact that you don't even know you're beautiful is insane. It's such a waste. You are stunning, darling. Even with that slightly mumsy new hairdo ...'

She stroked Lauren's bobbed hair and smiled to show she was joking. But it was no use. Lauren knew that she'd been quite good-looking back in the day. She'd never had any problems attracting guys and clothes had always hung well on her because she was tall but ... But those days were long gone. She was a mess now.

'And who is it that makes you think you're ugly, eh? It's that fucking Sebastardian C—'

'Don't say it, Kitty,' Lauren stopped her, knowing perfectly well what Kitty's nickname for Sebastian Hunter was. Swap the H for a C and ta da! The Sebastardian she could cope with, the next bit, not so much.

'And you keep sticking up for him!' Kitty was clearly exasperated. 'Be logical, Lauren. Why would a man like Sebastian choose you for his wife? And to be the mother of his children? You know what an egomaniac the man is. He needs to have a trophy wife, to go with his trophy cars, and trophy houses and trophy children. He knows he won the lottery with you. The truth is that you're the one who could always have done so much better than him. You could have had anyone. Everyone else can see that. Why can't you? Yes, he's got expensive clothes and a flash car and memberships to all the right clubs, but he's not even that good-looking. It's all front. He's the most false, cheesy wanker I've ever met. Take away his tan and his suits and he's just a scared little middle-aged man with short legs and a pigeon chest.'

'That's not true. Sebastian's a very good-looking man,' Lauren defended her husband.

'OK, so why does he hate other men so much?' Kitty demanded. 'You know, proper men. Like if you have builders in, or a plumber, or a gardener. He's always so rude to them. Or that time I brought Andre round for dinner? The male model? D'you remember? Sebastian faked a migraine and went to bed before pudding!'

Lauren shrugged. 'I never said he was perfect. He's a bit of a snob. I think he feels superior to them, I suppose.'

Kitty shook her head and stared at Lauren as if she was nuts. 'No, he doesn't feel superior. He feels *inferior*. Because those young guys look fit without a Savile Row suit on. Andre gets paid to take his top off. And the tradesmen? They take their tops off and wander around the house in front of you, showing you what you might have won. And Sebastardian hates it! Why the hell did he sack that window cleaner, eh? The one that looked like a younger David Beckham?'

Lauren allowed herself a little smile. 'Because he called me a MILF and Sebastian hit the roof.'

'You see, darling,' continued Kitty eagerly. 'Men still think you're beautiful. And Sebastian feels threatened by that so he tells you you're past it. He's fairly transparent, really. Nowhere near as clever as he thinks he is. It's juvenile mind games, not nuclear physics.'

'If I'm so beautiful, then why doesn't my own husband want to touch me?' asked Lauren, the smile fading from her face.

'Maybe he's having problems with his old man,' said Kitty. 'Can't get it up any more and he's too proud to admit it to you.' Kitty grinned, warming to the idea. 'God, that would kill him. I hope he's impotent. I really do. That would be hilarious!'

'I thought you said he was having an affair,' Lauren reminded her. 'How does that work?'

Kitty frowned. 'Oh, I dunno, darling. He's just such a twat to you. All I know is that you're the smartest, funniest, sweetest, best-looking woman I've ever met and he makes you feel this big.'

Kitty placed her finger and thumb two millimetres apart.

'Whether he's screwing around or not is irrelevant really. Although I'd bet my car on the fact that he is.'

This was a big stake for Kitty. She'd just bought a brand new Audi cabriolet and she was totally in love with it. Kitty continued.

'But even if he is faithful to you, the bottom line is he treats you like shit and you don't deserve it.' Kitty pouted and her voice developed a bit of a whine. 'I want the old Lauren back. The one that used to light up a room when she walked in, who went to war zones for photo shoots, who wore mini-skirts that barely covered her arse and sunbathed topless on Hampstead Heath. I feel like Sebastian Hunter killed my best friend.'

'He didn't kill me. Don't be such a drama queen, Kitty,' said Lauren, shaking her head at her friend. 'Look, I'm still here.'

She waved her hands frantically in front of her face. But Kitty shook her head. She looked really, really sad. Almost as sad as Lauren felt.

'You're not here, Lauren. Not really. You're like a shell of the woman you used to be and it breaks my heart. You think you're only worth something when he shines his light on you,' said Kitty. 'But you don't need him to make you shine. You were the shiniest girl in London when he found you. I think you've forgotten that.'

Sebastian drummed his fingers on the leather steering wheel of his new black Mercedes SLS AMG coupe. He was still parked up outside Rebecca's flat and he didn't know whether to drive off or not. Part of him wanted to go back up there and sort things out. He'd somehow got to the point where Becks was his only real friend and he knew, if this was it, that he'd miss her. She was smart and funny and even though she laughed at all his jokes, and hung on his every word, she didn't seem to be too intimidated by him. When he told her that he loved her company he meant it. He wasn't sure he actually loved *her*. But then Sebastian didn't really trust that word. Not any more. What exactly did it mean anyway? But he was very fond of her. He thought about her a lot and he was always checking his phone to see if she'd sent him one of her funny, cheeky, sexy text messages.

Unlike his staff, who arse-licked constantly, Rebecca didn't always agree with Sebastian. She teased him some-times about his clothes being 'square' (well, he was fifteen years older than her!) and she disagreed with him about politics (she was young and naive and still thought it was cool to be a leftie). To be honest, he kind of liked it because it was clear she adored him even when she didn't agree with him, and, anyway, their little tiffs always felt like foreplay. Invariably any disagreement would be resolved not through discussion but through sex. What's not to like about Becks? he wondered. He almost took the keys back out of the ignition then, so tempted was he to go back up there and lose himself in her perfect, soft, twenty-nine-year-old skin.

Shit, he realised, getting angry with himself, he'd started to rely on her a bit. That wasn't good. He had to be strong. She'd defied him and she had to learn. He'd told her not to ruin the time they had together by banging on and on about Lauren – when was he going to leave her, hadn't he said before Christmas, and now it was January, and hadn't she left her fiancé for him, and didn't he know she could have any man she wanted, and why should she wait around for him and blah, blah, blah-de-blah ... It was difficult to keep girls like Becks in check. She was quite up herself. The beautiful ones always were. You had to bring them down a peg or two or they'd start thinking they were the ones in charge. He'd seen it all before. The problem was, she was just his type – the type of girl that made heads turn wherever she went. He liked to have a girl like that on his arm. It made him feel big. And the added bonus with Rebecca was that she was completely and utterly filthy. Always up for it – whatever 'it' he fancied. Yup, walking away from this one would take balls of steel. It would be almost as difficult as it had been to walk away from ... no ... he wasn't going there. Not now.

Sebastian chewed his gum and scowled behind his sunglasses. It was grey outside but Sebastian always wore sunglasses. He didn't like it when people tried to look him in the eye. It made him uncomfortable. What were they trying to do? Read his mind? No chance! Not with his Ray-Bans and his blacked-out windows.

God, why couldn't Becks just go with the flow? Things were good between them. They were about to go on holiday, for crying out loud. He could have taken Lauren to St Barts, but no, he'd asked Rebecca. Didn't she realise what a big deal that was? How many risks he'd be taking? He had it all planned. He was going to wait until the day before and then tell his wife he had a business crisis in New York. And he was doing it all for Rebecca. It was the closest thing to commitment that she was going to get from him, that was for sure. Why ruin it by getting all het up about the future, and where this was going, and all that crap? What was her problem? It wasn't as if he was unfaithful to her, just because he was married. He told her he didn't sleep with his wife. It was the truth. He hadn't had sex with Lauren since he'd met Becks. Why would he when Rebecca was the same type of woman, only ten years younger? Why eat mutton at home when you can feast on spring lamb in Belsize Park, eh?

He wriggled uncomfortably in his seat. He was still horny as well as angry. It was a very uncomfortable feeling. Who the hell starts an argument with a cock in their mouth? There she was, halfway through one of her award-winning blow jobs and she suddenly stops, looks up at him with her eyes all hurt and tearful, and asks him if he'll leave Lauren after the holiday?

'Fuck her,' he shouted at no one. 'Fuck her!'

And then he turned the key in the ignition. Well, he would show her. He didn't need Rebecca. And he certainly wasn't going to put up with her giving him a hard time, or dishing out ultimatums in the middle of fellatio! Nor was he going to be manipulated by her tears. Women used tears as weapons. He hated it! And he was immune. Who the hell did Becks think she was? If she thought she was going to the Caribbean with him now she could think again. She was getting too big for her boots and that was dangerous. For now, the relationship was over. He would text her that later and then he wouldn't get in touch again. No matter how much she begged. And she would beg. Women were so predictable. No, he wouldn't get in touch again until he was ready. If she apologised enough, when he calmed down, then maybe he would reconsider. But for now, Sebastian no longer had a mistress. And that meant he could do exactly as he pleased. He sped away from her front door at break-neck speed. He knew she'd be watching from her window. Watching and snivelling and feeling sorry for herself. But he didn't look back. Knowing that she was watching was all he needed.

*

By ten o'clock Lauren had given up waiting for her husband
and had headed up to the bedroom. She was just about to get
undressed when she heard the front door slam. No! He was
home. Lauren tiptoed down the stairs tentatively. She felt
a little nervous, never knowing which Sebastian would be
walking through the door – cold Sebastian, angry Sebastian,
huffy Sebastian?

'Hello, darling!' called her husband brightly from the bottom of the stairs. 'I was hoping you'd still be up.'

Lauren nearly tripped down the stairs in shock. Darling?
It had been years since he'd called her that. She looked
down and saw him there, smiling up at her warmly, looking devilishly handsome in a navy Vivienne Westwood suit
and pale blue shirt. He was holding an enormous bunch of
exotic flowers in one hand and a bottle of champagne in
the other. Vintage Dom Perignon. Wow. She racked her
brain for a reason. It wasn't their anniversary. It wasn't her
birthday. What was going on? Oh God, what did it matter?
He was here. And he'd brought flowers. She skipped down
the last few steps in excitement.

'For you, gorgeous,' he said, presenting her with the
flowers. 'And this,' he continued, holding up the bottle of
champagne, 'is for us.'

'What are we celebrating?' she asked, grinning from ear
to ear.

'I told you. "Us",' he said. 'We might argue sometimes,
we might be getting a bit long in the tooth, and we might
not be love's young dream any more, but we're still together.
Still Mr and Mrs Hunter. And I think that's worth celebrating.'

Lauren thought her heart would burst with joy. She
wished Kitty could see this. This wasn't the behaviour of

a man who was being unfaithful, was it? Maybe he did still love her. Perhaps he was just a busy, stressed, complicated man who sometimes forgot to show his affection for his wife.

'And so …' Sebastian announced, as he opened the champagne with great pomp and ceremony. 'I am taking you on holiday, darling.'

'What?' Lauren asked, shocked. They only ever went on holiday with the girls. Twice a year – August and February half-term. It was their routine.

'We're going to St Barts, just the two of us,' he said, as if it wasn't that big a deal. But it was! They hadn't been away 'just the two of us' since Emily was born.

'When?' asked Lauren, with her head spinning and her heart singing and her face aching from smiling. 'Why? How?'

'Because I feel like it. Because we deserve it. Because it's freezing here and blissfully warm there. And we're going on Friday,' he said. 'So you can take my credit card to Selfridges tomorrow and buy yourself a whole new holiday wardrobe.'

'Thank you, Sebbie. Thank you so much … But … What about the girls?' asked Lauren. It was the middle of the school term.

'My mum's going to stay here,' he replied, calmly. 'It's all sorted.'

'Oh my God,' was all Lauren could say. 'I can't believe you've done this for me. I don't deserve you.'

Sebastian shrugged casually. Lauren wasn't sure if he was agreeing with the sentiment or not, but it didn't really matter. They were going on holiday, 'just the two of them', and it was going to save their marriage. She just knew it.

Lauren had been rendered speechless by the whole turn-around of events. But that didn't matter because Sebastian was always capable of enough conversation for two. When he was on form, her husband really was the most interesting, captivating and charming man she'd ever met. It was how he'd won her heart in the first place – and how he'd managed to keep making a profit in the property business while the competition went bankrupt all around him. He was magnetic when he was like this. He could talk his way into, and out of, anything.

They sat in the kitchen together, facing each other, knees almost touching, drinking the champagne and getting tipsy. It was something they'd done together often in the early days but hadn't done in years. Lauren hung on Sebastian's every word, utterly relieved, finally, to have been let back in to his world. He told her hilarious stories about the people at work and about his associates at the club. He was good at gossiping and always managed to make quite ordinary tales sound saucy or salacious. He always knew who was having an affair, or who'd had Botox, or who'd had to take their kids out of private school because they were about to go bust. OK, he was a little bit bitchy, and he did like to laugh at others' misfortune, but it was funny. It was undeniably funny. Sometimes laughing at Sebastian's jokes felt a little like siding with the school bully but tonight Lauren would have laughed at anything he said, however cruel.

'I'm getting to like your hair, by the way,' said Sebastian suddenly, lifting up his hand and tucking a stray blonde hair behind her ear. 'It suits you shorter.'

Lauren had to catch her breath as his fingers brushed her face. He hadn't touched her in so long. She stared into his eyes and willed him to kiss her. Sebastian's eyes were almond-shaped and so deep and dark that they were almost black. She'd been looking into them for twelve years, but Lauren could never quite fathom out what went on in there. If his eyes were the windows to his soul, then he kept the blinds down. Still, they were mesmerising. Hypnotising almost.

When his lips brushed hers, she gasped out loud and her knees almost buckled beneath her. It had been so, so long … And then his hand was gripping the back of her head and his tongue was probing her mouth and his hands were grabbing for her breasts and her bum. He feasted on her greedily, pushed her down over the kitchen island, pushed up her skirt, tore off her tights. He was being a bit rough, and her head banged against the granite worktop, but Lauren was so relieved just to be wanted by him, that she let him do whatever he pleased. It didn't take long, and it wasn't the best sex they'd ever had, but he'd touched her, he'd desired her and he'd made her feel just a little bit attractive again. Lauren couldn't have been more grateful.

Later, when Sebastian was asleep, Lauren sent Kitty a text.

O.M.G. All change chez Hunter. Seb's taking me on holiday. He bought flowers and bubbly too. And we had sex!!!! Feel so happy. Xxx

Kitty replied immediately.

Be careful, darling. He's up to something. I don't trust him. Just take care of yourself. Promise me. Remember, you don't need his light on you to shine. Xxx ps What about the back, sack and crack?

Lauren frowned at her phone. Why couldn't Kitty be happy for her? Talk about raining on her parade! Anyway, she and Sebastian had been so frantic that they hadn't even got properly undressed. She was still none the wiser about the, er, condition of her husband's pubic hair. What was the big deal? She tossed her phone back into her handbag without responding and climbed into bed with her husband. St Barts was going to change everything. She just knew it.

II

Valley of Fire, Nevada Desert

'And that's a wrap!' shouted the director. 'Well done, guys. Lexi, baby, you totally rocked!'

Lexi stretched like a cat and jumped down off the roof of the car she'd been standing on for the last six hours in the searing desert heat. She handed the guns she'd been holding to the props guy and kicked off her six inch spiky stilettos. Phew, they were having hot weather for January and she was wearing a tight black leather catsuit. Hardly beach-wear! She was light-headed with dehydration but Lexi never complained on set. Despite her wild-child persona, when it came to work, Lexi was a die-hard professional. She was shooting her latest movie – a super-cool indie production where she got to play a screwed-up, psychotic (but smoking hot, obviously) criminal on the run. She was loving it. Compared to the goody-goody parts she used to play for Disney, it was insanely fun! She'd had to dye her hair black, which she thought looked *way* cool, and she'd even had a real tattoo done – a pair of entwined serpents on the base of her spine, to represent her connection to Mal. Most of the piercings were fake though, except for the tongue ring she'd had done as a wedding present for Mal. That little bit of metal really excited him when she went down on him!

She high-fived the cast and crew as she sauntered back to

her trailer to change into something a little less restrictive. She downed a litre of water, tweeted a brief update for her fans and then peeled off the leather catsuit. Phew. That was better. Marissa, the make-up artist, popped by and removed the fake piercings, the false eyelashes and the heavy make-up she'd worn for the scene.

'So, what you gonna do with your two weeks off, baby girl?' asked Marissa, brushing the hairspray out of Lexi's hair gently, like a mother with her little girl.

Lexi could hardly contain her excitement. They'd finished filming the desert scenes and filming didn't start up again in LA for another fortnight. She bounced up and down in her chair.

'I am getting a flight to New York in ...' she checked her watch. 'Two hours. And then Mal has a surprise for me! I am so frigging excited, Marissa. I think he's taking me on honeymoon.'

'Careful, baby girl,' warned Marissa, brandishing her hairbrush. 'Sit still or we're gonna get all tangled up here. That sounds very exciting, Lexi. I wonder where he's gonna take you.'

'I have no idea but it doesn't matter. I have almost two whole weeks with Mal. Neither of us is working. It's the longest we've ever spent together and it's going to be amazing!'

Marissa smiled fondly at her.

'Well, you just make sure that man treats you right, baby girl. Don't you let him misbehave on your honeymoon. No drugs. Not too much booze and no loose women! Or he'll have me to answer to, OK? You tell him that from me. Tell him Marissa Jackson has your back. He knows me. We have history! He'll be quaking in his boots.'

Lexi giggled. Marissa must have weighed over 200lb and she was not to be messed with.

'That's right, you did his last video with him, didn't you?' remembered Lexi. Marissa was the best in the business. Anybody who was *anybody* had had their make-up done by her. 'He said he liked you.'

'Oh, Malcolm's a pussy cat, really,' smiled Marissa. 'Don't tell him but I kinda have a soft spot for that hairy manchild. It's his mother I'm scared of. That is one fierce dragon lady! She gives me the creeps the way she hangs around that boy of hers.'

'Yeah, you and me both,' replied Lexi, rolling her eyes.

By the time Lexi touched down at JFK, she was exhausted. She'd been too excited to sleep on the plane. But now, after a long day's filming, and an evening flight, she was walking through security like a zombie. She smiled as sweetly as she could for the paparazzi at the Arrivals gate and said, 'Yeah, thanks guys, it's so nice of you to capture me at my best!' But Lexi didn't really mind being photographed in her scruffy clothes, with her hair all mussed up and her make-up smudged. She figured she kind of suited the messed-up rock chick look and anyway, she always took a decent picture – it was why she'd been in the movies since she was nine.

And then Mal was there, grinning his big, dopey grin, and lifting her up with his vast arms, so that her face met his. Mal was six foot five; Lexi was five foot three. When he picked her up she felt like a tiny doll. She felt safe. And she loved it.

'I'm so tired, baby,' she moaned sleepily into his ear, once they'd shared a long, sloppy kiss.

'Don't you worry, petal,' he assured her. 'You go to sleep. I'll get you back to the hotel.'

'You need to shave, Malky. Your beard's all scratchy on

my cheek and you look like a cavemen,' was the last thing she remembered saying.

And then, much to Lexi's – and the paparazzi's – delight, Mal Riley strode out of JFK airport like a caveman, with Lexi Crawford thrown over his shoulder. He Man was taking She Girl back to his cave.

The Cave turned out to be a suite at the Mandarin Oriental. Lexi barely remembered the limo ride there, or being carried into the lift by Mal, or tucked gently into bed. But seven hours later she woke up to find him gazing down at her with a soppy look on his face.

'Aha, Sleeping Beauty awakes!' he announced, kissing her on the lips. 'Are you ready for breakfast, my sweetness?'

Lexi stretched, yawned and looked around. It was a beautiful suite. A tray was laid out by the bed, with a bottle of champagne in an ice bucket and a silver platter on it. The platter was covered by a domed lid.

'How long's that been there?' she asked, eyeing breakfast and then eyeing the clock. It was four p.m. New York time.

'Well, let's put it this way, poppet,' said Mal. 'Breakfast's been cold since midday and the ice melted three hours ago. Are you impressed by my self-control? I've been dying to open that bubbly for hours.'

'Aww, but you waited for me, baby. That is so romantic.' Lexi kissed him hungrily on the lips.

'I'm afraid I may have helped myself to a couple of sausages though, and there's no beer left in the mini bar.' Mal lifted up an empty bottle of Sol from the floor and burped. 'Oops,' he said.

Lexi sat up and shook the sleep from her head. Mal opened the champagne with a pop and Lexi giggled as the cork hit the chandelier and made it jingle. He placed a glass on the bedside table and then laid the platter on her lap.

'Open it,' he urged her, bouncing up and down.

'What? Why?' she laughed. 'How exciting can breakfast be? Especially if you've already eaten the sausages!'

'Go on,' he squealed. 'Open it.'

Lexi lifted the lid off the platter slowly. There, beside the congealed egg, and the cold, rubbery bacon, tucked into the toast rack with the stale wholemeal, was an envelope.

Mal looked at Lexi, his eyes brimming with anticipation.

'Is this my surprise?' she asked him, her cheeks aching from smiling. 'Shall I open it now, or tuck into this delicious feast first?' Lexi lifted up a half-eaten sausage and wrinkled her nose.

'Open it!' shouted Mal. 'Stop teasing me, Lexi. I've been waiting for you to wake up all day.'

She shoved the cold sausage into her mouth, wiped her greasy fingers on the silk bedspread and picked up the envelope. Slowly, ever so slowly, she opened it, and pulled out the little green card inside. On it was a picture of a palm tree and one word: Paradise.

'Paradise?' she asked Mal, quizzically. 'What's Paradise?'

Mal grinned proudly. 'Paradise, my darling, is a resort that does exactly what it says on the tin. At least I hope it is ... I mean, how can a place like Paradise be anything other than, um, erm, paradise? Put it this way, princess, I had about a hundred freebies this week, all offering us the honeymoon of our dreams, all five stars plus, all guaranteed sunshine, all promising privacy from the press and lashings of free champagne with a cherry on top and blah, blah, blah ... I wasn't sure which one to choose, so I chose Paradise because the owner's one of us – a celebrity. You might re-member him: Gabriel Abbot? He was always on TV when I was a kid. Remember? He was Ben Hudson's boyfriend! You must know who Gabriel Abbot is.'

Lexi shook her head and shrugged. No, she had no idea who this Gabriel Abbot was. And Ben Hudson? Maybe she'd seen a couple of his movies when she was a kid but wasn't he dead before she was born? Mal always seemed to forget that when he was a teenager she was still in diapers. But it didn't matter. He'd sorted out a honeymoon for them. And Mal never sorted anything out for himself – he had PAs, secretaries, agents and managers to do that sort of thing. Mal was a big kid. He hated responsibility and always preferred to just be told where he had to be and when. He never so much as ordered himself a taxi, so deciding on a honeymoon destination showed dedication. And to choose one with a fellow celeb in charge? Smart move. That would make avoiding the paps much easier. Ten out of ten for effort, Mr Riley, thought Mrs Riley with delight.

'Ooh, you are so frigging amazing, Malky!' she squealed, throwing her arms around Mal and knocking the tray of cold breakfast onto the carpet. She kissed him hard and passionately, losing her fingers in his thick hair, and losing her heart in his chocolate eyes. Before she knew it, Lexi found herself naked, with her thighs wrapped around her husband's waist, feeling his love and his passion deep inside her. She had never known such a feeling of complete and utter love and longing. And even better, she felt as though she belonged there, with him, for ever.

'I'm so happy, Mal,' she whispered, as he lay exhausted on top of her when they'd done. 'I never thought I'd feel like this about anyone. I thought it wasn't real.'

'What?' he asked, winking at her. 'You thought true love was just something you see in the movies?'

'I thought it was something I *acted out* in the movies,' she admitted truthfully. 'I thought it was something made up to make people feel better about their boring lives.'

'Me too,' agreed Mal. 'When I sang love songs, I never really felt it before. But now, when I do a gig and it's time for the cheesy stuff, all I have to do is think about you, princess, and the words just tumble out with so much meaning, so much depth. I can't wait to write my next album. You're my inspiration now, poppet, my muse.'

She snuggled into him contentedly. His muse. She liked the sound of that. It felt glamorous, sophisticated and very grown-up to be a musician's muse. And then a thought hit her.

'Malky?' she asked, sitting up. 'Where is Paradise, anyway?'

Mal scratched his matted hair and shook his head. 'Can't really remember, sweetness. St Lucia, St Martin, St Barts maybe? One of those swanky places in the Caribbean with that whole blue sea, blue sky and coconuts vibe going on.'

Mal stood up suddenly and started singing Beach Boys songs and swaying his hips, still stark bollock naked.

Lexi clutched her sides with hysteria and kept shaking her head.

'Come on, sweetheart; you must know this song,' grinned Mal, still jiggling.

'No, really, I don't think I do, but I think you should definitely perform that one at your next gig. The thrash metal boys'll love it!' Lexi suggested.

'Good plan, babes,' agreed Mal. 'Come on, pretty mama … Bermuda, Bahama, Key Largo, Montego, Aruba, Jamaica … I can't remember exactly where-a … but …'

'St Barth … Barthel … St Barthélemy …' said Lexi, struggling to pronounce the word she'd just found on her Google search for Paradise on her iPhone. 'Is that the same as St Barts?'

'Yup,' said Mal. 'That's the very fella. I remember now. And we are going to take Paradise by storm, Mrs Riley!'

Lexi's excitement grew as the afternoon wore on. They jumped in a cab to Bloomingdale's and spent a few thousand dollars each on new clothes for their honeymoon. Watching Mal trying to find some suitable swimming trunks was hilarious – even Bloomingdale's fashion-forward designer department didn't have black leather trunks and he wasn't exactly a Hawaiian print kind of guy. In the end Lexi managed to persuade him that a pair of plain black trunks were just about rock 'n' roll enough.

'But you need to do some hardcore sunbathing, baby,' she told him, shaking her head in amusement at his white body. 'Unless you get a quick spray tan now?'

'Princess,' replied Mal, patiently, 'I started showering regularly for you, I wear deodorant for you, I even bloody well shaved for you this morning, but I draw the line at a spray tan!'

They packed, together, down on their knees on the hotel floor, with their matching Louis Vuitton suitcases side by side. They could easily have got one of their staff to pack for them but it seemed so much better, more romantic, to do it together like a normal, married couple off on their first proper holiday together.

By the time they got to the airport, Lexi was literally jumping up and down with excitement. She'd made herself look suitably glamorous for this trip in a flowery, vintage 1950s dress, cat's-eye sunglasses, red stilettos, red lipstick, a huge beehive and a tiny black leather jacket. She strutted proudly through the Arrivals hall, clinging to Mal's arm, pouting for the cameras and throwing cheeky, charming little soundbites to the journalists, to go with the stories they would write about Lexi and Mal Riley's honeymoon.

Nobody knew where they were going exactly, of course. No one except their agents and their publicists. The couple were determined to have complete privacy this week. Nothing and no one was going to spoil Paradise for Lexi and Mal.

They settled in the VIP lounge, ordered more champagne and some oysters – which they fed to each other with their fingers. Mal seemed a little fidgety. He kept looking over his shoulder and checking his watch.

'What are you doing, baby?' Lexi asked finally, as her husband turned round to look at the door for the fifteenth time in fifteen minutes.

'Um, erm, ah ...' Mal shuffled uncomfortably in his seat. 'Another bottle of bubbly, babes?'

'Ye-eah, OK,' said Lexi, watching him closely now. Something was going on. He'd just changed the subject very obviously.

'Mal, is there something you want to tell me?' she asked him, narrowing her eyes.

Lexi had a sixth sense for Mal's bullshit. And her radar was going off. Big time!

'No, no, it's nothing, princess. Aren't these oysters delicious? Did you know, petal, that oysters can change sex during their lifetime? And they can make eggs and sperm with their gonads. Isn't that amazing?'

'Amazing,' deadpanned Lexi. 'Your mollusc knowledge astounds me.'

Mal stared at his plate and refused to meet Lexi's eye.

'Something certainly smells fishy,' she carried on. 'You're up to something, Mal. What's the story?'

Mal looked up at her, took a deep breath, and was about to open his mouth to say something when ...

'Malcom! Sweetheart! I'm here!'

'Oh shit,' said Mal, dropping his head into his hands.

'What the fuck?' asked Lexi, staring open-mouthed at the door into the VIP lounge.

There, bustling into the lounge, carrying the biggest piece of bright pink patent hand-luggage Lexi had ever seen, was Irene Riley. The Monster-in-Law. Oh. My. God. Irene was wearing a swirly fluorescent dress in an XXXL. Her chubby feet had been forced into white sandals. On her head, perched on top of her bubble perm, was a straw hat. She looked like a man in drag. She waddled up to where they were sitting, threw her arms around her son, and practically suffocated him in her more than ample bosom.

'What the hell is she doing here?' demanded Lexi, standing up and pushing her chair back.

Mal tried to speak but his mother wouldn't stop hugging him.

'You should mind your language, young lady,' warned Irene, waggling a podgy finger at Lexi. 'You have a lot of making up to do if you want to get back in my good books. Sneaking off and stealing my boy like that, without so much as a warning – never mind an invitation! I missed your wedding so I'm coming on holiday with you instead. This way I get to celebrate your marriage and get to know my new daughter-in-law too.'

She grinned at Lexi. It was not a warm smile. In fact, it felt more like a threat. Her front teeth were smeared in candy-pink lipstick. Lexi's stomach churned. The oysters were repeating on her.

'No way,' said Lexi, backing her chair away from Irene and Mal. 'No frigging way. This is insane. Mal! Mal! Tell her she can't come. This is *not* a holiday. It's our *honeymoon*, for Christ's sake!'

Lexi could see all her dreams of a Caribbean paradise turning to crap before her very eyes. Lexi, Mal and Irene on honeymoon together. How romantic was that going to be?

'Mal?' She stared at him with watery eyes, imploring her husband to tell her this wasn't happening. 'Mal, tell her. Tell your mother she cannot come on honeymoon with us!'

Mal attempted to talk, through a mouthful of his mother's chest.

'I didn't exactly invite her, princess,' he mumbled.

'Yes, he did,' said Irene smugly. 'Don't lie to your little wife, Malcolm. It's not a good way to start a marriage.'

'No,' said Lexi, the anger rising in her chest. 'Having your mother-in-law gatecrash your honeymoon is not a very good way to start a marriage!'

Mal finally managed to push his mother off enough to speak. 'Lexi, I didn't invite her. Mum, tell her. Tell her the truth,' Mal looked up at his mother, pleading with her to get him off the hook.

Irene ignored him. 'I don't remember exactly how the conversation went, Malcolm, but I'm here now, and my flight's booked and I've got myself into the very next holiday cottage to yours so ...' She squatted down, wedged her enormous backside into a chair, and got out a guide book. 'Let's plan what we're going to do. We haven't been on holiday together for years, have we, Malcolm? This is going to be so much fun!'

'I think I'm going to throw up,' announced Lexi, running from the table, towards the washrooms.

How the hell could Mal let this happen? Their first ever holiday together! Their frigging honeymoon! And he'd let his mother come along. Oh, Lexi knew that Irene would have given him little choice, but a man of thirty-three, still terrified of his mom? It was sick. It was just plain sick. Lexi leant her head against the cool mirror and tried to decide how to play this. There was no point in fighting Irene now. She was coming to St Barts with them whether Lexi liked it or not. So, the old battleaxe had evened the score for the blow-job phone call. Fair enough. Mrs Lexi Riley: one. Mrs Irene Riley: one. Lexi took a deep breath, fixed up her make-up and headed back out of the washrooms with a serene smile fixed on her face. This battle was lost, but the war had still to be won. And there was no way Lexi had any intention of losing Mal to Irene!

12

St Barthélemy, French West Indies

After her morning shift, Molly headed tentatively down towards the beach feeling like a gatecrasher at a society wedding. Gabriel had insisted that it was OK for the staff to use any of the hotel's facilities between shifts. So long as her work was done, and she wasn't getting in the way of the paying guests, Molly had permission to swim, sunbathe or even to use the spa. (Not that she would dare venture into spa territory. She'd seen the girls who worked there and they were beyond terrifying! And anyway, she had no idea what a thermae bath or a hot stone therapy entailed. She'd never even been in a sauna.)

She'd been at Paradise nearly two weeks now and this was the first day she'd felt brave enough to venture down to the beach. Still, her heart raced in her chest, and her legs felt wobbly. Molly was completely out of her comfort zone here. The scene was so breathtaking – the uninterrupted view of the ocean, the palms swaying gently in the breeze, the beautiful people lounging around, showing off their perfect bodies and spending their zillions on cocktails – that Molly felt as if she was walking into a movie scene. It was amazing but it was also scary. She tripped over her flip-flops as she made her way down the steep path that led to the beach and dropped her towel and her sunscreen. For the love of God, why was she such a klutz?

She collected her things, straightened herself up and tugged self-consciously at her denim shorts, feeling ridiculously scruffy and obscenely white compared to the bronzed goddesses who were already laid out, like reclining statues, on the wooden loungers. Right, she could do this. She was allowed to be here. It was OK … Oh, feck, no it wasn't OK! Look at these women. How did they get to look like that? It was as if they'd all got a memo from Mother Nature (or perhaps *Vogue* magazine) on 'How to be a woman'. But Molly hadn't received the memo back in Balymun. Before she'd left, she'd considered her sister Nula to be well groomed, but she now saw that Nula was a complete amateur in the glamour-puss stakes. Suddenly Molly realised how cheap her sister actually looked compared to the real deal, and for a second she felt sorry for Nula.

Molly took in the scene and noted what she should have been wearing had she got the memo. The women wore tiny string bikinis in white, gold or animal print on their taut, tanned, gym-honed bodies. Some swimwear was adorned with jewels, sequins or crystals. Kaftans came in turquoise, bright pink, jade green or pristine white. Long hair was either tied up in a top knot or swept back with brightly coloured silk scarves and headbands. Some wore straw hats – floppy, wide-brimmed ones, cowboy styles or trilbies. All wore oversized sunglasses. They also all wore delicate gold jewellery and a small amount of tasteful beach-appropriate make-up (waterproof no doubt). Sandals were either brightly coloured, gold or, again, jewel-encrusted. Mineral water and exotic, fruit-laden cocktails were brought to the women on silver trays by the waiting staff from the bar, poured carefully, and then handed to them so that they needn't move one perfectly manicured finger. Some read, some listened to their iPods, some smoked. None of them dripped with sweat. And none of them gaped open-mouthed and awestruck at their surroundings as Molly found herself doing now. This was a life they took for granted. Lucky cows, thought Molly. But she wasn't being bitter. As she headed towards the beach bar and the relative security of Jacques and Henri she found herself thinking what a lucky cow she was too.

'Good Golly Miss Molly!' sang Henri as she approached, flashing her his dazzling smile.

He'd started doing this every time he saw her and, although it was cheesy and she'd heard the same joke a thousand times before back in Dublin, it always made her smile. His familiarity with her made her feel accepted and, well, maybe even liked? Henri was undeniably the leader of the pack with the staff at Paradise. Even the Mean Girls got all giggly and coy around him. The other waiters, the concierge, the receptionists, the drivers – they all seemed to bow down to Henri in the hierarchy and it was clear to Molly that he was more than just the bar manager at the resort. She'd seen him having meetings with Gabriel. The two men would share a bottle of wine at a table in the shade of a palm most evenings. They'd lay out papers, consult diaries, and talk for hours. Jacques had told her that, unlike most of the French staff, Henri hadn't just left school or university. In fact Henri had squeezed a lot into his life already.

'He is one of those annoying people who is good at everything,' Jacques had explained, shrugging as if to say, *c'est la vie*. 'He was a very talented surfer on the west coast where he grew up, did some modelling in Paris, got a business degree from the Sorbonne and then he did something dull, but profitable, in finance for a while. And then Henri got bored. Henri, he is easily bored! He left his job, grew his hair and started running nightclubs in the South of France. He met Gabriel at a party in St Tropez the summer before last and now he is here. I think, when Monsieur Gabriel retires, he hopes Henri will become manager. Lately, he shares everything with Henri. It is like watching a professor with his favourite student.'

Molly wondered how old Henri was. He looked young. He had a smooth boyish face and a cheeky grin. At first Molly had thought he must be about the same age as her and Jacques (twenty-one, twenty-two?) but having listened to what Jacques had said, she realised that Henri must be nearer to thirty. The truth was, Molly had found herself wondering about Henri a lot. And every time she saw him now her tummy did a little flip. When he winked at her with those gorgeous hazel eyes she always felt a pang of something in her heart. What was that? Lust? Well, he was stupidly handsome. Longing? Molly had never really had a boyfriend. She'd had offers but none of the boys in Balymun had been her type and, besides, when had she had time for a relationship what with work and the family? Or maybe it was just this ridiculously romantic setting that had made her go all gooey. Whatever it was, it was daft. And a complete waste of time. She knew Henri was only friendly towards her because that was his way. He was a nice guy. And an outrageous flirt to boot. It didn't *mean* anything. The only thing Molly was sure about when it came to Henri was that a guy like that would never be interested in a girl like her. She was batting so far out of her league with this silly schoolgirl crush that she might as well set her sights on Orlando Bloom. So, Molly tried to act all nonchalant as first Jacques and then Henri leant over the bar and kissed her on both cheeks. It made her feel sophisticated when they did that.

'So Gorgeous Miss Molly,' grinned Henri, looking utterly swoonsome in his uniform of smart navy blue shorts and a white linen shirt, which he'd left undone to the navel. A tattoo of a dolphin poked out from underneath his rolled-up sleeve. 'Finally we have lured you to our lair! We thought you were never going to come to the beach.'

'I didn't want to lower the tone of the place,' half-joked Molly. 'I mean, look at the state of me. I've never been to a beach resort before, let alone lived at one, so my wardrobe's a blooming disgrace!'

She blushed in her denim cut-downs and her vintage U2 T-shirt, twisted her plaits self-consciously with her fingers and wondered why she'd worn her hair in this silly style in the first place.

Henri ignored her and busied himself behind the bar. But Jacques wrinkled his nose and shook his head. 'You are so silly sometimes, Molly,' he said. 'You look cool. Like you are going to Glastonbury.'

'Well, I'd certainly look more at home in a muddy field, that's true,' she conceded, watching Henri's back a little forlornly.

'For you, mademoiselle,' said Henri, suddenly spinning back round to face her and placing a bright red cocktail on the bar in front of her.

'What's this?' she giggled.

'Sex on the Beach,' replied Henri, poker-faced but with a naughty twinkle in his eyes.

Jacques rolled his eyes as if to say, *here we go again*.

'Ach, thanks a million, Henri, but I can't afford cocktails at these prices,' said Molly, glancing worriedly at the cocktail list. Fifteen euros! No fecking way!

'It's free, silly,' said Henri, shaking his head at her naivety. 'It's a present from me to you.'

'Oh.' Molly blushed again. 'Well, thank you. Thank you, Henri.' And then she added bravely, or foolishly, 'I've never had Sex on the Beach before.'

She couldn't believe she was being so saucy. It wasn't like her, but Molly forced herself to glance at Henri as she said it. For a moment their eyes locked and that little flip in her stomach turned into a full-blown gymnastics routine. Molly took a gulp of her drink to steady herself. She wasn't much of a drinker. As the daughter of an alcoholic she'd been put off the hard stuff at a young age, and she'd sworn she'd never use booze as a crutch like her dad had done, but what the hell. Needs must and all that. Get a grip, Molly Costello, she told herself. Henri looked away but he was still smiling to himself. Molly took another large gulp of her drink.

'You are supposed to sip cocktails,' whispered Jacques with a slightly concerned look on his face. 'It's not even lunchtime yet and the sun is very hot. And Henri, he is very generous with the vodka. Here.'

He handed her a straw. 'I am not carrying you home from the beach and explaining to Monsieur Gabriel that you are too sick to work later.'

Once again, Molly felt like she hadn't got the memo. She took the straw gratefully and sipped her drink slowly in the shade of the bar's canopy. She watched Delilah make her way down the path towards the beach. She was wearing a swirly blue and green one-piece, high-heeled sandals and nothing else, and she was walking down the steep incline as if she was on a catwalk.

'Now, *she* is something else,' said Molly. 'Delilah there. What is her story? She intrigues me.'

Jacques and Henri looked at each other and laughed.

'Oh, Delilah intrigues us all,' replied Henri. 'She is, um, unique. Yes, she is one of a kind. That is for sure.'

'Who is she? How long is she staying?' asked Molly. 'You all seem very familiar with her.'

'So we should be!' laughed Henri. 'Delilah's part of the furniture here. She's been in Paradise longer than that old tortoise of Monsieur Gabriel's!'

'What?' said Molly, perplexed. 'I don't understand. I thought she was a guest. She stays in room twelve, she sun-bathes every day, she uses the pool, she—'

'She is a guest,' grinned Jacques. 'But she is a permanent guest.'

'No, I don't get it.' Molly shook her head.

Jacques and Henri shrugged in unison.

'She lives here. Her life is a permanent holiday. *C'est la vie!*' replied Henri.

'But how does she pay for it?' asked Molly, shocked that anyone could actually live in a hotel, let alone one as expensive as Paradise.

The boys shrugged again, looked at each other and laughed.

'That is not our business, Molly,' said Jacques. 'She is close with the boss. They are friends from long ago. Delilah and Gabriel talk about the old days in LA a lot. Perhaps she doesn't pay at all. Who knows?'

'Was she an actress too?' asked Molly, fascinated.

'A model, I think,' replied Henri. 'She is still quite elegant I suppose. For her age.'

'How old is she?' whispered Molly, leaning over the bar, so as not to be heard gossiping. 'I've been trying to figure it out but I have no idea.'

'That is a state secret,' replied Henri. 'Nobody knows Delilah's real age. She tells people she is thirty-five; I have heard her. But I think maybe ten years older than that?'

'Hmph,' added Jacques, who was obviously not a fan. 'Twenty years older at least, I'd say.'

'No, don't be silly,' said Molly. 'She can't be over forty-five. Look at her. She's stunning.'

'She is frightening,' said Jacques. 'The Cougar of the Caribbean. Be grateful you are a girl, Molly. She won't want to get her claws into you.'

'Oh, she's not so bad,' Henri said kindly. 'She's a pussy cat really.'

'Really?' Jacques raised that eyebrow again. 'She didn't look like much of a pussy cat at the burlesque night last week. More like a killer tiger. She had you pinned against the wall with her claws for most of the evening.'

Molly felt a pang of jealousy at the thought of Henri being touched by Delilah.

'Or perhaps you were enjoying it, eh, Henri?' Jacques teased his friend. 'Actually, where did you go after that party? Did she drag you back to room twelve and maul you?'

Henri shook his head. 'Do not be silly, my friend. I would not touch Delilah with yours.' He pointed towards Jacques's crotch.

Jacques shrugged. 'Well, that makes a change,' he said. 'You have touched almost every other girl in the resort. Colette, Antoinette, Brigitte, Mimi ... And do not get me started on the guests.'

'Shut up, Jacques,' replied Henri, trying to sound jovial but obviously pissed off.

Molly swallowed hard. So he wasn't just a flirt. He was a player. She felt irrationally hurt and let down. Why was she being so silly? She barely knew the guy and, she reminded herself again, he was way out of her league. She glanced up at Henri. He was still smiling but his forehead was knotted in a frown. He refused to catch her gaze.

Molly slugged down the last of her cocktail, ignoring Jacques's advice, and said, as brightly as she could manage, 'Right, guys, I'm away to sunbathe. I'm going to try to get some colour on these lily-white legs of mine. I'll see you later. Thanks for the drink, Henri.'

The boys said goodbye and Molly headed off down the beach path, away from the crowds. She looked back at the bar briefly and noticed that Henri was having a go at Jacques about something. He looked quite angry. Perhaps the two weren't such good mates after all.

Molly paused at the beach boutique and stared wistfully at the exquisite bikinis and kaftans in the window. Oh, to own clothes like that! But she could see, quite clearly from the price tags, that she would never possess such glamorous things. Molly sighed and was just about to walk away when a gaggle of Mean Girls spilled out of the shop doorway, laughing and holding onto each other's arms. Their limbs were long and tanned, their manes of glossy hair bounced on their shoulders, their nails were French-manicured and they all wore clothes from the beach boutique. Molly knew all their names – Antoinette and Margot were waitresses, Elise was a receptionist, Renee worked at the spa and Mimi, the tallest, most glamorous, most terrifying of them all, managed the main boutique in the Plantation House. She also, Molly had gathered, worked as a burlesque dancer and a model. And, according to Jacques, something had happened with Mimi and Henri. Antoinette too. Molly watched the competition with a heavy heart. She knew when she was defeated. It was time to give up her silly crush on the bar manager and just concentrate on being his friend instead. Because if there was one thing Molly could do with at Paradise, it was friends.

'Hi, girls,' she said, lifting her hand in a limp wave as the Mean Girls brushed past in a cloud of perfume.

Margot and Elise at least acknowledged her presence with tiny, barely discernible nods, but the others blanked her completely as if she were invisible. Which, she guessed, to the likes of them, she was. Molly tried to keep her pecker up as she strolled further down the beach. It wasn't so bad. So maybe the other girls didn't accept her, and maybe the boy she had a crush on wasn't interested, but she had this place, this opportunity, and in the grand scheme of things Molly realised she was blessed. Molly remembered what her nan always said: 'There are always those more fortunate and less fortunate than you. Do not compare yourself to others, Molly. It can only lead to vanity or insecurity. And neither of those are good things. Just be happy with what the Lord gave you. He gave you those blessings for a reason. Make the most of what you've got, be the best Molly Costello you can be, and don't go wasting your time wishing you were someone else.'

Molly found a spot, as far away from the beach bar and the guests as she could. She was still in sight of the boutique, and the Mean Girls who were smoking and gossiping on the terrace outside. But they were taking no notice of Molly and, besides, she was boiling in her shorts and T-shirt. She stripped down to her black one-piece, spread her towel on the beach, slapped on some more sunscreen (factor fifty, naturally!) and was about to lie down when she heard them. Laughing. Cackling. Killing themselves at some joke or other. Molly looked up to see what was going on. And there they were, laying their towels out a few feet away, and whispering, laughing, nudging each other. The Mean Girls. Molly suddenly realised with a pang of despair that the joke was her. And her old-fashioned black swimsuit, and her pure white skin, and her stupid pigtails and everything about her that made her so different and inferior to them.

Molly lay face down on her towel, buried her head and tried to ignore them. She tried desperately to cling onto her nan's words of wisdom but it was so bloody difficult when the Mean Girls were right there, laughing at her and making her feel so damned small. She was thousands of miles from home, trying so hard to fit in to this glamorous, exotic world, and to make the most of this wonderful chance Gabriel had given her. But how could she do it when she was so clearly out of her depth? The Mean Girls knew instinctively that Molly Costello didn't belong at Paradise, so who was she trying to kid? For the first time that week Molly felt homesick. She wept into her towel and wished with all her might that she wasn't on this tropical island at all, but in her nan's tiny living room with Shane and Caitlin and, yes, even Joey. Joey might be a gobshite but at least he wasn't mean!

She lay there for what felt like hours, but must only have been fifteen minutes or so, listening to the rapid French conversation going on nearby. Molly had been quite good at French at school, and although she didn't have the confidence to speak the language (especially not with her thick Dublin accent), she did understand at least part of what was being said.

'Ses vêtements sont tellement laids,' one of them whispered, just loud enough for Molly to hear – her clothes are so ugly – and then the Mean Girls lowered their voices and all she could hear were their giggles.

She picked up the odd word, though – 'démodé' and 'elle est si pâle' – and she knew beyond doubt that they were talking about her. She had been deemed old-fashioned and pale. Molly wriggled into her towel and wished that the beach would open up and swallow her. Fragments of their conversation were being blown over on the breeze and, try as she could, Molly couldn't drown out their voices. They'd stopped talking about her now and were discussing their social lives instead. They talked about Nikki Beach and the Yacht Club and Les Tis St Barts. They name-dropped celebrities they'd met and been chatted up by. They talked about all the boys who fancied them. They discussed clothes and the fashion shows some of them modelled for. They bitched about the other girls who weren't on the beach with them at that moment. Girls who were on reception now, or waitressing the lunch shift, or working at the spa, or in the shops. Girls who would normally be in the same gang. In short, Molly realised, they were bitching about their friends. They talked about Paris, about shops and nightclubs they all knew from home, and about mutual friends they'd had at university. They talked about cars and horses and Papa's money and holidays in Monaco, Cannes and Juan Les Pins. Molly put her hands over her ears and wished she had an iPod to drown out their voices.

She tried not to prick up her ears when she heard Henri's name mentioned but she couldn't help herself. It was Mimi talking. The Head Mean Girl had a distinctive low, throaty, sexy voice and she spoke quite slowly as if it were all a bit of an effort. It was as if everything and everyone bored her a little. She was asking Antoinette if it would be a problem if she and Henri had a relationship. Antoinette was reassuring her that, no, of course it wouldn't be a problem, that nothing had really happened with her and Henri, and that it was obvious that Henri much preferred Mimi. Especially after the two of them had disappeared down to the beach together the other night. Mimi practically purred with contentment when she heard Antoinette submit like this.

Oh, she replied, she was so glad that Antoinette realised that Henri had never been serious about her; it could have been quite awkward and embarrassing had she carried on throwing herself in Henri's direction when everybody knew it was Mimi he really liked. But, of course, Mimi wasn't sure yet if she was interested. He was cute but, well, he was only a bar manager. Perhaps. Perhaps not. She had so many men interested in her, and some of them were very wealthy, very important, how was she to choose? Molly listened, horrified, as Antoinette agreed with everything Mimi said. How could she allow herself to be put down and humiliated like that by a so-called friend? The hierarchy at Paradise was far worse than any class system she'd come across in Dublin.

A few minutes later, Molly heard the Mean Girls pack up their things and announce that they were heading to the beach bar to hang out with Henri and Jacques. Once the sound of their giggles had faded to a safe distance, Molly breathed a sigh of relief and finally sat up. She glanced round at where they'd been lounging and was surprised to see Antoinette still sitting there alone. The French girl had her knees pulled up to her chin. She was smoking a cigarette and staring out to sea. A stray tear escaped from under her sunglasses and dripped onto the sand. Molly watched as Antoinette pushed her sunglasses up onto the top of her head, and wiped her eyes with the back of her hand. She looked as miserable and lonely as Molly felt. What a bitch Mimi was. And what a bastard Henri must be to play the girls off against each other like that. Molly wondered if she even wanted to be the guy's friend. No wonder Jacques got angry with him sometimes.

Molly was just about to look away, aware that she was invading another girl's private pain, when Antoinette glanced up and caught her eye. Molly smiled, partly out of sympathy and partly out of embarrassment at having been caught being nosy. For a moment Antoinette stared back blankly and then her features softened and she smiled back. It was just a small smile but it was something – a tiny thaw in the cold front, perhaps? A few minutes later, when Antoinette got up to leave, she took a few steps down the beach, paused, turned back and called, nonchalantly of course, 'See you later, Molly.'

'Oh, right, yeah, bye, Antoinette. I'll see you soon,' called back Molly, waving frantically.

She was completely aware that she was being ridiculously over-eager and grateful, but she was so relieved to have been spoken to by one of the other girls that she couldn't retain even a semblance of cool. And at least Antoinette knew her name. It wasn't much, but it was something.

13

St Barthélemy, French West Indies

Gabriel watched little Molly Costello from a distance. He was paddling, just up to his ankles, in the warm water to the very west of the resort, below his cottage. He'd rolled his trousers up to just below the knee and was well aware that he looked ridiculous. But none of the guests ever came this far along the cove, so from here he could admire his kingdom from afar without fear of being disturbed. He watched Molly now, alone a little further down the beach. So the other girls were giving her a hard time? It wasn't a surprise. It was a shame but it was to be expected, he supposed. The French girls he employed were very sophisticated and chic. They had to be in their roles. It was what the guests expected – beautiful, well groomed, articulate young people, with exquisite manners. Girls like Mimi – and she really was a snooty bitch, that one – spoke to the clientele as equals. They weren't intimidated by the rich or famous visitors to the resort and they knew instinctively how to act around wealth and glamour because they'd been surrounded by it their entire lives. There was no way they were going to welcome someone as lowly as Molly with open arms.

For Molly, the whole thing must be a terrible shock. To be suddenly thrust into this world was exciting but also terrifying. It would make or break her, he knew that. If she could handle this huge, sudden transition, then she would be able to handle anything life threw at her and she would rise, like a phoenix, from the flames of her past. Oh, how Gabriel hoped she would rise. And, oh, how he wished he could watch her ascent, but he knew already that she would have to do that without him. If she had the grit and the determination he suspected she had, Molly would be OK. But she mustn't let the likes of Mimi break her. It was her first real test. The truth was that Molly was worth ten Mimis. But did she realise that yet? Gabriel wondered. Definitely not. The poor girl was still just trying to get her head around being here, in Paradise.

Gabriel remembered how he'd felt when he'd first arrived in New York in 1959. He was seventeen. He'd never left London before. He had three dollars to his name and he knew no one except a rather strange, predatory old queen he'd met on the ship coming over. He stood on that dock with his legs literally shaking and thought, 'Well, Gabriel, what the hell happens now?' He'd come to America to become a great actor. It had always been his dream. But now he was there he had absolutely no idea how to go about finding a place to sleep that night, let alone how to become a professional actor. Julian Higgins – the predatory queen – must have seen him standing there, scratching his head with his legs shaking beneath him, because he appeared from nowhere and said, 'Right, boy, come with me.' And that had been that.

Higgins was not a kind man, as such, but he did take the young and very green Londoner under his wing and in his own, rather brutal way, he helped Gabriel start a new life. This was a decade before the Stonewall Riots and the start of the Gay Rights Movement and being a gay man, even in a place as cosmopolitan and sophisticated as New York

City, was not easy. What's more, it was illegal. Harassment, violence, blackmail and, of course, imprisonment were very real dangers back then. And in hindsight, without Higgins's help, Gabriel wouldn't have lasted five minutes.

Higgins owned a big old tenement building just east of Third Avenue in what Gabriel soon learned was a gay enclave of the East Side. It wasn't quite the Village – with its vibrant gay bars and nightclubs – but there were openly homosexual men on the streets, not kissing each other or holding hands (that would have got them arrested by the undercover vice officers who patrolled the area) but they would parade quite happily along East 57th with their dachshunds and poodles. And there were several gay bars, all with ornithological names, known collectively to their patrons as the 'bird circuit'. This was Higgins's world and it was soon to become Gabriel's too.

The tenement was populated with all sorts of gay men – florists, hairdressers, fashion designers, artists and, to Gabriel's delight, a couple of actors who proved very useful to Gabriel before long. Gabriel shared a tiny room in the basement with the cockroaches and the rats. But he was used to vermin. There had been plenty of rats in the slum East London terrace where he'd grown up. Gabriel's role was to amuse the older men in the tenement block and the wider community by basically being young, witty, good-looking and English.

'You are a beautiful boy, Gabriel,' Higgins would tell him. 'Forget the acting for now. Your face will pay for your upkeep.'

Gabriel usually didn't have to do much for his money. He would flirt with and flatter the older men and they would buy him gifts, or dinner, or theatre tickets. One of his middle-aged 'friends' managed the men's fashion floor of an upmarket department store in Midtown. Soon Gabriel was walking around Manhattan in mohair suits and Italian shoes with a silk cravat tied around his neck. Sometimes, with Higgins's encouragement, his 'friendships' went a little further than he was comfortable with. But Gabriel was young and naive. He was used to being told what to do. Besides, the men were all extremely kind to him, and their gifts really were very generous. It wasn't until years later that he admitted to himself that his first real job in New York was that of rent boy.

When Gabriel finally fell in love for the first time, with Timmy – a gorgeous Afro-American boy his own age – Higgins hit the roof. He forbade Gabriel from seeing Timmy and even tried to ground him. But by now Gabriel was eighteen, he'd been in New York for a year, and he'd not only started growing facial hair, but he'd grown some balls too. He defied Higgins at every turn, argued, shouted, climbed out of the toilet window when his bedroom door was locked and when, finally, Higgins beat him with a walking stick, Gabriel grappled that weapon from the older man and beat him right back.

Gabriel had to leave the East Side in a hurry. He and Timmy found a tiny apartment in the Village and every day Gabriel went up to Broadway to hang out with the actors he'd met and basically beg for parts in any play that would have him. He started getting small roles in terrible off-Broadway productions. They really were dire. But he was happy – completely, blissfully, sinfully happy. He and Timmy lived in the Village for almost a year before Gabriel came home one day and found his beloved boyfriend in bed with some other guy. It was the first time Gabriel had known what it felt like to have his heart broken and it crushed him. He didn't react well. He was very, very angry with Timmy.

And again, Gabriel had to leave in a hurry. This time he fled all the way to LA, where he set his sights on the big time – the movies! By the time he was twenty-one, he'd acted alongside Marilyn Monroe and James Stewart, and Higgins and Timmy and the East Side and the Village were all just distant memories. It was almost as though none of it had ever happened.

'Are you crying?' A voice startled Gabriel and dragged him back to the present with a jolt.

It was Molly, peering up at him with those pretty green eyes of hers. Gabriel wiped what did seem to be a stray tear from his cheek and said, 'It would appear so, my dear.'

And then he looked closer at Molly and saw that those lovely eyes were rimmed with red and that her nose was running a little and he said, 'Are *you* crying?'

She laughed weakly and said, 'It would appear so.'

Gabriel hooked his arm through Molly's and the pair stood silently for a moment, both looking out to sea as the water lapped their bare ankles.

'Why are you crying?' asked Molly, eventually.

'The past,' said Gabriel, truthfully. 'And why are you crying?'

Molly shrugged. 'The past, the present, the future ... Anyway, I'm not crying! Well, not really.'

She laughed at herself then and Gabriel's heart melted even more towards his new protégé.

'Is that all?' He squeezed her arm affectionately. 'It's the other girls, isn't it? I know they haven't exactly welcomed you with open arms.'

He watched Molly's face as she screwed up her button nose and blinked her long eyelashes. She was obviously determined not to cry in front of him. There was something about the firm set of her chin and the steely glint in her eyes that just oozed pride. He wondered if that came from her gypsy blood. There wasn't an ounce of arrogance in her body, not a hint of conceit, but there was something there, something resolute, something rock-hard in her core. Molly Costello would not break easily, Gabriel decided.

'Ach, I don't fit in with those glamour girls,' scoffed Molly, as if it was no big deal. 'Can you blame them for not wanting to be friends with me? I'm not their cuppa tea; it's as simple as that.'

'Their loss,' said Gabriel, squeezing her arm. 'I imagine they feel a bit threatened by you, my dear.'

'Threatened?!' Molly threw her head back and laughed as if it was the most hilarious thing she'd ever heard. 'Don't be daft. They're not threatened by me. They can see right through me, that's all. They know what I am and I'm not one of them.'

'So what are you, Miss Molly?' asked Gabriel, intrigued to find out how Molly saw herself.

She looked at him then, her eyes unblinking now, and said definitely and defiantly, 'Well, it's simple, Gabriel. I'm trash.'

She said the word without self-pity. It was a statement of fact, nothing more, nothing less.

'Trash?' Gabriel repeated the word, tasting it, feeling it, recognising it.

'Trash,' Molly confirmed.

'In what way?' Gabriel asked, frowning at her.

'I'm not only poor, common, badly educated and un-sophisticated,' stated Molly matter-of-factly. 'I'm also the daughter of a drunken, thieving gippo – those aren't my words by the way, that's just what people thought. I'm half gypsy. I wasn't accepted by my da's people, or by my mam's. My mammy died when I was six, and we weren't even washed properly after that. I was the lowest of the low in Balymun. And Balymun is no Paradise. So if I was low at home, what am I here in this beautiful, upmarket place? Trash.'

'No. You're Molly Costello,' Gabriel shrugged. 'Whoever she wants to be. You left all those ridiculous social stereotypes behind. You can reinvent yourself. Or just be yourself. Either. Both. Nobody need judge you here. You're free. And, anyway, if you're trash, then I'm trash too,' said Gabriel, thinking how similar his childhood had been to Molly's in some ways, despite the generation gap.

Molly gazed up at him, confused. 'But you're, well, you're posh, Gabriel,' she said, blushing a little. 'You talk beautifully and you're rich and successful and everyone looks up to you.'

'Nope,' said Gabriel, smiling at her now. 'I'm not posh, I'm just a good actor. It's been my life's work – to reinvent myself and fool the world. I was brought up in squalor, you see. I had no shoes, I was malnourished, I barely went to school. I was an outcast, a bastard.'

Molly looked at him uncertainly, as if she didn't know whether he was being serious. But Gabriel had never been more serious in his life. This was something that very few people knew – his real history – but for some reason he felt safe sharing the truth with Molly Costello.

'No really, I'm a bastard in the true sense of the word,' he continued. 'I have no idea who my father was, and I'm not sure my mother did either, God rest her soul. Some GI during the Blitz, I expect. Or a punter. She was a drunk and a prostitute. She had four children in all and none of us had the same father. Then, when my youngest sister was less than a year old, she killed herself. She was thirty years old when she died but she looked nearer sixty. There was no note, no explanation. She just checked out and left us to it. We were in and out of orphanages and foster homes for years. My brothers were adopted, separately, by different families, and I haven't seen them since. My baby sister … Well, it's complicated and rather sad, but that's another story … Now, my dear Molly, I don't mean to be competitive, but if that history doesn't make me even trashier than you, then I don't know what does!'

'I can't believe that,' said Molly, on the brink of tears again now, so full of humility and empathy for Gabriel's childhood that he wanted to pick her up and hug her. 'I'm so sorry. I had no idea. I'd never have guessed.'

'That's my point,' Gabriel continued. 'No one can guess because it's not what I show. And don't cry for me, Molly. It's not a sad story. It has a happy ending. I left London as George Bloom: a penniless East End bastard – and a homosexual to boot, can you imagine! – and arrived in New York a young, gay, aspiring actor called Gabriel Abbot. You don't have to change your name, Molly, but you can change your place in the world. When you leave your past behind, people can only judge you on what they see. You are what you show them. It's up to you now. You're in charge of your destiny and if you want to charm the other girls, that's in your control too.'

'But they're so mean!' said Molly, with half a smile, trying to lighten the conversation. 'I'm not sure I even want to be their friend. Antoinette seems OK, I suppose. But not Mimi. She's evil!'

'Do you remember what you said about that horrible boy in Dublin when he got away after trying to steal my briefcase and beating you black and blue?' Gabriel asked.

Molly nodded. 'I said he'll get his comeuppance,' she replied.

'Well, my dear little Molly, the same is true of Mimi and her gang,' he said. 'So don't let them get to you. No bad behaviour ever goes unpunished. And you're right, some of those girls are nasty pieces of work – don't think I don't see that. They'll get their comeuppance too.'

'What? Do you mean like karma?' asked Molly. 'Will the universe punish them for being so mean to me?'

She was smiling again now, teasing him slightly.

'If you like,' said Gabriel, thoughtfully. He had lived in LA in the sixties but he was no hippy. 'But it's not nature, or the universe that will punish them. Karma is man-made. Every action, or inaction has a consequence. Nobody gets away with behaving badly scot-free. Not in the end. Humans have a very strong sense of right and wrong. It's primal. If you behave badly and if you hurt the wrong person, then one day someone will make you pay.'

'Revenge?' asked Molly.

Gabriel shook his head. 'Not revenge, exactly, my dear Molly. Retribution.'

Molly shivered despite the heat. 'That sounds a bit sinister,' she said.

'No, retribution's not sinister. It's perfect. And it's completely fair. It's how things are meant to be.'

'I suppose ...' Molly didn't sound convinced. But she would be. Soon.

'Well, Miss Molly,' said Gabriel. 'I really must go. We have some very important guests arriving tomorrow and I have a lot to do to get ready.'

He paddled, not very gracefully, towards the water's edge and picked up his shoes. Gabriel couldn't remember the last time he'd been this excited. Tomorrow the plan got under way. His special guests were arriving at Paradise. And the truth was, Gabriel had never been so ready for an arrival before.

'Who?' asked Molly, all wide-eyed and excited. 'Who's coming to Paradise?'

'Patience, my dear, is a virtue,' winked Gabriel. 'You'll have to wait and see. But perhaps you should put on some make-up tomorrow, darling! You're a beautiful girl but you could easily be mistaken for a twelve-year-old.'

'What?' asked Molly, fixing Gabriel with a surprisingly steely stare. 'If I can't beat the Mean Girls, I should join them? Try to make myself more like they are?'

'No,' scoffed Gabriel. 'Don't be silly. I don't think you should join them. I think you should beat them at their own game.'

Molly cocked her head and gave him a thoughtful little smile.

'Maybe I will,' she replied. 'Maybe I will.'

'Well you can start on Friday night, my dear. I need you to waitress at a little soiree I'm throwing,' called Gabriel over his shoulder as he retrieved his shoes.

'Waitress?' asked Molly, still ankle deep in water, looking stunned. 'I can't waitress! I'm a chambermaid!'

'You can do anything you want, Molly Costello,' smiled Gabriel, knowing that he was right. 'I have complete faith in you. Anyway, that wasn't an offer, it was an order.'

'But ... ?' Molly called after him.

'No buts!' shouted Gabriel, raising his hand firmly. 'It's all decided. I'm the boss, remember? Now I must go. Adieu.'

Gabriel was satisfied. His work here was done.

14

It hadn't taken long for things to return to normal in the
Hunter household. Lauren had woken up with a smile on
her face, the morning after they'd made love. She'd curled
her arms around Sebastian's back and hugged him affectionately. The previous night had been heaven and she didn't
want it to end just because the alarm had gone off. She'd
felt his back stiffen. He'd lain there like a lead weight for a
few moments, letting her hug him but not moving, and then
he'd wriggled out of her arms and got out of bed. He'd stood
with his back to her, saying nothing. Lauren had watched
his back and felt the nerves start to jitter in her stomach
again. What was wrong now?

'Are you OK?' she'd asked him, tentatively. 'You seem a
bit tense.'

'For fuck's sake, give me a break, woman,' he'd replied
without turning round. 'I've only just woken up and you're
already whinging.'

'I'm not whinging,' Lauren had defended herself, trying
to keep the hurt out of her voice. 'It's just that last night you
were so affectionate and now you seem really distant again.
I'm confused.'

He'd walked towards the window, peeked out of the

curtains and shrugged. 'Yeah, well, you're always confused, Lauren, aren't you?'

'But ... I thought ... After last night ... And the holiday ... And ...' Lauren had started.

Sebastian had spun round then and faced her. He'd looked angry. His eyes were so narrowed that she could barely see his irises at all. 'This is what I can't stand about you, Lauren,' he'd spat. 'Everything's always so wet and needy and emotional. I feel like I can't breathe when I'm around you.'

'But ... ? What did I do?' Lauren's heart had been in her mouth.

'Lauren, we had sex last night. Big fucking deal. It doesn't mean I have to get the violins out this morning and sprinkle rose petals on the bed. I'm a busy man. I'm stressed. And now I have to work my arse off for the next couple of days because I'm taking *you* on holiday.'

'I never asked to be taken on holiday,' Lauren had reminded him.

'Ungrateful cow,' he'd muttered as he'd pushed past her and locked himself in the en suite. 'I don't know why I bother.'

She'd noticed that he'd taken his mobile phone with him and tried not to think about what Kitty had said the day before. Lauren had fed the girls and got their school bags ready. She'd fed the cat and made Sebastian his soya latte. She'd brushed her hair and put on her face for the school run. But inside her heart had been withering, dying. Sometimes it felt worse to be lifted back up onto the pedestal briefly. It meant she had so much further to fall when Sebastian pushed her off again.

He'd barely said a word as he'd eaten his breakfast that day. His forehead had been furrowed and his eyes had

166

darted around the kitchen, never focusing on one thing or another for long. He did this when he was thinking. Lauren had always thought it was a sign of his quick mind. She'd noticed him check his phone for messages four times in the space of seven minutes. She'd wondered if there was a problem at the office. He was obviously upset about something.

'Is everything OK at work?' she'd asked him, a little nervously in case he bit her head off.

'It's fine!' he'd snapped back. 'What the hell do you care about my business anyway? As long as you can spend it, you don't care where the money comes from. Here ...' he'd tossed a credit card onto the worktop. 'I suppose you'll want that if you're going to go shopping for the holiday.'

Lauren had stared at the credit card. She'd never asked him for money. She'd rarely bought clothes except for the kids. She hadn't even wanted the new car he'd bought her last month. She was still quite happy with the old one.

'I don't need anything,' she'd replied, pushing the card back in his direction.

He'd frowned, pushed it towards her again. She'd pushed it back. The girls had watched the credit card being passed backwards and forwards between their parents as if they were spectators at Wimbledon.

'Oh, for Christ's sake, buy some new clothes, Lauren,' Sebastian had snapped finally, standing up and putting the card in her handbag. 'There's no way I'm setting foot in public with you anywhere – let alone somewhere as sophisticated as St Barts – unless you get some decent gear. Go to Selfridges and see the personal shopper. You can't be trusted to choose things yourself.'

Lauren had bitten her lip and fixed her eyes on the ceiling. He'd done it again: managed to make her feel 'this' tall, as Kitty had put it. She couldn't bring herself to look at

Sebastian, or at Emily or Poppy. She was too ashamed.

When Sebastian headed for the front door, she'd followed him.

'That was mean,' she'd told him, staring at her shoes, still scared of the look in his eye.

'The truth hurts,' was all he'd said. And then, just as he was about to walk out the door, he'd added. 'And get your hair sorted. It's awful, Lauren.'

'But I thought you said it was growing on you!' she'd reminded him.

'I was slightly drunk and it was dark,' he'd replied, quick as a flash. 'It's the same reason I had sex with you.'

Then the door had slammed and he was gone. All he left was a waft of expensive aftershave in the hall. Lauren had felt something grow cold in her heart. It was just a tiny speck of ice in the midst of the burning pain but it was very definitely there. And, as she stared at the back of the door, it stopped her from crying this time.

Since that morning, things had gone from bad to worse. And now they were here, in the French West Indies, but Lauren felt a long way from paradise. The flight from London to St Martin had been a long and lonely journey for Lauren. Even as she'd packed her new things – the exquisite silk, bias-cut maxi dress, the bright turquoise swimsuit, the skimpy white beach dress, that ill-advised gold bikini that she already knew she'd never have the nerve to wear – Lauren had had a sinking feeling in her stomach. This was the first holiday she and Sebastian had been on alone together in years, but he had barely said a word to her in days and he'd been so moody and erratic lately that she was actually scared – yes, scared! – of being alone in his company. As she'd rolled the last few things into her case Emily had come into the bedroom. She'd put her arms around her mother's waist and just held her there for a few moments. Lauren had had to catch her breath. Her eldest daughter rarely showed affection these days and when she did Lauren drank in the warmth and cherished it for all it was worth.

'You'll be OK, Mum,' Emily had said, too old and knowing for her years. 'It'll be nice for you to sunbathe and relax. You'll probably meet some interesting people. And you can just ignore Daddy if he's, you know, in one of his horrid moods.'

Lauren had squeezed Emily then, bursting with love and determination that things were going to change. Her eleven-year-old daughter should not be worrying about the way her father treated her mother. It was all wrong. Somewhere deep down Lauren already knew that the holiday wasn't going to miraculously fix her marriage. But perhaps it would give her breathing space to reflect and think about what had to happen next. Divorce was out of the question, for now at least. She'd stuck by Sebastian this long and, for the sake of the girls' stability, she would see the marriage through until they were at least safely off to university. And besides, despite everything, she still loved him. He was her husband and as flawed as he might be she wasn't going to just give up on him now. Somewhere hidden deep beneath the sarcasm and the fake tan was a lovely, warm, funny man. Lauren remembered him well; she missed him, and sometimes she even got flashes of him now.

'You sound like a battered wife making excuses for her attacker,' was what Kitty had said, earlier that day, when they'd talked on the phone. '"Oh, but he's so nice when he's not beating the crap out of me. If I behave better then maybe he'll stop doing it to me. It's all my own fault."'

'That's not what I'm saying,' Lauren had tried to defend herself. 'He might be a bit vain and self-obsessed but you know he can be lovely sometimes. You liked him too when we first met him. I clearly remember you and Sebbie downing champagne from the bottle and dancing on the tables at the Atlantic Bar and Grill back in the day.'

'Maybe,' Kitty had conceded. 'Sebastardian was good-looking back then, and he was full of himself, and a bit flash, and a bit wild, and he played with people and wound them up, so it felt kind of cool to be in his gang. But it was like hanging out with the school bully. The minute he turned on you for the first time, I started to despise him. And I still do.'

'You thought he was fun,' Lauren had reminded her friend, remembering that she'd actually been worried by how well her boyfriend and her best friend had got on back when they'd all first met.

'Darling,' Kitty had said, patiently. 'Maybe I did think he was fun at first. But I used to think taking ecstasy was fun at college until I had a bad trip and ended up in A&E. Then I realised it was really, really bad for me. Toxic. And that's what Sebastian is for you. I've been saying it for more than a decade; you're not going to change my mind now.'

As always, the two friends had had to agree to disagree on the subject of Sebastian. Kitty had a habit of seeing everything in black and white. And besides, there was a reason she was still single at thirty-nine. In Lauren's opinion, she was far, *far* too picky and unrealistic. If Kitty's latest Mr Right wasn't Mr Perfect then he had to go. No excuses, no second chances. But Lauren was more realistic. If you love someone, she thought, if you *really* love them, then you accept them, flaws and all. Otherwise it's all just too damn conditional. Anyway, what the hell would she do without him? She was no one if she wasn't Mrs Sebastian Hunter.

But perhaps there was a way she could rebalance the

power? Why should Sebastian rule their home and their lives? At times he threw a dark cloud over the family with his sulky moods, temper tantrums and unexplained absences and then, fleetingly, he would shine his light on them again, with those brief flashes of charisma and good humour. He'd suddenly swan in to the house with a huge smile on his face, and a Wagamama take-away in his arms and microwave popcorn in his briefcase and he'd announce that they were all going to watch a movie together. They'd have this wonderful, perfect family evening, snuggled up in the smaller, more cosy living room. The girls would look as if they were going to burst with happiness and Lauren would sigh and smile and believe, briefly, that everything was right in her world. And then the next day it would be as though it had never happened. Sebastian would disappear off to work in a mood and none of them would see him again for days.

He ruled their world and he supported them financially, but he didn't always make them feel safe. Sometimes he made the earth shake beneath their feet and it left them feeling nervous and insecure. For the sake of the children, that had to stop. And Lauren was the only one who could do that. Oh, she knew it was difficult for Sebastian, having such a stressful career, and despite what he said to the contrary, she felt sure that the recession must be hurting him financially somehow. She wasn't making excuses for him. Kitty was wrong. And some of their problems were Lauren's fault. She wasn't the funky girl-about-town he'd met any more. How was that fair on him? Maybe if Lauren could find her confidence again then Sebastian would feel less pressured, happier with their relationship and more inclined to spend time at home? Perhaps he would remember what it was about Lauren that he'd loved in the first place? Maybe if she could somehow get her career back it would make her feel more complete and worthwhile? It was a crazy thought, a thought she hadn't even had the nerve to broach with Kitty, but ...

'Are you going to take your camera?' Emily had asked, spotting the dusty camera bag on the floor by the case. 'Really? Are you going to take photos?'

The look on Emily's face had taken Lauren by surprise. She'd looked proud. And hopeful. Lauren had barely picked up a camera since she'd had the children. The fear of taking bad photographs had been so great that she'd let Sebastian and the grandparents snap away with their digital cameras instead. The girls, and Emily in particular, were intrigued by the black-and-white photographs of actors, singers and sports stars that graced the walls of their home. Fascinated that in another time, and another world, before their birth, their mother had been someone talented, independent and maybe even a bit special. This camera, her only professional digital equipment (she hadn't even used digital cameras back in the olden days, when she'd been a professional photographer), had been a Christmas gift from her parents, five years ago now. It was top of the range and it must have cost a fortune, but it had been stored, gathering dust, on top of the wardrobe ever since that Boxing Day. Until now, anyway.

'I thought I might take it. Just in case,' Lauren had explained, picking up the camera bag and starting to dust it off uncertainly. 'The light in St Barts is supposed to be magical. It seems a shame to go there and not take any photos. But it's been such a long time.'

'Oh, Mummy, you must!' Emily had shrieked, more animated than Lauren had seen her in months. 'You absolutely must. It's the best idea you've had, ever.'

'Really?' Lauren had asked her daughter, feeling bashful and unconvinced.

'Really,' Emily had nodded enthusiastically. 'It would make me and Poppy really proud. And then when you get back you can take lots of pictures of us looking arty and interesting.'

Emily had posed then, head tilted up, her bone structure a perfect replica of her father's. Lauren had laughed and promised that she would do just that. There. It had been decided. The camera would go to Paradise.

But now, sitting in St Martin airport, waiting for the connecting flight to St Barts, with the camera bag at her feet, Lauren felt less convinced. Sebastian had laughed cynically when he'd seen the camera bag waiting neatly at the front door with the suitcases.

'Can you remember where the button is, dear?' he'd asked sarcastically.

He hadn't even asked why she was finally bringing her camera on holiday after all these years. But then he hadn't said much at all. Sebastian had spent the flight from London drinking champagne silently, plugged into his headphones, watching film after film after film. It had surprised Lauren how far away two people could sit from each other, side by side in an aeroplane. That was the beauty of first class, she guessed. If you can afford the bigger seats, you can more easily ignore your wife. She wondered how many other businessmen were thankful for this privilege. The only time Sebastian spoke was to be smooth and slightly flirty with the pretty young air hostess who brought him his champagne, his Perrier and his special healthy option meal. Every time she served him, the air hostess would then smile at Lauren as if to say, 'Aren't you lucky to have such a suave, charming husband?'

And now the arduous journey was almost over. Lauren looked around the small departure lounge in St Martin's airport. Sebastian was busy checking texts and emails on his phone, so Lauren amused herself by people-watching. A group of young American men lounged in one corner as if they owned the place, long legs crossed in front of them, expensive luggage scattered over three rows of seats. They were good-looking, well-bred, expensively dressed, loud and self-important. Their egos seemed to expand and fill the air around them. They talked and laughed so loudly and boastfully that Lauren now knew their names, ages, occupations and the reason for their trip. Dex, Mitchell, James and Lachlan worked on Wall Street. They were traders, lawyers and brokers in their early thirties. They'd met at Yale. They lived in the Upper West Side and their families also had homes in the Hamptons. Dex was getting married to Sexy Sabrina in two weeks' time. Sabrina was a hottie, almost thirty; she had a Harvard degree and blue blood credentials. Dex had done well for himself, was the general consensus. Sabrina was a fine young woman. But this was Dex's stag week and he should sow his wild oats as much as he possibly could.

What made Lauren feel most disconcerted was Sebastian's reaction to them. While their arrogance and casual sexism made Lauren's skin crawl, Sebastian was obviously thrilled by them. He kept looking up from his phone, glancing over at them, smiling to himself at their 'hilarious' conversations, and nodding in agreement as if he were part of their gang. Lauren hoped they wouldn't be staying at the same resort. She already knew that given half the chance Sebastian would 'adopt' these creeps and befriend them. They were just his type. Lauren frowned now as she watched them in their Ralph Lauren smart-casual wear, back-slapping each other at every supercilious remark. Yuk. She realised with a slight shudder that they kind of reminded her of Sebastian at that age and she found herself wondering, briefly, what it was she'd ever seen in him. If she found men like this so repulsive at thirty-eight, why had she found Sebastian so enthralling at twenty-six? But then she remembered that Kitty had liked Sebastian then too and Kitty was the arbiter of all things cool. No, she was just tired, jet-lagged and grumpy. Once they got to Paradise things would change.

To Sebastian's right, a man of about Sebastian's age was fast asleep with his head resting on his backpack. He was lying over four chairs with his feet just inches from Sebastian's best cream linen suit. Sebastian was definitely less thrilled by this fellow passenger than he was by the Wall Street brats. The sleeping man was wearing battered cowboy boots. Every now and then he stretched his legs in his sleep and his boots nudged Sebastian's finest linen. Sebastian would then tut, shuffle closer to Lauren, glare at her for daring to share his personal space, and then tut again.

Caught between a rock and a hard place, thought Lauren, trying to hide her amusement at her husband's dilemma.

Lauren couldn't see the sleeping man's face very clearly, but what she could see was interesting. He didn't look like the sort of guy who should be flying to a five-star Caribbean holiday resort. He looked like he should be climbing a mountain, or sailing a yacht, or driving across a desert in an old Land Rover. His body looked strong, as if it was made for outdoor pursuits. His white T-shirt had risen up a little and was flashing an inch or two of toned abs. His legs, which were clad in well-worn denim, were very long.

All the better for kicking Sebastian, thought Lauren, a little gleefully.

He was tanned but in a very different way from Sebastian. His skin looked weather-worn and wind-blown. He didn't look as if he'd been near a sunbed in his life, or a manicurist, or even a hairdresser, come to think of it. His hair was sandy blonde and tousled. His fingers were surprisingly long and rather elegant but his nails were a little grubby and very short. Lauren found herself wondering if he played guitar. He looked as if he should play guitar. She kept willing him to turn over in his sleep so that she could see his face. He looked as if he might be very handsome. Lauren hoped he would be handsome. Partly because she appreciated a handsome man as much as the next woman, but also, childishly, because it would annoy Sebastian even more than the suit-nudging business. There was nothing Sebastian loathed more than to be in a room with a man who was more handsome than he was.

The door opened then and disturbed Lauren from her thoughts. She watched, intrigued, as an enormous black man with a shiny bald head, a black suit, and a walkie-talkie strode into the room. He peered suspiciously at each passenger in the departures lounge, paced the room from corner to corner and then finally muttered something into his mouthpiece. He was clearly a bodyguard of some sort. It seemed the only explanation. St Barts was a very exclusive island, after all. Sebastian sat up straight beside her, his eyes popping out of his head.

'Somebody important is about to join us, mark my words,' he whispered, very excitedly, and a little patronisingly, to Lauren. Sebastian loved 'important' people.

She wanted to say, 'No shit, Einstein.' That's what Kitty would have said, but Lauren managed to bite her tongue. It was always best to pander to Sebastian's ego. Unless you wanted a tongue-lashing, of course.

Even the Wall Street brats had shut up now and everyone, except for the sleeping man, was watching the door in anticipation.

'Oh. My. God,' whispered Lauren as the new passengers finally walked in, surrounded by security guards and armed police. 'Now isn't that ironic?'

Sebastian's jaw was practically scraping the floor as Lexi Crawford and Mal Riley sauntered in, shades firmly in place, followed by a bustling, overweight middle-aged woman. Lauren's mind flashed back to the argument they'd had in the kitchen last week. It was these two unknown, untouchable celebrities who had instigated the fight. They'd been a metaphor for Lauren and Sebastian's own failings but never in a million years did Lauren think she'd ever actually meet the couple in question. And now here they were, in the flesh, just metres away.

'Perhaps they thought you might like to watch their car-crash of a marriage at close range?' whispered Lauren to her husband, knowing she was being facetious, but not being able to help herself. The argument was just too raw for her not to comment on this crazy coincidence.

'Oh, shut up, Lauren,' was all Sebastian said, before settling back in his seat with his eyes still firmly fixed on the new arrivals.

Lauren was transfixed too. She had met a lot of famous people in the old days, when she'd been a photographer, so she wasn't at all star struck. But both Lexi and Mal were such utterly beautiful creatures that it was almost impossible not to stare. Mal Riley was even taller than he looked on stage and on TV. He must have been almost six foot five. And he was undeniably handsome. He was scruffy but there was no way he could hide his wealth or success. His black clothes managed to look both battered and expensive at the same time. She imagined that his ridiculously tangled and dishevelled mop of black hair smelled sweetly of Aveda products if you got up close. His limbs were long and loose and he wore his confidence in an easy, friendly smile. Lauren had read all the stories about him – the drugs, the booze, the loose women, the cruel infidelities, the wild parties and the outrageous rock-star behaviour. And she was sure it was all true, but there was something likeable about the man. She'd watched him on *Jonathan Ross* just a few weeks earlier and had found herself warming to him, smiling and laughing at the things he'd said. He'd seemed pretty smart and self-aware, to be honest. And although he was cocky, the swagger seemed almost put on, as if he knew he had to act that way in his role as Rock God, but that underneath he was actually a pretty decent bloke with a half-decent brain and a good heart. She watched him now, with his hand placed gently on the small of Lexi's back. He kissed the top of his new wife's head tenderly as she sat down in her chair.

Lexi Crawford was an exquisite little doll of a girl. She was much smaller than Lauren had imagined but, despite the dyed black hair, the heavy eye make-up and the tongue piercing, she was properly beautiful in the true old-fashioned Hollywood sense of the word.

'She looks like a young Liz Taylor,' Lauren found herself whispering to Sebastian.

For once he agreed with her. He just nodded and said, 'That's exactly what I was thinking. What the hell is she doing with that oaf?'

'Oh, I think Mal Riley's quite sexy really,' replied Lauren. 'All those screaming fans can't be wrong.'

'Urgh!' was all Sebastian managed to say. Lauren swallowed her smile. She was right: Sebastian did not like being the second best-looking man in a room.

Lauren watched as Mal settled his wife and the older woman into their seats. He was being equally attentive to both women and Lauren guessed that the busty, Hyacinth

Bucket lookalike must be his mother. Every now and then, when the mother wasn't looking, Lexi threw a filthy glare in her direction. And then, when Lexi was busy searching for something in her bag, the older woman did exactly the same thing to her daughter-in-law. The hatred between the two was palpable. Mal, meanwhile, seemed a bit jumpy, fussing over one and then the other in a slightly manic, nervy manner. So the hot-shot rock star was a mummy's boy. Poor Lexi. Lauren already knew whose side she was on in this one. The poor kids had only just got married. What the hell was Mal's mother doing on their honeymoon?!

Just then the sleeping man stirred, yawned, stretched his legs, and kicked Sebastian in the hip.

'For fuck's sake,' muttered Sebastian. 'What the hell is someone like *that* doing here, anyway? He looks like a tramp.'

The sleepy man did not look like a tramp. He looked weary and well-worn and a little scruffy, maybe, but he had an aura of importance and worth that Sebastian had clearly missed. When she used to take photographs, it wasn't always the most obvious people that Lauren enjoyed shooting the most. Some people just had a kind of magical glow around them that Lauren found she could capture through her lens. This man was one of those people. She knew that already. Lauren watched the man as he turned finally onto his back and showed his face for the first time. And then she grinned to herself. Yup, he was handsome all right. He was so bloody handsome and chiselled and perfect that neither Sebastian, nor even Mal Riley, was the best-looking man in the room any more.

'Do you mind?' snapped Sebastian at the man, as he stretched one more time and then opened his eyes.

'Huh?' The man squinted at Sebastian, rubbed his eyes,

sat up. 'I'm sorry, did you say something, buddy?' He was American, of course. As American as Clint Eastwood, John Wayne and the Marlboro Man.

'I said, do you mind not kicking me please,' replied Sebastian tersely, sounding very uptight, very pissed off and very English. Lauren felt suddenly rather embarrassed to be sitting next to him.

'Jeez, I'm so sorry, man,' said the American in a slow, sexy drawl. 'I'm just so frigging zonked, must be the jet-lag. I was totally out of it there. Here, d'you wanna beer? By way of an apology?'

The guy reached into his backpack and offered Sebastian a Budweiser.

'No, thank you,' said Sebastian coldly and ungratefully. 'I don't drink beer.'

'Oh, OK,' said the American, scratching his head and opening the beer anyway.

Lauren watched as he downed the Bud. Part of her wanted to say, 'I'll have a beer with you.' The American looked laid-back and easy-going. She imagined he'd be good to chat to. But of course she would never have the nerve to do that.

Sebastian sat with a distasteful look on his face. His lip curled as if something smelled bad, and his fingers drummed impatiently on his crossed thighs. God, he really hated men who were different from him, Lauren realised. Perhaps there was something in what Kitty said. Maybe Sebastian felt inferior to 'real' men, who let their stubble grow and their clothes get dirty and their guard down.

'Clyde?' Mal Riley suddenly shouted across the room. 'It is you, mate! Fucking hell, it's been years.'

Mal strode towards where Sebastian and Lauren were sitting, walked right past them as if they were invisible and threw his arms affectionately around the sleepy American. Wow, both men were so tall! Lauren could practically feel Sebastian's inferiority complex growing beside her. Sebastian told everyone he was six foot tall but Lauren was five foot ten, and she hadn't been able to wear high heels for twelve years because even the tiniest kitten heel raised her above her husband's head.

Mal and the American, Clyde, back-slapped each other and hugged for a while. Lauren pretended to read her magazine but she couldn't help listening. The two men hadn't seen each other in six years. They'd last bumped into each other on a TV show in LA. Mal apparently loved Clyde's work and wondered why he hadn't done anything new lately. He asked Clyde how his wife was. Clyde muttered something about divorce and Mal gave him another man hug. Then he ushered his friend over to where Lexi was sitting in 'celebrity corner' and Lauren and Sebastian were left alone. Lauren hadn't recognised this Clyde fellow. She wondered what it was that he did for a living that Mal Riley 'loved' so much.

'Do you know who that was?' Lauren asked Sebastian, a little tentatively.

'Yup,' said Sebastian abruptly.

Silence.

Lauren took a deep breath. 'Well, who?' she asked.

Sebastian sighed, as if she were a complete irritation to him. 'I think it must be Clyde Scott,' he said impatiently.

Clyde Scott. The name was familiar to Lauren but she couldn't pinpoint where she'd heard it before.

'Who's he?' she asked, unwilling to let the subject go.

Sebastian sighed again, rolled his eyes. 'The thriller writer,' he said.

Aha, Lauren remembered now.

'Oh right!' she said brightly. 'That's brilliant. You love his books, don't you, Seb? You used to read them all the time.'

Sebastian took a sharp intake of breath, pursed his lips and narrowed his eyes. 'Nope,' he said, defiantly. 'I was never a fan.'

Lauren couldn't help but smirk. Oh my God! He was so childish sometimes. And such a compulsive liar! She knew perfectly well that Sebastian had devoured every one of Clyde Scott's novels. She remembered them clearly, sitting on his bedside table. He'd even put those books on his Christmas list! But now, because he'd thought the man was annoying, and he'd called him a tramp, and he'd refused to share his beer or even strike up a conversation with the guy, Sebastian was going to pretend he didn't rate his writing at all.

She looked around the departures lounge and watched her fellow passengers closely, one by one. In a few minutes' time Lauren would get on a tiny twelve-seater light aircraft with all of them – the Wall Street brats, the Rock Star, the Child Star, the Mother-in-Law, the Thriller Writer and The Husband. St Barts was a tiny island and she was going to be there at the same time as all these people. Lauren felt a tingle of excitement run up her spine. She suddenly realised just how far away she was from the school run and the coffee mornings, the endless washing and the weekly Waitrose shop. Whatever happened with Sebastian, the next few days were going to be an adventure. And that was something Lauren hadn't had for a very, *very* long time.

PART TWO

The Destination

15

The beach bar, Paradise

Clyde sat at the circular bar and nursed his JD and Coke silently. He'd politely declined the free welcome cocktail that the blond Adonis behind the bar had offered him, and had politely declined the cheerful banter on offer too, but he had gratefully accepted this drink instead. He was pleased to note that Henri – as the Adonis had introduced himself – was rather generous with the liquor measures and smart enough to spot when a man wasn't in the mood for small talk. It was ten thirty a.m. and this drink was the closest thing to breakfast that Clyde could stomach.

He looked up, took in the chalk-white beach, the turquoise waves lapping the shore, the bronzed bodies reclining on loungers, the palm trees, the white fluffy clouds in the impossibly blue sky, the pelicans flying overhead and although it was all undeniably beautiful he felt ... well, nothing. He was completely detached from his surroundings. It was as if he was looking at a postcard, as if he wasn't really here at all. This was not Clyde's world. It was so damn far from the cold Colorado winter, from his kids, and his home, and his beloved Shiloh that he'd never felt so out of place in his life. What the hell was he doing here? It was the craziest, most dumb-assed idea ever. He would kill Berkowski for talking him into this. There was no way he was going to get inspired in St Barts. So he might as well just get smashed instead.

'I'll have the same again, please, buddy,' said Clyde, sliding his empty glass down the bar to Henri. 'And put this one on my room. Room one.'

'Sure,' said Henri, brightly. 'A Jack Daniel's and Coke coming up. I'll start a tab for you.'

'And get me your biggest, flashiest, fruitiest, most mind-bending cocktail please, sir!' boomed a familiar English voice behind him. 'With one of those paper umbrella thingies in it. Ooh, and a sparkler! And put it on my room. Not that I've got a fucking clue what room I'm in. You'll have to ask the missus once she's decided which bikini to wear. She should be here by sundown ...'

'Room five, sir,' said Henri confidently. 'You are very definitely staying in room five.'

'Am I?' asked Mal, vaguely. 'If you say so. And forget that "sir" business. It's Mal, for crying out loud. Oh, and when my mum gets here, tell her I'm drinking one of them virgin cocktails – you know, all fruit and no booze. She's a bit funny about me drinking before lunchtime, bless her. Morning, Clyde, glad to see you're having a liquid breakfast too.'

Clyde couldn't help smiling to himself. Mal Riley was just one of those guys who made you smile, even when the last thing you wanted was company. He turned round and grinned at Mal, realising that he was grateful to have at least one ally on the resort. Despite his dark mood, Clyde almost laughed out loud when he saw Mal's version of beach attire. The singer looked completely ridiculous. Mal had squeezed himself into a pair of tiny, tight, black Lycra bathers. His hair was as huge and dishevelled as ever. He was wearing lots of chunky silver jewellery, guyliner and black leather thong sandals. His giant body was pasty white and covered in tattoos and thick black body hair. Talk about a fish out of water! For a man who looked so cocky and cool on stage, Mal Riley sure as hell looked silly on a beach.

'I know, I know!' said Mal loudly, seeing the look on Clyde's face and sliding onto the barstool next to him. 'I look like a complete prick. I feel like a pork chop at a Jewish wedding! An International Rock God does not take to beach chic naturally. Can you believe I couldn't find black leather swimming trunks, even in New York?!'

Mal grinned and eyed Clyde up and down. The guy didn't take himself too seriously. That was what made him so cool, Clyde guessed.

'Mind you, I think I'm making more of an effort than you are, cowboy,' said Mal. 'Aren't you bloody well sweltering?'

Clyde was wearing his usual uniform of jeans, a T-shirt and boots. He hadn't even thought to pack anything other than a spare pair of jeans, some underpants, socks and two spare T shirts in his backpack. Those things, along with his toothbrush and his laptop, were all he'd brought to the West Indies. What else did he need?

'Nope, I'm just fine as I am,' replied Clyde, not quite sure if he was ready for a conversation yet, even if he did like Mal a lot.

But Mal had a way of lifting your mood even if you were determined to wallow. He spoke in a kind of humorous stream-of-consciousness, without pausing for breath or passing what he was saying by his brain. The guy had no filter and no volume control and the resulting monologue (which could be heard halfway down the beach) was absolutely hilarious, if completely un-PC.

'My, you're a very good-looking boy, aren't you?' he was now saying to Henri. 'Are the staff here employed straight from modelling agencies? Cos those girls in reception ... Fucking hell, they're hot! And the one who served me breakfast. And that little cutie who came to turn down our beds last night. D'you know the one I mean? Tiny little thing with black hair and green eyes. Even my missus commented on how pretty that one was. Irish, I think she was.'

Henri was nodding now and although Mal didn't hear him say, 'That's Molly,' Clyde did. Henri placed the finishing touches – the obligatory umbrella and sparkler – on Mal's cocktail and handed it to him.

'This one is on me,' the barman smiled. Mal was right. He did indeed look like a male model.

'Wow! Very exotic,' said Mal, eyeing his drink cheerfully. 'Thank you. What is it?'

'It's a Happily Ever After,' replied Henri. 'Seeing as you are on your honeymoon.'

'Oh, I love this guy!' Mal grinned, turning to Clyde. 'He makes bespoke cocktails. What's your name, mate?' He turned back to Henri.

'Henri Prideux, bar manager, at your service,' said the French guy, bowing.

'Well, Henri Prideux, it is a pleasure to meet you. I am Malcolm Riley – as you may know – but you can call me Mal. Now would you be kind enough to make a cocktail for my good friend Clyde here? He's a miserable bugger, as you've probably gathered already. Didn't used to be. In fact he used to be a bit of a laugh but, alas, people change. Because he's such a miserable sod, he's here on his own, and he's just got divorced for the second time. See what you can come up with for that.'

And then Mal's eyes lit up and he started bouncing on his stool, clapping his hands like an over-excited five-year-old. 'I know, I know! Let's do this for everyone who comes to the bar today. Let's make up cocktails that suit them. Brilliant! A drinking game. I love drinking games! You up for that, Henri?'

Henri grinned and nodded.

'Clyde?' asked Mal eagerly.

'I don't like cocktails,' muttered Clyde, knowing he sounded grumpy. 'And I don't like games. I'm forty-two years old and this may be a holiday camp but it ain't a kindergarten.'

'Oh, do be quiet,' scoffed Mal. 'Don't talk bollocks. Anyway, me and Henri are playing our game and you're going to join in whether you like it or not. So Henri,' Mal continued, ignoring Clyde's wishes, 'that old codger there. The one with the comb-over. What are you making for him?'

Clyde watched the elderly gentleman sitting alone at a table at the other side of the bar with a little concern. He was minding his own business, reading his *USA Today*, and sipping a coffee quite contentedly in the morning sunshine. Clyde hoped Mal wasn't going to start picking on pensioners. That would just be mean.

'Ah, that is Walter,' grinned Henri. 'He is one of my favourites. He comes here every year from Florida – Tampa I think. It is quite a sad story really. Gabriel told me. Walter used to come with his wife, but she died a few years ago and so now he comes alone. He stays in the same room, sits at the same table for dinner as he did when she was alive, wearing the same suit and ordering the same red snapper dish. He has drinks at the library bar after dinner, asks the pianist to play his wife's favourite song while he sips a single glass of rum, and then goes to bed alone. In the daytime he relaxes here with me at the bar. He is my friend. We must not be cruel to Wally.'

'I'm not being cruel!' shouted Mal. 'Wally looks like a

really cool old dude. I am digging that comb-over actually. I might need to resort to that soon myself. Fuck knows what's going on under here.'

Mal fingered his own huge hair. It was impossible to see whether he was thinning or not under all that backcombing and hairspray.

'Keep your voice down, Mal,' said Clyde, embarrassed for his friend and for the elderly gentleman. 'You'd better hope Walter is deaf or he'll have heard every word of that.'

'Thankfully, he is quite deaf,' Henri interjected.

'Just as well,' mumbled Clyde. 'Don't pick on the old guy, Mal. Please.'

'I'm not!' Mal insisted. 'I want to make his day. Bring a smile to his lonely old face, put a spring in his step and maybe even some lead in his pencil ... So what are we giving him, Henri? You're the expert.'

Henri pondered for a moment, considered his three long rows of liquors and then said, 'I've got it! I'll make him a Love in the Afternoon. I think it's time Walter had a little romance in his life. He has been eating dinner alone for too long.'

'Ahhh, French romance. How wonderful. You see, Clyde? Henri's not being mean, he's playing Cupid,' said Mal, with his head on one side, working a soppy smile.

'I hate to rain on your parade, Henri,' said Clyde. 'But are you sure love is what Walter needs? Sounds like he's still in love with his wife. And anyway, it's still the morning. What good is Love in the Afternoon to him?'

Henri glanced at his watch. Clyde noticed it was a vintage Patek Phillipe. Not what the normal surf dude bartender wears.

'Is after eleven now,' he shrugged. 'Is almost the afternoon and, besides, this morning he will read his newspaper; this afternoon he will find love.'

Clyde laughed and shook his head. It was difficult to argue with a laid-back guy like Henri.

'So, Henri,' Mal leant across the bar, 'how's your love life? I bet you get jiggy with the ladies all the time, you lucky bugger. I'm a married man now, got to behave myself, but if I was a single bloke I'd be like a pig in shit around here ...'

Henri shrugged again. 'I cannot complain,' he replied casually, shaking Walter's cocktail and pouring it carefully over ice. 'Now I must give Walter his love potion. Excuse me.'

'Put it on my tab,' called Mal after him. 'Put everybody's drinks on my tab today. I'm an International Rock Sensation. I can afford it!'

Mal's voice seemed to bounce off the palm tress and reverberate around the beach. Clyde winced a little and shrank behind a wooden post to avoid the stares from the sunbathers. Mal seemed oblivious.

'You're a single man now, Clyde,' continued Mal, turning back towards Clyde. 'You've got to go on the pull here. Please. For me. You can fill me in with all the filthy details and I can live vicariously through you. I've got my wife *and* my mother with me so I can't even ogle properly. But look ...' Mal pointed at the beach. 'Look at all that perfect female flesh. It's a crime to be a single man in a place like this and not feast on the delectable delicacies on offer.'

'Mal,' asked Clyde, patiently, 'do you ever think about anything other than sex?'

'Nope,' replied Mal cheerfully. 'Do you?'

The truth was that Clyde rarely thought about sex any more. He rarely thought about anything other than how badly wrong his life had gone. He had no interest in having a relationship. Not because he didn't like women – he loved women – but because he knew he was in no fit state to get involved with anyone. He was broke, washed up, angry and depressed. What the hell did Clyde Scott have to offer anyone? No, he was much better on his own.

'I'm not in the market for a relationship right now, Mal,' Clyde explained, downing his second JD and Coke.

'Relationship?' Mal's top lip curled disapprovingly. 'I never said anything about a relationship. You've only just got divorced! A relationship's the last thing you need. Eurgh! No, no, no! What you need, mate, is to have a few flings. Get back in the saddle. You're into horses, aren't you? You must know a thing or two about getting back in the saddle.'

'Horses I can handle,' replied Clyde, with a rueful smile. 'Women, they're far too complicated for me.'

'So what are you here for, mate?' asked Mal. 'This place is a pussy fest. What the bloody hell are you going to do with yourself in this tropical island paradise if you don't get shagged?'

'Work,' said Clyde, flatly. 'Apparently. According to my agent.'

'Work?!' Mal almost fell off his barstool. 'What a fucking stupid idea that is! And I thought my agent was a plonker. Why d'you need to come here to work?'

'Because I sure as hell ain't doing any work at home, I guess,' said Clyde, truthfully.

'On a bit of a downer, eh?' asked Mal. He kept his voice cheerful but his eyes were full of warmth. He wasn't being judgemental, just concerned.

'You could say that,' Clyde conceded. 'Writer's block. The worst frigging case of it anyone ever had.'

'Oh dear,' said Mal, shaking his head. 'I thought I hadn't had one of your books in the post for a while.'

'A while?! It's been years, Mal,' said Clyde. 'I haven't published anything in six years to be exact.'

'Six years!!!!' Mal screeched so that half the beach turned round and stared at the two men propping up the bar. 'Christ, Clyde, I thought I was an idle bugger but that's just plain lazy! Even I've managed an album every couple of years and I've had to fit rehab into my busy schedule. What have you been doing with yourself, mate?'

'It hasn't exactly been a holiday,' mumbled Clyde, feeling his cheeks burn. 'And keep your voice down. I don't want the whole world knowing my business.'

Clyde stared at his glass in shame. He knew Henri had heard every word, although the bartender was busying himself with making another drink and pretending not to listen. He felt angry at Mal for being so loud and for taking his troubles so lightly. Oh, he knew he was being unfair – how could anybody understand the real reasons behind his writer's block? And six years of doing absolutely nothing must sound incredibly lazy to most people. But still, the anger brewed in his chest, bubbling and boiling. He sighed deeply and tried to swallow his resentment at Mal's comments. His anger was misplaced. Clyde wasn't annoyed at Mal – not really – he was mad at himself and lashing out at everyone else. He thought briefly about Nancy and how many times she'd told him just that: 'Stop lashing out at me, Clyde,' she'd pleaded. 'Stop shouting and hollering and cursing at me when none of this is my fault!' Clyde ran his fingers through his hair. He wasn't a lazy man. He wanted to work. But how on earth was he supposed to write one damn word when the last words he'd written had caused so much damage?

'I'm a fuck-up, Mal,' he said quietly. 'A complete fuck-up.'

'No, you're not,' said Mal, shaking his head. 'You're brilliant. I used to hate reading but I love your books. That's a massive compliment, mate. That's like me getting a classical music geek to appreciate rock. It's a gift.' Mal patted Clyde's arm. 'And now I understand why fate has thrown us together again, my friend. My role here is to lighten you up, fill you with fun, drop you in the shallow water before you get too deep.'

'Edie Brickell and the New Bohemians,' muttered Clyde, remembering one of Mal's other favourite games – guess the song reference.

'Correct for ten points,' grinned Mal. 'Ah, here's your cocktail!'

Clyde eyed the brown drink that Henri had placed in front of him suspiciously.

'What is it?' he asked Henri.

'A Dark and Stormy, of course,' replied Henri, all wide-eyed faux innocence. But Clyde knew when he was being teased. And he was man enough to know he had to take it. He was a moody bastard these days. That was a fact.

'Brilliant!' Mal slapped his thighs in delight. 'I love this guy! He's got you down to a tee already! Now sup up, Clyde, there's a good boy. I'm going to make you enjoy yourself in Paradise if it fucking kills me!'

'Well, good luck, buddy,' mumbled Clyde. 'But you've got your work cut out. It's going to take more than a bit of sunbathing and a few cocktails to sort my head out. I've lost everything. And I have no one to blame but myself. I ran out on it all – my marriages, my kids, my career and even my frigging horse. How you going to fix that for me, eh?'

Mal looked thoughtful for a moment. Serious, almost. And then he said, 'All I can impart are some words of wisdom that I once heard in a song – "I ran out of places and friendly faces, because I had to be free, I've been to Paradise but I've never been to me ..." You're in Paradise, Clyde, now all you have to do is find *you*.'

Clyde sighed, shook his head in defeat, and felt an involuntary smile play on his lips.

'You are such an asshole. You've had too much therapy,' he told Mal. 'And bad therapy at that, if all you can do is quote cheesy song lyrics at me.'

'So ... ?' asked Mal, expectantly. He had a game to play.

Clyde laughed despite himself.

'The song's called "I've Been to Paradise" but I have no clue who sang it,' he said.

'Her name was Charlene, it was a hit in 1982, and she was a one-hit wonder, bless her cottons,' replied Mal, surprising Clyde as always with his vast musical knowledge.

Clyde took a sip of his Dark and Stormy. It tasted good. Maybe Mal had a point. Perhaps if he could just lighten up a bit, he'd find his way back. But how the hell did he do that when the truth of what he'd done was so terrible? Clyde wondered briefly if Mal might be the person to finally offload on. He'd almost told Nancy many times, knowing that she deserved an explanation for the sudden change in her husband and in her life. But he knew she wasn't strong enough to understand and, besides, he wasn't certain that she loved him enough to deal with the truth and stand by him. So he'd kept schtum. He'd thought about telling Berkowski too. Of everybody, he was the one who most deserved an explanation for the writer's block. But again, he wasn't sure even Ron would grasp the reasons why, the circumstances that had led to it happening and the utter failure Clyde felt as a result. The only living creature who'd heard the whole sorry story was Shiloh. And she sure as hell wasn't going to breathe a word!

But Mal had lived. He'd done bad things in his life, hurt people, lost his way and survived to tell the tale. He'd been in rehab and sex therapy and he'd had all his darkest secrets dragged through the tabloids. If anyone understood that good guys could do bad things it was Mal. Maybe this was Clyde's chance to be honest.

He watched Mal slurp up the last of his cocktail and burp loudly. He watched him wink at a couple of pneumatic blondes in white bikinis as they sashayed by. He watched him sign an autograph on a beermat for a giggling teenage girl, order another cocktail and wolf-whistle at the waitresses who'd just turned up for the lunch shift at the beach restaurant. And Clyde realised, with a slightly heavy heart, that he wasn't going to tell Mal what was really going on in his head. Mal was fun. He was essentially a good guy. It was probably a blessing that he'd turned up here, to keep Clyde company in the Caribbean, but Mal was not going to save Clyde's soul. It would take someone deeper than Mal Riley to do that. But for now, at least, Clyde had a buddy to hang out with. And that was something.

The two men had first met over a decade ago on a US chat show. They'd hit it off in the green room over a shared love of whisky, rock music and crime stories. After that they'd met up a few times. Mal had invited Clyde to a couple of gigs. Clyde had invited Mal to the premiere of the movie of one of his books. Mal would send Clyde promos of his latest albums. Clyde would send Mal signed first editions of his thrillers. It was one of those casual friendships that men excelled at. No Christmas cards or detailed emails about how their lives were going. Just the odd text or drunken phone call, followed by long absences and then last-minute hook-ups if they happened to be in the same city at the same time. They checked up on each other on Facebook occasionally but the truth was they hadn't actually seen each other in years. Not that it mattered. Mal was just one of those guys who never changed. Clyde felt sure that he could go twenty years without seeing Mal and their conversation would still be easy and familiar. It had been a long time since Clyde had hung out with anyone other than his drinking buddies in the bar back in Colorado. Maybe Berkowski was right about something, Clyde accepted grudgingly. Maybe Clyde did need this change of scene.

'Right, what are you making me this time, Henri?' demanded Mal loudly, disturbing Clyde from his thoughts. 'I've had my Happily Ever After and I want to live a bit now.'

Henri shrugged nonchalantly. 'It depends what you are after, Monsieur Riley,' he mused.

'Mal!' shouted Mal at Henri. 'Call me Mal!'

'Uh, OK, Mal,' Henri blushed slightly. 'A Hanky Panky, perhaps?'

'I wish,' grinned Mal. 'But the missus would kill me.'

'So I guess you don't want a Slippery Nipple, or a Screaming Orgasm, or a Blow Job either?' Henri kept a straight face but his eyes were laughing.

'No! No! No!' cried Mal. 'Lexi will be here any minute and she can't catch me having any of those things. Not again ...'

'OK,' said Henri finally. 'I shall keep it simple and give you a ...'

'Yes?' Mal asked eagerly.

'A Paradise,' announced Henri, finally reaching for the brandy. 'Seven parts gin, four parts apricot brandy, three parts orange juice. Simple but delicious and a house speciality of course.'

'Phew,' said Mal, settling back in his seat. 'I thought you were going to get me in trouble there.'

'Unless of course I could interest you in a Redheaded Slut?' Henri added.

'Henri!' shouted Mal. 'I'm a little worried you may be a very bad influence on me. Now what are you going to get my friend here? He's the one who needs to get laid.'

'No, I don't,' Clyde interrupted. 'I need to work!'

'I have the perfect cocktail for a writer who needs inspiration,' said Henri, reaching for the rum. 'A Hemingway Daiquiri, sir. That should get the creative juices flowing.'

Clyde nodded in agreement. He was rather impressed with Henri. The guy was certainly more than just a pretty face. And since Clyde already knew he would spend most of his time in Paradise right here, propping up the bar, it was good to know that the bartender was good company.

'OK,' said Mal, spotting a couple of newcomers to the beach. 'Those two from the plane yesterday. See, Clyde? Henri? Over there. The smooth dude and his trophy wife.'

'Oh yeah,' said Clyde, spotting the grumpy English moron from St Martin airport. 'I kicked him by accident and he nearly wet his pants. Uptight asshole.'

'Well, Clyde, if you are going to go around kicking total strangers ...' teased Mal. 'That might be the done thing in America but we Brits don't stand for it, you know.'

Clyde laughed. 'Yeah, OK,' he conceded. 'Maybe he had a point. I'll give him another chance. What are you making for him, Henri?'

'I can't decide,' mused Henri. 'I am torn between two – a Millionaire Cocktail No. 1, because the man is obviously very wealthy. Or perhaps ...' Henri paused. 'An Agent Orange?'

Clyde felt himself laugh, genuinely, for the first time in months. He'd forgotten how good male camaraderie could feel. The uptight English guy obviously styled himself on

007 and there was no denying that his tan had an orangey glow.

'That's brilliant!' said Mal, excitedly. 'Do it. Make him one of those and then send it over. But what abut the wife? She looks nice, doesn't she? Beautiful lady, a bit shy maybe. See, she's the one bird on the beach in a one-piece swimsuit, bless her, and she's tasty so there's absolutely no need for that. What a terrible waste of a good body.'

Clyde followed Mal's gaze to the sun loungers where the English couple were laying out their towels. He hadn't really noticed the guy's wife at the airport. He'd been half asleep and then Mal had suddenly appeared and whisked him off to meet Lexi and his mom. But Mal was right. The wife was beautiful. Very, very beautiful. She was tall and elegant with a fabulous curvaceous figure, blonde hair cut neatly to her jawline, and the most amazing bone structure. Compared to the glitzy, showy Miami model types on the beach, she looked like a really classy lady. A proper English rose among the thorns.

'She kinda reminds me of Princess Diana,' Clyde heard himself say out loud before he could stop himself. God, he sounded wet! Where had that come from?! It must have been the cocktails.

But Mal and Henri both nodded in agreement. 'She does indeed,' mused Mal. 'I think we all like Mrs Orange, don't we? Let's be nice to her.'

'I could make her a Blue-Eyed Blonde cocktail?' Henri offered. 'Or a Polished Princess?'

'Nah,' said Mal, shaking his head and grinning wickedly. 'She's the one who needs a Screaming Orgasm. I reckon that husband of hers hasn't given her one of them in years! Go on, Henri, send her over a Screaming Orgasm. Put a smile on the poor girl's face. I told you, we're going to be extra nice to her.'

Clyde and Mal watched excitedly, like a couple of naughty schoolboys, as Henri first mixed the cocktails and then carried them over to the new arrivals on a silver tray. The bar manager chatted to the English couple briefly before returning to the bar and filling his new friends in.

'Their names are Sebastian and Lauren Hunter. They live in London. And they are here for one week,' announced Henri, proudly. 'And, yes, she does look a little like Princess Diana, but perhaps even more beautiful I think.'

Clyde took one last look at Mrs Lauren Hunter from London. Her husband had plugged himself into his iPod and was busy texting or emailing on his phone. She was struggling to rub sunscreen on her back. He noticed that she didn't ask her husband for help and that he didn't offer. Why was it that all the most gorgeous women seemed to be married to jerks?

'Aha!' shouted Mal suddenly. 'Here she is. My little sexpot. And after three hours of deliberating over her suitcase, she's chosen to wear ...' Mal scratched at his messy hair and looked confused. 'What is that ensemble exactly? From here it looks like dental floss!'

Clyde turned to where Mal was looking, up the path that led from the cottages to the beach. And there, strutting sassily to some inaudible theme tune in her head, was Lexi. Rihanna probably, thought Clyde. Or Kesha, maybe. Lexi was wearing the most minuscule silver string bikini Clyde had ever seen. Nothing was left to the imagination – not the tanned toned thighs, or the gym-honed abs, or the pert young breasts. Clyde looked away a little uncomfortably. He was not a lecherous man, and the fact that Lexi was only a year older than Clara (his daughter from his first brief and disastrous marriage to his high school girlfriend, Lori) made it difficult for him to see her as anything other than a child. That, and the fact that his kids had been watching Lexi Crawford on TV since she was about ten, made it hard for Clyde to get his head round the fact that Mal was married to this child at all. Still, Lexi seemed like a sweet kid. A little bit stroppy, pouty and immature maybe, but then, Clyde reminded himself, so was Clara. They were teenagers. It was their job to be immature! Clyde wasn't into younger girls. He found it a struggle to meet women his own age who understood him. What on earth did Mal and Lexi find to talk about?

Lexi said a brief hi to Clyde and then jumped onto Mal's lap, wrapping her legs around his and her arms around his neck. She kissed him so long and hard on the lips that Clyde didn't know where to look. So he stared at his boots until the newlyweds had finished smooching.

'Where's Mum?' asked Mal, finally coming up for air.

Lexi pouted. 'I dunno,' she shrugged. 'It's bad enough having to be in the same resort as her without keeping tabs on the old bat.'

'Dear,' Mal reprimanded her. 'The old dear, you mean.'

'Whatever,' said Lexi, popping her chewing gum loudly. 'Actually I drowned her in the hot tub.'

'Don't be silly, cupcake, Mum's three times the size of you,' grinned Mal. 'She'd have buried you under the deck first.'

Lexi rolled her eyes. 'Yup, I guess,' she said, sounding bored. 'But a girl's allowed to dream. Mommy *dearest* is probably still struggling into her swimming girdle, I imagine. Yuk! What a gross thought.'

'Alexis ...' warned Mal, sounding more like a father than a husband. 'That's enough. I need you and Mum to play nicely this holiday, OK? We've talked about this.'

Lexi sighed. 'OK,' she conceded.

Clyde watched the lovebirds with interest. Even with the age gap, their crazy transatlantic lifestyles, and with Mal's overbearing mother tagging along for the ride, they seemed genuinely happy. Mal's eyes brimmed with affection (and also clearly with lust) when he looked at Lexi, which he did often, with a big soppy grin on his face. Meanwhile Lexi clung onto Mal like a shipwreck victim to a life raft. She never took her eyes off his face, or her hands off his body. The girl was obviously infatuated with her new husband. The stroppiness was just an act, Clyde decided. Lexi probably thought it made her look more in control of Mal. But she wasn't in charge. Mal obviously wore the trousers. Or the black Lycra bathers, at least! For reasons known only to the newlyweds, the balance worked for them. Perhaps because Mal (who'd been behaving like a teenager for twenty years) was getting to be the 'grown-up' for the first time in his life, or perhaps because Lexi (who'd been working for a living since she was a very young child) was finally being protected and looked after like the kid she still was. Clyde smiled to himself. Maybe it would work. This could be the real deal. Who was he to judge anyone else's relationship? It wasn't as if any of his own relationships had worked out.

His marriage to Lori had only lasted two years (and had cost him a million times that in alimony since!) and although his marriage to Nancy had survived the best part of a decade the good times had been painfully brief. He still kicked himself sometimes for the way things had turned out with Nancy, especially when he thought about his sons, Ethan and JJ, but he couldn't blame himself for what happened with Lori. They'd been just naive kids when they got hitched. Life had been all about drinking and partying with their buddies. The truth was they'd barely known each other, really. They'd shared a love of Tom Petty and pepperoni pizza but it hadn't run much deeper than that. And then suddenly there had been bills to pay and a baby to feed and clothe. Clyde had worked such long hours on the newspaper back then, trying to make a name for himself as a journalist, that Lori must have felt lonely and overwhelmed stuck at home with Clara. Then when Clyde did finally get home from work, he used to stay up half the night working on his first thriller. Still, it was no excuse for the way she treated him. He used to tell her that the good times would come if she could just be patient. But Lori had had no faith in Clyde. She used to get really angry. Boy, that woman could be mean, telling him that his writing was a waste of time and asking him who the hell he thought he was, trying to write a goddamn book. She'd flirt with other men and constantly belittle him in front of their friends and family.

She'd walked out on him eventually and moved back in with her mom, taking Clara with her and refusing to let him see his baby daughter more than once a week. It had broken Clyde's heart. But he'd channelled his pain into his work, and he did nothing but write for the next six months. Within a year of her leaving he got his first book deal. Of course, Lori wanted him back then, once he'd hit the jackpot, but it was too late. Clyde missed Clara desperately but he didn't miss Lori at all. It was a nasty divorce. He fought her tooth and nail for access to Clara and she fought him tooth and nail for access to his ever-increasing wealth. In the end they'd both won – or lost, depending on which way you looked at it. To this day the bitch was still living off his success. But at least he had a good relationship with Clara. But Lori was going to have to find a new cash cow now, wasn't she? Because Clyde Scott no longer had a dime to his name.

Lexi's squeals disturbed Clyde from his thoughts. Mal was tickling her bare back and nibbling at her ear as she wriggled delightedly on his lap. Clyde suddenly felt like a gooseberry.

'Right, guys,' he said, standing up. 'I think I might go explore Paradise a bit.'

'Oh ...' Mal's face fell. 'But what about our game?'

'What game?' asked Lexi suspiciously.

'Nothing for you to worry your pretty little head about, darling,' said Mal, pinging his wife's bikini strap.

'I'm sure you and Henri are more than capable of carrying on without me for now. Maybe we'll hook up later, huh?' suggested Clyde.

'There's a welcome party tonight,' announced Lexi. 'We got an invitation under our door from Gabriel Abbot. Dinner, dancing and entertainment, apparently. You coming, Clyde?'

Clyde opened his mouth to say that he wasn't sure, thinking that a party was the last thing he needed right now, but Mal answered for him.

'Course he's coming,' he said. 'We'll hook back up later, OK?'

Clyde said, 'Maybe,' high-fived Mal, pecked Lexi on the cheek and waved goodbye to Henri.

'See you later, guys,' he said, strolling off up the path away from the beach, to the sound of Lexi's squeals and Mal's loud demands to Henri for a Slow Comfortable Screw for his good lady wife.

Clyde hadn't even felt the sand between his toes yet. But he was in no hurry. This tropical beach thing was going to take some getting used to. And anyway, Paradise wasn't going anywhere. He passed by a group of loud-mouthed New Yorkers whom he recognised from the flight from

St Martin: guys in their late twenties or early thirties, who stank of fast money, good breeding and bad manners. Clyde found himself wondering which cocktails Henri would be serving them. He wasn't sure if it was the sunshine, or the rum, or Mal's company, but as Clyde wandered back up the hill towards the Plantation House he found he had a slight bounce in his step.

16

Gustavia, capital of St Barthélemy

Molly fingered the little packages of powders and creams nervously, bit her lip, picked up a pink blusher, tried to read the French description and then gave up. She glanced over towards the incredibly chic shop assistant, but the girl was busy chatting on the phone and was studiously ignoring her customer. Molly replaced the blusher and started running her finger along the lines of lipsticks instead. She recognised the brands – Chanel, Yves Saint Laurent, Lancôme – but she didn't know where to start when it came to buying make-up. Ach, she wished Nula was here. Nula would know what to do and she wouldn't be intimidated by the glamorous shop girl either.

She spotted a beautiful red Chanel lipstick in pretty black and gold packaging. She took a deep breath, picked it up and waved it in the direction of the assistant, who was still chatting fifteen to the dozen on her mobile.

'Excuse me?' called Molly.

The girl ignored her.

'Excuse me?' Molly called again, louder this time.

The girl glared at her, as if Molly was the one being rude, said '*Excuse moi*,' into the phone, and then barked, '*Oui?*' impatiently at Molly.

'How much is this, please?' asked Molly, shyly.

'Twenty-eight euro,' barked the assistant.

'Oh,' said Molly, feeling the shame creep up her cheeks. She could never spend twenty-eight euros on a lipstick. That was insane. She put the lipstick neatly back in its place and, without daring to look back at the snooty shop assistant, she started edging towards the door.

'Try the supermarché across the street,' shouted the shop girl, loudly. 'The cosmetics, they are cheap there.'

'Thank you,' mumbled Molly, shuffling out of the shop feeling tiny, stupid and inferior.

As she left, she could hear the girl in the shop laugh hysterically into her phone and Molly just knew that two more French girls were now cackling over her complete lack of sophistication.

It was hot this afternoon. And humid. Molly's T-shirt clung to her skin and her hair stuck to her forehead. Gustavia was hardly a sprawling metropolis, more of a quaint little harbour town, dotted with pretty, white-washed wooden houses with red roofs. It looked very Scandinavian because, as Molly had learned during her research, although the island had originally been a French colony, it was actually sold to Sweden for a while in the 1700s, before returning to French rule a hundred-odd years later. The Swedish architecture remained. In fact, if it weren't for the designer stores on the main street, the 500-ft yachts in the harbour and the thirty-five-degree heat, Molly could easily have been walking through a small, rural fishing town in Scandinavia. Gustavia's population was only 8,000 – the same as Rush, for crying out loud, and that was just a tiny wee seaside town north of Dublin – but St Barts had 200,000 tourists a year. All of them visited Gustavia. Most of them visited between December and March. And they all seemed to be wandering the narrow cobbled streets of Gustavia that day.

Molly dodged and side-stepped the glamorous tourists, who seemed to glide effortlessly down the streets, flitting in and out of cafes and boutiques, never raising their voices or breaking a sweat. She wondered how the women managed to walk in those heels, and how the men managed to look so ice cool in this heat. She gaped and gawped and apologised and blushed as she almost trod on their toes and their minuscule dogs. It was all such a mystery to her still. How did the women tie their hair up in scarves like that? How did they do such complicated things with sarongs? How did the men drape their sweaters over their shoulders without looking daft? How did they wear their feet bare in those loafers and deck shoes without getting blisters? And, for the love of God, could a real dog honestly be that tiny? Or was it a rat? And why was it wearing a diamond-encrusted dog coat in this heat? Molly still felt like such an outsider here: as if she had no right to be in this amazing spot. Well, she'd certainly had no right to be in that make-up shop today. Twenty-eight euros for a lippie! That was ridiculous.

She sat down on a bench for a breather and gazed across the harbour at the yachts and catamarans that bobbed in the calm blue water. It was so breathtaking that Molly felt as if she'd been accidentally dropped right into a holiday brochure. She took a moment to appreciate how lucky she was just to be here at all. She thought about what Gabriel had said, about how it was up to her to make herself belong. About how she could only be judged by what she showed the world. She took a deep breath and held her head up high. It was up to her to change things.

Suddenly, a dark shadow fell over the sea and Molly noticed the black clouds collecting just offshore. Uh-oh, it was going to pee it down any minute. Molly had barely been on the island two weeks but she could already predict the weather. It did this often, even in the dry season. The sky would be cloudless and blue one moment and then suddenly rain clouds would appear from nowhere, the heavens would open and three inches of rain would fall in ten minutes. Then the clouds would disappear, the sun would come out again, and it would be as if it had never happened. Molly kind of liked it. The rain here was not like the rain back home. It wasn't the kind of dreary, cold drizzle that seeped under your skin and chilled your very bones. It was the kind of rain you could keep swimming in, or sit with a cocktail on the beach and laugh as your face got drenched in the warm tropical shower. And it kept the island lush and green. And if there's one colour the Irish love, thought Molly, it's green! She smiled then, and breathed in the smell of the rain that was about to come. Then she got up from her bench, brushed her hair off her face, and ran across the road to the supermarket as the first fat drops of water fell from the sky.

It was a long shower for St Barts. Twenty minutes later, Molly was still sheltering under the awning outside the supermarket, waiting for the rain to stop so that she could walk back to the bus stop. She hadn't thought to bring anything as sensible as an umbrella with her to St Barts! She was reviewing her purchases thoughtfully – one black eyeliner, one pink lipstick, one red lipstick and one black mascara. There, what else could she need? And all it had cost her was twelve euros for the lot. Who needs designer boutiques, eh? Now all she had to do was figure out how to put the stuff on her face! She opened her iced coffee and sipped it, feeling rather sophisticated suddenly. Molly Costello was sipping an iced coffee in the Caribbean. Who'd have seen that one coming?!

A horn beeped loudly right in front of her and made Molly jump. She didn't look up. This was Gustavia. Who the hell did Molly know in Gustavia? The horn beeped again and then lots of horns started beeping impatiently.

'Hey, Miss Molly! Are you getting in or are you going to cause a traffic jam?' shouted a male voice.

'Henri!' yelled Molly, far too enthusiastically to sound cool. 'Um, er, yes please. Are you going back to Paradise?'

She scrambled into the jeep beside him, spilling her coffee all down her front and then realising too late that the passenger seat was soaking wet. She was sitting in a puddle of water.

'Sorry about that,' said Henri. 'The roof leaks in the rain. We can take it down now. The rain has stopped. We will soon dry.'

Molly noticed that Henri's blonde hair and bare chest were all damp and she had to look away. Henri was a friend. Only a friend. And he could only ever be a friend because a) he was out of her league, and b) he was a complete womaniser, Molly reminded herself sternly. Still, she took one last quick glance at his six-pack. Well, she was only human.

'I need to just pick up two more passengers and then we will get back,' he said, lighting a cigarette and winding down the roof while he steered the jeep with his knees. 'Whoops!' he said, swerving to avoid a moped coming the other way along the narrow street.

Molly swallowed hard and tried to think of something interesting to say. Was it her imagination or did Henri seem a little less flirty these last few days? He hadn't invited her back to his place, or to Nikki Beach, or even offered her a Sex on the Beach cocktail for ages. Maybe he was seeing Mimi properly now, she thought, trying not to frown.

'I'm waitressing tonight,' she announced, hoping that she didn't sound naive or boastful. 'It's my first time.'

'Ah, of course,' replied Henri, cheerfully. 'It is the welcome party this evening. Monsieur Gabriel likes to throw parties when VIPs arrive. You have seen the VIPs?'

'Mal Riley and Lexi Crawford? Yes, they were in their room when I turned down the beds last night. They seemed nice.'

'I have just left them on the beach,' said Henri. 'They have been at the beach bar all day. He is a really funny man – he has been buying cocktails for everyone all day and now all the guests are drunk! And Lexi is very cute, very young but very cute. But his mother, *mon Dieu*! What a scary lady. And why is she on their honeymoon? My mother wouldn't dream of doing that. What kind of relationship must she have with her son?'

'I have no idea,' said Molly, genuinely shocked. 'I didn't realise they were all together. She doesn't *look* like Mal Riley. Is she the, erm, rather large lady in room six? Next door to them?'

'Yes, she is right next door,' Henri shook his head. 'Can you imagine? She will hear everything!'

'I thought she was a bit of a battleaxe,' admitted Molly. 'She made me wait outside for fifteen minutes until she was ready for me. Lexi was lovely though. She gave me twenty euros! I just spent it on make-up.'

She held up her bag from the supermarket and then snatched it down again, remembering that buying cosmetics from the discount store was not very sophisticated behaviour.

'Make-up? Waitressing? Good golly Miss Molly, what has happened to you?' Henri laughed to show he was joking but Molly cringed in her damp seat. He thought she was a kid. That was quite clear.

'No, I am joking, Molly,' Henri continued, smiling at her, in a kind of big brotherly way. 'That is very good. You are too nice to be hidden away changing bed sheets. You should be meeting the guests.'

'I'm nervous,' Molly admitted truthfully. 'What if I drop something? What if I serve the wrong meal to the wrong table? What if I get an order wrong or spill red wine on the tablecloth?'

'You will be fine. Monsieur Gabriel obviously has faith in you, otherwise he would not give you the chance,' said Henri, reassuringly.

Molly nodded. He was right. Why would Gabriel ask her to waitress unless he thought she was up to it?

'We are here,' announced Henri, parking up outside the back of a rather unassuming building on the opposite side of the harbour from where Molly had been sitting earlier. 'Come on!'

'Where's here?' asked Molly, climbing out of the jeep and following Henri.

'The Yacht Club, of course,' said Henri. 'It's a bar, restaurant, club. Very exclusive.'

'Really?' asked Molly, confused. There was no grand entrance as far as she could see.

Henri laughed at the look on her face.

'Most people, they arrive from the front,' he explained. 'It looks very different from there.'

Molly still didn't understand. The front? But the building was on the sea.

'On their yachts.' Henri grinned as he watched the penny finally drop in Molly's brain. 'They moor up outside and step straight from their boats into the club. This back entrance is for us lesser mortals who cannot afford to own, or even hire, a yacht!'

'So why are we here?' asked Molly, tiptoeing gingerly behind Henri, as he entered the building.

Henri appeared not to hear her as he rushed off ahead. Molly had to trot to keep up. She felt as if she was trespassing. The sofas and chairs were so pristinely white that she felt dirty just squeezing past them, especially with her soggy bottom. Urgh, her denim cut-offs were soaking and they squelched as she moved. She followed Henri as quickly as she could, trying to hide behind him as he made his way between the low tables and white leather sofas until they finally arrived outside again on the wooden deck. It was late afternoon now. Several yachts were moored in front of the club and beautiful people in bright kaftans and white linen and lashings of gold were settling into the chairs and sofas to enjoy their first sundowners of the evening. They had a stunning panoramic view of Gustavia and the ocean as it twinkled in the last of the day's sunlight.

But Molly didn't take in the view. She stared at her feet, wishing the ground would swallow her up. She guessed everybody must be looking at her, wondering how a waif and stray like her got washed up in a classy joint like this! Why hadn't Henri just made her wait in the jeep? Why were they here anyway? He must have known how out of place she'd look. Molly wished, suddenly, that Henri had never driven past and that she was safely sitting on the bus, heading back to work with all the other chambermaids. And then, just as she thought it couldn't get any worse, Molly heard a low, throaty voice call: 'Hey, Henri! *Bonsoir sexy! Nous sommes ici!*'

And there she was – Mimi – lounging provocatively across an entire sofa, sipping a mojito and smoking a slim Sobranie cigarette. Her turquoise kaftan had ridden up to reveal a mile of tanned leg and a tiny pair of matching bikini bottoms. At the front, the lacing of the kaftan was undone just enough to show a line of bare brown flesh right down to her navel. She was not wearing a bikini top. A dainty silver sandal dangled from her perfectly pedicured toe. Molly's heart sank to the pit of her stomach. Why did Mimi have this effect on her? She felt slightly relieved to see Antoinette sitting on the chair next to Mimi.

'Hi, Antoinette,' Molly ventured, hoping that their brief exchange on the beach meant that they were now on speaking terms.

Antoinette nodded, slightly, in Molly's direction and then she glanced immediately at Mimi to gauge her reaction. Mimi gave Antoinette a glare so cold that it would have frozen the fires of hell. Molly swallowed hard and mumbled to Henri that she would see him back at the car. And then she stumbled off the terrace, ran past the tables and chairs and sofas, and back out into the street behind the club. Why did Mimi hate her so much? What the hell had she done to that girl? Nothing! Nothing!

Molly fought back the tears. She was not going to cry over Mimi. She was going to listen to Gabriel and she was going to keep control. She took a few moments to regain her composure and then climbed back into the passenger seat of the unlocked jeep to wait for the others. God, how she wished she was on the hot, sweaty, overcrowded, unreliable bus now.

When Henri, Antoinette and Mimi finally appeared fifteen minutes later, Molly realised that she'd made yet another faux pas. Mimi walked round to the passenger side and stared, uncomprehendingly at Molly, as if she had a very bad smell under her perfect retroussé nose. Antoinette meanwhile had climbed into the back. It took a few uncomfortable moments before Molly realised her mistake: Mimi did not travel in the back of jeeps. Molly grabbed her supermarket bag of make-up and clambered inelegantly over the seat and into the back beside Antoinette. The only thing that made the move less humiliating was the knowledge that the front seat was wet and that Mimi's pert little derrière was about to become soggy.

'Urgh! This seat, it is soaking Henri!' shrieked Mimi, right on cue. 'Henri! Do something!'

He threw her a towel with casual shrug. Antoinette tutted loudly.

'Mimi and Antoinette have been on a yacht trip today,' Henri ventured, either oblivious to the frosty atmosphere, or trying to thaw it with conversation.

'That's nice,' said Molly, not meaning it for a moment.

'They were invited by one of the guests at the hotel. That is a perk of working in a place like Paradise,' he said cheerfully.

'Yes, but only if you are a certain type of girl, Henri,' snapped Mimi, impatiently. 'Why you are telling a chambermaid this I have no idea.' She waved her hand in a dismissive gesture and tutted impatiently.

'Molly is going to waitress at the party tonight, actually,' said Henri.

Mimi snorted with laughter and said something very quietly and very quickly in French that Molly didn't catch.

'Pardon?' asked Molly, bravely. She was not going to let Mimi treat her like this. Not after her conversation with Gabriel. 'What did you say, Mimi?'

Mimi turned round then and looked Molly directly in the face. Her eyes were ice-cold grey.

'I said,' she replied, slowly and clearly, 'that Monsieur Gabriel is desperate for staff this evening because the prettiest waitresses are appearing in the fashion show with me. Aren't you, Antoinette?'

Mimi turned to her friend. Antoinette nodded but refused to meet either Mimi's or Molly's eyes.

'And that means he is short of staff. You are his last resort. It means nothing. Tomorrow you will be changing dirty sheets and cleaning toilets again.'

And then Mimi turned back round to face the road. She launched straight into a fast, fluid conversation in French that Molly couldn't follow. Molly sat in silence all the way back to Paradise, staring at the coast as it faded in the twilight. Mimi had been a complete bitch to her again but this time she didn't cry. The little ball of anger that had been planted in the pit of her stomach on the beach that day had started to grow and burn. It flared now, like a raging fire, and she could feel the determination to succeed rising in her as if it had a life of its own.

Mimi talked incessantly all the way back. She kept planting her hand firmly on Henri's thigh and every now and then she leant her head against his shoulder. Molly remembered the conversation she'd overheard on the beach and wondered if Mimi had decided that Henri was boyfriend material after all. Perhaps the man who'd taken her on the yacht today wasn't rich enough, or handsome enough, or interesting enough for Princess Mimi, thought Molly bitterly. She wondered also how Antoinette must be feeling, watching her so-called best friend stroke and fondle the man she'd liked.

Antoinette was very quiet all the way home. She said nothing except for the odd, '*Oui*' and '*Non*' when Mimi demanded a response. As they pulled up outside the Plantation House, Molly felt a gentle poke in her ribs. She turned to face Antoinette, who had clearly done the poking, expecting a rude comment, or a sneer. But Antoinette just smiled at her, rather sweetly and shyly, and mouthed the word,

'Sorry.' Molly nodded, understanding, and appreciating the gesture. 'It's OK,' she mouthed back. Antoinette was scared of Mimi, Molly could see that quite clearly. Mimi was the head Mean Girl and to be in her gang meant to bow down and grovel to her every whim, even if that meant getting hurt along the way. Antoinette was very much in Mimi's gang. And from the outside it looked as though she was second in command. But Antoinette obviously wanted Molly to know that she didn't always approve of Mimi's behaviour. Molly remembered how her own friends sometimes used to disappear when she got bullied at school, too scared and intimidated to back her corner. She'd understood then, as she understood now, that standing up to the tormentor is never easy.

Antoinette didn't wave goodbye, she didn't wish Molly good luck for tonight (as Henri did), and she didn't even look back over her shoulder as she strutted into the Plantation House behind Mimi. But she had handed Molly another olive branch. And Molly had accepted it gratefully. In Paradise, Molly needed all the friends she could find.

17

Room five, Paradise

Lexi shut the door to room five behind her, resting her back against the cool wood for a moment, and heaving a huge sigh of relief. Phew! She had survived day two of Irene's company without killing her. Yes, she had been tempted to drown her mother-in-law several times, and yes she had made the odd slightly inflammatory remark (the complaint that Irene was blocking out Lexi's sun went down particularly badly) but, hey, no blood had been spilled and that was something.

'Did I do good, Malky baby?' she asked her husband, who had just thrown himself on the enormous corner sofa with the TV remote in his hand.

'You were fine, cupcake,' he replied, flicking from football, to soft porn, to MTV. 'I think you might not want to ask my mother where on earth one buys swimsuits in *that* size again, but otherwise, petal, you were good as gold. Well, ish ...'

'She did steal my sun, though,' pouted Lexi. 'And you know how tetchy I get about shadows when I'm sunbathing. Anyway, you and Henri were the ones making her drink those cocktails – wasn't that last one called a Fat Lady's Ass? I mean, purlease, Malcolm, if I'd come up with that suggestion I'd have been in serious trouble!'

'Hmm ...' was all Mal said, as he watched himself on-screen, performing at last year's Glastonbury Festival.

'Right,' said Lexi, jumping onto the sofa beside Mal and bouncing up and down. 'What shall we do now? We have two hours till the party.'

'Mmm?' murmured Mal, still engrossed in his own performance on TV.

Lexi sighed. 'Come on, Malky!' she yanked at his arm. 'This is our honeymoon. We have two hours without your mom around. We're in this kick-ass fucking hotel, in the best suite ever. We have a Jacuzzi and a plunge pool. We have the choice of two bedrooms – one with a mirrored ceiling. Hell, we even have a frigging bed on the terrace. So let's not waste time watching TV!'

'Huh?' Mal said, without taking his eyes off the hundred-inch plasma screen. 'Did you say something, angel?'

Lexi snatched the remote from his hand and snapped off the power button. She had agreed to be polite (ish) to his mother, she had (almost) forgiven him for allowing Irene to gatecrash, and she had even promised not to tweet rude comments about the old witch. OK, she'd crossed her fingers behind her back when she'd made that promise and she'd already sneaked off to the washroom to tweet a couple of times today but it was the thought that counted. Anyway, Lexi had made more than enough sacrifices this week; she was not about to spend their first two hours of privacy watching frigging MTV! The screen went black.

'Eh? What did you do that for?' Mal turned to face her, looking crestfallen. 'That was my best Glasto performance ever, baby.'

'And this is our only honeymoon ever, baby,' Lexi mimicked him and frowned. 'You have that gig downloaded on your phone. You can watch it any time. Mal, we never get to spend time together. We're usually on two different continents, for fuck's sake. When we do see each other, that cock-sucking agent of yours is always following you around like a salivating puppy dog. Actually, come to think of it, I'm surprised you didn't invite Blaine on our honeymoon too ...'

Mal grinned and opened his mouth to speak but Lexi put a finger firmly on his lips. 'No, Mal. Don't even joke about the fact he's arriving tomorrow because I swear on my unborn children's lives that if Blaine Edwards sets one foot on Caribbean soil this week I will personally kill you – and him too just for the fun of it.'

Mal sniggered and tried to bite Lexi's finger.

'I'm serious, Mal,' she continued sternly. 'We've never had a holiday together before. And even here I have to share you with your mom, so can we please not waste one minute more watching TV?'

Mal took Lexi's finger in his mouth and sucked hard. His big brown eyes had softened and the pupils were dilating. He'd obviously got the message! Lexi felt the familiar yearning for him in her groin. God, he was hot. And now she had his full attention she was going to screw him senseless. With his free hand Mal tugged at the string of Lexi's bikini top until it fell onto the sofa. His tongue moved from her hand to her arm, along her collarbone, biting, kissing and caressing, until he found her nipple. Lexi let out an involuntary sigh as he pulled her nipple into his mouth and sucked and flicked and tickled her with his tongue. God, he made her wet. The minute he started touching her, she just melted into a hot, sticky, horny mess! Lexi glanced down and saw Mal's enormous cock straining against the Lycra of his bathers. Her stomach lurched and her pussy ached for him, but not here, not on the sofa. Not when they had this amazing shag pad all to themselves.

She slid her hand down to his groin and gripped his erection firmly. 'Come with me, big boy,' she demanded, leading him by the cock towards the patio doors.

This time Mal didn't protest. He followed her happily, with his erection in her hand and a look of pure, unadulterated lust in his eyes.

'Where are you taking me, Mrs Riley?' he asked, impatiently.

'Outside,' she replied. 'I'm going to screw my gorgeous husband under the starry tropical sky and no one is going to stop me!'

Room two, Paradise

'Ouch,' said Lauren, rubbing after-sun into her pink shoulders. 'I think I overdid it a bit today.'

Sebastian said nothing. All Lauren could hear was the sound of the cicadas singing in the foliage outside.

'Maybe you could rub some cream on my back for me?' she ventured tentatively.

Either her husband didn't hear her, or he ignored her. Sebastian was standing in the open patio doorway with his head turned towards the ocean, so that Lauren couldn't help but admire his refined profile. God, he looked devilishly handsome tonight, in his best black suit trousers and a crisp white shirt. His bow tie was hanging loosely around his neck. The top three buttons of his shirt were still undone, revealing a tanned chest that had gone three shades darker after today's sunbathing. He held a glass of champagne in his hand just so. His short hair was still black and damp from the shower. Lauren watched him and sighed under her breath. This was Sebastian at his best – tanned, rested, surrounded by opulence, sipping champagne and wearing black tie. It didn't matter what Kitty said, Lauren still thought her husband was pretty damn sexy. She wished he would turn round now and see her in her new underwear. She wished he would admire her and desire her and offer to rub after-sun all over her tender skin. She wished he would be overcome with passion and rush over to her and kiss her hard on the lips ...

But that wasn't going to happen, was it? Lauren rubbed the cream into her back as best she could and then gave up. She didn't try asking Sebastian for help again. She'd hoped that their sex life might get back on track after that brief night of passion in the kitchen but since then Sebastian had been as aloof and uninterested as ever – even more so, maybe. Lauren felt sure something bad was going on at work, and subsequently felt guilty for having him all to herself here in St Barts. He wasn't being as rude or sarcastic with her as usual. He was just incredibly subdued and distracted. He kept checking his texts and wandering off to make phone calls in private. She'd tried asking him if everything was OK at the office but he'd just frowned and told her it was nothing he couldn't handle. And now he was obviously a million miles away. He was right there, just a few feet away from her, but as Lauren watched him staring out into the hot, Caribbean night with a faraway look in his eye, she knew he was beyond her reach.

Lauren made up her face carefully: dark, smoky eyes, lashings of black liner and mascara and a pale, nude lipstick. She sipped her champagne and wondered if she might be a little drunk already. She'd had three cocktails on the beach and this was her second glass of bubbly. Oops. She fluffed up her newly re-cut hair with her fingers and almost smiled at her appearance in the mirror. The cut was shorter than she'd ever had it before but Sebastian had been right: it paid to go to the best salon in Mayfair that money could buy. The new style made her look fresher, younger and funkier and it lifted her face. The make-up had been a present from Kitty – freebies from her last shoot when she'd styled Kate Winslet for *Vogue* – and she'd applied it tonight in exactly the same way Kitty had demonstrated.

Sebastian wandered out onto the terrace and disappeared from view. Lauren felt herself deflate a little further. Here she was, naked but for the La Perla underwear she'd bought in Selfridges, with a beautiful new haircut and perfectly applied make-up and her husband hadn't so much as glanced in her direction. She took the long, midnight-blue dress out of the wardrobe. It really was exquisite – floor-sweeping, curve-enhancing, cleavage-flashing, pure silk and obscenely expensive. Lauren slipped it carefully over her head and zipped it up. She got her new matching Jimmy Choo sandals out and gazed at them for a moment before putting them on for the first time. They were beautiful but they had a four-inch stiletto heel and Lauren hoped that Sebastian wouldn't be cross if she was just a smidgen taller than him tonight. But a dress like this needed heels. A discerning man like Sebby would understand that. And besides, wouldn't he want his wife to look glamorous on his arm at the party? It was such an exclusive resort, and the other guests were all so good-looking and successful that she felt determined to shine tonight.

Lauren took a deep breath, checked her reflection in the mirror one more time, decided that yes, she did look pretty bloody good for a thirty-eight-year-old mother of two and then walked on slightly wobbly feet (it had been a long time since she'd worn heels this high) towards the patio doors.

Sebastian was reclining on a lounger, pouring himself another glass of Veuve Cliquot.

'How do I look?' she asked, a little nervously, as she walked out onto the terrace.

Sebastian turned to face her. He narrowed his eyes as he always did when he was summing up a situation. Lauren had butterflies in her tummy. She thought she looked good; she just needed Sebastian to confirm it.

'You look quite nice actually,' he said, with a little surprise, but without much enthusiasm. 'I told you you needed to go shopping. The dress is quite well cut. It hides all your bulges. And thank God my salon fixed your hair. It was bloody awful before.'

And then he turned away again, back to his own thoughts. That was it. His reaction to her two-thousand-pound spending spree, the four hours in the hairdresser's chair, the highlights, the lowlights, the layers and the make-up. She looked 'quite nice'. Quite fucking nice? Lauren shook her head, utterly deflated. What was the point? What was the bloody point of trying to impress Sebastian?

Lauren had a sudden flashback to the first year of their relationship. She remembered with complete clarity something that she hadn't thought about in a long, long time. It was the way Sebastian used to lie on her bed in her Notting Hill flat and watch her try on dress, after dress, after dress, before an evening out. It was a kind of ritual they'd got into, on his insistence. He told her he loved nothing more than to watch her dress, undress and parade in front of him. Sometimes he'd jump on her when she stripped off, telling her that she looked amazing in the dresses but even more stunning out of them and explaining that he couldn't keep his hands off her a moment longer. Often they'd been two hours late for the party because they'd ended up naked in bed instead. She could hear him now, telling her that it didn't matter what she wore, she would be the hottest girl in the room anyway, that she'd look sexy in a black bin liner. Now he didn't even think she looked sexy in an Alberta Ferretti gown. The memory made her sad. What had happened? What the hell had happened to that chemistry over the years?

She watched him now, tapping his foot impatiently in his brand new imported Italian leather shoes, wearing his bright, straight-out-of-the-box, white shirt with the extra big collar, with his teeth freshly whitened and his shiny gold Rolex newly serviced and cleaned. Sebastian liked everything to be brand new and shiny. He loved the latest gadgets and had to be the first to get his hands on the smartest smart phone, or the fastest car, or the most innovative computer system. But he tired of things quickly. If it wasn't new, it was worthless in Sebastian's eyes. That's what had happened to the chemistry, she realised. She'd stopped being shiny and new. Lauren stroked the silk of her dress. What had she been thinking? Her clothes might be brand spanking new, and her shoes and her haircut and even her lipstick, but she was still the same old Lauren underneath. She wasn't going to fool Sebastian by giving herself a makeover.

The truth was that Sebastian had been looking at Lauren for so many years that these days he couldn't see her at all. She was invisible to him. And because she had no role in life other than that of Sebastian Hunter's wife, and the mother of Sebastian Hunter's children, that made Lauren Hunter invisible, full stop. Somehow, over the years, she had faded and disintegrated and eroded, until she barely existed at all. Lauren bit her lip hard and swallowed the lump that had formed in her throat. But if she was invisible, if she was so bloody inconsequential and powerless and weak, why did she have this burning pain in her heart right now? If she could feel this acutely, then surely she was still alive.

She watched her husband closely as he casually sipped his Veuve Cliquot, oblivious to her tormented soul, and this time it was Lauren's turn to narrow her eyes. He was wrong. Lauren Hunter still existed. She knew she was still alive. She was right here in front of him, even if he couldn't be bothered to open his eyes and see that. She could feel the blood pumping through her veins. She could still feel the need to be desired and cherished and longed for. She could almost reach out and touch the dreams that had floated out of her grasp over the years. Her dreams were still there, somewhere, and Lauren didn't want to let them float away for ever on the warm Caribbean breeze. She wanted to grab them now, to repossess them, and nurture them and one day she still wanted to make them all come true. Lauren downed her glass of champagne in one. She was filled with a sudden desire to get drunk. She glared at Sebastian angrily. She would show him. Tonight she would remind him that his wife was not invisible after all.

Room five, Paradise

'Oh my God, Mal. Christ!' screamed Lexi, as Mal disappeared between her thighs.

She stared up at the stars in the crystal-clear sky, as the muslin drapes fluttered in the breeze and felt the waves of ecstasy flood her body. Lexi Crawford was in paradise – both literally and metaphorically! God, when Mal went down on her it was just the best feeling ever. Ever! She gripped the mattress of the four-poster bed and shouted, 'Yes, just there, baby. Oh yeah, oh my God, right there. Yes, yes, yes! Oh fucking hell, Malky, faster. Just there. Yes! Faster, baby, faster … I'm going to … I'm going to … Oh Jesus fucking Christ I'm going to …'

'Malcolm!' shouted a shrill voice, suddenly disturbing Lexi from the brink of orgasm. 'Malcolm, what on earth do you think you're doing? Don't be so disgusting! Get up right now!' bellowed the voice.

Lexi was confused. She was still in the throes of sexual heaven as she felt Mal pull away from her pussy. She gripped the mattress hard, gritted her teeth and shouted, 'Oh, for fuck's sake!' this time out of frustration rather than elation.

She was lying, stark naked, under the fairy lights that lit up the outdoor bed on the terrace. She watched Mal stand up. She watched his face fall. She watched his erection droop immediately. She watched him open his mouth and stutter.

'M … Mu … Mum! What are you doing here?' he stammered, his face turning crimson.

Lexi rolled onto her stomach and glared up at him, furious that her climax had been so rudely interrupted. But Mal wasn't worried about Lexi's orgasm any more. Like a teenage boy ashamed at being found with a copy of *Penthouse* in his grubby little paws, Mal was only worried about the fact that his mother had just caught him having oral sex. With his wife! On their frigging honeymoon! Like that was a crime?! Lexi's blood was boiling. She could practically feel the steam coming out of her ears. Argh! She bit the pillow, punched the mattress and desperately tried to think about what her anger management therapist would say right now. She couldn't even look in Irene's direction, knowing that the sight of the woman would make her blow immediately. Lexi tried to stay calm and centred. She attempted to regroup and count to ten. But as she spotted Mal bowing and grovelling as he backed away from the bed, covering his cock with one hand and holding his other hand up in a submissive gesture of apology to his mom, Lexi thought she would explode. She couldn't hold it any longer. She sat up, not caring that she was naked, and glared at Mal's repulsive, obese, overbearing mother. Irene's sneer of disgust barely masked her delight at having ruined the newlyweds' sex life.

'Why the hell can't you ring the bell like a civilised human being?' Lexi yelled at her mother-in-law. 'What did you do? Climb into our garden from yours? This is not your suite. This is private property and we are entitled to our privacy!'

'Don't you dare speak to me like that, young lady,' warned Irene. 'For your information I did knock on the door but you were obviously too busy molesting my son out here to hear me.'

Lexi's eyes were popping out of her head. What the fuck? What the crazy, messed-up, infuriating, unfair, fuck? Molesting her son? Her son the former sex addict who'd bedded half of the frigging Western world? Lexi was his wife. She was the only one not trying to molest him. She loved him. She'd never slept with anyone else but him in her life. And this was their honeymoon. This was so unfair. Screw what her therapist would say. Lexi jumped up onto her feet and stood, stark naked, with her hands on her hips facing her mother-in-law.

'Mal is my husband,' she shouted at Irene. 'What we do in our own time, and on our own property, is our business. This is sick, Irene. You are sick!'

'I'm sick?!' spluttered Irene, clutching her enormous chest as if she'd been mortally wounded. 'I am not the one doing unspeakable, disgusting things! You're a slut! Nothing but a revolting, cheap, despicable slut! Are you going to let her talk to me like this, Malcolm? I've never been so insulted in my life. I'm so upset. Oh dear. Oh dear, dear, dear. I think I'm having one of my funny turns. Malcolm? Malcolm darling. Please, I need water and a seat. I feel quite faint.'

'It's OK, Mum,' said Mal softly, tying a towel round his waist and handing her a bottle of Evian. 'Here, drink this and sit down. I'm sure Lexi didn't mean those things. I'm sure she's sorry. She's just embarrassed that you caught us like that.'

Lexi watched her husband fuss around his mother in utter disbelief. And she watched Irene lap up his attention, faking her heart palpitations, fanning her sweaty face with her hands. But Lexi could see right through Irene. The glint of triumph in her eyes was quite clear.

'No, I'm not sorry!' hollered Lexi, grabbing the pillow and throwing it on the deck out of sheer frustration. 'I'm not sorry. Mal, your mother just called me a slut. Why are you fussing around her? She called your wife a slut. Are you going to let her do that?'

'You called me sick!' Irene snapped back at her like a snake spitting venom. 'And control your temper, young lady! I won't stand for violence!'

Violence? She'd thrown a fucking pillow. How much damage could that do? Malcolm seemed glued to the spot. He stood, frozen, between his mother and his wife, clearly paralysed by confusion and torn loyalties. He opened his mouth but no words came out.

'I'll make this really simple for you,' said Lexi to her mute husband. 'Your mother is loving this, Mal. This is what she wants – to come between us and to destroy the little privacy we have. You can either let her speak to me like that and allow her to destroy our marriage or you can ask her to apologise to me and to leave our suite. Now!'

Finally Mal found his voice.

'Come on, babe,' he cajoled her. 'It's all just a silly

misunderstanding. Nobody's to blame and we've all just got a bit heated. It's daft. Just say sorry to Mum and we'll put it behind us and have a nice evening together, OK?'

'No, it's not fucking OK!' screamed Lexi. 'She called me a cheap slut. How can that ever be OK?'

'Hmmph,' snorted Irene, sitting back smugly in her chair, crossing her arms over her immense bosom and shaking her head. Lexi could see her double chins wobbling.

'She didn't mean it, Lexi,' said Mal, standing behind his mother's chair now. He'd obviously picked his team – Team Irene. 'Poor Mum had a fright, that's all. Look, this is ridiculous. You're making a scene about nothing. Go and have a shower and calm down.'

She watched as Mal patted Irene's shoulder fondly and something snapped. Lexi had never felt so let down or humiliated in her life. Why couldn't he stand up for her? Why couldn't he stand up to his mother? Why couldn't he see how wrong this was? Tears of rage and injustice poured down her cheeks as she grabbed the nearest thing – a beer bottle Mal had abandoned on the table by the daybed – and threw it as hard as she could across the terrace. The bottle smashed as it hit the teak floor, spraying shards of glass and sticky beer all over the pristine white furniture. Lexi stood and stared at the mess, with her fists clenched, her heart pumping in her chest and tears stinging her eyes.

'Well, there we go, Malcolm,' announced Irene. 'The girl obviously has serious mental health problems. I told you you'd made a mistake.'

Lexi wanted to say so much. She wanted to tell Irene that she wasn't a 'mistake', that she loved Mal with every molecule in her body, that he loved her too, that they made each other happy and that they were a team ... But now Mal was staring at her aghast with his hand on Irene's shoulder and Lexi realised they weren't a team at all. She was on her own here. So instead of saying all the loving, sweet words she shouted, 'Fuck you! Fuck you both!' instead and then she ran into the cottage, into her suite, into the bathroom and locked the door.

The tears of pain and shame and regret came thick and fast – they always did after she'd lost her temper. The red mist had engulfed her, again, and even though Lexi knew she'd been in the right to begin with, she'd lost her rag and made herself the villain. It would be so easy for Irene to demonise her now. She'd let the old witch get to her and she'd lost control, and now she looked immature, violent and crazy. But Lexi was none of those things; she was just a girl who'd never known whom to trust, or whom to turn to. All she wanted was to be scooped up, looked after and loved. She slumped down onto the bathroom floor, buried her head in her hands and sobbed. Some honeymoon this was turning out to be!

18

The Grand Ballroom, Paradise

The scene was set perfectly. The floor was so highly polished that Gabriel could see his reflection in it; the tables were laid in thick starched white cotton table linen; the finest silver cutlery was placed neatly at every setting; tropical blooms adorned each one of the eight round tables; the staff had been briefed and all looked suitably elegant in their black and white uniforms; the seating plan was displayed proudly on a silver stand by the door; and the pianist had arrived and was arranging his music at the grand piano in the corner. Yes, it was all going precisely to plan, but still Gabriel's hands trembled.

He hadn't expected to feel quite this anxious when the day finally arrived but here it was, and here he was – a nervous wreck. Silly old fool! What was he afraid of? Being rumbled? That was ridiculous. He was an actor, for crying out loud. He'd fooled the world his entire life; surely he could keep up the act for a few days more. The old cliché ran through his brain: 'You can fool some of the people some of the time but you can't fool all the people all of the time.' What if the cliché was true, as clichés usually were? What if 'he' was the one man who could see straight through Gabriel? That would ruin everything.

No, he was being paranoid. Gabriel had glimpsed the

most important of his special guests briefly during the last two days but only from a distance. He somehow had less of an aura in the flesh than Gabriel had constructed for him in the shadows of his mind. He had become Gabriel's nemesis and he had taken on superhuman proportions in Gabriel's head. But Gabriel had been a little surprised when he had first spied the man through the palm trees. He was undeniably handsome, yes, but he looked, well, disappointingly human really. Almost normal, Gabriel had realised. He had felt as Dorothy must have felt when she discovered that the Wizard of Oz was just an ordinary man – a little disenchanted.

Still, just because he didn't have ten horns and seven heads, it didn't mean he wasn't the Devil. Gabriel remembered a terrible off-Broadway production he'd appeared in back in '61 in which he'd played a modern-day Lucifer. It was set in Hell's Kitchen, New York. How subtle the writer had been! Some of the plot had stuck with Gabriel. He recalled that the Devil was actually an angel of God's – the most beautiful angel in heaven – who had defied the Lord and had been cast out of heaven. Most of the lines escaped him now but he d id remember clearly that, in this play at least, the Devil was handsome, powerful and charismatic and that he used these powers to woo women and charm men before taking them over to the dark side. It all felt eerily familiar suddenly. Gabriel sighed at the strange coincidence. But then, he guessed, there was no such thing as an original plotline in life, fiction or even religion.

'Gabriel, do I look OK?' whispered a voice behind him.

Gabriel jumped, taken by surprise, and looked round. He had to look down before he realised it was little Molly, gazing up at him with those questioning green eyes.

'Do I?' she asked again, her eyes widening even further. 'Do I look OK?'

Gabriel's heart melted and he beamed at her. She looked adorable and really rather grown-up and sexy in her tight black pencil skirt and neat white blouse. And was that a smidgeon of make-up she was wearing?

'Molly Costello, you look ravishing!' Gabriel announced, bending down and kissing her on both cheeks.

She giggled and blushed as he held her at arm's length and admired her further. 'I feel like a father who's suddenly realised that his little girl is a woman. Proud but a little unsettled. I shall have to keep a close eye on you and make sure the menfolk don't take advantage of you.'

Just then Delilah swept into the ballroom in a haze of green chiffon and cigarette smoke. It was still legal to smoke indoors in St Barts, although Gabriel (who suffered from chest problems) really wished it wasn't. Of course he could have banned smoking in his own hotel but Delilah would have defied the rule and kept puffing away regardless. She was not one for rules.

'Delilah, darling, you look heart-stoppingly wonderful as always,' said Gabriel, kissing her on both cheeks too. 'Now, Delilah, what do you think of young Molly here? All grown-up in her waitress's uniform. It suits her, don't you think?'

Delilah took a step back from Molly, sucked hard on her cigarette and circled her finger bossily, indicating to Molly that she should turn round to be examined at all angles. Molly spun round slowly. Twice. And then stood there, patiently, looking awkward and embarrassed, waiting for Delilah to make her judgement call. Delilah took several more drags on her cigarette, cocked her head to one side, and then to the other, and then finally she nodded firmly.

'Bravo, darling,' she announced. 'You scrub up very, very well. I see why Gabriel has singled you out as his little favourite now. You really are as cute as a button, aren't you?'

Molly's poor little face melted with relief. Gabriel understood that a woman like Delilah must be an intimidating prospect for a girl like Molly. But Delilah wasn't scary. Not really. Not underneath the mask of make-up and lies.

'But we must do something with your hair. You can't possibly wear it like that in a schoolgirl ponytail. Come here, quickly, before the guests arrive,' said Delilah.

Gabriel watched proudly as Delilah got a comb and some hairpins out of her clutch bag. She pounced on Molly and started running the comb through the girl's long, thick dark hair. She pulled it, twirled it and wound it up high on Molly's head, before securing it into an elegant topknot.

'There, *très chic!*' declared Delilah, satisfied with her own handiwork. She kissed Molly's cheek, quite tenderly and then gave her a little nudge. 'Now run along, darling. Back to the kitchen before chef wonders where you are and gets cross.'

Gabriel watched Delilah fondly with slightly damp eyes. It had been a long time since he'd seen her maternal side. He missed it. It was the part of herself that she'd buried most deeply.

Suddenly Serge appeared, sliding hurriedly across the floor with a look of abject horror on his face.

'Mr Gabriel,' he said breathlessly. 'I'm afraid we have a problem with one of the guests!'

The Foyer, Paradise

'This is ridiculous!' said Clyde, for the fifth time, trying to keep the anger out of his voice. 'I'm on a beach holiday, man. I didn't expect to have to wear a damned dinner jacket!'

And I didn't even want to come here in the first place,

he thought to himself, resenting the fact that some jumped-up little French student in a suit was telling him what he could and couldn't do. He read the guy's name from the badge on his lapel. The words swam in front of his eyes for a moment. Shit, he was slightly smashed. He'd started the day on cocktails and had a momentary high. He'd even taken his darned memory stick to the library and printed out his manuscript, thinking for a minute there that he might actually be able to start considering work. What a crazy idea that had been. As if!

But he'd only got five pages into the book before the whole godforsaken nightmare had seeped back into his brain. As he'd read the words all he could do was remember where they'd led. Shit, how much damage had those words done? And it was all his fault! He was an evil, dangerous son-of-a-bitch. And all that novel did was remind him of that fact. Clyde Scott was damned. He was damned to hell and back again. Even a place like Paradise was hell when you had a thing like that weighing on your soul. Clyde had spent the rest of the day emptying the complimentary bottle of rum that had been left in his room. And now he was here. The truth was that the main reason he'd turned up for the party at all was for the free booze.

'So, Jacques,' he said, finally making out the name. 'Tell me, what do I do? The proprietor has invited me to this party. If I don't attend I'm rude but if I do attend, in the only clothes I've brought with me, I'm barred for flouting the dress code. This sucks.'

'I am truly sorry, sir,' said the Jacques boy. 'But I must abide by the rules. Men must wear jackets and ties for dinner in the formal rooms. It is acceptable in the restaurant on the beach to wear jeans but not here, not in the ballroom. I am so very sorry.'

'Forget it,' said Clyde. 'Send my apologies to your boss and get someone to bring a club sandwich and a bottle of JD to my room. Who the hell wants to wear a dinner jacket in this heat anyway?'

'But, sir, I am sure we can find a solution. Wait, sir! Serge has gone to talk to Monsieur Abbot,' called Jacques.

But Clyde had had enough. He strode purposefully towards the exit, ignoring the boy's pleas. He'd tried but he didn't even want to go to some stupid party with a bunch of jumped-up assholes. He'd only decided to turn up because of the booze, and because Mal had been so insistent, and because the old boy that owned the hotel was putting him up here for free. He was some sort of fan, apparently, and Clyde couldn't afford to lose any more fans – or to pay for the hotel room! But what kind of company would he be tonight anyway? No, it would be best for everyone if he just sloped off back to the privacy of room one. He was halfway out of the door when the boy caught up with him and grabbed his arm.

'Please,' he said to Clyde, a little desperately. 'Come back in, Monsieur Scott. Monsieur Abbot is waiting for you.'

'Oh, for fuck's sake,' muttered Clyde under his breath. For a moment he'd thought that he'd escaped the dumb-ass party and now he realised that he might not have got away after all.

Clyde sighed deeply and followed the young Frenchman back inside reluctantly. A distinguished-looking old guy in a smart black tux, with white hair and a deep tan was waiting by the reception desk smiling. He had an air of importance about him and as Clyde got closer he realised that the face was familiar. But from where? He couldn't quite place it. It was the drink, he reminded himself; it muddled his brain.

'Mr Scott, I am Gabriel Abbot, the proprietor, and I am

absolutely thrilled to meet you. I have been a huge fan of yours for many years and it's my privilege to welcome you here as my guest at Paradise Resort and Spa.'

The old dude spoke as if he had marbles in his mouth. And he was as camp as Christmas. Almost despite himself, Clyde kind of liked the guy immediately.

He shook Gabriel's hand firmly, concentrated on not slurring his words and said, 'Thank you, Mr Abbot. I'm very pleased to meet you too. Sorry I'm not going to make it to your party tonight.'

'Don't be silly,' scoffed the old guy. 'Of course you're coming to the party. You're on my top table and the evening simply won't be the same without you. I have a solution. Henri is on his way with a dinner suit in your size. Luckily, I believe you're around the same height and build as our bar manager. *Et voila!* Problem solved.'

'Thank you,' Clyde managed to say through clenched teeth. What was he? Some sort of frigging charity case? Christ, a man might be washed up but he still had pride. A free holiday? A borrowed suit? The shame crept up Clyde's cheeks as he forced a polite smile.

'Hey, man!' said Henri, the cocktail guy from the beach bar, jogging into the foyer wearing a waiter's uniform and carrying a suit bag and a pair of black shoes. He high-fived Clyde and then handed him the clothes. 'I bet you did not know I provide menswear as well as cocktails! There is a men's room on your right. You can change there.'

Gabriel Abbot smiled warmly and clapped his hands together twice. 'Right, minor crisis over, it seems! Thank you, Henri. Mr Scott, I shall see you in the ballroom at your convenience.'

Clyde nodded and muttered a thank you, although he was not feeling remotely grateful.

'I frigging hate suits,' he muttered to Henri as he headed off towards the washrooms.

'So do I,' agreed Henri, indicating his uniform. 'But Monsieur Gabriel, he loves to have rules. It is just his way. Go with it, Clyde. All resistance is futile, believe me!'

19

Room five, Paradise

'Lexi?' Mal called through the bathroom door. 'Lexi? Are you OK? Have you calmed down, baby?'

'Fuck off, asshole!' came the response.

That would be a no, then. Mal sat down with his back against the bathroom door and wondered what to do next. He hated it when Lexi cried, and he could hear her crying now. She'd been locked in there for an hour and although he'd been cross with her earlier, now he just wanted to kiss and make up. So Lexi and his mum had a few issues. It was no biggie. They were both strong women. It wasn't surprising that they clashed sometimes. They would get used to each other. They'd have to. They were the two most important people in Mal's life.

'Mum's gone back to her room,' he ventured, hoping that would cheer Lexi up. 'We've to call for her when we're ready for the party. We need to go soon though, cupcake. We're already late.'

'I'm not going to any fucking party with you, bastard!' she yelled. 'And definitely not with your bitch of a mother. She can burn in hell for all I care!'

Right, this was going to be trickier than he'd first realised. Mal chewed his lip and then lit a cigarette. He tried another tack.

'Come on sweetheart, get your glad rags on and let's do what we do best – let's party!'

'No!' screamed Lexi. 'Fuck off and grow a pair, asshole! Take your freaking mother to the party! She's the frigging boss of you!'

Grow a pair? Mal rubbed his balls gently. They were huge! His mum's timing had been priceless earlier. Neither he nor Lexi had managed to climax and now he was barely going to be able to walk this evening as it was. Mal stubbed his fag out in his empty beer bottle. He'd have to remember to put that bottle in the bin. He didn't want Lexi throwing it at him when she came out of the loo. Right, he had one more idea.

'Mum said you wouldn't go to the party,' he ventured. 'She said you'd be too ashamed to show your face in public after what you did ...'

'After what I did?!' screamed Lexi, even louder and angrier now. 'After what I did?! I cannot believe that woman. I'm not the one who behaved badly. She called me a slut and I'm the one who should be ashamed?! I'm not fucking ashamed of anything except my frigging mother-in-law!'

Mal smiled to himself and lit another cigarette. He'd got her talking at least. Well, screaming anyway ... He leant his head back against the door and said, 'I can't hear you, babe. You'll have to speak up.'

It was a lie, of course. He could hear Lexi yelling quite clearly. He expected that the whole resort could. Possibly the entire island.

'I said,' bawled Lexi at the top of her lungs, 'that the only thing I'm ashamed of is—'

'Nope, can't hear you, honeybun.' Mal sniggered quietly to himself. He counted silently in his head. Five, four, three, two, one ... He heard the lock snap open and finally Lexi peered her tear-stained, pouting (but still very pretty) face out from behind the door. Bingo!

She opened her mouth to speak, or yell, but Mal beat her to it. 'Come here, little one,' he said softly, standing up and holding his arms out open to Lexi.

For someone who'd been screaming her lungs out, Lexi didn't look very angry suddenly. She looked horribly hurt and upset. And she looked frighteningly vulnerable and young. But not angry. Mal felt a sharp pang of guilt in his chest and for perhaps the first time in his life he also felt a sense of responsibility for another human being. Hell, he'd never quite managed to be responsible for himself, let alone anyone else! But who did Lexi have looking out for her if she didn't have him? Her parents were greedy, money-grabbing bastards who'd basically sold her to the highest bidder, her agent was even more immoral than Mal's (and that was saying something because Blaine Edwards was pretty much as immoral as they come) and she didn't really seem to have any friends. Girls always wanted to hang round her when she was out at parties and clubs but they were never there for her when she needed a girlfriend to talk to.

Mal tried to wrap his arms around Lexi, but she took a step back into the bathroom and glared at him. He wasn't sure if she was going to cuddle him or stab him. Lexi was like an injured animal. She looked so cute and needy sometimes that all Mal wanted to do was pick her up and make her better. But the minute she got cornered she lashed out. She'd spit and snarl and hiss and howl. She was wild and she was hard to tame, this vixen!

He felt for her, he really did. But the difficult thing was, Mal genuinely hated it when Lexi was rude to his mum; she had no idea how much his mum had sacrificed for him over the years. Lexi had such a short fuse. And she swore like a

Geordie builder. It was no wonder his mum got the wrong idea. Sometimes it felt as if Lexi didn't even know what she was saying. But Lexi was all mouth. She didn't mean to be rude. Her heart was good. It was big, pure and full of love and Mal knew that it was all his. He wished his mum could see the good in Lexi. But all she saw was a cocky, loud-mouthed child star in a short dress. Or no dress at all in the case of this evening ... Oh God, what a bloody mess!

'Come on baby, let's make up,' he cajoled Lexi. 'I'm a lover, not a fighter, you know that.' She took a tiny baby step towards him.

Mal knew the situation wasn't entirely Lexi's fault. His mum could be difficult. He wasn't stupid, he could see that. His mum was getting on a bit, she was set in her ways and she thought the sun shone out of Mal's arse. That couldn't be easy for Lexi to deal with. But Mal's mum had no one in her life except him. He was an only child, born after years of trying for a baby. His dad had left when he was a kid (he'd only re-emerged fifteen years later once his son was famous and Mal had given him short shrift). Irene was no oil painting, even Mal could see that, and she hadn't had a man in her life for years. She was lonely. Mal was her universe and Lexi was a threat. Somehow he had to get the two of them to at least accept each other. Better still, he had to get the two of them to bond. But how the hell did he do that when they hated each other with such passion?

Mal reached out and stroked Lexi's tear-stained cheek. She looked up at him with huge, scared, cornflower-blue eyes.

'It's OK, petal,' he said. 'Everything will be OK. I'm going to fix things. I promise.'

Lexi nodded then, finally trusting him again, and she let herself fall into his arms. Mal could have sworn he could actually feel her spirit calm as he hugged her. He was a bit slow sometimes, Mal – he was the first to admit that about himself. And he hadn't really got the whole marriage thing until tonight. Lexi was his wife. He loved her. He really fucking loved her. There was no way he'd have put up with that vicious temper of hers if it wasn't the real thing! So she was his responsibility now. He really had given up his freedom for the woman he loved. Wow! That was quite something. It felt grown-up, like a rite of passage. Mal gave himself a metaphorical pat on the back. It felt kind of cool to finally be a man. He would write a song about that when he got back to the studio. Maybe he'd call it 'Grow a Pair'! He chortled to himself.

'What's funny?' asked Lexi, warily.

'You are,' he replied. 'Grow a fucking pair? Ooh, you're dead romantic, you are!'

'Well, you do need to grow a pair,' Lexi pouted, wiping her tears on his clean shirt.

'I know, baby,' he whispered into her hair. 'You're right. I need to grow the biggest, fucking hairiest pair of balls in the entire universe so that I can protect my princess for ever.'

'Yes, you do,' said Lexi.

'I do,' repeated Mal. 'I do, I do, I do, I do, I do ...'

He couldn't remember saying those words in the chapel in Las Vegas. He couldn't really remember anything about his wedding at all. But tonight those words felt perfect and Mal meant them with every molecule of his being.

Room two, Paradise

Sebastian checked his phone one last time. Perhaps there was something wrong with the reception? Or maybe she'd lost her phone. Or broken it again. She was always in a rush, that girl, running from meetings, to the television studios, to hair appointments, and dinner parties, and although she was incredibly elegant she could be surprisingly clumsy sometimes. She'd once dropped her phone down the loo at Gatwick Airport in her rush to text him that she'd landed back safely from covering a story in New York. Yes, that must be it, thought Sebastian. Rebecca had broken her phone.

Becky was a TV reporter. She only did silly, fluffy celebrity stuff on one of those *News Lite* programmes for Sky. But although Sebastian teased her about being an airhead and a bimbo, he was secretly rather proud that his mistress was a minor celebrity. He remembered the first time Becky had come on their television screen at home, how rewarding it had felt to watch her familiar face beamed into his own kitchen, knowing that later in the day, that same beautiful face would be lying in bed next to him, gazing at him lovingly. Sebastian had also been fascinated by the way Lauren had watched Rebecca's slot, quite happily, completely oblivious to the fact that the glamorous presenter was her husband's mistress.

Oh, Rebecca, why are you being so silly? he wondered. Maybe he should call her, just to see whether the phone would ring? That way he would know for sure whether she was ignoring him or not. But what if it rang and she didn't answer? How humiliating would that be? Sebastian shuddered at the thought of being the one who was dumped. No, surely she wouldn't deliberately ignore him. She'd never blanked him before and he'd finished with her lots of times. He reconsidered what he'd texted her since last week. He had sent her a simple message after their argument telling her that it wasn't working, that he didn't like how things were going and that he was obviously making her unhappy so it was best that they went their separate ways. She hadn't replied and at first he'd been rather impressed by her self-respect. He had expected at least one grovelling, desperate, pleading response.

The days had passed, and Sebastian had become increasingly uncomfortable with the fact that Becky seemed to have simply let their relationship go this time. Worse, he began to feel a little scared that he'd lost control of her. He even imagined her on a dinner date with another man or calling her ex-fiancée and making things up with him. The thought of those long legs wrapped around another man's torso killed him! Finally he did something that was completely against his own rules: he sent her another text. He was kicking himself for it now – never double text; it's a clear sign of weakness! All he'd done was send, 'Hi Becky, I hope you are OK? Xx' but still, it was embarrassing. That was two days ago now and still she hadn't responded. He didn't understand. Last time he finished with her, just before Christmas, he'd received endless texts and phone calls pleading with him to give her another go. She'd promised to stop pressuring him and once they'd got back together she'd been good to her word. It had bought him time. Until last week, of course, when she'd started moaning on about him leaving Lauren again. It was all her own fault. If only she could relax and just enjoy what they had then they'd both be happy.

Should he call her? Just to make sure? Sebastian checked that Lauren was still busy touching up her make-up and then walked outside. He slid the patio doors closed behind him and then he dialled. The phone rang and rang but Rebecca didn't reply.

'Bitch!' muttered Sebastian, under his breath. 'Ungrateful

bitch!' He kicked one of Lauren's flip-flops angrily off the terrace. Why was Becky doing this? And why did he feel so bad about it? He heard the patio doors open.

'Why did you close the doors?' asked Lauren.

'Because the air-conditioning is on inside and it's boiling out here,' he snapped, irritated by her stupid questions.

He glared at Lauren, resenting her very presence here. This trip had been meant for Rebecca and now he had to go to dinner with Lauren and listen to her dull conversation about 'the girls' and 'school' and 'Kitty's last trip to Hollywood'. Yawn.

'So? Shall we go, darling?' asked Lauren, oblivious to his thoughts.

Darling? Why the hell did she still call him darling?

'Yup,' he said, shoving his phone in his jacket pocket and making a deal with himself that he would never call or text Rebecca again. She'd blown it this time. She'd humiliated him and nobody did that to Sebastian Hunter.

'And you're sure this dress looks all right?' asked Lauren, trying to hold onto his arm.

He pulled his arm away and snapped, 'You look fine, Lauren. I told you that before.'

Sebastian didn't look at his wife. There was no need. He knew what Lauren looked like: she looked like the albatross that had been hanging round his neck for the past twelve years.

Belsize Park, London

'Any more texts?' asked Becky hopefully, the minute she walked into her flat, before she'd put her bag down or taken her coat off.

Luke lounged on the sofa in the living room, watching *The Only Way Is Essex* repeats and eating the box of Ferrero Rocher that Becky's gran had given her for Christmas. Luke was Becky's self-proclaimed GBF (gay best friend). He had a key to her flat and she often found him here when she got in from work. He had also taken possession of her mobile phone. Not her work phone – that she was allowed to keep – but her other one. The personal one. The one that 'the c**t Sebastian' (as Luke often referred to Rebecca's lover) used to contact her.

'Nope,' said Luke, popping another chocolate in his mouth. 'No texts today.'

'Ohhh,' said Rebecca, deflating immediately.

She'd spent her entire day at work thinking about nothing other than whether Sebastian had been in touch again. She couldn't contact him on her work phone because she only had his number saved on the other mobile. Neither did she have his number written down anywhere. It was safest that way; Sebastian had explained that. The fewer loose ends lying around, the less chance that they'd get caught. Rebecca sighed. She felt really sad. She didn't even know where Sebastian was. It was horrible being out of contact. He'd told her he'd cancelled the trip to St Barts but he could be anywhere – here in London, or in New York, or Germany, or France, or Dubai on business. She'd really hoped he might text again today.

'He did call though,' added Luke, casually.

'He called!' Rebecca shouted, excitedly. 'Oh. My. God! He called? He never calls!'

'Yup,' replied Luke. 'About five minutes ago. You just missed him. Not that I'd have let you answer anyway ...'

'Did *you* answer?' asked Rebecca warily, perching on the sofa beside Luke's legs and watching him closely.

'Yes, I told him you were otherwise engaged,' said Luke, innocently. 'I told him you were with Dan.'

Dan was Becky's ex-fiancé – the man she'd left for Sebastian. The man whose heart she'd crushed in her rush to be with The Dashing Mr Hunter (as Luke referred to Seb when he wasn't calling him something worse).

'You did not!' screeched Becky, praying that Luke was pulling her leg. That would just be *the worst*. Seb would never speak to her again if he thought she'd gone straight back to Dan.

'No, I did not,' agreed Luke. 'I ignored the bastard. Just like you would have done if you'd been here.'

Rebecca chewed her lip. Maybe she'd huffed long enough. All she wanted to do was make the point to Sebastian that he couldn't dump her every few weeks and then come back when he felt like it. Every time he did it she fell to pieces. But she missed him. She missed him so much. All she really wanted to do now was to hear his gorgeous, sexy, velvety voice.

'Can I have my phone please, Luke?' she asked as non-chalantly as she could.

'Nope,' said Luke, shoving another chocolate in his mouth.

'Oh, come on, please,' begged Becky. 'It's my phone.'

Luke turned round to look at her now. He shook his head firmly and swallowed down his chocolate. 'No way, Becks,' he said. 'I have confiscated your phone for your own welfare. You have no idea how to play this guy so I am going to have to force you to do it my way. You need to go cold turkey. No contact!'

'But I want to speak to him. He's my boyfriend!' replied Becky, a little desperately.

'He's not your bloody boyfriend,' said Luke, with an

incredulous look on his face. 'He's some other poor woman's husband. And he treats you like complete shit.'

'But I love him,' said Becky, feeling the tears welling up in her eyes again.

'Maybe,' said Luke. 'But the only way you're ever going to get the upper hand with this guy is to play hardball. He's been around the block a few times, Becks. He's not like Dan. He's not some young pup who thinks you're the most amazing woman he's ever met. Dan would die for you. Sebastian Hunter wouldn't even dye his hair for you. Look, you're clearly not capable of playing the game on your own, so I am going to have to help you.'

'Where's my phone?' demanded Rebecca, searching under the cushions and lifting up Luke's leg to see whether or not he was hiding it there.

'Somewhere you will never find it, my darling,' grinned Luke. 'Listen, Becks, I know what I'm talking about. If you call him now things will just go back to the way they were. He likes it like this. He has the little wifey at home cooking and washing and looking after the kids and he has you to shag senseless and to make other men jealous – but only in faraway places where no one he knows will catch him having an affair. You see? For him, the job's a good 'un! He has no reason to change. But for you? For you this situation sucks. It's horrible. You will never be anything more than his mistress while you play by his rules.'

'I have to be patient,' argued Becky, remembering Sebastian's words to her. 'He will leave but he'll leave when he's ready and he'll do it for himself, not for me. If I put pressure on him it will only push him away.'

'I'm not telling you to put pressure on him, Becks,' Luke reminded her. 'I'm telling you to walk away. Ignore him. Let him stew. If he loves you enough, he'll come. If he doesn't come? He doesn't love you and you're better off without him.'

Rebecca sighed. She knew Luke was right. But it was so hard. And it was such a gamble. What if he didn't come? What would she do then? She'd never loved anyone the way she loved Sebastian and the thought of life without him ... well, it wasn't worth thinking about. Now she wished she'd just kept her mouth shut last week, instead of banging on about Lauren again. Yes, it was frustrating never knowing where she stood or what the future held. But this wasn't much fun, was it? She was supposed to be on holiday with Sebastian right now and instead she was here in her poxy little flat with Luke. Much as she adored Luke he couldn't compete with Sebastian. No one could.

'Where have you been today, anyway?' asked Luke. 'I thought you'd be at home. I've been here since lunchtime waiting for you.'

'Where d'you think I've been? I've been at work,' replied Rebecca, sinking back into the sofa and grabbing a chocolate.

'But I thought you'd taken this week off?' said Luke.

'I cancelled my leave,' answered Becky, flatly. 'No point in taking a week's holiday just to mope around London.'

'We could have gone somewhere,' replied Luke. 'You get some great last-minute deals at this time of year.'

Rebecca shrugged. 'I didn't think,' she said, truthfully. 'It's probably best I save my leave for next time though.'

'Next time what?' demanded Luke. He sounded cross.

'Next time I get the chance to go somewhere with Sebastian,' she explained.

Luke stared at her as if she had three heads. 'You're nuts,' he said. 'You're completely fucking mental, Becks. You have your entire life on hold for that man. I bet he's not sitting around moping over you right now. I bet The Dashing Mr Hunter is at some fabulous party somewhere, smarming over women and sipping lashings of champagne.'

'Don't be so cynical,' said Rebecca. 'If you think that then you don't know Sebastian. You don't know him at all.'

'Hmph,' snorted Luke. 'The scary thing is that I think I know him a hell of a lot better than you do. And I've never even met the man, remember? Because you're such a big, dark, dirty secret that he can't even meet your friends. How can that be right, Becks? How can that be love?'

20

The Grand Ballroom, Paradise

Molly placed the plate of sautéed froie gras scallops carefully in front of Mal Riley and hoped that the mega-star didn't notice her hands shaking.

'Thank you, sweetheart,' he beamed at her. 'You're doing a top job!'

Molly caught Gabriel's eye briefly as she placed the second plate in front of Lexi Crawford and the faint smile on his face told her she was doing OK. Phew.

'That looks delicious,' said Lexi Crawford, sweetly. 'Thank you so much.'

Molly was surprised at how gracious and polite the celebrity couple were being. She'd been terrified that they would be arrogant and rude (Mal Riley had quite a reputation as a hell-raiser in the press) but the truth was they were much more pleasant than the 'ordinary' guests at the next table. Gabriel had put Molly in charge of serving the top table and the table directly to its right. Gabriel's hand-picked guests were a glamorous bunch. Well, except for Mal Riley's mother – she looked like a normal middle-aged mam from back home.

Along with Gabriel and Delilah on the top table was a couple from London who were just so sophisticated and stylish that Molly couldn't help staring. Gabriel had mentioned that the man did something important in property but to Molly he looked more like James Bond. He was very dashing and charismatic and every time Molly served the table he seemed to be the one telling a witty and amusing anecdote. His wife was breathtaking in a midnight-blue silk gown but she seemed very subdued compared to her husband. Then there was the author, Clyde Scott, wearing Henri's suit and shoes (news like that travels fast around the staff room in a place like Paradise). He might have been wearing borrowed clothes but the writer was properly handsome in Molly's book. A little bit drunk maybe, and not the most talkative, but very, very easy on the eye.

And then of course there was Mal and Lexi, who were so famous that Molly had to pinch herself to remind herself that this was actually real. She really was here, in St Barts, serving dishes she'd never heard of to stars she'd only ever seen in newspapers or on TV. It was a hot night and the one place in Paradise that the air-conditioning didn't work properly was in the ballroom, so Molly was sweltering. Her eyes itched from the make-up she'd applied and stray wisps of hair kept falling out over her face. She was starting to worry that she looked a fright. But there was no time to check in a mirror. She nodded politely to Lexi Crawford and hurried back to the kitchen to get the next dish.

As she served the American men at the next table, Molly felt a hand pinch her bum. She tried to ignore it, concentrating on not spilling the food, or knocking over the champagne but her cheeks flushed and her heart raced. Who'd do a thing like that in a place like this? The men were drunk already. Molly had heard from Jacques that this group were on a stag party and that they'd been behaving pretty obnoxiously, chatting up the female members of staff and rolling back into the resort at three a.m. after hitting the clubs in Gustavia with some young girls in tow.

Molly also knew that the groom, whose name was Dex, had already 'visited' Delilah in her room. She'd spotted him leaving this morning. And he'd spotted Molly too. He'd caught her eye, just for a moment, but in that instant he'd acknowledged that he knew Molly knew. It had left her a little shaken, to be honest. Being a chambermaid meant having a key to every room in the resort. And having a key was a bit like having a secret camera. Usually nobody noticed the maids. They were so insignificant that they were almost invisible to the guests. But the maids saw everything. Molly hadn't realised quite how naive she'd been until she came here to Paradise. She'd seen a few sights in the Dublin Grand but nothing compared to what she'd seen here.

Delilah alone was like a character from a soap opera. Molly had seen the bottles of pills in her bathroom cabinet and knew that Gabriel medicated her every morning. She had absolutely no idea what was wrong with Delilah but she guessed it must be something pretty serious. She slept a lot and sometimes when Molly entered her room she didn't even wake up, no matter how many times Molly knocked or called out. She'd just lie there, comatose, on her bed. One morning Molly had been so convinced that Delilah was dead, or at the very least in a coma, that she'd actually pinched the woman until she'd flinched. And still she hadn't woken up! Molly had learned to clean around her.

When she wasn't sleeping Delilah often entertained gentleman callers. Most were married and they all sneaked into and out of her room by the back door. Delilah was a complete enigma to Molly. Sometimes she was very friendly and chatty, sometimes she said nothing, other times she'd look through Molly as if she couldn't see her at all. And then tonight she'd been amazing – really supportive, even fixing Molly's hair. But what was the deal with all the toy boys? Why would a stunning, rich, mature woman like Delilah behave like such a nymphomaniac? Molly was baffled.

As a maid, Molly knew which guests were getting on or arguing. The elegant married couple from London were obviously not intimate any more. Their bed always had two distinct sleep marks in it, one on either side, with a good two feet of space in between. Mal and Lexi, on the other hand, had made a bit of a mess all over their enormous suite. But then they were on their honeymoon, so who could blame them? Clyde Scott, the author, hadn't brought any women back but he did drink too much. She'd seen the empty bottles in his room. And although Molly found him terribly handsome for an older man she was also wary of him. She knew from her da that drunks could be violent and unpredictable and she wasn't taking any chances.

And then there was this lot – the stag party from New York. They left all the lights and the televisions on when they left room eight. They left porn channels playing and dirty magazines on the floor. There were boxes of condoms on every bedside table and Molly had had to retrieve a pair of knickers from the ceiling fan this morning. And now one of them had his hand on her bottom. She thought it was probably Mitchell, the shortest and least handsome of the group, but didn't want to give him the satisfaction of turning to face him.

'Excuse me,' she said, politely but firmly, squirming out of his grasp.

'Hey, cutie,' leered the one called Lachlan. 'What time d'you get off work? D'you wanna come and party back at our pad? Would you like that? I bet you would, eh?'

Molly bit her tongue and swallowed the words she wanted

to say (*feck off, you filthy bastards*). Instead she placed their starters in front of them carefully and said, 'No, thank you' in as polite a voice as she could muster.

'Are you OK?' asked Henri, as she rushed back into the kitchen.

Henri was head waiter tonight and he looked so blooming hot in his uniform that Molly couldn't look him in the face without blushing. She was trying really hard to treat him as 'just a friend' and he really had stopped flirting with her now, so there shouldn't have been any problem. Well, no problem apart from the fact that every time she clapped eyes on Henri, a string quartet of Cupids started playing love songs in her head!

'Eh?' she asked him, blankly, forgetting what he'd just asked her.

'I asked if you are OK, Molly,' he repeated. 'When you came back in to the kitchen then, you looked a bit upset.'

'Oh,' said Molly. 'That. It's nothing really. Just the guys on table two, they're giving me a bit of a hard time is all. Nothing I can't handle.'

'How?' asked Henri, frowning. 'What are they doing?'

Molly blushed. 'Ach, they're only messing around but I don't really like it. They're pinching my bum and asking me back to their room and stuff like that. I'm sure it's all very innocent and normal and I expect Antoinette and the girls are all used to it but I wish they'd stop it.'

'I shall speak to them,' announced Henri, looking genuinely angry. 'That is quite unacceptable.'

'No!' said Molly. 'No, don't do that, Henri! Please. This is my first time serving. I don't want to make a fuss. I want everything to be perfect for Gabriel.'

Henri nodded, understanding, but he was still frowning.

'OK, Miss Molly,' he said. 'But if they do anything worse,

you must tell me. I can wait until after the party and then I can have a word with them. In private!'

Molly nearly swooned. She really did. Right there in the boiling hot kitchen with her make-up melting on her face with a plate of half-eaten bread rolls and melted butter in her hand. Maybe it was Henri's French accent, or maybe it was just the fact he was absolutely the best-looking boy Molly had ever laid eyes on, but hearing him offer to fight for her honour like that made her weak at the knees. Ach, she had to stop this ridiculous fantasy about Henri. Molly pulled herself together and carried on with the job in hand.

The pianist had started off playing quiet, melodic background music but now he was getting louder and more upbeat. The guests, who had had a fair amount of champagne by now, were also getting louder and more upbeat. The noise of voices chattering in French, English and American accents rang in Molly's ears as she cleared up the starters, served the main courses and then cleared those away too. Table one seemed to be having a lovely time. The sophisticated English lady had relaxed and she was chatting away to Clyde Scott quite happily now. Her husband, meanwhile, was having a whale of a time with Mal Riley and Lexi Crawford. All three were laughing their heads off. Mal's mother had been bending Gabriel's ear for hours now, and Delilah? Well, Delilah appeared to have sloped off.

Every time Molly approached table two she had to take a deep breath. The fondling had continued – a hand up her skirt, a brush of her breast, a squeeze of her waist. The comments kept coming too: 'Hey, baby, how would you like some American Pie for dessert?' The stag party repulsed Molly. She could tell they were rich and from well-to-do families – they wouldn't be in a place like Paradise if they weren't – but they were low. She realised, suddenly, with a flash of pride that she'd learned from Gabriel already. They could touch her and lech at her and make lewd comments but in her heart Molly knew it was these rich, spoilt boys who were trash, not her. Not Molly Costello.

As coffee and petits fours were served a group of other musicians joined the pianist. There was a saxophonist and a guitar player and a singer. The entertainment was about to begin and Molly wasn't sure she was ready for it. She'd seen the girls already – Mimi, Antoinette and three other waitresses from the resort – strutting around in the kitchen in their flimsy kaftans and high heels, flirting with Henri and the other waiters and getting under the chefs' feet. There was to be a fashion show, featuring the clothes from the resort's boutiques, and the models were raring to go.

The band started playing a sexy jazz tune and suddenly the lights in the ballroom went down. A loud, 'Ohhh ...' came from the guests and then a spotlight hit the back of the room and there she was – Mimi! Molly watched her sashay into the ballroom, tossing her hair, swaying her hips and working the beautiful clothes. The audience cheered and clapped. There was no denying that Mimi was a great beauty. Molly looked away and continued pouring the coffee.

The girls modelled a series of outfits from the boutiques, each outfit smaller and sexier than the last, until finally Molly found herself, sweating and dishevelled, clearing away coffee cups as Mimi strutted past her in a thong bikini and five-inch heels. Even the stag party had stopped leching at Molly now. With a near-naked Mimi in the room, Molly Costello was invisible once again.

21

Lauren smiled a little sadly to herself at the way the men reacted to the models. They were so predictable, weren't they – men? There was Mal Riley, just married to the exquisite little Lexi, and he was staring at the girls in their bikinis as if he'd never seen a pair of breasts before. Honestly, his tongue was practically hanging out of his mouth. Lexi seemed to be pretty cool about the whole thing and was clapping and whooping at the dancing girls too. And at least Mal had the good sense to turn round and give his wife a kiss on the cheek every few minutes. Lauren supposed that if you were Lexi Crawford, Hollywood star and world-renowned sex bomb, then insecurity about other girls probably wasn't much of an issue.

The group of loud Americans at the next table had been manhandling the poor waitress all night and now they were shouting and leering at the models as if they were in a Las Vegas strip club. And then of course there was Sebastian. Sebastian was far too controlled to leer or shout out at the models but Lauren knew him too well. He was watching their every move, with his eyes narrowed, taking in their long, young limbs, their bouncing breasts, their pert bums, their glossy, tumbling hair. She saw his tongue poke out of his mouth, just a little, and he almost licked his lips. Then he stopped himself, sniffed the air, and recomposed his features.

To the untrained eye he was merely appreciating the fashion show but Lauren felt her stomach churn. How long ago had she first noticed the eerie way he looked at attractive women? It was a long time ago now, probably when she'd been pregnant with Emily. He hadn't found her attractive when she was pregnant. In fact he'd made her feel repugnant. Sex had stopped abruptly the minute her bump had started to show. Lauren had felt horribly unattractive and unwanted, and she'd started watching Sebastian more carefully, a little paranoid about being fat and unsexy. That's when she'd first seen it. Sebastian didn't look at women in the same obvious, almost tongue-in-cheek way that Mal was doing now. He did it so furtively and secretly and with such a cold look in his eye that it made Lauren feel sick. It was the same way that he looked at cars when he visited Monaco, or prize racehorses when he went to Ascot. Rather than merely appreciating it, he looked as if he wanted to own and possess the beauty before him.

But Sebastian had certainly cheered up. Actually he'd more than cheered up. He'd been on top form tonight, laughing and joking with Mal and Lexi, talking business with Gabriel Abbot and even having a brief chat with Clyde Scott about literature. The other guests all seemed to like him, the way they were laughing and hanging off his every anecdote. Lauren wished she could switch her moods so easily. She was still feeling angry about earlier and her irritation hadn't been helped by a conversation she'd overheard between Sebastian and Gabriel Abbot.

The owner of Paradise had quite clearly stated to Sebastian that they would 'enjoy themselves tonight and get down to talking business tomorrow'. Lauren had realised, with a familiar feeling of being let down and lied to, that this romantic, 'surprise' holiday was probably a business trip. She remembered now that Sebastian had been talking about investing in the tourism industry for some time. He wanted to own a slice of paradise, he'd explained. She'd assumed that his business trips to Dubai and Abu Dhabi had meant he would be investing in the Middle East, but he'd obviously decided to check out the Caribbean too. St Barts had some of the most expensive pieces of real estate in the world – with some slices of land selling for more than £60 million. And Sebastian always liked to possess the flashiest and the best. Lauren wondered if he'd even paid for this holiday at all, or if they were actually here as Mr Abbot's guests. That would certainly explain Sebastian's sudden change of behaviour. Her husband could always turn on the charm offensive if there was a business deal to be struck.

Gone was the moody man who'd scoffed at Mal and Clyde at the airport, and here was Sebastian Hunter, raconteur, comedian, debater and the celebrities' new best friend. He'd still barely said a word to Lauren, but at least he'd seemed cheerful and relaxed. Mind you, Sebastian always was at his best with new people.

The models had finished their fashion show now and had changed into elaborate burlesque outfits – their perfect bodies were adorned with white feathers and sequins and they wore huge headdresses on top of their shiny hair. They danced, fairly well but not expertly Lauren thought, through the room, and each girl stopped beside a table. A tall, beautiful girl stopped beside theirs and started wiggling sexily and provocatively right in front of Sebastian's face. Lauren recognised her as one of the waitresses from the hotel. Antoinette, Lauren remembered – she'd read the girl's name badge at breakfast when Sebastian had flirted with her in French. Now Antoinette took hold of Sebastian's hand, stepped onto his knee and jumped up onto the table, to continue her dance there. She was flirting right back at him – young girls often did that, impressed by his expensive suits, his Rolex and what they perceived to be his sophisticated worldly charm. Lauren caught Sebastian's eye briefly. A self-satisfied smirk played on his lips.

Lauren forced a smile but she felt hugely uncomfortable, mainly because Sebastian was being arrogant and full of himself, but also because she couldn't help watching the way all the men in the room were leering up at the young dancing girls. Lauren wasn't a prude and neither was she jealous of other women's beauty – she could quite happily admit that Lexi Crawford was stunning without a hint of envy. It was the unnecessary titillation she didn't understand. Maybe it was her age. Lauren was getting older. She was aware that she wasn't as attractive as she'd once been but she was wiser and more insightful these days. She supposed she wished that men would appreciate women for more than just youthful good looks. Otherwise what did experience or life lessons count for in this world? She'd hoped that knowledge and perception might be worth something. She'd hoped it might be all about more than just sex. But as she watched Mal, and the stag party, and her own husband drool over the nubile young flesh on offer Lauren wasn't convinced.

'Look,' whispered Clyde Scott in her ear suddenly.

The writer was a bit drunk but Lauren had been talking to him a lot this evening and she'd found him to be a fascinating man – just as she'd hoped he would be when she'd watched him at the airport. He was a little bit down and moody, maybe, but he had an attractive self-deprecating sense of humour and even his depression seemed appealingly deep and intense. Lauren liked him. And he was incredibly handsome to boot. Lauren half-smiled to herself as she realised what a hypocrite she was being: there she was damning the men at the table for ogling the dancers while she was quite happily drinking in Clyde Scott's rugged good looks. But of course that was different, wasn't it? He was attractive because he was intelligent and interesting. Not because he was handsome. Or, at least, not *just* because he was handsome.

'Look here,' he whispered again.

Lauren turned round in her chair to see that, while all the other men were gawping at the naked dancer on top of the table, Clyde had disappeared underneath the tablecloth.

'What are you doing?' she asked, perplexed, leaning down to see what he was looking at.

'Shh,' he said quietly, ushering her down lower. 'Don't scare her. She's only a baby.'

'Who?' asked Lauren.

'My new friend,' he grinned.

And there, under the tablecloth, eating a scallop from Clyde's hand, was a little black kitten. Lauren was amazed. While all the other men in the room were ogling the dancing girls, Clyde Scott was playing with a cat!

'Aww,' said Lauren, melting. 'She's so cute. What is she doing in here though?'

'I don't know,' whispered Clyde. 'There are cats all over the resort. I've got one that keeps walking in my room and jumping into bed with me. That's cool; I love animals. But I'm not sure this little one's meant to be in the Grand Ballroom. She's got expensive tastes, though. She's loving this scallop.'

Lauren and Clyde stroked the kitten, their fingers touching every now and then, and giggled like a couple of naughty schoolkids keeping a secret from the teacher.

'Hey, dude!' shouted one of the obnoxious Americans

from the next table. 'Dude! What are you doing down there? You're missing all the pussy!'

Clyde sat up slightly, grinned at the younger man, and said, 'No, I'm not. I've got my own right here!'

Lauren and Clyde dissolved into fits of hysterical giggles. Antoinette, the dancing girl, looked down at them and frowned, obviously annoyed that they were ignoring her show. And even Sebastian looked round then. He narrowed his eyes at his wife. He looked from Lauren to Clyde and then back to Lauren again and then he shot her the filthiest look she'd ever seen.

'My, oh my, I think somebody's jealous,' Clyde whispered in her ear.

Lauren was shocked. She'd barely felt any emotion from Sebastian lately. But Clyde was right: Sebastian definitely looked, if not jealous exactly, then certainly disgruntled. Maybe it was childish of her but Lauren couldn't help but smile smugly back at her frowning husband. After the dismissive way he'd treated her earlier, revenge tasted awfully sweet. You see, Sebastian, she thought to herself, maybe I'm not invisible after all.

But Lauren's smugness was short-lived. She should have remembered that it was impossible to get one over on Sebastian. He always won. It was just the way it worked. If anybody hurt him, even if it was just the tiniest slight, he would lash right back with a much more forceful blow. The punishment was always greater than the crime. Sebastian stood up and carefully flattened the creases from the front of his trousers. He took off his bow tie and placed it neatly in the pocket of his jacket, which was hanging on the back of his chair. He undid the top two buttons of his shirt and ran his fingers through his dark hair. Lauren watched him closely. He was preening himself – peacocking, as Kitty called it. What was he about to do? She watched as Sebastian held his hand out to the girl dancing on the table. Antoinette flashed him a simpering smile, took his hand gladly, stepped down from the table and allowed Sebastian to lead her to the dance floor. Naturally, Sebastian was an excellent dancer. He placed one hand on the naked flesh at the small of the girl's back and the other on her bare shoulder, pulled her close to him so that his cheek was almost touching hers and spun her around the dance floor with such poise and such passion that all the other dancers moved to the edges of the floor to watch.

Lauren bit her lip. Sebastian was making a point and he was doing it very publicly. She might be able to chat to another man at a dinner table, but he could take over the whole party by dancing with a beautiful, semi-naked model who was young enough to be his daughter. Lauren felt herself shrivel up inside. She caught Gabriel Abbot's eye and could have sworn that he was looking at her pityingly. How humiliating! To be the dried-up, boring, old wife of the life and soul of the party.

'Let's dance!' announced Clyde Scott enthusiastically, obviously seeing her pain and trying to ease it.

Lauren shook her head. She couldn't think of anything she wanted to do less than share the dance floor with Sebastian and that girl.

'Thanks, but I'm not much of a dancer at the best of times,' she lied. 'And tonight I'm wearing high heels and a long dress. That's a recipe for disaster. I'd only trip up and embarrass you.'

Clyde shrugged. 'I don't get embarrassed easily,' he said. 'And anyway, I don't believe you. You walk like a ballet dancer. I watched you on the beach.'

'No, it's OK,' replied Lauren, blushing because he'd

admitted to watching her on the beach. 'Actually, I have a bit of a headache. I think I might call it a night.'

'Let me walk you to your room, then,' offered Clyde. 'I believe we're next-door neighbours so I'm going that way anyway.'

Lauren glanced in Sebastian's direction, nervously. 'Um ... ?'

Clyde followed her gaze. 'Your husband doesn't look like he's ready to stop partying any time soon,' he observed.

It was true: Sebastian was in his element, spinning the young girl round the floor, whispering in her ear and making her throw her head back in fits of laughter. He probably wouldn't even notice that Lauren had gone.

'OK,' said Lauren. 'That would be very kind of you, Clyde. Thank you.'

While Clyde said his goodbyes to the kitten, Lauren said her thank yous and goodbyes to Gabriel Abbot and the other guests and asked Mal Riley if he would kindly tell her husband that she'd gone to bed with a headache.

'Sure thing,' said Mal, cheerfully. 'Hope you feel better soon.'

Lauren noticed the saucy wink that the rock star gave Clyde as he followed Lauren towards the door and cringed. Oh God, did this look bad? She was leaving the party with a man who was practically a stranger – and a very good-looking one at that – while her husband dirty-danced with a scantily clad burlesque dancer. The Hunters might as well have worn T-shirts stating, 'Our marriage is a disaster!' But Lauren had to get away. She couldn't watch Sebastian one minute longer. And Clyde was only being a gentleman, offering to walk her back to the cottage.

It was a sticky night and the air felt close and heavy. It smelled of the sea and of tropical flowers and the hint of rain. Lauren could barely make out any stars in the black sky. The cicadas were singing their night song and in the background the waves lapped to shore in a gentle, rhythmic hush.

'It's so beautiful here,' she sighed.

'It is indeed. You don't seem very happy here though,' replied Clyde.

The pair were meandering slowly along the path, walking close to each other, but not touching.

'Don't I?' replied Lauren, a little defensively. Was it that obvious? 'I'm having a wonderful time. Really, I am,' she protested. 'I just have a sore head tonight, that's all.'

Clyde smiled at her, knowingly. 'Your husband's a Grade-A asshole, if you don't mind me saying,' he stated matter-of-factly. 'I can see why a woman might be less than happy in your shoes.'

'I'm fine,' snapped Lauren, annoyed by Clyde's audacity. 'You don't even know Sebastian.'

Clyde shrugged. 'I know his type,' he said. 'I'm a pretty good judge of character. It's what I do.'

'I thought you were a writer,' snapped Lauren, still annoyed at him for being so personal. Bloody Americans! Why were they so forward? What right did this guy have to criticise her marriage?

'Exactly, I write about people,' he said. 'I observe people. I talk to psychologists, psychiatrists, profilers, therapists. I think I have a pretty good handle on most folks. And your husband's clearly an asshole.'

'Really?' scoffed Lauren. 'Because from what you told me over dinner you've got two divorces under your belt, three children you rarely see and a career that's ground to a halt. Perhaps you should use your remarkable insight to fix your own life before you go judging other people's.'

Clyde laughed. 'Touché, Mrs Hunter!' he said. 'It may well be a case of physician heal thyself; you're right. But then it's always easier to see what's wrong with everybody else's life than it is with your own. Anyway,' he nudged her playfully with his elbow, 'I never said I wasn't an asshole too. I'm just a different type of asshole.'

Lauren felt herself thawing a little. At least Clyde was laughing at himself. That was something Sebastian never did.

'Talking of assholes ...' whispered Clyde, suddenly grabbing Lauren's arm. 'Look!'

Lauren followed his stare and gawped, open-mouthed, at what she could see. There, in the shadows, creeping hand in hand towards room twelve, was the bridegroom from the stag party and Delilah, the glamorous socialite from the dinner party.

'The Cougar of the Caribbean strikes again!' whispered Clyde. 'According to the guys at the beach bar, that old broad has a different victim practically every night.'

'Shhh ...' warned Lauren. 'They might hear us.'

Lauren and Clyde fell back into the shadows. Clyde was still holding Lauren's arm. They waited there, clinging to each other and trying not to laugh until Delilah and Dex had disappeared up the path to her room.

'But he's getting married in a couple of weeks,' said Lauren, once they'd gone. 'He told me all about his fiancée and the wedding plans and the apartment they're renovating in Manhattan at dinner last night. What a bastard!'

'Another Grade-A asshole,' agreed Clyde. 'I believe I'm a bit of an amateur on the official asshole league table. I'm barely a Grade C compared to Dex and your husband.'

Lauren let go of Clyde's arm abruptly. What was his problem with Sebastian? It was OK for Lauren to get angry with her husband but she didn't like it when virtual strangers had such negative opinions.

'You don't know anything about my husband,' said Lauren, frostily. 'You only met him two days ago.'

'I know what I see,' replied Clyde, stopping in his tracks and turning towards her.

They were almost at the path that led to Lauren's door now.

'And what do you see?' asked Lauren. 'Tell me, oh wise one.'

Clyde put his head on one side and smiled at her almost affectionately. 'Honestly?' he replied. 'I see a beautiful, classy lady in a knockout dress, with sad eyes. And I don't like it.'

Lauren blushed and stared at her new Jimmy Choos. What was she supposed to say to that? She didn't know whether to enjoy the compliment or be insulted by his brass neck.

'You're wasted on him, Lauren,' continued Clyde, lighting up a cigarette and sucking on it hard. He stared at her intently. 'He doesn't appreciate you, that's crystal clear. The guy has absolutely no idea what he has. Which makes him not only an asshole but an idiot as well.'

'You're drunk,' said Lauren, flatly.

There was a low rumble of thunder overhead.

'Yes, I am,' agreed Clyde. 'And I always talk the most sense when I'm drunk.'

He lifted up her hand and kissed the back of it gently. 'Goodnight, beautiful,' he said as the first drops of rain started falling.

Lauren laughed despite herself. 'Goodnight, Grade-C Asshole,' she retorted and then she ran down the path to escape the rain.

Lauren lay awake in bed for a long time that night.

She thought about Sebastian and the way he treated her; she thought about Clyde and about what he had said; she thought about her daughters back home and wondered how they were getting on without her and she wondered if she might have the nerve to pick up her camera tomorrow and start taking photographs as she'd promised Emily she would do. Yes, Lauren lay awake for a long time that night. She lay awake until it had gone three and still Sebastian hadn't come back.

22

The kitchen, Paradise

Molly's evening of being a waitress was almost over. The tables were cleared – which was just as well because she'd noticed that Mimi, Antoinette and the lesser Mean Girls had started dancing on them. Gabriel had left his guests and was in the kitchen now, calmly but firmly ordering the staff to clear this and wash that. The guests were up dancing too, although not on the tables, thankfully. Only the wine waiters were still required to keep the champagne flowing until the party-goers were ready for bed.

'You may finish now, Molly,' said Gabriel, rubbing her back affectionately. 'You did really well tonight. Thank you.'

Molly felt exhausted but satisfied. She'd got through her first night of serving and apart from the odd grope from the horrible stags she'd survived unscathed.

'No, thank you, Gabriel,' she said. 'For giving me this chance. I really hope I can do it again sometime.'

'Of course you can, my dear girl,' he smiled. 'You were marvellous.'

Molly went to the staff toilets and checked her reflection in the mirror. Holy Mother of Mary, she looked a sight! Her eyeliner and mascara were halfway down her cheeks, her topknot had slipped and was now more of a halfway-down knot, her white blouse was splattered with food and her face was bright scarlet from a combination of heat and sunburn. How the hell did those French girls stay so chic-looking working in a place this hot? It was beyond her. She splashed her face with cold water, rubbed off the worst of the make-up and let her hair down. What did it matter what she looked like? She was only going to collapse in a heap in bed now. She knew the rest of the staff would carry on partying after the official party was over. They would drive to Gustavia and go clubbing, or head down to the beach, or all pile into Jacques and Henri's place. Only Molly would go to sleep but she doubted anybody would miss her.

The music was quieter now, some of the guests were already making their way out of the Plantation House and back to their rooms, and Molly guessed that the party was winding down. She left the toilets and started heading down the corridor towards the staff exit. As she passed the empty library, she noticed that a light was on. That wasn't right. She was just about to pop her head in, to see if anybody was there, when she heard voices. It was a girl's voice, speaking hushed French – an instantly recognisable, deep, smoky, sexy voice. Mimi, thought Molly, backing away from the library door. And then she heard Henri. He sounded anxious, frightened almost. Molly stopped in her tracks, knowing she was eavesdropping but unable to walk away. She needed to know what was going on between Mimi and Henri.

Molly peered through the crack in the door. She could barely see a thing so she gently pushed the door a little further open with her foot. It creaked slightly and Molly had to hold her breath, terrified that she'd be caught, but thankfully neither Mimi nor Henri seemed to notice. Mimi was standing facing in Molly's direction. She was still wearing her fancy burlesque costume and she looked stunning but Molly could see quite clearly that the French girl was crying. Her shoulders were shaking and tears were streaming down her face. Henri was holding her shoulders but Molly couldn't see his expression because he had his back to her.

'*Ne pleure pas; tout ira bien,*' he was saying. Don't cry; everything will be OK. '*Ne paniquez pas, Mimi.*' Don't panic, Mimi.

Molly had no idea what was going on but it looked very private and intimate. Henri pulled Mimi towards him, then, and wrapped his arms around her. He kissed and stroked her hair tenderly. Molly felt her heart sink. So she had the answer to her question. Yes, Mimi and Henri were a couple. And whatever was going on here was none of Molly's business. She let the door close silently and left the French lovers to their privacy. Ach, she'd been daft letting her little crush on Henri get out of control. All this tropical sunshine must have gone to her head.

She wandered slowly down the corridor, staring at her feet and feeling a bit sad, dejected, and very, very silly. She didn't see the stag party until it was too late. Three of them appeared in front of her suddenly, roaring with laughter, carrying bottles of Gabriel's champagne that they'd obviously just helped themselves to from the wine cellar. Only the bridegroom, Dex, was missing.

'Oh lookie here, boys,' said the one called Lachlan. 'It's the little leprechaun waitress.'

He blocked the corridor by leaning against the wall in front of her. Molly had no way past. She backed away from them, horrified to find herself alone with the stag party. She was sure that back home in New York these young men knew how to behave impeccably but here, let off their leads, they had a wild pack mentality, like feral dogs.

'Let me past, please,' said Molly as bravely as she could, glancing back over her shoulder to see if any of the staff were around to help. But the corridors were empty and Molly was alone.

'Don't you want to talk to us, Molly?' asked Mitchell, the short one, who creeped her out the most. 'I know you're called Molly. I checked you out on the staff webpage.'

'I'm tired,' replied Molly, trying to keep the fear out of her voice. 'I've worked a long shift and I just want to go to bed now.'

'So come to bed with us,' suggested Mitchell, licking his lips repulsively.

'Come on, dude,' said James, the least drunk and least offensive one. 'Let her go. You've had your fun.'

'No,' replied Mitchell, petulantly. 'I want Molly to be a little more friendly. I'm sure her boss would like her to be friendly to the paying guests.'

Mitchell tried to grab her arm but she snatched it back and started walking away from them, back towards the library. Lachlan laughed as if it was a game and ran past her, blocking her from the other side. Now Molly was trapped.

'You're scaring me,' she admitted, hoping to shock them back to their senses, but only James seemed to have any sense.

'Come on, guys,' he said to Mitchell and Lachlan. 'She's just a kid. Leave her alone. Let's go back to the room and get smashed.'

Mitchell stared at her for a while, slowly eyeing her up and down. God, he gave her the creeps! And then finally he dropped his arm.

'OK,' he said. 'But we'll see you tomorrow, Little Miss Molly. You don't get away from me that easily. I know you want me really.'

She was just about to push by and escape when he shoved his hand between her legs, squeezed roughly and grinned at her.

'What the hell are you doing, you pervert?' she shouted, pushing him hard in the chest.

Molly couldn't believe what had just happened. She'd never felt so violated in her life. She might have been spat at, and bullied, and even beaten up by her own father, but no one had ever made her feel so debased. How dare he touch her like that! The rage burned in her belly and before her brain had time to kick in, she'd punched him right in the face. The corridor fell deathly quiet as Mitchell stared at her in disbelief. In turn, James and Lachlan stared at Mitchell's bloody nose in disbelief. Blood trickled out of his nostrils and dripped onto his white dress shirt and onto the floor.

'Holy fuck, what have you done to me, bitch?' demanded Mitchell, his eyes blazing.

'You kinda deserved that, bro,' half-laughed James nervously.

But Mitchell obviously didn't agree. Molly saw the look of sheer hatred on his face. He clearly couldn't believe that she – a lowly waitress – had punched him, Mr Bigshot Manhattan banker, or wanker, or whatever he was. Molly had always lived on her instincts – fight or flight – and she knew when it was time to flee. She took off down the corridor in a sprint without looking back. But she could hear Mitchell yelling after her all the way to the door.

'You're not going to get away with this, you little whore,' he shouted. 'Let's see what your boss has to say about you punching the guests, shall we? Huh? Huh? I'll sue your scrawny little ass. Yours and the whole damn resort. Let's see how your boss likes a lawsuit, huh? Bitch! You fucking crazy, psycho bitch!'

Molly ran out into the steamy, black, stormy night. Rain lashed down at her but she kept running up the path, away from the Plantation House and the awful American men.

Tears streamed down her face and merged with the rain as she muttered to herself, 'You stupid fecking cow. What have you done, Molly? What the hell have you done?'

She ran into the staff block, ignoring the sounds of the other girls chatting and laughing, took the stairs two at a time to the second floor, struggled with her key in the lock and then finally threw herself onto her bed and wept, and wept, and wept, until her pillow was sodden with tears. She'd blown it. Her one shot at a new life and she'd damn well blown it over some daft fecking eejit groping her. Of course Mitchell would tell Gabriel that she'd punched him, and of course, Gabriel would have to sack her. It didn't matter that Mitchell had been perving over her all night, or that he'd grabbed her privates. It would be her word against his. His friends would back him up and that would be that. Where was her evidence, anyway? Where were her marks and bruises? There were none. He hadn't even touched her for long. The whole thing had been over in an instant. But Molly? Molly had gone and punched the bastard so hard in the face that he'd got a bloody nose! How could she talk her way out of this one? No, Molly Costello would be back in Balymun by the end of the week.

Lexi watched the group of guys from New York walk towards her and narrowed her eyes. The one with the bloody nose was cursing and swearing, making all kinds of threats about what he was going to do to the waitress who'd just smacked him in the face. They had no idea that Lexi had seen and heard the whole thing: the way they'd groped and harassed the poor Irish girl all evening as she'd tried to do her job, the way they'd trapped her in the corridor, disrespected her and then the way that pervert had grabbed the poor girl's pussy. What a fucking despicable moron. Lexi had lost her bearings on the way back from the washrooms. She'd disturbed the cute bar manager making out with one of the dancers in the library. That had been embarrassing! And then she'd heard a young girl's voice further down the corridor, shouting, sounding scared. Lexi had followed the noise and turned the corner just in time to see the waitress try to get away from the stag party. She would have jumped in and stopped the guys if she'd been closer but she was too far away and it had all happened so fast. So she'd hidden round the corner and watched from a distance.

That bastard Mitchell had deserved the punch in the face. Hell, if he'd done that to Lexi, he'd have been kicked in the balls too, not to mention what Mal would have done to him if he'd known. He was the one who had assaulted the girl. But here he was now whining and moaning and feeling sorry for himself.

'I'm going straight to Mr Abbot's office in the morning and I'm going to make a formal complaint,' he was saying to his friends now, as they approached Lexi. 'Look at me! I'm bleeding! That psycho bitch is going to pay. Just watch me. If I'm feeling generous I'll just get her fired but if I'm still feeling this fucking angry in the morning I swear I'll have her banged up. I've got half a mind to call the cops right now.'

'Well, you'll look pretty stupid, Mitchell,' said Lexi, stepping out from her hiding place. 'Getting beaten up by a tiny little girl like that? The cops'll just laugh in your face. It made me laugh, watching.'

Mitchell and his two friends stood frozen to the spot. Lexi liked this power she had over 'ordinary' people. They never quite knew how to act around her because she was a superstar. Ha! Well, sometimes it paid to be a celebrity.

'And don't even think about laying one finger on me, you frigging pervert, because my husband is just back there. If I holler, he'll come running and you don't want to fuck with Mal Riley, do you?'

Sometimes it paid to have an incredibly tall husband too, especially one who was renowned for trashing hotel rooms and punching photographers. Mitchell shook his head but remained mute.

'You're not going to talk to Gabriel Abbot in the morning, are you, Mitchell?' she demanded, standing very close to him and talking very slowly and clearly.

'That's what I told him,' one of his friends jumped in.

'Shut up, you,' snapped Lexi. 'I'm talking to Mitchell, here.'

Mitchell swallowed hard.

'The problem you have, Mitchell,' Lexi continued, 'is that I witnessed you sexually assault that poor girl. And all I saw her doing was protect herself in an attempt to get away from all three of you.'

'Bu ... but,' Mitchell tried to speak.

'Shut up!' yelled Lexi. 'You get that poor kid into trouble with her boss and I will personally report you to the local police, *comprendez?*'

'Look, I'm a lawyer,' one of the guys started to say. 'And—'

'How many times?' demanded Lexi, stamping her foot. 'Shut, the fuck up! I'm talking. I don't care who you are. I'm Lexi Crawford. I have lawyers who'd eat you for breakfast, believe me! All I need is for Mitchell the sex fiend here to apologise to the girl he so brutally attacked and promise me, on his life, that he will not be making any complaint about that waitress to the management.'

Mitchell stared at his feet. He couldn't look her in the eye. Like all bullies he was a coward, really. Lexi shrugged nonchalantly.

'I have the sexual attack video recorded on my phone,' she said. 'Maybe I'll go show Mal and see what he thinks. I'm pretty sure he'd tell me to go straight to the authorities. Either that or he'd beat the crap out of all three of you himself.'

'Just do as the lady says,' said the tallest guy, nudging Mitchell's arm. 'You don't want to get into any trouble, dude.'

Lexi yawned. 'I'm bored,' she announced. 'I'm going back to talk to Mal about all this. Show him the video, see what he thinks.'

There was no video footage of course, but what the hell. Lexi was a good actress. She started wandering back down the corridor.

'No!' shouted Mitchell suddenly. 'No, wait! It's OK. I'll do it. I'll apologise to the girl and then I'll forget the whole thing. Happy?'

'Ecstatic,' replied Lexi. 'Now fuck off out of my sight before I change my mind, freak!'

She watched as the three men practically ran out of the building into the rain outside. Lexi grinned to herself and headed back towards the ballroom. That was fun! Now all she wanted to do was grab Mal and drag him back to bed. They had unfinished business from earlier!

'Come here, poppet,' shouted Mal excitedly as he spied his wife re-entering the ballroom. 'Look at this!'

Lexi sat down on Mal's lap, helped herself to one last glass of champagne and said, 'What, baby? Look at what?'

Mal grinned his sexy, lopsided grin, and pointed at the dance floor. 'I think Mum's found romance in Paradise,' he laughed.

'O.M.G!' giggled Lexi, her eyes popping out of her head. 'Now that is a sight I never thought I'd see.'

There, slow-dancing to the band, was the oddest sight.

Irene Riley – all 280 pounds of her – had her arms around the neck of a tiny, skinny little old man. Irene, who was wearing a floral dress the size of a marquee, was almost a head taller than her dance partner. They weren't dancing so much as shuffling, completely out of time to the music, but both were wearing doe-eyed expressions of sheer bliss. Lexi had never seen her mother-in-law looking so soft before. It was as if an alien had invaded her body. A nice alien! Lexi and Irene had studiously ignored each other all evening, save for the odd filthy look they'd flashed in each other's direction. Irene had then monopolised Gabriel Abbot all evening and Lexi had heard her tell the proprietor that Americans were terribly crude. Especially her daughter-in-law. And that it was so nice to have a conversation with a fellow, civilised Brit. But now, the Monster-in-Law was smooching with her little Yankee boyfriend and she didn't seem to be complaining at all.

'That,' said Mal, 'is Mr Walter Howard Esquire, from Tampa, Florida. Widower and multi-billionaire. And I think he may be the answer to all our prayers! He just introduced himself to Mum, told her he couldn't take his eyes off her all night and asked her to dance. I've never seen her looking so happy before!'

'Halle-fucking-lujah!' said Lexi, raising her glass to Mal's. 'Let's drink to Walter Howard.'

Mal chinked his glass against Lexi's. 'And to dreams coming true in Paradise, baby,' he added.

'Well, you can make my dreams come true right now, lover boy,' demanded Lexi, grabbing Mal by the shirt and pulling him up from his seat. 'By coming back to the suite with me. I believe we have some unfinished business. Now, where were we when your mother so rudely interrupted us earlier?'

'I believe,' replied Mal, following her eagerly out of the ballroom, 'that I was somewhere between your luscious thighs, Mrs Riley. And I was just about to give you the biggest, bestest, most mind-blowing screaming orgasm that you've ever had in your life.'

'I think you might be right, Mr Riley,' giggled Lexi.

And then they ran as fast as their legs would carry them through the tropical storm, back to their lavish room, and to their enormous bed, and to their precious privacy, back into the blissful comfort of each other's arms.

23

It was only six a.m. but Molly had been lying awake, staring at the ceiling, for hours, wondering what to do for the best. Perhaps she should go straight to Gabriel and tell him her side of the story while Mitchell was still sleeping off his hangover? Would that be the right thing to do? She could go to room eight, knock on the door and say sorry to Mitchell in person, appeal to his better nature and get herself off the hook, maybe? But then she remembered the blood on his face and the look of hatred in his eye and she decided that that would be a very stupid thing to do. And besides, she wasn't sorry. Not really. The truth was she never wanted to see that man again. Ach, she knew she'd been wrong to punch him. She should have been strong enough to turn the other cheek. But he'd been so rude to touch her like that. Molly shuddered at the memory. Maybe she should write a resignation letter to Gabriel now, push it under his door and then run away. But run away where? She had no money for a flight back to Dublin and she knew no one on the island other than the people here. Or should she just get up, get on with her shift and pray that Mitchell had changed his mind about telling Gabriel overnight?

Molly opened the shutters to watch the sunrise. Last night's rain had washed away the clouds and it was going to be another perfect, blue-sky day in Paradise. She opened the window and leant right out so she could feel the warmth on her face and see the turquoise blue of the sea. Pelicans were fishing just offshore. The air smelled of tropical blooms. Molly did not want to leave this place.

'Please God,' she prayed. 'I know I did a terrible thing, but please God, let me stay.'

She decided to get into her chambermaid's uniform and get on with the day. Whatever would be would be (as her nan would have sung), or *que sera sera* (as Henri was fond of musing). She thought about how she'd seen Henri wrap his arms around Mimi last night and Molly's heavy heart sank a little deeper into the pit of her stomach. But there was no point in staying here, feeling sorry for herself and staring at the view all morning. She might as well make herself useful while she still had a job to do.

Molly always started with the empty cottages, the rooms that had just been vacated and were about to be filled with bright, shiny new guests at lunchtime. It was too early to clean any of the rooms that had residents sleeping inside them. But by eight thirty she'd finished in the empty rooms. Molly had to then make a judgement call about which guests would get up early and go for breakfast, or to the gym, and which ones would lie in until noon. The gay couple in room eleven were always a good bet because they had breakfast on the terrace early and then spent the next hour in the hotel gym. As usual their room was empty and almost pristine. It took Molly no time at all to clean room eleven. Next she headed to room six, where Irene Riley was staying.

Mrs Riley had been abrupt, bad-tempered and critical every time Molly had encountered her so far, so she took a deep breath before knocking on her door.

'Good morning, my dear!' sing-songed Mrs Riley,

cheerfully, as she opened the door with a warm smile. 'Isn't it just the most beautiful day? I've been sitting on my veranda and counting my blessings this morning.'

Molly smiled back, confused. What had happened to the scary lady who'd been in this room yesterday? This lady looked the same – she was tall, fat and wearing an incredibly bright frock – but she'd clearly had a personality transplant.

'Good morning, Mrs Riley,' ventured Molly, wondering how long this good mood would last. 'Is it OK if I come in and start cleaning now or would you like me to wait until you're ready to go to breakfast again?'

For the last two mornings Molly had been ordered to wait but today Mrs Riley said, 'No, no, don't be silly. Come in, come in, my dear. I'm sure my son and his wife will be ready shortly. I'll just wait outside in the sunshine. I've got a pot of tea on the go. I brought proper tea bags with me from home. You just can't get decent tea abroad, can you? Would you like some tea? You must miss a good cuppa living out here.'

Would she like some tea? Molly scratched her head. No one had ever offered her tea while she cleaned before and Irene Riley was the last person on earth that she'd expected this from.

'Um, actually, that would be lovely,' Molly accepted. 'I do miss a good cuppa, it has to be said. Thank you. Thank you very much, Mrs Riley.'

'You're welcome, dear,' replied Mrs Riley, pouring a fresh cup of tea and handing it to Molly.

Five minutes later, Irene was still hovering around Molly as she swept the floor. She'd said she would wait on the terrace but she was showing no signs of leaving Molly to it. It was almost as if she wanted to chat.

'So, um, what are your plans today, Mrs Riley?' asked Molly.

Irene's face broke into a delighted grin as if she'd been waiting for Molly to ask.

'I'm going on a date,' confessed the older lady excitedly. 'Mr Walter Howard has invited me to go sailing on his yacht.'

'Ach, that's grand!' exclaimed Molly, meaning it, too. 'Mr Howard's a lovely gentleman. You'll have a blast, I'm sure.'

'Actually, dear,' said Mrs Riley, suddenly looking a little embarrassed, 'I was wondering if you could help me decide which outfit to wear. I'd ask my daughter-in-law but we had a bit of a disagreement yesterday and I'm not sure she's forgiven me yet.'

Molly nearly fell over. Was this really the same woman who'd asked her to re-scrub the toilet three times yesterday when it was already pristine? Now she wanted fashion advice. From Molly!

'Um, yes, of course, Mrs Riley,' said Molly. 'Whatever I can do to help.'

'Thank you, my dear. And do call me Irene,' said Irene. 'And you are?'

'Molly,' said Molly.

'So, Molly, I can either wear this ...' Irene indicated the flowery tent she was wearing.

Molly wrinkled her nose. The dress was truly hideous – garish, sack-like and hugely unflattering.

'What else have you got?' asked Molly, trying to be diplomatic.

'Well, I did buy something in Gustavia yesterday,' replied Irene. 'But I'm not sure it's very me. Shall I show you?'

Molly nodded, enthusiastically. The older lady was quite sweet really. Molly had obviously got her all wrong. Irene disappeared into her bedroom for five minutes and then reappeared wearing a rather glamorous black and white zebra-striped kaftan, over a black one-piece swimsuit, with a red silk scarf tied round her hair, gold wedge sandals and huge black Jackie O-style sunglasses. She stood in front of Molly looking a bit bashful and embarrassed.

'Is it too much?' she asked. 'Truthfully? Am I too old and too fat?'

Actually, Molly thought Irene looked rather chic.

'You look radiant, Irene,' replied Molly, truthfully. 'Mr Howard is a very lucky fella to be taking you out on his yacht today.'

Irene smiled then. Her face was full of relief. Molly got the feeling that Irene Riley hadn't had much to smile about in a very long time.

'Mum! Mum!' Mal Riley strode in the back door without knocking. 'You ready for brekkie?'

The singer stopped dead in his tracks when he saw his mother, took off his gold aviator sunglasses, scratched his head and said, 'Eh?'

Molly stifled a giggle as she busied herself plumping the cushions on the corner sofa.

'What do you think, Malcolm?' asked Irene, twirling around proudly in her new outfit.

'I think someone's kidnapped my mother and replaced her with one hot mama!' replied Mal, looking genuinely shocked. 'What happened? Did Gok Wan pay you a visit while I was sleeping?'

'No, don't be ridiculous,' scoffed Irene. 'I'm going on a date with Mr Howard today, Malcolm, and I wanted to look my best. Molly here helped me to choose my outfit.'

Molly looked up at Mal, shyly.

'Good work, Molly!' grinned Mal. 'Chambermaid, waitress, fashion adviser – you're a very talented girl! I might have to steal you from Mr Abbot and put you on my payroll.

I've got an agent with terrible dress sense who could do with your help.'

Molly blushed. Mal Riley, International Rock God, was bantering with her and paying her compliments. She might be out of a job in a few hours but at least she'd have some good stories to tell her family when she got home. If she could find a way to pay for her flight home ... Molly sighed. Why couldn't everything just go right for once? She really, really didn't want to leave Paradise. Not when things like this happened here.

Just then Lexi Crawford appeared at the back door. She didn't come in. She just peeked, tentatively, round the door, and waited on the deck, kicking her feet and chewing her gum.

'Just a minute,' said Irene, heading in Lexi's direction. 'There's something I need to do.'

Molly didn't mean to be nosy but Irene had a loud voice and the patio doors were wide open.

'I'm sorry if I insulted you yesterday, Alexis,' she heard Irene say to her daughter-in-law. 'But you have to understand that Malcolm is all I have in the whole world. It might seem silly to you, what with him being thirty-three, but he's still my baby and it makes me over-protective sometimes.'

'I understand that, Irene,' replied Lexi, politely but coldly. 'But that's no excuse for calling me a slut.'

Whoah. Molly flinched. So Irene really could be a grumpy old cow sometimes. Imagine calling her daughter-in-law a slut. Imagine calling Lexi Crawford of all people a slut!

'I'm trying to apologise, Alexis,' Irene continued. 'You don't always make it easy for people to be nice to you. You can be quite abrasive.'

Molly heard Lexi's gum pop. 'Whatever,' said the actress dismissively.

Mal wandered around the room, humming one of his own songs, pretending to look at the pictures on the wall and studiously ignoring the debate going on outside between his mother and his wife. He might as well have put his hands over his ears and sung, 'La, la, la, I can't hear you.'

'Look, Alexis – Lexi,' Irene's voice softened. 'Let's try to put all the arguments behind us. Malcolm obviously loves you and I'm sure, once I get to know you better, that I'll become very fond of you too. Whether you and I like it or not, we're family now. So let's just try to get along, shall we?'

'You gatecrashed our honeymoon,' Lexi reminded her mother-in-law. 'Forgive me if I'm finding it a little crowded around here.'

Irene sighed. She was obviously finding it quite difficult to swallow her slice of humble pie but she was trying, she was really trying. Molly found herself willing Lexi to soften for a moment and give the older lady a chance.

'I realise that it might have been a bit selfish of me to come here with you and Malcolm. In hindsight it might not have been my best decision. But we're here now, so let's just try to enjoy ourselves,' said Irene. 'I'm going out with Mr Howard today so that will give you and Malcolm some peace.'

'Cool,' said Lexi. Pop went her gum.

'Look, I'm trying to say sorry and make amends here, Lexi,' said Irene.

There was a long silence and then finally Lexi replied: 'OK, Irene. Let's call a truce. I'm sorry too.'

'Thank you, dear,' said Irene. 'I'm glad we had this little chat.'

The conversation appeared to be over and Irene stepped back over the threshold into the suite.

'But if you ever walk onto our property without knocking

again, I can't promise not to be doing unspeakable things to your son!' shouted Lexi from the terrace.

Molly looked up, shocked, not sure whether she'd heard what Lexi had said correctly. She caught Mal's eye. He grinned, mischievously, and shrugged as if to say, 'Well, that's life when you're an International Rock God.'

Lexi entered the room then, looking rather pleased with herself. Molly couldn't help but giggle.

'Ready, girls?' asked Mal cheerfully, turning to his mum and his wife. 'May I escort these two beautiful creatures to breakfast?'

They said goodbye to Molly, Mal handed her a ridiculously generous fifty-euro tip, and then the Riley gang started heading out of room six. As they got to the door Lexi told the others she'd catch up with them, that she just had something to do quickly.

'I'll only be a minute,' she called, closing the door behind Mal and Irene.

Molly wasn't sure what was going on. Lexi Crawford was staring at her now. Had she done something else wrong? Molly racked her brain but couldn't think of anything she might have done to upset Lexi.

'It's Molly, right?' asked Lexi.

Molly nodded. She must have looked terrified because Lexi said suddenly, 'Oh God, don't be scared. It's nothing bad. In fact I think I've got some good news for you.'

Molly just kept staring at the actress. She had absolutely no idea what the girl was talking about.

'I saw what happened last night,' explained Lexi, stepping towards Molly. 'With those bastards from New York in the corridor. I was there, Molly.'

'Oh,' was all Molly could say as she desperately tried to work out what this meant.

'They're not going to cause you any problems, Molly,' said Lexi. 'I promise you. You're not going to lose your job. I told them I'd seen everything and that I'd report them to the police for sexual assault if they caused you any trouble. They're not going to tell Mr Abbot. Your job's safe. I just thought I'd let you know.'

Molly didn't know what to say. She stood glued to the spot, unable to speak or move as she tried to digest what the actress was saying.

'But why would you do that for me?' asked Molly, confused.

'Because those guys are disgusting perverts!' said Lexi, getting fired up now. 'I'm not going to stand by and let jerks like that treat us girls in that way. You're my age, aren't you?'

Molly nodded. 'I'm twenty-one,' she said.

'And I'm nineteen,' said Lexi. 'And I know how it feels to be a long way from home and a bit lonely and a bit lost. The last thing you need is to have a heap of shit piled on you by assholes like that.'

Molly thought about what this meant. So she wasn't going to lose her job? And she wasn't going to have to leave the resort? And in a couple of days the stag party would leave Paradise for ever and she'd never have to see their repulsive faces ever again?

'I can't thank you enough, Miss Crawford,' said Molly, with tears of relief and gratitude rolling down her face. 'I definitely thought I was going to get sacked. I thought I might even get arrested. And at best I thought I was going back to Dublin with my tail between my legs ...'

'Nah, you're fine, Molly,' smiled Lexi. 'There's nothing to worry about any more. And for fuck's sake call me Lexi – you're older than I am!'

'Well, thank you, Lexi,' said Molly. 'I won't forget this. And if there's ever anything I can do for you ...'

'Can you arrange for Wally Howard's yacht to get shipwrecked today?' asked Lexi, grinning. 'I could do with Irene getting stranded on a desert island for the rest of the week.'

Molly laughed.

'Right, I'd better catch up with the others. I'll see you later, Molly. And don't go punching any more assholes while I'm gone. It's my turn to beat up the bastards next time, OK?'

After she'd finished her morning shift Molly changed and took herself down to the beach bar. She ordered a piña colada from Jacques and chatted to him for a while – deliberately avoiding the subject of Henri (where was he anyway? In bed somewhere with Mimi?). And then, feeling brave after her cocktail, Molly headed boldly into the beach boutique. It was time to get out of her old-fashioned swimsuit and get herself a proper tan. Molly felt as if she'd been given a second chance here at Paradise and she was determined to make the most of it. It was the first time she'd dared to enter the shop and as the bell tinkled above the door she felt her courage dissolve. The Mean Girl who worked there eyed her like a hawk as she sifted through the swimwear.

You'd think I was a shoplifter rather than a member of staff, thought Molly, starting to get jittery.

She fumbled with the price tags on a couple of bikinis she liked and then tried to hide her shock as she realised they were over a hundred euros each – for four tiny triangles of Lycra! The stunned look on her face must have been evident because the Mean Girl shouted, 'There's a sale rail at the back of the shop.' She was clearly enjoying Molly's discomfort.

Molly swallowed her pride and went to the sale rail.

She fingered the bikinis carefully. Gold? Nah, too flashy. Turquoise? Hmm, pretty but not until she had more colour. White? Definitely not until she had more of a tan! Black? Too safe. Red? Too *Baywatch*. Finally she stopped at a beautiful coral-coloured bikini with tiny, silver, shell-shaped beads threaded onto its strings. Molly checked the size. It was a small. Perfect. And then, crossing her fingers and praying, she checked the price tag. Forty-nine euros and fifty cents. Yippee! There was indeed a god of swimwear. Who knew? Molly smiled and hugged the bikini to her chest. Today was a good day after all. She imagined what her nan would think of her spending so much money on such a teeny weeny bikini and winced. Ach, but this was a different world and people here lived by different rules. In Paradise this bikini was a bargain.

'I'll have this one, please,' she said chirpily to the Mean Girl behind the desk. She handed over the beautiful bikini and the fifty-euro note that Mal had given her as a tip earlier.

'*Oui*,' replied the Mean Girl, ungraciously. She snatched Molly's money, checked it carefully to make sure it was real, and then reluctantly shoved the bikini unceremoniously into a bag.

'Bye,' called Molly cheerfully over her shoulder as she left.

'Hmph,' grunted the Mean Girl.

Molly Costello knew that the likes of her was not supposed to walk into Paradise Beach Boutique and buy such an exquisite piece of swimwear. As she walked along the beach path, swinging her shopping bag by her side, Molly thought her heart would burst with pride.

24

Belsize Park, London

Rebecca had thrown all the cushions off the sofa, she'd been through the cupboards in the kitchen, she'd pulled all the towels and sheets out of the airing cupboard and she'd spent the last half-hour down on her hands and knees, crawling around the hard wooden floorboards of her flat looking under every chair, table, bookcase and bed. And still she couldn't find where the hell Luke had hidden her phone. She needed to speak to Sebastian. She needed to speak to him now! It had been over a week since they'd been in contact and the ache in her heart had grown into a monster. The pain and longing had taken on a life of its own and it squirmed and wriggled in her stomach like a serpent. She couldn't eat, she couldn't sleep, she couldn't concentrate properly on work.

Just then Becky heard the familiar click of a key in the front door. Luke! She jumped back onto her feet and ran to the door. Her best friend had barely stepped over the threshold when she pounced on him, thrusting her hands into his pockets, grabbing his satchel, emptying the contents onto the floor and then frisking him like an over-enthusiastic police officer.

'Becky!' screeched Luke, half laughing, half annoyed. 'Have you gone completely bloody mental? What are you doing? Get off!'

'I need to call him, Luke,' she replied desperately, still manhandling him. 'I need to speak to Sebastian right now. Give me my phone.'

Luke shook his head and wriggled away from her. He ran into the living room.

'What the hell happened here?' he asked incredulously, seeing the mess. 'Have you been burgled? You're never going to find it, babes. I'm far too clever to hide your phone somewhere you'll actually discover it.'

Becky ran her fingers through her hair and pleaded with Luke. 'Please, Luke. Give me my phone. I'm a grown-up and I can make my own decisions. I need to speak to Sebastian.'

Luke was carefully placing the cushions back on the sofa.

'You're not phoning him,' he replied calmly. 'You sound like a drug addict begging for more smack. He is addictive, he is bad for you and I am not going to let you have another fix. This is rehab, Becky. I'm putting you through cold turkey whether you like it or not.'

'No, you're not!' screamed Becky. 'You don't get to decide, Luke. I know you're my friend but you're not God. You don't get to control me.'

'No,' retorted Luke. 'Only The Dashing Mr Hunter gets to control you. And someone has to cut the strings. You're not strong enough to do it yourself so I'm doing it for you. I am your friend, Becky. I love you like a sister and I am not going to let you sacrifice yourself at the altar of Sebastian fucking Hunter! He's not worth it.'

The serpent in Becky's stomach reared up in a fiery rage. 'Give me my fucking phone!' she yelled. 'I hate you, Luke. I hate you!'

Becky had never argued with Luke before. She wasn't one to lose her temper with friends or to cause a scene. She rarely swore or raised her voice. She had always been the smart, together, capable career girl in their group: the one others depended upon in times of crisis. She was logical, calm, intelligent and wise. She was the one who mopped up tears and sorted out other people's disagreements. She was the one who worked out how to split the dinner bill at restaurants, who organised hen weekends and wedding gifts, the one who booked weekend breaks and remembered birthdays, anniversaries and the names of all her friends' babies. Becky was Mrs Dependable. She was sanity personified. At least, she always had been in the past. But now Becky felt mad. She felt completely and utterly and insanely out of control. Only Sebastian made her feel like this. He was the only one who made her cry when they argued and who messed up her head when he wasn't around. She couldn't live without him. She had to get her hands on that phone. She lunged at Luke again, grabbing at his coat with tears streaming down her face. She tried to hit him but Luke was a big guy. He grabbed her by the shoulders and pulled her to him, forcing her into an involuntary hug.

'Calm down, babes. I'm doing this for you. You'll thank me in the long run,' he said quietly, into her ear. 'This has been going on long enough, Becky. I'm not going to stand back and watch you destroy yourself over him. You've sacrificed enough.'

He was trying to soothe her but Becky didn't need to be comforted. She needed her bloody phone! She wriggled out of his grasp and threw herself on the sofa, pulling her knees up to her chin defensively.

'That's my choice,' she said, still angry with him. 'It's up to me. I'm the only one getting hurt.'

'Really?' said Luke, tartly, spinning round to face her. He looked stern and disapproving now. 'What about Dan? What about Sebastian's wife? They've been hurt. Dan loved you. He was good to you. He thought he was marrying you, for fuck's sake! You just tossed him aside without a second thought the minute your lover came on the scene. And Sebastian's wife? You claim to be a feminist, Becky, but you're screwing another woman's husband. That's hardly one for the sisterhood, is it? You seem to be completely blind to what you're doing.'

'His wife doesn't—' Becky started to say but Luke interrupted her.

'What?' he snorted. 'His wife doesn't understand him? Really?! That's not much of a cliché, is it, Rebecca? No one's ever heard that one before! And I thought you were supposed to be intelligent. Christ! What is wrong with you?'

'I wasn't going to say that,' replied Becky, feeling suddenly very small and very alone. She wasn't used to Luke being angry with her. 'I was going to say that his wife doesn't want to know. She doesn't really care and she doesn't love him either. It's a marriage of convenience for her as much as it is for him.'

'And she's told you this in person, has she?' asked Luke, sarcastically. 'That couldn't possibly be Sebastian feeding you a pile of bullshit to carry on getting his leg over, could it?'

'I believe him,' was all Becky could find to say.

'Yes, well you'd believe anything that man says because otherwise you just might have to face the fact that you've made a mistake. And Little Miss Perfect doesn't make mistakes, does she?'

Luke's words swam around Rebecca's brain. She knew there was some truth in them. She was well aware that sleeping with a married man was immoral and against everything she believed. But this wasn't some sordid little affair. This was Big Love. Sebastian was The One and he felt the same way about her. It was all just a case of confused timing. When he left Lauren and the dust settled everyone, including Luke, would see that it had all been for the best and that this was how it was supposed to be.

'Becky,' said Luke, kneeling down in front of her and placing his hands gently on her knees. He made her look in his eyes. 'Do you remember a story you told me right at the start? About how Sebastian reacted when his wife called one night?'

Becky shrugged dismissively, but she did remember. She didn't want to remember. She'd pushed the memory to the very back of her mind because it didn't quite fit with the rest of the picture.

'She called in the middle of the night, didn't she? When he was in bed with you?' Luke asked.

Becky nodded. They'd been making love in some soulless hotel just off the M25 somewhere. It had been about two a.m. His phone had rung and rung. Sebastian had tried to ignore it but eventually he'd had to answer it, just in case there was an emergency at home. Becky shivered suddenly. She tried to look away from her friend but Luke held her chin and turned her face back towards his. 'Look at me, Becky,' he said. 'This is important.'

Becky did as she was told but for some reason looking Luke straight in the eye was very, very uncomfortable.

'She was crying, right? Really crying. You could hear her,' Luke continued.

Becky sighed, nodded again. She wished she'd never told Luke about this. But it had been a long time ago, right at the beginning, and she hadn't realised then quite how difficult her friends would find it to understand about her relationship with Sebastian. He'd told her not to confide in anyone. He'd said they wouldn't understand. And he'd been right. Sebastian was always right. Now Luke was like a dog with a bone.

'His wife was asking him when he would be home, pleading with him to come home,' he continued. 'She was apologising for some argument, wasn't she?'

It was true. It was the only time that Becky had ever heard Lauren's voice and the woman had sounded inconsolable, but that didn't really mean anything, did it?

'Why would she do that if she didn't love him?' asked Luke, almost reading Becky's mind. 'Why was she so upset if their marriage is a sham?'

Becky didn't have an answer. She tried to remember how Sebastian had explained it away but she couldn't recall now exactly what he'd said. But it had made sense. It must have done.

'He's a liar, Becks,' said Luke, patiently. 'So no, I'm not giving you your phone back. Not until you come to your senses.'

'You don't understand,' said Becky, hearing the weakness in her voice. 'It's so much more complicated than you realise. Me and Sebastian, we're *meant* to be together. We don't want to hurt people but we can't fight our feelings. We *need* to be together.'

'Really?' asked Luke. 'Then where is he now? Why isn't he here, banging the door down trying to get to you? Where was he on your birthday, Becky? And when you had that kidney infection last year? I seem to remember that I was the one who sat up all night with you. It seems to me he only *needs* to be with you when he's feeling horny.'

'That's not true,' argued Becky, but her voice faltered. 'He loves me.'

'Then where is he?' demanded Luke again.

Becky shrugged and squeezed her knees closer to her body. She felt cold, exhausted and empty.

'I'll tell you where he is,' continued Luke. 'He's somewhere with his wife and children, getting on with his life – his *real* life. You're just a fantasy to him. He has no intention of ever making your relationship – if you can even call it a relationship – real. You're not the one who cooks his meals, or irons his shirts, or sends birthday cards to his mother, or who remembers to pay the gas bill. His wife does all that. I'd bet my entire shoe collection on the fact that he's with her right now.'

Rebecca shook her head slowly and firmly. 'No,' she said. 'You've got it wrong. You're not in it. You don't understand it.'

Luke sighed deeply. He looked as if he might cry with frustration and defeat. Becky hated to see her friend upset over her situation but she also knew that she was the one who was right. He would understand one day. They all would.

'I don't know what has to happen to make you wake up and see what's going on here, Becky,' said Luke. 'But one day something will happen and the scales will fall from your eyes.'

He tried to hug her again but she sat stock-still and didn't return his affection. Rebecca couldn't let anyone in but Sebastian.

'Give me my phone,' she repeated, knowing she sounded cold and unfeeling.

And that's when the first tear trickled down Luke's cheek. Becky felt the shame creep up her face: she'd made her best friend cry. This wasn't what she wanted. She didn't want to push Luke away but ... ? How the hell could she make her friends understand? It was one of those situations that unless you'd actually lived it, you couldn't possibly know how it felt.

'I don't want to argue with you or upset you, Luke,' she continued. 'But Sebastian is very, very important to me. He'll be upset that I haven't been in touch. I love him and I am not going to hurt him. So give me my phone.'

Luke stared at her then, as if she'd grown two heads.

'I give up,' he said, eventually, wiping a tear from his cheek. 'You can have your stupid phone. You can call your stupid lover and ruin your stupid life. I thought you were better than this, Becky. When you left Dan I stood by you. All our other friends thought you were a bitch. Christ, your own mother didn't speak to you for a month! But I stuck up for you and I tried to understand and I gave Sebastian the benefit of the doubt. But it's over now. He's strung you along for far too long. I don't believe he will ever leave his wife and I can't stand around and watch you make a fool of yourself. I've tried. God knows I've tried. But I give up.'

He left the room for a few minutes and returned carrying Rebecca's iPhone. She still had no idea where it had been hidden all this time but she didn't care. She had it back and now she could call Sebastian. It was all that mattered. Luke tossed it onto the sofa beside her with a look of sheer disgust on his face.

'There,' he said. 'I hope you and your precious phone will be very happy together. Because that's all he is: a series of text messages, snatched phone calls and the odd booty call.'

'Thank you,' said Becky, ignoring Luke's glare, picking up her phone and cradling it like a newborn baby. 'That's all I wanted.'

Luke gathered his wallet, his phone, his notebook, his comb and all the other contents of his bag from the floor where Becky had scattered them. He slung his satchel over his shoulder, sniffed up the last of his tears and headed towards the door.

'You will come to your senses, Becky,' he said, finally, with his hand on the door handle. 'I don't know how and I don't know when, but it will happen. And I'll be there for you. I'm still your friend. But while you're deluding yourself like this, I can't be around you. You won't listen to me and you won't let me help and it's doing my head in. Take care of yourself, babes. Because Sebastian Hunter certainly won't.'

Rebecca barely took in Luke's words or heard the door slam behind him. She was already dialling Sebastian's number. Her heart hammered in her chest and beads of sweat formed on her top lip. She couldn't wait to hear his voice. Everything was going to be OK now. The nightmare of the last week was over. The phone rang. It was the unfamiliar beep of an international ringtone. Business, she thought. New York. Dubai. Business. Not with his wife. Luke was wrong.

25

Room two, Paradise

Lauren watched Sebastian glance at his ringing phone. A self-satisfied grin played on his lips and then he pressed the reject button with relish.

'Who was that?' asked Lauren, wondering why he'd taken such great pleasure in cutting someone off.

'Business,' he smiled, leaning back in his lounger on the terrace and admiring his tanned torso. 'Just some idiot who thought I'd wait for an answer on a deal. But they left it too long. I'm not interested any more.'

Lauren nodded, unsurprised. She knew Sebastian was a tough businessman. He wasn't the sort of guy who liked to be messed around or left hanging. Quite why he had to have so many business calls on holiday she wasn't sure but, still, at least he'd ignored that one. She picked up her book again and tried to get back into the plot, but there was a question swimming around her mind that wouldn't go away. Their morning had been peaceful and relaxed. Sebastian hadn't talked much over breakfast and he hadn't wanted to go to the beach, preferring to plug himself into his iPod here on the terrace instead. But at least he wasn't being actively unpleasant. Neither of them had mentioned last night. Not the fact that Sebastian had danced and flirted so publicly with that young French girl. Not the fact that Lauren had been

303

walked home by a handsome and rather drunk American author. And not the fact that Sebastian hadn't got back to the room until, well, Lauren didn't know what time, did she?

'Where did you go last night?' she blurted out, knowing already that it was the wrong thing to say if she wanted to continue their peaceful morning.

Sebastian turned towards her and cocked his head. Even behind his sunglasses, Lauren could tell that he'd narrowed his eyes in that way he always did. He was daring her to continue, already up for the fight.

'Pardon?' he asked, although Lauren had spoken very clearly.

'Last night,' she continued, trying to sound only mildly interested. 'You got back to the room very late. I just wondered where you went. What you were doing ...'

'I was at the beach bar with several of the other guests,' he retorted impatiently. 'Not that it's any of your business. You sneaked off early with that obnoxious American. You made me look like a complete prat! What do you think people thought? Not to mention the fool you made of yourself. Do you really think a man like that would be interested in you? He's rude and uncouth but he's fairly successful and well known. He doesn't want middle-aged women throwing themselves at him. God, I was so humiliated watching you drool over him like that.'

Lauren's mouth fell open involuntarily. What the ...? She couldn't believe what she was hearing. She hadn't thrown herself at Clyde! And she wasn't bloody well middle-aged! At least she didn't feel it. Not now, lying here in her gold bikini, with the beginning of a rather good tan. She felt, well, kind of sexy actually. Maybe it was the sunshine, or the fact she'd now had a few days' rest, or the compliments

Clyde had paid her, but something in Lauren snapped. She was not going to let Sebastian talk to her like this any more.

'For your information, Clyde was the one who offered to walk me home. He was being a gentleman because I'd had enough of watching you doing your *Dirty Dancing* impersonation with a girl not much older than Emily. I was the one who was humiliated by *your* behaviour. And I was the one in bed by midnight waiting for you to come back. Again!'

Lauren felt as if she was jumping off a cliff top and free-falling without a parachute. She had no idea whether she'd land safely or not, but what the hell. She'd been standing at the top of that cliff for years, wondering what would happen if she jumped. Now it was time to find out.

'So did you sleep with her? The dancing waitress? Antoinette, I think her name is?' Lauren asked bravely.

In all the years she'd been married, Lauren had never before come right out with it and asked if Sebastian had been unfaithful. Oh, she'd wondered. What else was a wife to do on all those cold, lonely nights in bed, waiting for him to come home? But she'd lied to herself, deluded herself and convinced herself that he would never do that to her. She'd argued with Kitty to the point of almost losing her friendship at times. She'd stuck up for Sebastian until she was blue in the face. She'd bought every excuse and believed every story. She'd even accepted every consolatory bunch of flowers and she'd stayed firmly at the top of that cliff, resolutely refusing to jump, but for some reason now the whole charade seemed ridiculous. Laughable, even. Of course he'd been unfaithful to her. And the strangest part was that suddenly Lauren felt nothing. There were no tears and no pain. Just a sudden moment of clarity.

Sebastian spat out the mouthful of Evian he'd just gulped

down and stared at Lauren as if she'd just cut up his favourite Vivienne Westwood suit.

'What?!' he demanded. 'What did you just say? Have you gone completely mad, Lauren? How dare you accuse me of something so disgusting!'

Lauren shrugged casually. 'I'm not sure I even mind if you did sleep with her, Sebastian,' she said, truthfully. 'I was just wondering. I thought it would be rather novel to hear the truth for once.'

Sebastian reared up in his lounger like a wild animal. 'I swear on our children's lives that I did not sleep with Antoinette,' he roared. 'I didn't so much as kiss that girl. And I never would! I have never been so insulted in my life, Lauren. Never! I don't know what's got into you. What's all this sudden talk about sleeping with other people? Perhaps I should be asking you if you slept with the author?'

'Nope,' replied Lauren, quite chirpily. 'Of course I didn't. But then I'm not a compulsive liar and a cheat, am I?'

'No,' retorted Sebastian, his face still scarlet with fury. 'And neither am I! But you are quite clearly certifiable. I'm sending you to Harley Street the minute we get home. You're obviously unwell.'

'Oh, fuck off, Sebastian,' she snapped. 'I'm not sick, I'm just sick of you. I don't actually give a damn what you did last night. For all I care you might as well have had an orgy with the entire waitressing staff. I don't know why I even asked.'

She got up off her sun lounger, threw her book on the deck and headed towards the room. Lauren didn't want to spend one more minute in Sebastian's company.

'Where are you going?' asked Sebastian to her retreating back. He sounded almost disappointed that she didn't want to continue the argument now it had finally come to the fore.

Lauren realised, with a slightly smug sensation, that she hadn't heard those words coming out of Sebastian's mouth for years. He never asked her where she was going, or what she was doing, or where she'd been, because she had always been exactly where she was meant to be: at home with the girls. She ignored him as she sauntered towards the patio doors. A smile played on her lips.

'Where are you going?' he demanded, louder this time, like a Victorian father talking to his wayward daughter.

'None of your business,' she called back. 'You never tell me what you're up to. So why should I tell you?'

'Well, I don't care anyway,' he shouted after her, sounding incredibly petulant and about six years old. 'I've got a business meeting with Gabriel Abbot anyway. You didn't think this was just a holiday, did you? Did you?!'

'No shit, Einstein!' she called back at him as she entered the cottage.

Sebastian's face was a picture. He looked genuinely perplexed by the change in his wife's behaviour. For a moment she thought she saw something approaching fear in his eyes before he replaced his sunglasses and cut off his emotions again.

'Fine. You go,' he muttered. 'But be careful what you wish for, Lauren. You'd be nothing without me. Nothing. Do you hear me?'

Lauren closed the patio doors behind her and blocked out Sebastian's voice. She had no interest in hearing him. Surprise, surprise, Sebastian had a business meeting in Paradise. Like she hadn't figured that one out already! This was no romantic holiday to save their marriage; it was just another opportunity for Sebastian to make a deal of some sort. Ah well, 'whatever', as Emily would say. Lauren threw her white beach dress over her bikini, picked up her camera bag and slammed the door to room two behind her. As she wandered happily along the path towards the beach, with the sun on her face, Lauren felt suddenly free. As free as a bird. A bird of paradise. She grinned to herself, with her camera bag swinging by her side and walked faster, faster away from Sebastian.

'Where are you off to, looking so cheerful, Mrs Hunter?' called out Henri, the cute barman, as she strode past the bar towards the beach.

'I'm going to draw a line in the sand,' replied Lauren. 'And then I'm going to take a photograph of it. Just to remind myself that it's there.'

Henri shrugged at her and flashed her a bemused smile. He probably thought she was crazy. Maybe she was crazy. Sebastian certainly thought she was. But as Lauren slipped off her sandals and walked barefoot in the sand, she felt more sane than she had done in years.

26

The beach bar, Paradise

'I think today, everyone, they have gone mad!' announced Henri to Clyde as he slid onto the barstool that had become his regular perch since arriving at the resort.

'Really?' asked Clyde, only half-interested.

His head hurt. Why had he stayed up half the night reading the frigging manuscript and drinking rum? It hadn't got him anywhere. It never did! Except here again: hungover, disillusioned and in desperate need of the hair of the dog.

'Make me something strong and appropriate, Henri,' said Clyde to the barman. And then, because he realised he was being rude, he added, 'So what's all this about people going nuts?'

'Well, first there is Delilah,' explained Henri, looking perplexed. 'Now Madame Delilah, she is not so, um, how you say it? Normal. She is not so normal any of the days. But today. *Mon Dieu!* I am out here early, before anybody else, getting the bar ready, putting up the shades, you know?'

Clyde nodded. He liked Henri. His manner was easy and laid-back and his stories were always entertaining.

'And she is there, on the beach,' Henri pointed towards the shore. 'Talking to herself, marching up and down, and she is completely naked, Clyde! I did not know where to look! She is older than my mother. Now I know this for a fact because today she was not wearing any make-up. And let me tell you, without her make-up Delilah is not so young.'

Clyde laughed despite himself. The thought of the crazy old broad with all that plastic surgery, wandering around in her birthday suit was hilarious.

'What did you do?' asked Clyde, wide-eyed. 'Call for the men in white coats?'

'*Non*.' Henri shook his head as he shook a cocktail shaker. 'I was worried that some of the guests might start to arrive, and that she would scare them, so I go down to her and wrap a towel around her shoulders. I sit her on a lounger and then I call Monsieur Gabriel and he comes and he takes her away. He does not even behave as if this is a strange thing. Gabriel, he seems to understand Madame Delilah, but I do not know what goes on in that lady's head. She is crazy. But today, she is not the only one!'

Jeez, this place was a bit of a nuthouse! That Delilah was seriously screwed up; Clyde was expert enough to have worked that out from the start. He felt sorry for the old girl, really. It was clear that she was mentally ill and only functioning on a normal, sociable level because she was on strong medication. He could see it in the glazed look in her eyes. And even Gabriel Abbot's behaviour rang alarm bells in Clyde's head. He had such a God-like presence around the place that everyone did exactly what he wanted them to do at all times without complaining. Even Clyde had done what he was told, when he'd tried to avoid the party. Gabriel had ensured there was no way he could get out of the invitation. Clyde had the owner of Paradise down as a real Svengali character. Gabriel was very calm and polite but Clyde wondered what he would do if someone disobeyed him. He suspected it wouldn't be pretty.

Something about the set-up at Paradise made Clyde feel uneasy. Why had Abbot invited him here in the first place? What was this free holiday all about anyway? Berkowski had said Gabriel was a fan but the old guy had barely asked Clyde about his work. In fact, Abbot seemed far too busy and distracted to spend much 'quality' time with any of the guests. No, Clyde wasn't convinced that anything was as it first appeared in Paradise.

Half the girls who worked here seemed to be borderline sociopaths, sniffing out party invitations, private yachts and potential husbands as they served breakfast. Mal was a recovering sex addict, drug addict and alcoholic with a complete inability to detach from his mother and even Lexi's anger issues were *way* off the scale.

And as for Sebastian Hunter, well, OK, maybe Clyde was biased here, but Christ, that man was a narcissist! What was it that defined narcissistic personality disorder again? Clyde tried to remember. Ah yes, that was it: lack of empathy, a willingness to exploit others and an inflated sense of self-importance. Sebastian to a tee! Clyde had spent time researching novels in USA's toughest prisons, mental institutions and psychiatric hospitals but he was darned sure that Paradise had just as many interesting characters for him to draw on as any of those institutions. Perhaps if he ever did get around to writing another book it should be set somewhere like this instead of on the mean streets of New York, Detroit, LA or Vegas. The poor, the downtrodden, the uneducated and the hungry had excuses to behave crazily sometimes, but what excuse did this lot have? Too much leisure time? Too much sun to their heads? Too much money? But what the hell? Who was Clyde to criticise? He'd had it all and let it turn to horse shit. He was nothing but a dried-up, depressed drunk. Seemed like he fitted in here just fine. Perhaps Paradise was just a ridiculously overpriced nuthouse.

'Who else is nuts?' asked Clyde, warming to his own theory now.

'Well, you will not believe the new romance,' continued Henri. 'That is crazy too. You remember Wally?'

'Sure,' said Clyde. 'The lonely old dude whose wife died. Of course I remember Wally.'

'Well he has found love after all!' exclaimed Henri, his eyebrows rising to his blond hairline. 'And I do not know, maybe it is my fault. I make him a Love in the Afternoon cocktail and the next thing he is walking along the beach, hand in hand with Mal Riley's mother. Mrs Riley! The very big, scary lady. It is incredible! Perhaps I have a gift. I am half bartender, half Cupid. Maybe I should put up my prices.'

Clyde snorted and pointed at the menu.

'Henri, back in Colorado I could have a three-course meal and a bottle of wine for the price of some of your cocktails,' he said.

'Yes, but you do not get romance thrown in for free,' grinned Henri, handing Clyde his first cocktail of the day. 'I'll put this on your tab, yes?'

Clyde nodded and tried not to think about how the hell he was going to pay that bar tab at the end of his trip.

'So, what's this?' he asked, eyeing the drink suspiciously. 'It better not be a love potion!'

'A Dirty Cowboy,' replied Henri, eyeing Clyde's now rather dusty jeans and sand-covered boots. 'You want to borrow some shorts? Flip-flops? You have worn my best suit already so why not my other clothes?'

'I'm just fine as I am,' said Clyde, feeling suddenly grumpy again. Why couldn't everyone just butt out of his business?

If he wanted to wear jeans and boots on the beach, what was it to them?

'OK, Clyde,' said Henri pleasantly. 'But the weather forecast says it's going to get even hotter tomorrow and you are going to be one very dirty, *smelly* cowboy if you are not careful.'

'Fuck you,' said Clyde, forcing a grin to show the younger man that he was joking, but also letting him know that that conversation was dead.

Henri shrugged. But then Henri always shrugged. It was his thing. He tapped the bottle of vodka in his hand.

'I am only trying to help. Spiritual guidance, my friend,' he said. 'It is my calling.'

'Very funny, Henri. So who else is crazy today?' asked Clyde, sipping his Dirty Cowboy and trying to change the subject away from his choice of attire.

'Even our beautiful princess seems a little cuckoo,' replied Henri. 'Can you believe it? Normally she is so quiet.'

Clyde's ears pricked up. The beautiful princess? Lauren? Clyde remembered last night, how she'd let him walk her home, and how as he'd tried to read his manuscript later, back in his room, he couldn't really concentrate because he kept thinking about her.

'Lauren?' he asked, trying to keep the interest out of his voice. 'Um, I mean, Mrs Hunter?'

'*Oui*,' nodded Henri. 'Since she arrived she look so sad but today, just five minutes ago in fact, she is marching past here with a huge smile on her face and saying she is going to make lines in the sand, or something like that. I don't know. She was not making so much sense to me. And then she is going to take photographs.'

Clyde opened his mouth to ask which way she'd gone but Henri interrupted.

'Even Mal is being strange today,' he said. 'He just asked me if I could close the beach on Friday. He says he needs it all to himself – the beach, the bar, the restaurant, the ocean! I mean he is a big star and I like him a lot but close the beach? This is a small, exclusive resort. The guests are used to seeing celebrities. There is no one here to bother him. Why does he need the place to himself? I told him to ask Monsieur Gabriel. I am only the bar manager. Me, I am merely a disciple. Gabriel, he is God of Paradise.'

But Clyde was only half-listening to Henri; his mind had already wandered down the beach after Lauren. He strained his eyes against the sun, staring down the sand in one direction and then the next, trying to spot her. The beach was quieter than usual today. Only a few glistening, bronzed bodies littered the loungers. But there was no sign of the beautiful Mrs Hunter. Clyde found himself wondering how many more days she would be here. Not many, he guessed. And he felt a new sadness fill his soul. It had been a very long time since a woman had piqued Clyde's interest and wasn't it just his luck that the lady in question was married. Not to mention the fact that she lived in England!

Clyde nursed his cocktail, ordered another and then another. He watched Henri work. The young Frenchman was always full of quips and compliments, jokes and smiles whenever a customer came to the bar, but Clyde noticed that every time Henri turned away from the public his face fell. Henri kept biting his lip and sighing deeply. His normally smooth, tanned forehead kept furrowing into a deep frown. Every now and then he dropped a piece of pineapple, or a cherry, then he would slop some liquor onto the bar, curse at himself and the frown would deepen. This was not like Henri at all. The guy was normally so agile and co-ordinated. And then, as soon as he heard someone approach, he would spin round and turn back on that mega-watt smile. Clyde knew he wasn't good at much these days. In fact, he was pretty much good for nothing. But what he could still do, and what he had always been able to do, was study people and make a pretty good judgement call about what was going on in their heads. It was why he'd made such a good thriller writer. He somehow saw beneath the façade and knew instinctively what the real story was.

'You OK, buddy?' asked Clyde eventually, feeling Henri's pain and wanting to help. 'Because I know when someone's faking a smile and you seem to have something on your mind today.'

There was that shrug again, and the easy false smile.

'I am OK,' replied Henri. 'It is my job to be always happy. But I am only human. Some days I don't feel so good. Maybe later, when I finish work, I will cry into my pillow, eh? Or perhaps I am just crazy too. It is a full moon on Friday night. Maybe we are all lunatics, going slowly insane.'

Henri grinned then, trying to convince Clyde that he was joking, but Clyde wasn't easily convinced. He knew the look of a man who was troubled – Christ, he saw it every time he looked in the mirror! And Henri definitely had something more than full moons on his mind.

'Girl trouble?' asked Clyde, refusing to drop the subject.

Henri shrugged nonchalantly as usual but the shadow in his normally sparkling eyes gave him away. 'A little, maybe,' he said. 'But it is nothing I cannot handle.'

'If you say so,' replied Clyde. 'But if you want to talk anything through, I'm here.'

'You are always here!' laughed Henri. 'I am thinking I will rename this place Clyde's Bar.'

'No, seriously Henri,' Clyde said firmly. 'You might think I'm just a washed-up old drunk but I've been around the block a few times. I've made mistakes and I've screwed up lives but I've lived and I've learned. If you want to talk to anyone, I'm all ears, OK?'

'OK,' said Henri, nodding his head. The false smile had faded. 'Perhaps later, once I have finished work, we will talk. But for now the show must go on!'

Clyde watched Henri turn to a group of glamorous young girls who'd just arrived from New Hampshire. He made them giggle and blush as he offered them Sex on the Beach and Slow Comfortable Screws with a look of faux innocence on his young, handsome face. Oh to be that age again, thought Clyde. Whatever problems Henri had, Clyde felt sure they could be easily fixed.

Gabriel's cottage, Paradise

Gabriel read the letter from the hospital again, ensuring that he had understood every word correctly. He sighed and felt a smidgeon of regret that things had turned out this way. Well, there it was in black and white: what the doctor in Dublin had told him was true. He'd been to see surgeons in Miami, New York and London too but the trip to the Irish specialist had been his last hope. Now that too was gone. If he had had any doubts about the course of action he must now take then this letter had erased them. It was as if the plot had been written by someone else's hand. Gabriel was merely following the path that fate had thrown before him. Why would this letter arrive now, while HE was here? Surely it was a sign. There was very little time left for Gabriel to right those wrongs. He knew what he still had to do and then his work here would be done.

Gabriel didn't feel as ill as the letter implied. Yes, he was

316

often short of breath. Yes, he found it hard to wake up in the morning and harder still to fall asleep at night. Yes, his joints ached and he sometimes felt cold, even when it was thirty-five degrees outside. But dying? Was this really how it felt to be the walking dead? He already had it all arranged: what would happen to the people he cared about once he had gone. Delilah would be just fine; he would make sure of that first. And Henri. Henri was like a son to Gabriel. He would never leave that boy in the lurch. But there was Molly to consider now too. Gabriel hadn't known the girl long but there was something about her that had got right under his skin. Again, it felt like fate, that she should be thrown into his life just at the end. He had barely taken in the news from the surgeon when he'd met her in Dublin. She had fought for him and defended him and it was his duty to do the same for her. He had the chance to save one more lost soul before he died. Yes, he would have to think hard about Molly. He would never rest in peace unless he knew she was safe and cared for. But there wasn't much time left to figure that one out.

Gabriel placed his panama on his head and walked back out into the daylight. He winced. The sun hurt his eyes now. It was almost too bright for Gabriel to bear. He headed slowly, with aching legs, towards the beach bar. Not a living soul here knew that he was ill, let alone dying. So, for now, Gabriel had to keep up appearances. He had taken bookings for weddings later in the year, and arranged parties for next Christmas, knowing perfectly well that he wouldn't be here. All these things were being done simply to confuse the rest of the staff. There was no way that Gabriel could let anyone know the truth. He even had a business meeting arranged with Sebastian Hunter this afternoon. The Englishman was keen to invest in the island. He wanted to buy a small pocket of undeveloped land that Gabriel owned to the west of Paradise. And who could blame him? This was undoubtedly the most beautiful spot on the planet. But Gabriel was not really going to be able to help Sebastian Hunter, was he? He wouldn't be around to sign any land deals later in the year. No, Gabriel was merely going through the motions so that nobody got suspicious. He was acting again. Just like he always had done.

The beach bar, Paradise

Clyde had been drinking all afternoon. He had chatted briefly with Mal but his friend had seemed distracted and busy and hadn't stayed long. He tried to think about the novel, just as Ron Berkowski had ordered him to do, but every time he got to the part in the plot where his inspiration had dried up he got stuck again. How the hell did he get over that one? Clyde knew that it would take more than a change of scene to cure his writer's block. It would take a frigging miracle.

He watched Gabriel Abbot and Sebastian Hunter share a bottle of white wine as they discussed some unknown business deal at a table a few feet away. None of it seemed real somehow. Sebastian was such a fake. Clyde could smell that a mile off. No man plucked his eyebrows and dyed his hair or dressed up in all those expensive clothes unless he had something to hide. And the guy never looked anyone in the eye. He hid behind his sunglasses all the time and even inside, when he had to take them off, he narrowed his eyes and looked away. Clyde had met lots of men who refused to make eye contact and most of those had been in prison.

Clyde glanced once more in Sebastian's direction. The

guy was deep in conversation with Gabriel and it didn't look as though he was moving any time soon. He was far too busy enjoying the sound of his own voice. In fact, both men were taking turns to interrupt and talk over each other and neither of them seemed remotely interested in what the other one was saying. Battle of the ego, eh? Some productive business meeting that must be! Clyde downed the last of his drink and slid off the barstool.

'Are you leaving?' asked Henri.

'Thought I'd just take a little stroll down the beach,' replied Clyde, trying to sound as if it was no big deal.

The truth was Clyde had yet to step foot on the sand and both he and Henri were well aware of this fact. Clyde never got any further than this stool at the beach bar.

'Well, change into these first,' said Henri, leaning under the bar and reappearing with a neatly folded pair of swimming shorts and some flip-flops in his hands. 'I keep these under the bar in case I want to swim after work. You can borrow them. I cannot let you walk down Paradise beach in your jeans, cowboy. It is against the rules. Not Monsieur Gabriel's rules, but my rules!'

Clyde sighed and reluctantly accepted the clothes. He guessed the kid was right this time.

'Um, Henri?' he asked, trying not to blush. 'I don't suppose you noticed which direction Lauren Hunter went in, did you?'

Henri grinned and this time his smile looked genuine. 'I was wondering how long it would be before you asked about the princess,' he laughed. 'She went that way. Round the headland, away from the resort. But that was hours ago. She could be anywhere by now.'

'Thanks,' mumbled Clyde as he headed towards the men's room to change into the shorts.

He was a little drunk and a little light-headed, having forgotten to eat breakfast, or lunch, or anything other than the alcohol-soaked fruit in his cocktails all day. And he had absolutely no idea why he was going off in search of Lauren Hunter. But it felt like the right thing to do and Clyde Scott had nothing left to live by other than his instincts.

27

The beach bar, Paradise

Henri spotted Molly strolling up the beach long before she looked up and waved at him and Jacques. He watched her, without her knowing it, for the longest time. She was stepping carefully towards the beach bar, barefoot in the hot sand, carrying her beach towel and her battered old rucksack, trying desperately not to kick sand in anyone's face. She'd bought herself a new bikini. She managed to look smoking hot and a little bit embarrassed at the same time. Henri shook his head. He had to stop thinking about Molly like this. But it was hard. It was so fucking hard. He wished that Clyde hadn't disappeared. It might have been useful to talk to the older, wiser man today. Clyde drank too much but he was smart and he talked sense. And God knows Henri could do with some sensible advice right now!

He couldn't take his eyes off her. Molly had the most perfect neat, curvy little body that Henri had ever seen. He loved the way that her back curved into her pert bottom. He loved the way her bikini bottoms rose up as she walked and she had to stop every few paces to pull them back down and keep herself decent. He loved the way her long black hair swung down her back, brushing her naked skin. He loved her smooth, flat stomach, her slim shapely legs, the fullness of her thighs and the roundness of her hips. He loved her pretty little bare feet, even though she didn't wear nail varnish on her toes. He loved the way her lips pouted like red rosebuds in bloom. He loved the way that her silver St Christopher necklace dangled between her magnificent breasts. And most of all he loved the way she had absolutely no idea how unbelievably beautiful and sexy she was. Other men noticed her too. Henri could see that as their heads turned to watch her make her way across the sand. But Molly remained oblivious.

There was nothing false or showy about Molly. Her beauty was untainted, natural and pure. She didn't wear make-up to the beach like the other girls. Her skin was clear and smooth and completely unblemished. Henri always wanted to reach out and stroke the bit where her neck met her jaw. He wondered if she would be tickly there and if she would laugh that sweet, tinkling little laugh of hers, if he ever found the nerve to try. Henri adored Molly's voice. She talked in a sing-song that sounded to Henri more like music than language. He loved the fact that she had absolutely no idea how funny and interesting and engaging her conversation was. Sometimes he didn't understand her dialect and he missed whole chunks of what she was saying but it didn't matter. He loved to listen to her anyway. But most of all, more than any of those things, Henri loved to stare into Molly's eyes. Henri had stared into many pairs of eyes in his time but he had never seen eyes this colour before. They were the same shade of bright, vibrant green as the lush foliage on the island. Her irises were clear and pure. If the eyes were the windows to the soul, then Molly Costello had the purest, clearest, most perfect soul in all the world.

But Henri had to stop himself from looking into Molly's eyes. He'd been trying to stop doing it for ages. He'd stopped flirting with her too and it was killing him. He knew she liked him. Molly wasn't the type of girl who could easily hide her emotions. The knowledge that his feelings for her were reciprocated just made the whole situation even more frustrating. God, wasn't it just his luck that now, when he'd finally met a girl he actually liked, that he couldn't have her. And he had no one to blame but himself. He'd gorged on all the fancy cakes in the patisserie and now he'd made himself sick. He'd either kissed or slept with half the girls in the resort, not to mention the odd celebrity guest. And now he was paying the price. Henri couldn't have Molly because he didn't deserve her. She was too good for a bad boy like him. But it was such a shame. Henri felt sure that if he and Molly had been given a chance he would have been a good man for her. He wouldn't be tempted by other girls if he had Molly by his side. But it was too late. That was never going to happen now. Mimi had made sure of that.

'Put your tongue back in, Henri,' whispered Jacques into Henri's ear as Molly approached. 'She's far too sweet and innocent for you. Although that bikini's a bit sexy! Anyway, you're taken, remember? I wouldn't want to be in your shoes if Mimi caught you looking at Molly like that – especially not in that bikini!'

Henri blushed and looked away from the young Irish girl. It was as if his friend could read his mind.

'Hi, boys,' called Molly in her gorgeous sing-song accent. 'How's it going today? Bejesus it's hot, is it not?'

'Hi, Molly, hottest day in six months,' replied Jacques knowledgeably. 'And they say it's going to get even hotter tomorrow. It might even break the record, according to some.'

'Ach, listen to us, blathering away about the weather like old folks,' she said. 'Hello, Henri.'

Henri nodded in Molly's direction but refused to look her in the eye. He knew that if he did he would just see hurt and confusion at his coldness and he couldn't bear to see those emotions in Molly's beautiful eyes.

'What have you been doing this afternoon?' Jacques asked her.

Molly giggled and blushed. 'Believe it or not, I've been a model for Mrs Hunter. She found me on the beach and asked if she could take some photographs of me. Did you know she used to be a celebrity photographer? I've no idea why she wanted to take pictures of the likes of me, but I guess she didn't have much of a choice. The beach was quiet today. Did you notice? Anyway, it was kind of fun and she seemed to be happy with the results so ... Have I got time for a quick drink before my shift, d'you reckon?'

'I'll get you something,' muttered Henri.

He wasn't at all surprised that Lauren Hunter would want to photograph Molly. She was exquisite.

'So, what's going on here? Have I missed anything?' she asked, climbing up onto a stool and dumping her rucksack on the bar.

'Well, there is a staff party tomorrow night, isn't there, Henri?' said Jacques, poking Henri in the ribs.

Henri nodded again and handed Molly the special cocktail he'd made her. She beamed at him and said, 'Ta,' but still Henri couldn't smile back.

'Mmm, what's that?' asked Molly, sipping her drink gratefully. 'It's a bit minty.'

'Irish Eyes,' mumbled Henri. 'Because that is what you have.'

He hoped she would know, somewhere deep down, that what he really meant was that she had the most beautiful eyes in the world.

'It's delicious,' she announced. 'So, what's the party for? Any special reason?'

Jacques gave Henri a furtive glance. He was obviously wondering if Henri would tell Molly the truth. Jacques was too perceptive for his own good sometimes. Henri opened his mouth to speak, hesitated, still unsure of what to say and then ...

'It is our engagement party!' came a familiar, throaty rasp from the other side of the bar.

Henri jumped, Jacques rolled his eyes, and Molly spluttered on her cocktail.

'Mimi!' Henri managed to say. 'I didn't see you there.'

'*Non*,' pouted Mimi. 'You were busy on the other side of the bar.'

'Your engagement party?' asked Molly, in a slightly shaky voice. 'I, um, I didn't realise. Congratulations. Both of you. Really, I'm made up for you.'

Henri felt his cheeks burn with shame.

'*Henri, rapide, allez. Nous devons aller maintenant!*' barked Mimi. Henri, quick, come on. We need to go now.

'Where are we going?' he asked Mimi. 'My shift doesn't finish for ten minutes.'

'*Nous avons besoin de parler*,' she said. We need to talk.

Henri was sick of talking to Mimi. They'd done nothing but talk since she'd dropped the bombshell. What more could they say? His future was written in stone now.

'You go,' Jacques told Henri. 'I can manage here. It is just me and Molly anyway. I'm sure we can look after each other, eh, Molly?'

Henri allowed himself to glance, very briefly, in Molly's direction. She was nodding at Jacques and forcing a smile but those gorgeous, pure, innocent green eyes were full of uncried tears. Henri followed Mimi away from the bar, and away from Molly, with legs of lead and a heart of stone.

28

The beach, Paradise

'Oh God, you made me jump out of my skin!' squealed Lauren, clutching her chest with her hand. 'You nearly gave me a heart attack!'

'What?' asked Clyde. 'The sight of me in a pair of bathers is so freaky you almost had a coronary?'

Lauren laughed and let her hand fall to her side. Actually, the sight of Clyde Scott in nothing but a pair of Hawaiian-print swimming trunks (that clearly belonged to someone else) was rather lovely. He had the body of someone who spent a lot of time doing proper 'man's' work. His wasn't the smooth, sculpted torso of a twenty-something male model. Nor was it the pampered, preened and gym-honed body of her vain husband. There was a deep scar low on Clyde's stomach (appendicitis perhaps?) and his chest hair was greying a little. No, he wasn't 'perfect' but he looked strong and capable, and like a man who could look after himself – and anybody else who came along. Lauren suddenly had a vision of him on his ranch in Colorado, riding horses, chopping wood and wrestling bison, all with his top off and his muscles rippling. The picture was doing nothing to lower her heart rate. She had to stifle a giggle.

'No, silly,' she said, trying not to stare. 'You look, erm, fine. You just took me by surprise. I didn't see or hear you coming. I thought I was alone here. What are you? A professional stalker?'

'It's one of my many talents,' replied Clyde, taking off his aviators and looking her directly in the eye. It felt like he was almost challenging her to fall into his soul.

Lauren blushed and looked away. She wasn't used to being looked at like that. Sebastian was all about avoiding eye contact at all costs. A little butterfly fluttered around her tummy. And then she realised that her model had been scared off by the interruption.

'Oh no!' she said. 'My pussy ran away!'

'Your pussy ran away?' Clyde mocked her with his eyes. 'What the hell are you up to, Mrs Hunter?'

Lauren lifted up her camera to show him.

'I was taking photos of one of Paradise's many cats,' she explained. 'I did have a real human being to shoot earlier but she had to get back to work. Molly. You know? That gorgeous little Irish girl. God, she photographs well. Those eyes!'

'I'm impressed, Lauren,' smiled Clyde, perching on a rock. 'I thought that's what you and I had in common – both washed-up has-beens, too scared to get back to work. You told me last night that you used to be a photographer but that now you're just a mom.'

'Just a mum is quite a busy job!' replied Lauren, knowing she sounded defensive. 'But the kids aren't here, the light is amazing and my husband's otherwise engaged, so why not?'

She picked up her camera and fired off a couple of shots of Clyde. He didn't seem to mind. He nodded and watched her carefully with his head on one side. Lauren wondered what went on in his brain. There was clearly always some deep internal monologue happening that she wasn't party to.

'Are you trying to steal my soul?' he teased her. 'Isn't that what the Australian Aborigines believe?'

'I'm not trying to steal your soul,' she laughed. 'But you scared the cat away and I have no one else to shoot here now.'

'No, it's good. You look right with that camera in your hands,' he said, slowly and thoughtfully. 'It's real good. I'm happy for you. You've taken a big step today, I guess. After what you told me last night. I tried to get back into work too but I just ended up cursing at my computer and heading back to the bar.'

Lauren couldn't remember exactly how much she'd told him last night. The champagne had been flowing and the music was loud. She felt suddenly very exposed. She barely knew this man but she'd obviously confided in him about her career – or lack of it. What's more, she suddenly realised, she was standing in front of him wearing nothing but a tiny gold bikini. She folded her arms over her chest and hoped he couldn't see the stretch marks on her stomach.

'So what are you doing here?' she asked. 'I thought you were surgically attached to that stool at the beach bar.'

Clyde shrugged and for the first time he avoided eye contact. 'Just thought I'd have a little stroll,' he replied, almost too casually.

They were a good kilometre from the bar now, on the very edge of Gabriel Abbot's estate. Lauren had waded through the sea, round a headland, and clambered over rocks to find this cove. Only to discover that it was where the staff came to sunbathe away from the guests. Luckily for Lauren only the beautiful Irish maid had been here today and that had worked out perfectly. Molly had proved to be a wonderful model. But what was Clyde doing here? She let herself wonder if perhaps he'd come looking for her.

It was a flattering thought but also one that made her feel uncomfortable.

'And what are you doing out of your jeans?' she asked. 'People might think you're actually enjoying your visit to St Barts if you dress like that. I thought you told me you were here against your will: cast away on this tropical island by your cruel, tyrannical literary agent.'

Clyde laughed easily, and his face broke into a warm, broad smile. 'You make it sound so much more romantic and dramatic than it actually is. Maybe you should finish my damn novel for me with an imagination like that,' he said.

'What's stopping *you* doing that?' Lauren teased him.

He'd given her all the peripheral details last night, about how he'd over-stretched himself financially with the ranch, how greedy his first ex-wife was, how his second wife had left him and remarried, how much of a failure he felt and how he knew he was drinking too much. But he hadn't actually told her what had gone wrong with the book he'd failed to finish. Clyde stared at his feet, picked up a stick, started drawing circles absent-mindedly in the sand, opened his mouth to say something and then changed his mind.

'Why couldn't you finish it?' she probed. Lauren had a feeling that Clyde had been keeping something to himself for a long, long time and that maybe, just maybe, if he spoke his fears out loud then he'd be free of them.

'It's complicated,' he muttered. 'And it's not pretty. I don't write fairy tales, Lauren. Some of my subject matter is pretty dark: paedophilia, incest, gang rape, human trafficking, torture and always, always murder. That's what sells. Sex and death. You meet some nasty people researching that sort of stuff. You live in a cruel world. You meet kids who've been abused. Guys in prison who have no conscience about taking another life. You meet boys who were initiated into gangs before they could write their names and girls who've been sold for sex before they reached their teens. Girls younger than my daughter or even your little girls ...'

He trailed off. And Lauren felt suddenly very green and naive. Who was she to give advice to this man, this expert in his field, who'd lived more lives, and seen more human suffering than she could ever imagine?

'I'm sorry,' she said. 'I understand if you don't want to talk about it. It must be really difficult for you.'

'Don't feel sorry for me, Lauren,' said Clyde. 'I'm no victim here. I made money out of all that suffering. A lot of money. I did my research, spent months with those people, and then I ran off back to my ranch, and my fancy horses and my fucking seaplane and left them in hell!'

'So, if you got disillusioned, why didn't you just put that book to one side and write another one instead? Change genre? Try something new? Authors do that sometimes, don't they?' Lauren asked.

Clyde stabbed the sand with his stick. 'I have to finish that book. One day. I can't just give it up. I owe it to someone to tell that story. But it's tough. It's so fucking tough.'

'Whom do you owe it to, Clyde?' asked Lauren.

He was such a tortured soul, she really wanted to help. Clyde looked up at her then and gave her that same unwavering stare. But this time he looked as if he was challenging her to walk away, to give up on him like everyone else had done.

'I killed someone,' he said finally, in a quiet, uncertain voice. 'A young girl with her whole life in front of her. I took what I needed from her and then I left her to rot. I used her and I abused her and finally I killed her. Not with my own hands, maybe, but as good as dammit. So how do I move on from that? How do I write her story when I'm responsible for the tragic end?'

330

Clyde threw the stick into the shallows. His brow was knotted and Lauren noticed that a vein pulsed in his temple. She didn't know what to say. She didn't know what to think. She didn't know where to look. She was so far out of her depth here that she was drowning. What did Clyde mean that he'd killed a girl? He seemed like such a nice guy. It didn't make any sense.

Clyde stood up. 'I'm gonna leave you to it, Lauren,' he said, sadly. 'You're a lovely lady and it's been a real pleasure meeting you but I don't think you need to be speaking to the likes of me. I'm sorry, ma'am.'

He nodded at her, very politely. If he'd been wearing a Stetson, Lauren felt sure that Clyde would have raised it in a gesture of goodbye.

'No, wait, Clyde,' she said. 'You don't have to go. You can tell me the rest. I'm not going to judge you. I'm sure whatever happened wasn't really your fault.'

'I wish you were right,' he replied, already walking away across the sand towards the headland. 'But I'm toxic. Everything I touch turns to horse shit. Stay away from me, for your own good.'

Lauren watched Clyde until he disappeared around the corner. Part of her wanted to run after him and tell him that it was OK; that whatever he'd done, she still wanted to listen and to help. But another, more sensible, part made her stay right there on the beach. She barely knew the man.

Clyde stormed back along the beach, grabbed two bottles of Scotch from Jacques as he passed the beach bar and barked, 'Put them on my tab,' before stomping all the way back to room one. He no longer cared about how he would pay the bill. His life was screwed. And if he was going to go down, he might as well do it in a puddle of whisky. Clyde slammed

331

the door behind him and opened the first bottle before he'd even kicked Henri's stupid flip-flops off his feet.

What the hell had he been thinking even talking to Lauren Hunter? Why would he want to soil a classy lady like that with his sick problems? He'd been waiting to talk to someone about what had really happened with the book for the longest time but why had he just offloaded it on Lauren? What must she think of him now? What a jerk he was. He wasn't good enough to clean the shit from that woman's shoes. Oh, she'd tried to be nice about it. She'd tried to understand and to say the right thing but he'd seen the confusion in her eyes. He'd thought talking to someone might ease his guilt but all it had done was more damage. His disease was contagious and now he'd spread it to Lauren. Clyde downed a quarter of the first bottle in two swigs.

The doors and curtains were shut. Outside the birds sang their evening song, the cicadas had started their nightly chorus and the sun was sinking lazily into the deep blue ocean. Soon the black night would be filled with stars, the almost full moon would light up the sky and the guests of Paradise would put on their glad rags and eat and drink and dance and chat their night away. But Clyde could never be part of that. It wasn't his world.

Instead he lay on the bed, without even turning on the television, and spent the next few hours staring at the ceiling fan as it whirred around and around, getting steadily out of his broken, fucked-up mind. The anger, frustration, guilt and disappointment boiled in his veins until Clyde felt as if he would explode with the pain.

29

Room two, Paradise

Lauren and Sebastian had spent an uncomfortable dinner in the à la carte restaurant, sharing a table with Mal Riley, Lexi Crawford, Irene Riley and Wally Howard. Lauren hoped that the cold atmosphere between her and her husband hadn't been too obvious to the other guests. Luckily, the older couple only had eyes and ears for each other, which was rather sweet and heart-warming at their age. And Lexi and Mal were both big talkers, constantly grappling with each other for the limelight.

'No! I've got the talking stick now,' Lexi had squealed at one point, trying to stop her husband from interrupting her.

'No you haven't, sweetness,' Mal had retorted, grabbing a grissini from the table. 'I think you'll find *I* have the talking breadstick. Now where was I?'

Their behaviour meant that any awkward silences had been quickly filled with tales of Hollywood and gigs and movie sets. Lauren couldn't have wished for a better distraction. She'd found herself laughing along despite the worries on her mind. Sebastian, of course, was being utterly vile to her but completely charming to the others. Lauren felt sure that she'd caught Lexi giving her pitying glances once or twice over dinner as Sebastian had made yet another cutting remark about Lauren and tried to pass it off as a joke.

'Creole mutton stew?' he'd mused, reading the menu. 'No thank you. I've had my fill of mutton. Rib of tender spring lamb for me this evening I think,' he'd joked to the pretty young waitress.

But it was no joke. He was obviously fuming about their argument earlier and Lauren knew he was deliberately trying to hurt and humiliate her.

He was lying on the bed beside her now, reading a book with his back turned determinedly towards her. Lauren was quite happy to let him huff, though. She had no interest in discussing the disagreement with him or resolving anything. What was the point? She'd learned, years ago, that the only way of making up with Sebastian was to take full responsibility for her 'bad' behaviour and then to apologise until she was blue in the face. But Lauren wasn't going to apologise this time. She wasn't sorry at all.

A strange, unfamiliar word had been floating around her mind for days now. It was as if she had a rebellious little devil hiding somewhere deep inside her head and it kept chanting, 'Divorce, divorce, divorce ...' The chant had started on the journey here. It had begun as a whisper, but it had got louder and louder and now the naughty devil was shouting at her to listen to his advice. Divorce. It was unthinkable. Impossible. Too complicated. Too difficult. It wasn't for the likes of Lauren Hunter. It wasn't the answer. It couldn't be the solution. It would be too messy, too expensive, too painful for the children. Lauren could never divorce Sebastian. Could she?

Suddenly a loud bang came from somewhere outside. Lauren jumped, and so did Sebastian, but neither of them said a thing, so determined were they to ignore each other. Lauren tried to get back into her book but it was no use; her mind was filled with thoughts of fantasy divorces and intriguing American authors. She'd hoped to see Clyde at dinner so that she could show him she wasn't shocked or put off by what he'd told her earlier. But he wasn't there. Neither was he at the piano bar, or in the library. Perhaps he was still perched on his stool at the beach bar, drinking into the night with the friendly barman, Henri. Maybe Lexi and Mal had joined them and he was laughing and joking around now with his friends. Lauren hoped he was there. She didn't like to think of him being lonely.

The words Clyde had told her earlier were still swimming around her mind. He'd said he hadn't actually killed the girl with his own hands. And he'd never been to prison so he couldn't have done anything wrong legally. Lauren suspected that Clyde was beating himself up for something that really wasn't his fault. He was difficult and depressed and moody but Clyde had a good heart. Lauren could see it when she looked at the photographs she'd taken of him earlier that afternoon. His goodness shone through his eyes. Eyes: windows to the soul. Sebastian had always had the blinds drawn but Clyde certainly didn't. When he looked Lauren in the face she knew there was nothing to hide.

And then there was another bang. Much louder this time. And a weird strangled cry and then a thump and a thud.

'What the hell?' muttered Sebastian to himself, getting up off the bed and walking to the patio doors.

Sebastian opened the doors. Whoah, it was hot tonight. The tropical heat flooded into the room and obliterated the air-conditioning instantly. Above the sound of the waves lapping to shore and the cicadas chanting came more crashes and bangs. A loud and distinctive American voice could be heard cursing and swearing. Lauren's heart sank. It was Clyde's voice and he sounded in a bad way. His cottage was next to theirs and the noise of breaking glass floated into her bedroom on the warm evening breeze.

'What is that bastard doing?' shouted Sebastian as he walked out onto the terrace. 'He's trashing the place. He's completely mad!'

'Leave him, Sebastian,' called Lauren, jumping out of bed now too and rushing out onto the terrace after her husband. 'It's none of our business.'

Sebastian spun round and glared at her. 'Oh, poor little Clyde,' he sneered. 'Are you worried about him? I know you were with him earlier, you slut. I saw the photos of him on your camera. Did you have a lovely time on the beach together?'

'Clyde's a nice guy,' Lauren defended herself and her new friend. 'He's interesting. I like talking to him, that's all.'

'Of course you do, darling,' snarled Sebastian, coldly. 'Well, why don't you go and shut your "friend" up if you're so close? Great choice of friend, by the way. A raving lunatic. Good work, Lauren!'

The peace of the still night was shattered again by another loud bang.

'You obviously haven't made your friend very happy, have you?' said Sebastian. 'One day with you and he's gone stark raving bonkers. Christ, he should try twelve years in your company! It's a miracle I'm not in a padded cell by now.'

'Oh fuck off, Sebastian,' snapped Lauren. 'I'm not even going to have this conversation with you. It's ridiculous. Let's go back inside and get some sleep. We'll talk tomorrow. There are things I have to say to you but they can wait until the morning. And it has absolutely nothing to do with Clyde Scott. Whatever's going on in room one is none of our concern.'

'Sleep?' raged Sebastian. 'How am I supposed to sleep with that going on next door?'

Right on cue, a loud roar came from room one.

'Right, I've had enough of this,' said Sebastian. 'I'm going to sort the lunatic out.'

Sebastian stormed off in the direction of the next-door cottage. Lauren followed him through their garden, over the low hedge that separated the properties and then into Clyde's garden. She was barefoot and wearing nothing but a flimsy silk nightie that barely covered her bottom. She stepped on sharp cacti, tripped over water sprinklers in the dark and stubbed her toe on an unseen rock.

'Sebastian, this is silly, leave it,' she whispered as they got close to Clyde's patio doors. 'What good are we going to do?'

'We'll shut the prick up!' said Sebastian.

Crash! Something else had just been broken in room one.

'I don't like this,' said Lauren, getting frightened now.

What had got into Clyde? It sounded as if he was trashing his room like some drug-addled rock star. If Mal Riley was behaving like this, no one would be too surprised, but this was an award-winning novelist! Sebastian banged on the closed patio doors. Lauren hid behind a bush. Silence. He banged on them again, harder this time. Finally the doors slid open.

'What the fuck do you want, asshole?' demanded Clyde.

Even from her hiding place, Lauren could see that Clyde's hair was matted, his eyes were bloodshot and his common sense had left him entirely. He was still wearing nothing but a pair of swimming trunks. The stench of alcohol and cigarettes poured out of his room.

'I don't know what you're up to in there, Scott,' replied Sebastian, coldly and calmly. 'But whatever it is, you are disturbing me. Shut up right now, or I shall call reception and have hotel security remove you from the premises.'

'Screw you, bastard!' shouted Clyde, slamming the door and disappearing back into his room.

Sebastian turned towards the bush where Lauren was hiding and shrugged as if to say, 'See? He's insane.'

Just then the patio doors slid open again and a large object hurtled past, inches from Sebastian's head, before landing with a crash on the terrace.

'What the hell are you doing? You could have killed me!' shouted Sebastian, picking up the broken bottle of whisky that had just missed him.

A cowboy boot came flying out of room one, followed by another one, and then a coconut from the fruit bowl and a pineapple, a mango and a passion fruit. Lauren had to stifle a giggle as she watched Sebastian duck and cover his head. There was something rather satisfying about seeing her husband being bombarded with fruit.

'That's it, Scott!' bellowed Sebastian, cowering away from the patio doors, still being hit by the occasional flying papaya. 'I'm calling security. You're going to spend the night in the cells, mark my words!'

Sebastian strode purposefully back towards room two but Lauren stayed glued to the spot. There was one more almighty crash on the terrace, followed by the fluttering sound of paper on the wind. The patio doors slammed shut, the light went off inside and suddenly there was silence from room one. Lauren watched as hundreds of sheets of A4 cascaded and danced in the breeze. Some bits landed on the terrace, others in the bushes and trees. A rogue sheet of paper blew towards Lauren and caught in her nightie. She picked it up and strained her eyes in the dark. 'Chapter Twelve' it said on the top of the page. She realised immediately that this was Clyde's manuscript. And however little he thought of his work right now, she knew it was too important to throw away. Lauren leapt onto the terrace and started collecting the pages as best she could. She stepped carefully over the shattered whisky bottle, the battered fruit, the cowboy boots and the smashed laptop computer that littered the terrace. It took her a long time to gather together all the pages and she knew that a few must have escaped, blown into the ocean or high up into the palm trees. But she'd done her best.

She held the manuscript together as best she could, tucked it under her arm and tiptoed back over the hedge and towards her own room. Lauren hid the document under a deep pile of beach towels at her own back door. She didn't want Sebastian to find it. He'd probably burn Clyde's work. She wondered if this was the only version left of the book now that Clyde had smashed his computer to smithereens. Even if it wasn't the only version, the manuscript was still precious to Lauren. She would read it tomorrow and then maybe she would be able to figure out what had happened to Clyde to make him so eaten up with guilt and self-hatred.

'Did you call security?' Lauren asked Sebastian, as she slipped back into bed.

'Yes, but they've just called back and said that everything is quiet in room one and that Mr Scott appears to be asleep,' he replied huffily. 'I got the distinct impression that they thought I was exaggerating.'

Lauren smiled to herself, closed her eyes, and drifted to sleep thinking about one thing: freedom.

30

Room five, Paradise

Lexi lay on her stomach on the huge bed and flicked from TV channel to TV channel. She was bored. *Again.* Bored. Bored. Bored. Bored. BORED! This was her honeymoon, for fuck's sake, so where was her useless asshole of a husband? Oh, he'd been perfectly attentive at first. And Lexi had been literally in paradise in Paradise. But then suddenly Mal had gone AWOL. What was the frigging story here? Was he tired of her already? She knew Mal had a pretty short attention span – hell, so did she! – but surely he couldn't be bored with his new wife already?

Mal had been running around like a headless chicken on acid for the last couple of days. If he wasn't on the phone to that jerk of an agent of his, Blaine, then he was chatting to Gabriel Abbot, or to the bar manager or even to the frigging piano player. He was busy hanging out with anyone but her it seemed! Now that they'd finally got Irene out of the way – offloaded so perfectly onto that doddery old fool from Florida – Lexi had thought they'd finally get some time alone together. But no. Even last night she'd had to endure dinner with the geriatrics and that couple from London. She seemed OK, the wife, Lauren. But the guy. Urgh! Sebastian. What a tosser. If Mal ever spoke to her the way that jerk spoke to his wife, Lexi would chop his balls off with a blunt knife – and then feed them to him with relish! They'd managed to have an early night, at least, and they'd played some pretty wild games in the bedroom before going to sleep. But then she'd woken up late this morning and Mal had already done a disappearing act. What was going on in his head? Did he really want a testicle sandwich?

She flicked through the menu from the spa, picked up the phone by the bed and booked herself in for a few therapies. A hot lava shell massage, a hydrodermabrasion facial and, having glanced at her naked body, a Brazilian, an underarm wax, a full leg wax, an arm wax, an eyebrow threading and a nasal pluck. It had been almost a week since she'd last seen her beauty technician in LA and her grooming wasn't up to its usual standard. But Lexi knew already that a few hours in the spa wouldn't make up for another day spent without Mal. The truth was she felt sad and lonely. Why didn't he want to spend all his time with her? She'd have happily been marooned on a desert island with her husband for the rest of her life. There was no one for Lexi but Mal. But, even now, she couldn't help worrying that he didn't feel the same way about her.

Molly was still reeling from what she'd found out yesterday afternoon at the beach bar. Mimi and Henri were engaged. It was unbelievable! One day Molly had been wondering whether Henri was dating the Head Mean Girl and the next day it turned out that they'd been planning a wedding together. Molly felt bewildered, confused and very, very naive. How could she not have realised they were a proper couple? How could she have thought that Henri was flirting with her? Why had she let herself spend all those hours day-dreaming about kissing him? God, she was a fool. Nothing but a green, ignorant, immature, fecking fool! Jacques had said that the whole thing was very hurried and a bit of a shock but, still, no one got married completely out of the blue. Even Molly knew that much.

She rolled her cleaning cart out of room six and closed the door. She was done for this morning. She guessed she would just get rid of this stuff, go back to her room and mope. She would re-read the letter that had arrived from her nan yesterday. She would think about Shane's amazing mock results and Caitlin's new boyfriend and about the fact that her useless fecking youngest brother had got himself sentenced to five months in a young offenders' institute. Nan hadn't even mentioned her da in the letter and Molly guessed that was for the best. There was no way the old boy was up to anything worthwhile. Yup, she would lie on her bed and wallow in self-pity, homesickness and broken-heartedness. Ach, she'd been stupid to let herself fall for Henri. But fall for him she had and now she had to lick her wounds. Just for a day or two. Then she'd be OK. Surely she'd be OK. It wasn't as if she'd even kissed Henri. The whole silly romance had happened entirely in her own daft little head.

Molly took the cart back to the maids' room at the back of the Plantation House. She chatted in her now semi-decent French to a couple of the other chambermaids who were heading home to look after their kids before returning to Paradise later for the night shift. What did she have to complain about, really? Molly thought. At least she had plenty of free time on her hands. Free time to mope! She didn't even have to work the late shift tonight. Gabriel had given her the evening off so that she could go to the staff party. But the truth was Molly would rather be cleaning toilets than celebrating Henri and Mimi's engagement. But she'd guessed she would have to go. She had to put her brave face on, as her nan used to tell her when she got bullied at school. There was no need to let the whole world know she was in love with Henri. As she was leaving, the head of housekeeping asked her to drop off a pile of clean towels to the spa.

Molly loved walking into the spa area of the hotel. Going through the tall wooden gate was like walking into another world. The Paradise Spa was closed off from the rest of the hotel on three sides, but at one end it was completely open, leading out to a teak deck that surrounded a perfect, still (and usually empty) infinity pool that clung to the edge of the cliff. Molly imagined that you could swim in that pool and look straight out to the ocean and the sky beyond, with an uninterrupted view. It must feel like having all the world to yourself. Not that Molly had ever swum in the spa pool. Not that she ever would

The air in the spa smelled of expensive perfume from the beauty products and of warm wood from the saunas. It felt as though a soft down pillow smothered the place, muffling the noise from the beach and the bars. The atmosphere was so calm and hushed that Molly always whispered when she was in here.

'Hey, Mols!' shouted a very loud American voice, from beneath a parasol by the spa pool. 'What you up to, girlfriend?'

Molly peered under the parasol. There, lying glistening with oils, was a topless Lexi Crawford, chewing on her gum and sipping on a piña colada. Molly almost dropped her towels. Lexi had been even more friendly since she'd warned off Mitchell and his friends, but it still took Molly by surprise that a Hollywood star would talk to her in such a matey manner.

'I'm just dropping these towels in and then I'm clocking

off,' whispered Molly, a little bashfully. 'What are you up to?'

'I just got my pussy waxed,' explained Lexi, very loudly, without embarrassment. 'And all my other bits. And I had a facial and a massage. It was kinda cool, I guess, but now I'm just ...' She looked down at her taut, bare stomach and laughed. 'I'm just navel-gazing I guess. Which is kinda boring and kinda dumb.' Lexi grinned up at Molly. 'You wanna hang out?'

Did Molly want to hang out with Lexi Crawford? Is the Pope a fecking Catholic, as her da would say!

'Um, yeah, sure,' replied Molly, sounding much more casual than her racing heart felt. 'I'll just get rid of these.'

'Sure,' said Lexi, popping her gum. 'Then we'll hang. It'll be fun to chill with someone my own age. You're the only girl round here who doesn't have claws!'

Lexi glared at one of the girls who worked at the spa as she walked past.

'Jeez, how do you work with these girls?' asked Lexi, so loudly that the whole resort must have heard. 'I've never met such a bunch of princesses in my life. And I know the Kardashians.'

Molly giggled. 'Wait a minute,' she said to Lexi and then she practically legged it to the spa reception to dump the towels.

When she got back, Lexi had wrapped herself in a colourful sarong and slipped her feet into a pair of jewelled flip-flops.

'Ready?' she asked Molly. 'Let's paint Paradise red, girl-friend!'

'Um ...' Molly looked down at her maid's uniform. 'I need to go back to my room and change. I can't go anywhere like this.'

'Where's your room?' asked Lexi.

'Up the hill, about ten minutes away,' explained Molly. 'I'll be half an hour. Why don't you wait at the beach bar for me?'

'Nah, that sucks,' said Lexi bluntly. 'I don't like waiting. If I'm gonna have fun, I wanna have fun now. Let's go to one of the boutiques. You can buy new stuff rather than trekking back to your room.'

Molly swallowed hard. It seemed like the girls had come across the first stumbling block in their fledgling friendship.

'I can't afford to buy anything from the boutiques here,' whispered Molly, blushing. 'I don't get paid that much.'

'I'll pay,' said Lexi, casually. 'I'm the one who can't be bothered waiting for you to change, so I should pick up the tab. It's no biggie, baby girl. I buy my girlfriends stuff back home all the time. It's one of the perks of being me!'

'I don't know,' said Molly, uncertainly. She didn't enjoy feeling like a charity case. She might be a lowly chambermaid but she still had a bit of pride.

'No arguments,' said Lexi, grabbing Molly's hand and leading her out of the spa. 'I wanna hang out. Hanging out with girlfriends means shopping, lunch and cocktails. I'm not taking no for an answer just cos your pay cheque's not big enough. Screw that! Money's there to be spent, Mols, and I've got shit loads of the stuff.'

Molly didn't feel like she was in a position to say no to the starlet when she put it like that. Lexi dragged Molly by the hand and headed straight for the resort's main boutique. Molly dug her heels into the tarmac.

'No, Lexi, not that boutique. Please. Let's go to the one on the beach,' she begged.

'Why?' asked Lexi. 'This one's bigger and better. It's got some really cool stuff.'

Molly stared at her feet. Mimi worked in this boutique and Molly wasn't sure she could face Mimi today without bursting into tears.

'I don't like the manager,' whispered Molly to Lexi. 'She's horrible to me.'

'Great!' announced Lexi. 'All the more reason to buy you loads of hot new clothes. Make her jealous. Which one is it, anyway?'

Lexi pushed open the door to the boutique. Molly followed her reluctantly. Mimi was leaning on the desk painting her nails. She looked up and narrowed her eyes at Molly as she entered. In Molly's head, Mimi's long, wavy hair turned into Medusa snake-heads and began to hiss.

'That one?' whispered Lexi, still being a little too loud.

Molly nodded.

'Thought so,' said Lexi. 'I've seen her around. She's a fucking bitch. Queen bitch!'

'I call her the head Mean Girl,' Molly confided in Lexi.

Lexi threw her head back and laughed loudly while Mimi looked on suspiciously. Molly realised with a warm feeling in her stomach that Mimi must be hating this – seeing her, Molly Costello, shopping with *the* Lexi Crawford.

'So, what do you need, honey?' asked Lexi, fingering the rails of beautiful clothes. 'A bikini if we're going to the beach, a beach dress of some sort, some sandals, jewellery and then maybe something special for another occasion?'

Molly opened her mouth to argue that it was all too much but then she caught the look of sheer hatred on Mimi's face and she immediately shut her mouth again. The curtain opened from the changing room and Lauren Hunter stepped out wearing an exquisite pale blue halter-neck dress. She said hello shyly to the girls.

'Buy it, Lauren baby!' exclaimed Lexi across the boutique.

'You look smoking hot in that. I thought you said you had children. You must be lying, lady! There's no way you've had two kids with a body like that!'

Lauren blushed.

'Do you think?' she asked, nervously. 'It's not too young for me? Not too short?'

'No,' scoffed Lexi. 'What are you talking about? You're not old. And if I had legs as long as yours I'd be walking around naked. Buy it!'

Lauren smiled at the girls and disappeared back into her changing room. Molly realised that despite her brash, loud behaviour, Lexi Crawford was a total sweetheart. Lauren Hunter was undeniably attractive, but for some reason she obviously lacked self-esteem, and Lexi had just gone out of her way to boost the woman's confidence. Lexi started grabbing armfuls of clothes off the rails and handing them to Molly.

'Try this, and this, and this ...' she kept saying as she laid more and more bikinis, dresses and kaftans over Molly's arms. 'Right, that's enough for now. Let's hit the dressing rooms.'

Lauren Hunter was paying for her dress now, still looking a little bashful and unsure.

'How is Mr Hunter?' Mimi was asking, cattily. 'He is such a nice man. So interesting, so handsome, so beautifully dressed, so charming and so funny. Tell him that Mimi says a big hello.'

Lauren mumbled that she would, waved goodbye to Molly and Lexi and then left the shop.

'That bitch screwed Lauren's husband,' said Lexi matter-of-factly as they entered the sanctuary of the changing rooms.

'No way!' said Molly. 'Mimi's engaged to Henri.'

'What? The blonde hottie at the beach bar?' asked Lexi, popping her gum. 'No way! What the fuck is he doing with her? He's gorgeous.'

Molly shrugged. 'I'm sure she has her charms. Somewhere.'

'Well, I don't care who her boyfriend is, that girl out there, she definitely screwed Sebastian Hunter. It was written all over her face there. That's why she was saying that stuff to Lauren. She was getting off on her conquest,' announced Lexi. 'Believe me. I might be young but I know these things.'

Molly said, 'Maybe,' but she didn't believe Lexi for a minute. There was no way that Mimi had slept with Lauren Hunter's husband. Lexi had it all wrong. Anyway, it was Antoinette who was flirting with Sebastian Hunter at the party the other night, not Mimi.

It took a very long time and a lot of trying on before Lexi decided which items of clothing she was going to purchase for Molly.

'Isn't she just the most stunning girl you've ever seen?' Lexi asked Mimi as Molly paraded around the shop in a backless black silk dress. 'Wouldn't you just kill for a figure like that?'

Mimi barely tried to hide her disdain. 'I prefer to be tall,' she sniffed. 'That dress, it is too long for her.'

'No, it's not,' drawled Lexi. 'All the girls are wearing them like that in LA. Anyway, if you're too tall, you look like a man in drag the minute you put on a decent pair of heels.'

Lexi and Mimi eyed Molly as she turned around in front of the mirror, one with a smile on her face, the other with a scowl. The dress was to die for. But it was six hundred euros. Lexi passed Molly a pair of snakeskin, strappy sandals with five-inch stiletto heels. They had bright red leather soles.

'Louboutins,' she said. 'Every girl needs a pair of Loubs.'

They were another eight hundred euros. Molly walked in the shoes very, very carefully. Partly because they were worth so much money and she didn't want to scuff them but mainly because she'd never walked in heels so high in her life. God, how Molly loved shoes. Oh, to own a pair of Louboutins! But, hey, she was getting to try them on and that was something. Even if she did have to hand them back to Mimi in a minute.

'Mols, you truly are the prettiest girl in the whole world,' declared Lexi. 'Mal and I were talking about it the other day.'

'Shut up!' giggled Molly, mortally embarrassed.

She knew Lexi was only trying to wind Mimi up, but still.

'No, I'm serious!' shouted Lexi. 'Mal did say you're really, really hot. And such a natural beauty too. You don't slap on the make-up and the false lashes like some girls do.'

Lexi glanced at Mimi, resplendent in full make-up and false eyelashes. 'I don't mind Mal talking about you like that, Mols,' Lexi continued, as Mimi squirmed. 'I'm not jealous of him appreciating other girls if they're worth appreciating. Anyway, you're a friend. We were saying that if you were in LA you'd have been snapped up by now. You'd be a movie star.'

Molly could practically see the steam coming out of Mimi's ears.

'We'll have all this, please,' said Lexi to Mimi, dumping a mound of clothes on the counter.

'Lexi!' squealed Molly. 'You can't buy me all that.'

'Why not?' asked Lexi. 'Anyway, you can't tell me what to do. I'm Lexi frigging Crawford. We'll have that dress and the Loubs as well.'

Molly stood open-mouthed in the middle of the shop. 'Lexi, have you seen the price of this dress and these shoes?' she asked.

'No, but I very much doubt it's something I can't afford,' she laughed, handing her Gold Amex to Mimi. Lexi threw a white bikini and kaftan to Molly. 'Get out of that dress and into this beachwear, baby,' she said. 'It's time for lunch and cocktails! You can wear the gold sandals, I think. The gladiator ones. Yes. And this necklace ... and this headscarf and ...'

Molly thought her head would explode with the madness of it all. Lexi Crawford had just spent several thousand euros on her. Was it right to accept it? The poor girl from Balymun didn't know. But when she looked at the bright smile on Lexi's face, Molly knew Lexi had got something out of it too.

'I don't have many girlfriends, Mols,' Lexi confided in Molly, as they skipped arm in arm down the path towards the beach. 'Thanks for going shopping with me. It meant a lot. I had a real good time.'

31

Room two, Paradise

Lauren hid the bag containing the blue dress at the back of the wardrobe. She didn't want Sebastian to see it, or its extortionate price tag. Lauren had no idea when she was going to wear something so frivolous or girlie but it had felt right. Impulsive and extravagant yes, but definitely right! And anyway, Lexi Crawford had told her to buy it. You don't refuse fashion tips from a Hollywood actress.

Sebastian had made himself scarce straight after breakfast and she hadn't seen him since. Maybe he'd been worried by her suggestion that they 'need to talk'. Everyone knows what that means. Had it crossed his mind that she was considering divorcing him? The thought would appal him. Not because he loved her. Lauren had completely given up on the fantasy that her husband had any such feelings for her any more. But a divorce would be expensive for Sebastian and it would tarnish his reputation as a wholesome family man. Yes, a divorce would hit Sebastian where it hurt most – in the wallet and the ego. Hmm, the more she thought about the idea, the more Lauren warmed to it. The girls would be OK. Maybe they would even understand. Hadn't Emily told Sebastian to his face that she wished Mummy would leave him? Did she mean it? Or was Lauren justifying the unjustifiable to herself?

She went out to the terrace and collected the manuscript from where she'd hidden it. Lauren had spent most of the morning on the terrace reading the pages – all one hundred and forty-three of them. She'd lost seven pages last night but she was pretty sure she hadn't missed any of the most important stuff. And she knew now why Clyde was in such a mess.

The man was hugely talented. His writing style wasn't flowery or complicated. He didn't use big words or complicated sentences but what he did do was create images and characters that jumped out of the page and came alive in the reader's mind. Lauren had been drawn into the plot immediately and she'd been unable to put the manuscript down until she'd come to the end of what he had written. It was the story of a teenage girl in New York, born into extreme poverty to a heroin-addict mother who died of Aids before the child was two. The heroine, Simone, was tough and foul-mouthed but she had such courage and heart that Lauren fell in love with her.

The story followed her sordid life of drug abuse, violence, prostitution and crime. The villain of the story was the girl's terrifying, violent and psychopathic pimp. The suspense revolved around whether or not the girl would escape her terrible life. So many times she nearly found a way to get out but her pimp would track her down, beat her up and drag her back in. Lauren willed the girl to escape with every page she turned and then the story stopped abruptly. There was no happy ending and, sadly, Lauen suspected she already knew what had happened to Simone. Clyde had told her on the beach yesterday.

Lauren had tried to talk to Clyde the minute she finished the manuscript but when she'd peeked through the patio doors to his cottage she could see that he was still fast asleep on his bed. Sleeping off last night's hangover no doubt! Broken glass, rotting fruit and his smashed laptop were still strewn across the deck as a reminder of his behaviour the night before. Clyde was in a total mess but Lauren wasn't scared of him. This time she really felt she could help.

She'd killed time by browsing in the boutique and 'accidentally' spent several hundred euros on that dress in the process; but now it was mid-afternoon, surely Clyde would be awake? With the manuscript under her arm, Lauren sneaked back through from her own garden to the one next door. She nearly jumped out of her skin when she spotted Clyde there, clearing up pieces of broken glass and plastic from his terrace. He looked absolutely dreadful. His face was ashen and he had huge bags under his eyes. Lauren's heart broke for him. She hesitated for a minute, hiding behind that bush again, and then she took a deep breath and stepped out into his garden.

'Hi, Clyde,' she called chirpily.

Clyde looked up, smiled at first, and then frowned.

'You shouldn't be here, Lauren,' he said. 'Leave me alone. I'm an asshole. A drunken, fucked-up asshole.'

'Stop feeling so bloody sorry for yourself, Clyde,' she replied cheerfully. 'There's nothing wrong with you that a good kick up the arse won't fix.'

'What?' Clyde's face was a picture. 'You can't talk to me like that, Lauren.'

'Yes, I can,' she replied, stepping onto the deck and gingerly making her way past the broken glass. Lauren sat down on a lounger and placed the manuscript on her lap.

'I've been reading this,' she said, patting the document. 'You're good, aren't you, Mr Scott?'

'It's a pile of crap,' he snapped. 'And you had no business reading that. It's private property. It's mine.'

'You threw it out,' she reminded him. 'Along with your laptop and the entire contents of your fruit bowl.'

'I think I hit that idiot husband of yours a few times.' Clyde allowed himself to smile a little.

'Oh, you remember that? So you weren't as drunk as you were pretending to be, then?' she teased him.

'Are you kidding? I was completely smashed,' said Clyde, shaking his head in shame. 'I vaguely remember seeing you hiding behind a bush in a tiny negligee though. Or was that a dream?'

'That was definitely a dream,' replied Lauren.

Clyde stood up and shook his head. 'I'm real sorry, Lauren,' he said. 'I'm ashamed that you saw me like that. I guess that's what they call rock bottom, huh?'

'Well, you have to hit the bottom before you can climb back up to the top,' said Lauren, smiling at him, hoping that he could see that she didn't think any less of him. 'I think you've been beating yourself up for nothing though, Clyde.'

Lauren lifted up the manuscript. 'I've read it all. I think I get it. The girl you talked about. It was Simone, wasn't it?'

Clyde sighed deeply, a dark shadow crossed his face and his knees seemed to buckle beneath him. He flopped down on the lounger beside Lauren.

'Sharona,' he said quietly. 'Her real name was Sharona. And she was the gutsiest kid I've ever met. She had so much life burning in her eyes that sometimes I thought she'd burst into flames right before me. How could that die? How the fuck could I let that die?'

'What happened?' asked Lauren. 'What happened to Sharona?'

'I met her in a hostel in New York. I was looking for teenage hookers to talk to. Research, you know, for the novel. I wanted to set a thriller in that world. There are so many criminals and psychos, and the girls, their stories really tug at the heart strings. And I thought I'd totally lucked out when I met Sharona. Her story was more harrowing than anything I could have dreamed up. She was sassy and smart and real funny. And her pimp was the biggest piece of lowlife scum who ever walked the mean streets of New York. Even her back story was like something out of a movie already ... Well, you must know that. You've read the first half.'

'And then she died?' asked Lauren, placing her hand gently on Clyde's arm. 'When you were still writing?'

His whole body was shaking. He nodded.

'By getting her involved, I killed her,' he said. 'I wanted to save her but instead I destroyed her. She trusted me. She told me all her deepest, darkest secrets. I was supposed to protect her. But I didn't keep up my end of the bargain. I was too selfish, too greedy, too self-obsessed.'

'What happened, Clyde?' asked Lauren again. 'How did Sharona die?'

'I made a deal with her. We plotted for weeks. In return for her story I was going to pay her fifty thousand bucks. That was enough for her to disappear.' Clyde looked into the distance, lost in his memories. 'She was going to move to Denver. I had it all set up for her. I'd even found her a job. A friend of Nancy's had a diner and she said she'd give Sharona a chance as long as I vouched that she was clean. And she *was* clean. She stopped using weeks before any of this happened.'

'So what went wrong?' asked Lauren, feeling devastated for the girl she'd read about. Poor Sharona had come so close to escaping. How on earth had it gone so horribly wrong?

'I wouldn't give her the money until she'd finished giving

me all the details about her pimp and his associates. There was some really hardcore stuff – human trafficking, bent cops, underage girls being snatched from their homes in Mexican border towns. And there were connections with some serious drug lords. You don't mess with guys like that. Sharona knew that she was living dangerously, talking to me about it all, and I was scared she'd do a runner. I didn't want Sharona to take the money and then freak out and disappear before I had the whole story.'

'That's understandable,' said Lauren. 'You were just insuring your story.'

'Maybe,' said Clyde. 'But wait, it gets worse. So ...' he took a deep breath. 'Finally we finish. She gives me everything – and I mean *everything*. This plot was the best ever – mesmerising, exciting, heart-wrenching. No one would believe it was based on pure fact. It was the perfect plot. We finish on the Thursday. I tell her I'll have the money set up in a brand new bank account for her by the Friday lunchtime. By Friday evening, she was supposed to be on a plane to Denver. Nancy was going to meet her at the airport and take her to some digs she'd sorted out. The whole frigging thing was planned so that nothing could go wrong.'

Clyde took another deep breath, ran his fingers desperately through his tousled hair and continued. 'That night, the Thursday, I go out in Manhattan with some buddies to celebrate. I think I've got the best fucking story of my career under my belt! I get smashed and I mean *totally* smashed. I'm so frigging pleased with myself. We go to a restaurant, then a club and then finally I go back to my hotel and I sleep for, like, ten hours. My stupid phone's run out of juice, I don't even know when, so I don't even get it charged up until gone eleven on the Friday. And that's when I get the messages.'

'The messages?' asked Lauren, seeing the tears well up in Clyde's eyes. 'What messages?'

'From Sharona,' he sobbed, turning round to look at Lauren. 'Five, six, seven messages, each one more desperate than the last. "Please, Clyde, he's coming for me. He's gonna kill me. I need to get out now. I know we said tomorrow but I can't wait. Can I come to your hotel? Please, Clyde. Save me, Clyde. He's gonna kill me this time."'

Clyde dropped his head into his hands and sobbed.

'But how is that your fault?' asked Lauren. 'You said Friday. She obviously left those messages on the Thursday night.'

'Yes,' said Clyde, tearfully. 'And if I hadn't been in some noisy club I might have heard those calls, and if I'd checked my battery before I went out, and if I'd even plugged the damned phone in when I got back to my hotel then maybe it would have been OK. Maybe I could've saved her.'

'You'll never know that, though, Clyde,' said Lauren softly, stroking his hair now, trying desperately to soothe him. 'How could you have known her pimp was after her?'

'I dunno. All I know is what happened next. So, I get the messages and I jump straight in a cab to her apartment,' Clyde continued, reliving the hell. 'And when I get there, the cops are all over the street and there's a coroner's van outside. I'm shaking now and I'm asking anyone who'll listen, "What happened here? What's going on?" Some kid tells me a girl's been found dead, that it's no big deal, just another junkie who's OD'd in that crack squat there. And for a moment I think, well, maybe that's not Sharona because Sharona doesn't use any more. Then they bring out the body and the guys from the morgue, they're laughing and messing around, because what's one more dead junkie to them? The frigging bag's not even done up properly and the girl's arm is hanging out and it's Sharona's arm. I see her tattoo on her wrist, and the ring she always wears and I see her short, little bitten nails and I know it's Sharona. And I tell you what, I don't care what it says on that coroner's report – that girl did not OD. If she died of a drug overdose then her fucking pimp injected her.'

'Did you tell the police?' asked Lauren, almost in tears herself at the desperate sadness of the story.

'Of course I did!' said Clyde. 'I gave them every last detail. I thought because of my work and my reputation in the field that they'd take me seriously, but they didn't want to know. Teenage junkie prostitute ODs. One fewer street kid for them to worry about. End of frigging story.'

'But it's not the end of the story,' said Lauren. 'You can still write Sharona's story. You're the only one who can make sure she didn't die in vain.'

'It's my fault she's dead!' shouted Clyde, the colour rising in his cheeks. 'I killed her!'

'No, you didn't!' Lauren shouted back, equally angry. 'That's just ridiculous. Her pimp killed her and you don't even know whether that had anything to do with her talking to you. It might have been over anything. You didn't break your deal with her. Did you have her bank account set up with fifty thousand dollars in it?'

'Yes, I did,' nodded Clyde, calmer now.

'Did you have her plane ticket to Denver booked?'

'Yes.'

'Had you found her a job?'

'Yes.'

'And somewhere to live?'

'Yes.'

'So ... what more could you have done?' asked Lauren,

pleading with him to see the reality of what had happened. 'Do you know what I think, Clyde?'

He shook his head.

'I think you've spent the last six years so eaten up with grief and misplaced guilt that you can't even see the truth. You did nothing but help that girl. You tried your absolute damnedest to save her. You had more faith in her and you gave her more hope and more of a chance than anyone else had ever done. You must have made her feel happy, proud, hopeful. I know it's a tragedy that you couldn't give Sharona her dream. But you gave her hope before she died. And that was something. That really was something, Clyde.'

Clyde was crying now. Sobbing hard into his hands. Lauren hoped that somewhere in those tears he was purging the guilt he'd held onto all these years.

'Hindsight's a great thing, Clyde,' said Lauren, stroking his hair. 'But regret's a waste of time. None of us can go back and change things. All we can do is go forward as best we can. Live for the present and the future; don't wallow in the past. You need to finish this book. It's brilliant. And if Sharona was half the feisty, big-hearted heroine you say she was, then she would want you to write her story. Was she excited that she was going to be in a book?'

Clyde looked up and his sobs subsided a little. He almost smiled as he remembered, 'She was so frigging excited. She said it would be the best book ever written, that it would be made into a Hollywood movie and she'd go to the premiere in a silk dress and diamonds. She said she was going to be a star.'

'So make her a star,' said Lauren. 'Give Sharona her dream. It's not too late. She might not get to go to any movie premiere but she can get into millions of heads. You're the only one who can do that. You didn't kill her,

359

Clyde. But you can make her immortal. You have to do it for Sharona and for the sake of your own sanity. Don't you see that? Let go of the guilt and pay tribute to her. It's the only way forward.'

Clyde nodded. 'I've never thought of it like that before,' he said. 'Oh Jesus, I've just realised how angry Sharona would be with me right now. She's probably up there hollering at me to get a fucking move on! She's waited six years for her movie already and I haven't even written the damned book yet!'

'Exactly,' smiled Lauren. 'So between us, me and Sharona are going to kick your backside until you get it done.'

'How?' asked Clyde, staring at her. His tears had dried up now. 'How are you going to kick my butt if you're in England and I'm in the States?'

'That's what emails are for,' retorted Lauren, sensing that Clyde was going somewhere a bit scary with this. 'And Skype and telephones and texts.'

'And what about taking your own advice?' he taunted her. 'About having no regrets and making the most of the future.'

'I don't know what you mean,' she said, defensively, knowing exactly what he meant.

'Your marriage,' he said, taking her hand gently in his. 'You're not happy. Your husband's a Grade-A Asshole, as we've already established, and you're just staying there, trapped in your miserable marriage by what? By your own fear? Or guilt for your kids? Or what?'

'You're right,' replied Lauren quietly. 'But it's going to take time to sort that one out. I have been thinking about it, though. Since I've been here. I've thought about, you know, the "D" word.'

'You can't even say it out loud,' laughed Clyde. 'You

English are so uptight. Divorce! It's nothing to be scared of. I've done it twice and I survived.'

'Just,' giggled Lauren. 'You look like the walking dead but you're definitely still alive. Just!'

'Come to Colorado with me, Lauren,' said Clyde suddenly.

'Don't be ridiculous,' replied Lauren, snatching her hand from his. 'That's madness. I only met you a few days ago.'

Clyde shrugged. 'I thought you said we should live for the moment and make the most of now.'

'I didn't mean—' Lauren began to say but Clyde stopped her. He placed his finger gently on her lips. His free hand reached for her hair. He pulled her face carefully towards his. Lauren held her breath as his beautiful, full, sensitive mouth came closer and closer to hers. His lips brushed Lauren's, her heart leapt, her stomach flipped and for a moment she allowed the warmth of his kiss to overcome her. It was just the briefest of embraces. Clyde's tongue barely touched hers before she came to her senses. But in that moment her destiny was sealed. Whatever happened, she could never kiss Sebastian again. She'd tasted something better now. She'd tasted something real. Lauren pulled away.

'No,' she said. 'I can't do this. I'm married. It's not right. It's not what I do.'

Clyde nodded and allowed her to pull away. 'I'm sorry,' he said. 'I shouldn't have done that. It was dumb. Why would a woman like you be interested in a guy like me?'

Lauren laughed. 'I didn't say I wasn't interested,' she replied. 'And I didn't say I wasn't tempted and flattered and confused and … All I'm saying is I'm still married.'

Lauren exhaled deeply. The pair sat in silence, side by side on their lounger.

'So, what now?' asked Clyde finally.

361

'We wait and see?' suggested Lauren, hopefully. 'We email each other, keep in touch. In a year, two years, who knows?'

'Jeez, you've got tickets on yourself, lady,' teased Clyde. 'You think I'll wait two years just to kiss you?'

Lauren blushed. 'No, I didn't mean that. Oh God, I'm no good at this sort of thing. I meant, can you give me some time? You need time to sort yourself out too. And then, if our friendship has grown, and we've kept in touch, and if you haven't run off with the latest Miss Denver, then maybe we can meet up in the future?'

'OK,' agreed Clyde, smiling now. 'I'll make you a deal. One year from now, you meet me in New York. No excuses. No maybes. No what ifs. I'm sure Miss Denver will understand that I have a prior arrangement.'

'No,' replied Lauren. 'I've got a better deal. You finish your book and I'll meet you in New York. If it takes a year, two years or another six years. You finish Sharona's story and I'll be on a transatlantic flight. That's a promise.'

Clyde's face broke into a wide grin. 'I reckon that's an even better deal. I'm pretty sure I can finish that novel in six months with you and Sharona kicking my butt!'

Clyde hugged her close to him. She breathed in the musky smell of him, felt his muscles rippling under his shirt, and the warmth of his breath on her neck. She drank it all in and hoped that it would be enough to keep her going until she saw him again.

'Friends,' she said. 'For now.'

'Friends,' agreed Clyde. 'But friends with benefits some time in the not too distant future, maybe?'

'Maybe,' whispered Lauren into his ear. She couldn't yet let herself believe that might be true. There was so much she had to do before she could be free.

32

The beach bar, Paradise

Lexi and Molly had eaten burgers and chips with their fingers at a table on the sand. They'd washed their lunch down with a bottle of champagne and now they were getting stuck into the cocktails. Molly was well aware that Henri was behind the bar only ten feet away but she'd stubbornly refused to look in his direction. She'd been relieved when it was Jacques who'd come to take their order. Still, her mind kept wandering to Henri. Every now and then she spotted a glimpse of his blonde hair out of the corner of her eye. She wondered if he'd noticed her new clothes. She wondered why she cared.

'Is it just me or is it getting hotter and hotter in this place?' asked Lexi, fanning herself with her hand and looking around the bar. 'I can't believe that Mimi bitch has bagged Henri,' Lexi continued, eyeing Henri and guzzling her third cocktail. 'I mean, look at him. That boy is be-a-utiful with a capital B! If I wasn't a happily married woman ...'

Molly forced a smile and tried to hide her feelings.

'What's up, Mols?' asked Lexi. 'You like the guy?'

'No,' said Molly too quickly, shaking her head far too enthusiastically.

'You do too!' replied Lexi, her eyes widening. 'Why don't you go bag him for yourself, baby girl? I don't usually agree with stealing other girls' men but that Mimi is one cold fish. She deserves everything she gets. He can't like her. I mean, she's quite good-looking, I suppose, but her personality is so ugly. Yuk!'

'I can't compete with Mimi,' replied Molly, truthfully. 'I'm not in her league.'

'What?!' Lexi spat out half her mojito. 'You are so far out of that girl's league that she's not even in the same ball park! You're crazy if you can't see what you've got going on.'

'Thanks, Lexi,' replied Molly. 'But it's complicated. Henri's not available so there's no point in me even thinking about him like that.'

'Crap,' said Lexi bluntly. 'Go and get us some more cocktails from him now.'

'Noooo!' squealed Molly. 'I can't. I won't.'

'You wiggle that cute little ass of yours up to the bar, flash those crazy green eyes and get us a couple of complimentary drinks. Go!' ordered Lexi.

Molly was caught between a rock and hard place: argue with a girl who'd just spent several thousand euros on her, or make a fool of herself in front of a guy she fancied who was engaged to someone else. She chose the latter. Lexi scared her more than Henri did.

'Work it, baby!' shouted Lexi as Molly walked towards the bar.

Molly blushed and prayed that Jacques would serve her.

'Hello, Molly,' said Henri. 'You look very nice today.'

Molly's knees almost buckled beneath her as she raised her eyes to meet his. As always, she almost melted.

'Thank you,' she managed to say.

'So, what can I do for you?' asked Henri.

Leave Mimi, fall in love with me, live together happily ever after, thought Molly.

'Um, why don't you surprise us with your special cocktails?' she managed to say instead.

'OK,' he said.

There was definitely an atmosphere. Molly felt awkward for obvious reasons – her heart was beating at about a million beats per minute – but why was Henri being so off with her? He'd been really unfriendly yesterday, too. Molly's heart hurt.

'Are you coming to the party later?' he asked her, obviously just trying to make polite conversation.

'Yes, if that's OK,' she replied, wishing she could say no without sounding rude. The last thing she wanted to do was celebrate Henri's engagement to Mimi.

'It's not what I'd planned,' he said, suddenly.

'What? The party?' asked Molly, confused.

'No, no, no, the engagement,' said Henri. 'It's not the way I thought things would work out.'

Henri trailed off. He looked troubled, almost sad.

'Mimi's a stunning girl,' was all Molly could think of to say.

Henri shrugged as usual, but the twinkle had gone from his eyes. He handed Mimi two champagne cocktails.

'That one is yours,' he said, pointing to the glass with strawberries in it and a rose petal floating on top. 'They're on the house.'

'Thank you, Henri,' said Molly, carefully picking up the glasses with shaking hands.

She started to walk away and then remembered something. 'What is this cocktail, by the way?' she asked, turning her head back towards Henri.

'True Love,' he replied, staring right into her eyes.

They looked at each other for the longest time. Was Molly going mad or had Henri just told her that he'd made her a True Love cocktail? Henri, whom she'd fancied since the minute she'd arrived at the resort. Henri, who'd never so much as tried to kiss her. Henri, who was marrying fecking Mimi! He was the most infuriating, sexy, confusing, gorgeous, annoying man she'd ever met! Molly stared at her new sandals, glued to the spot for a moment. Her head was spinning and her heart was racing. For the love of God, what was going on in that boy's head? Or was the confusion in her head? Had she just imagined that whole thing? Suddenly, an unfamiliar voice brought her back to her senses.

'Um, excuse me, miss,' the voice was saying, a little nervously. 'But I've been, erm, admiring you from afar all afternoon and I wondered if perhaps you'd like to join me for a drink one evening?'

Molly looked up and came face to face with a rather sweet-looking guy in his mid-twenties. She'd seen him arrive yesterday. Jacques had mentioned something about him being a film-maker from LA but he looked more like a college student with his creased linen shorts and his round, wire-rimmed spectacles.

'I'm here all week,' he added hopefully.

Molly glanced towards Henri to see whether he was watching. He was. Intently. Molly could have sworn that his mouth formed an involuntary '*non*' to the guy's question. Who the hell did he think he was? Henri had just got engaged and yet he had a problem with Molly accepting a date? Well, stuff him.

'That would be lovely, erm … I'm sorry, I don't know your name,' she said as loudly as possible just to make sure that Henri heard.

'Frank,' grinned the young man. 'Tomorrow? Here? At sundown?'

'Sure,' nodded Molly.

'The bar's closed tomorrow,' shouted Henri, almost petulantly.

Molly threw him a withering look. Closed? Really? Since when was the bar ever closed?

'No problem,' continued Frank, oblivious. 'We can meet on the terrace at the Plantation House instead.'

'Good plan,' nodded Molly, smiling smugly at Henri.

Oh my God, what was she doing? She didn't even want to go on a date with Frank – sweet as he seemed. She just wanted to make Henri feel jealous. Molly and Henri stared at each other almost angrily.

'So I'll see you tomorrow?' asked Frank, uncertainly, watching Molly, watching Henri.

Molly dragged her eyes away from Henri's. 'Yup,' she replied. 'It's a date. Now, I must get back to my friends. See you tomorrow, Frank.'

Molly glanced once more at Henri. He shrugged a sad little shrug and turned away from her. She swallowed hard. She felt sure she'd made him jealous but it felt like a rather hollow victory. Molly somehow managed to get back to the table without dropping the drinks. Thankfully Lexi was deep in conversation with Jacques and didn't notice Molly's bewilderment.

'What do you mean he took a taxi to the frigging airport?' Lexi was screeching at Jacques.

'I do not know,' Jacques was saying. 'Monsiuer Riley, he just say he has to collect a friend from the airport and he gets Serge the concierge to order him a cab.'

'When was this?' demanded Lexi in a rage. 'I'm going to fucking kill him!'

'About an hour ago,' said Jacques, backing away from the furious actress. 'I am sure he will be back soon. The airport, it is not so far.'

'I don't know what the fuck Mal is up to but he's not answering the phone,' yelled Lexi to Molly. 'Why is he at the airport? I don't understand. God, that man drives me crazy!'

Lexi was shouting so loudly that half the beach had turned round to listen to her rant.

'I mean, we're on our frigging honeymoon and first he brings his mother with us and now ... Oh. My. God. Noooooo!' screamed Lexi, staring up the path with a look of sheer horror on her face.

Molly followed her stare. Mal Riley was sauntering happily towards the beach bar beside a short, fat man with a green Mohawk hairdo. The man was wearing a fluorescent pink shirt, bright orange shorts and red Ray-Ban Wayfarers.

'Malcolm Riley, what the fuck is that bastard doing here? Malcolm! I'm going to rip your fucking testicles off!'

Mal shrank behind his companion. The short, fat man marched cheerfully up to Lexi, either oblivious to her fury, or enjoying it, Molly wasn't sure.

'Lexi, baby, you're looking mighty fine as always,' said the man in an Australian accent. 'Come and give Uncle Blaine a big fat kiss.'

'Go to hell, Blaine,' spat Lexi, folding her arms grumpily and refusing him her cheek.

'She loves me really,' said the fat man, turning to Molly with a lecherous grin. 'This is just her idea of foreplay. And who are you, gorgeous?'

'Molly Costello,' replied Molly, not knowing how else to behave under these weird circumstances.

'Blaine Edwards,' said the fat man, leering down towards her face. 'Celebrity agent and fixer extraordinaire. Stick with me, baby, and I'll make your dreams come true.'

He tried to kiss her hello on the lips but Molly managed

to turn her face just in time and got a big, fat, wet smacker on the cheek instead.

'Hi Molly,' said Mal, sheepishly, kissing her a little less lavishly on the other cheek. 'Thanks for looking after Lexi for me.'

'I am here,' snapped Lexi. 'You don't have to talk about me in the third person. I'm here and I'm really, really frigging pissed, Mal. What is Blaine doing on our honeymoon?! Christ, could this get any worse?'

'Babe, babe,' interrupted Blaine. 'I was on St Kitts; it's right next door. I just thought I'd pop over for twenty-four hours and say congrats to my fave clients in person.'

'I'm not your client. You're not my agent,' Lexi reminded him sternly. 'And if I get my way you won't be Mal's agent for much longer either, you odious little toad!'

'Calm down, Lexi,' said Mal, squeezing in beside her and trying to give her a cuddle. 'Blaine's just popped by to say hello. Isn't that nice?'

'Nobody "pops" to St Barts,' replied Lexi tartly. 'We're in the middle of frigging nowhere. And whatever it is Blaine professes to do, or be, nice certainly isn't a word I'd ever use to describe him.'

'Oi! You! Blondie!' shouted Blaine to Henri. 'A jeroboam of your finest champagne. *Tout suite!*'

Blaine snapped his chubby fingers impatiently at Henri, his gold sovereign rings glinting in the sunshine. Molly shuddered at the man's rudeness and began to see why Lexi was so upset.

'So, Molly,' said Blaine, squeezing his enormous backside into the seat beside her. 'What is it you do, lovely?'

'Ach, I clean toilets,' replied Molly, hoping that would make him lose interest pretty quickly. 'Anyway, I need to get off and get ready for a party. See you guys later.'

Molly got up to leave. She picked up her three bags of new clothes and started to walk as quickly as possible away from the table.

'And I need to help her get ready,' added Lexi suddenly, jumping up and following Molly. 'Bye, Mal.'

The two girls ran up the path, arm in arm, away from the beach bar as fast as their slightly drunken legs would carry them, laughing their heads off at their naughty schoolgirl behaviour.

'Isn't Blaine the biggest jerk you ever met in your life?' asked Lexi, breathlessly as they reached the top of the hill.

Molly nodded. 'I would kill my husband if he brought someone like that on my honeymoon.'

'You don't have a husband,' giggled Lexi.

'Oh yeah,' laughed Molly. 'I forgot about that for a minute there.'

'Come on,' said Lexi, grabbing Molly by the arm and pulling her along the path. 'Get ready at my place. There's more room. And I can help you with your make-up. We're going to make Henri eat his fucking heart out tonight.'

Two hours later, Molly walked, on slightly shaky legs (due to the absurd height of her heels), back to the beach bar. Most of the staff were there already, looking even more glamorous than usual in their best party clothes. Molly felt a bit shy in her brand new black dress and the fancy make-up Lexi had put on her face. When she'd looked in the mirror she could hardly believe the sophisticated young woman in the reflection was her. Lexi had done her hair so that it bounced in waves over her shoulders and down her bare back. She knew she looked quite pretty but she wasn't really sure that she looked like Molly Costello.

'Wow, Molly, you look amazing,' said Antoinette, rushing

up to her. 'Come and have a drink with me and Jacques. We are sitting over here.'

'Thank you, Antoinette,' said Molly with relief.

Antoinette had been sweet to Molly in private in the past but it took Molly by surprise that the waitress was being so public with her friendship. Molly glanced around the bar. She felt Mimi's eyes on her immediately. If looks could kill, Molly and Antoinette would both have been dead on the spot.

'Oh dear, someone's not happy about us hanging out together,' said Molly to Antoinette.

'Do not mind Mimi,' replied Antoinette with a flick of her hand. 'We are not friends any more. I am here for Henri. Although I feel very sorry for him.'

Molly said, 'Oh.' It was all she could think of to say.

She kissed Jacques hello, gratefully took the glass of wine he offered her and sat down at the table. She glanced around the bar, searching for Henri and spotted him chatting to a couple of the waiters at the other side of the circular bar. He didn't look her way. Was he ignoring her on purpose? She wondered if he thought she was stupid now, after her behaviour earlier. It must have been so transparent that she'd only accepted Frank's invitation in a childish attempt to make Henri jealous. She didn't even want to go on the date and had been thinking up excuses to get out of it ever since. God, she was an eejit!

Molly noticed that neither Antoinette nor Jacques seemed to be in the party spirit either. They gulped at their wine, frowned at Mimi and shared furtive looks of disapproval every few minutes. Something was going on but Molly was damned if she knew what it was. Every now and then the pair had quick snatches of conversation in hushed French. Molly couldn't hear what they were saying and as the evening wore on she felt more and more left out.

After an hour of sitting in virtual silence, Molly excused herself to go to the loo. She stared at her reflection in the mirror and wondered why Cinderella had made so much effort for the ball if Prince Charming was already engaged to one of the Ugly Sisters. As she squeezed past the party-goers on her way back to the table, somebody grabbed her arm. Molly spun round and found herself face to face with Henri.

'You look breathtaking tonight, Miss Molly,' he said.

Molly's heart lurched. Why was he doing this? Why was he suddenly paying her compliments when he was marrying Mimi?

'Thank you,' she said, trying desperately not to look at him.

She didn't trust her face not to give away her feelings. Molly tried to pull her arm away but Henri held his grip.

'This is not what I want, Molly,' he whispered in her ear. 'I have no choice but to marry Mimi. But I want you to know that if I had a choice ... if there was another way ... then I would choose you. When that guy asked you out earlier, I hated it! I think you know that.'

'I don't understand, Henri,' said Molly, honestly.

She allowed herself to look him straight in the eye. 'I'm not very sophisticated and I'm not worldly-wise. I don't know much about life or love or anything much really but I do know what's right. And I don't think you're being very fair, Henri. You're engaged to Mimi and you're saying this stuff to me. And it's confusing me. I don't like being played with. I know you enjoy flirting and that it's just a bit of fun for you but it's not fun for me. It's not fun at all.'

Molly felt the tears sting her eyes. She didn't want to cry in front of Henri, or in front of any of these virtual strangers.

Molly snatched her arm from Henri's grasp and ran away, through the crowds.

'Molly!' Henri shouted after her, but she kept running, tripping over her high heels and scuffing her precious new shoes.

She glanced back, just once, as she reached the edge of the beach. She saw Henri coming after her and then she saw Mimi step in front of him and block his way. Henri gave her one last desperate look. But what did it mean? What did any of this mean? She turned her back on the party and fled up the path that led away from the beach and the music and the party and Henri.

33

The Plantation House, Paradise

'Come in, come in, Henri,' said Monsieur Gabriel, ushering Henri into his private office in the Plantation House. 'Please, sit down.'

His face was grim, and whatever it was that he needed to speak to Henri about so urgently was obviously serious. Henri worried that perhaps his occasional weed-smoking habit had been found out, or that one of the married guests had complained about him flirting with his wife. But he rarely got stoned and when he did it was always back at his place with Jacques, far from the guests. And as for flirting with the wives, well, he'd hardly done that since Molly arrived. He'd worked out she was a good girl straight away and he'd been trying to impress her ever since. Well, until Mimi dropped the bombshell and his whole life went tits up ...

Henri felt sick to his stomach. How could he have been so stupid? Mimi was pregnant. Pregnant! God, the word still felt so alien. Henri had always wanted to have children. One day. In the dim and distant future. With a woman he loved. But not like this. Not now. And not with Mimi! But what choice did he have?

Mimi was a Catholic, so abortion was out of the question. And her father was a very important man in the French

374

government. There could be no scandal and no illegitimate child. Mimi had made it very clear that Henri's life would be made impossible if he didn't do the right thing here. How could Henri wriggle out of responsibility for this mistake? He had no choice. He'd done the crime and now he had to do the time.

It was true they'd had sex a few weeks ago and Henri couldn't remember being particularly careful. It was around Christmas and he'd been very drunk. They'd had a few drunken snogs since but that was it. Mimi was a stunning girl but Henri did not love her. Christ, he wasn't even sure he *liked* her very much! She could be a real bitch to the other girls and she was the ultimate spoilt princess. Yes, Henri liked to party with Mimi – they all did – because she knew everyone who was anyone on the island. She made heads turn wherever she went and she never had to queue to get in anywhere. If you went out with Mimi you always ended up in the VIP area, or at some private party on a Russian oligarch's yacht. Being with Mimi had felt crazy and wild and fun for a time, but now? Now Henri felt like he'd been thrown in prison – and Mimi was his jailer. No, it was definitely not love. It was a life sentence.

'*Bonsoir*, Henri,' came a voice from across the office, startling Henri back to the present.

'Antoinette?' Henri was surprised to see his friend there.

His friend? Was Antoinette his friend? he wondered. She was Mimi's friend, definitely. And a girl he often hung out with, but a friend? The truth was Henri had been a bit awkward around Antoinette ever since he'd drunkenly kissed her one night. Oh God, why hadn't he had more willpower? He suddenly thought of all the pretty girls he'd drunkenly kissed and realised that he'd have given every one of those kisses up for the chance of just one kiss with Molly. What a fool he'd been. Was he in trouble for kissing Antoinette? Why would he be? What was going on? How could his life get any worse?

'Antoinette has found some things that might be of interest to you, Henri,' explained Monsieur Gabriel, patting the spare chair by his desk.

Henri sat down, a little uncomfortably, beside Antoinette and opposite his boss. The office was dark. Only one dim brass lamp was glowing on Monsieur Gabriel's desk. It gave the elderly gentleman a strange, ghostly hue. This all seemed a bit creepy. The party had been in full swing when one of the receptionists had suddenly appeared and told him that Monsieur Gabriel needed to see him *immediately*. Henri had followed the girl up from the beach and had found the Plantation House in complete darkness. The restaurant was closed and so was the library bar. The pianist had long since stopped playing and the last of the guests had retired to bed. Now, they were here: Henri, Gabriel and Antoinette, crowded round the old mahogany desk, talking in whispered voices. It all seemed very cloak and dagger.

'What is all this about?' asked Henri nervously.

'You'll see,' replied Monsieur Gabriel solemnly. 'Antoinette, you may show Henri the articles you have found; there's a good girl.'

Antoinette was holding a small, flowery bag of some sort. A cosmetics purse perhaps. She opened it slowly and took out a packet of tablets. Henri shrugged.

'I do not understand,' he said, shaking his head. 'What are these? What have they to do with me?'

'These,' said Gabriel, rather dramatically, 'are Mimi's contraceptive pills. And, if you look carefully, you will see that they are up to date. Each tablet has a day of the week on it, see? Thursday. She's a very thorough girl; she's taken today's of course.'

'*Non*,' said Henri, shaking his head. 'Mimi is pregnant. I am sorry to break it to you like this, Monsieur Gabriel, but Mimi and I, we are having a baby. Anyway, what are you doing with Mimi's toilet bag?'

Henri noticed that Gabriel and Antoinette shared a knowing look and he suddenly felt rather stupid. What was he missing here?

'Antoinette brought these things to me because she found something out that made her feel very uncomfortable,' explained Gabriel.

Antoinette looked at Henri and nodded. 'I was scared to confront Mimi. I spoke to Jacques. He said to tell Monsieur Gabriel. That he would know what to do.'

'What to do?' Henri scratched his head. 'About what? What did you tell Jacques?'

Henri's head was spinning. Antoinette. Jacques. Mimi. Contraceptive pills. Why was Mimi still taking the pill if …

'Mimi is not pregnant, Henri,' said Gabriel finally. 'She has been lying to you in an attempt to trap you. It's one of the oldest tricks in the book but it's still pretty damn efficient, clearly. I can't believe you fell for it, boy. She tells you she's pregnant, you agree to marry her, then a few weeks later she claims to have a miscarriage. She'll be heartbroken, you'll feel sorry for her and so guilty that you'll marry her anyway. It's such a cliché! I thought you were smarter than that, Henri!'

Henri's first emotion was one of pure relief.

'Oh my God, that is so good. That is amazing. This is the best news ever!' he started to say, and then the doubts set in. 'But maybe these are old pills? How do we know they are from today?'

'I share a room with her, Henri,' replied Antoinette, quietly. 'I do not mean to spy but Mimi, she is not as clever as she thinks she is. I see everything. I know everything. Look.'

Antoinette took a half-empty box of tampons out of the bag. 'She had her period last week. All I had to do was look in the bin. It is true. She is not pregnant. She is just a liar and a bitch. I can't watch you throw your life away for lies.'

'Thank you,' said Henri, genuinely touched. 'Thank you, Antoinette.'

'You may go now, Antoinette,' said Monsieur Gabriel. 'Thank you, my dear. And remember, not a word of this to Mimi. I'll deal with her myself.'

'Of course, Monsieur Gabriel,' said Antoinette. 'Thank you.'

And with that she left. Henri sat there with his head swimming. He knew Mimi was a bit of a player but this?! This was outrageous! He couldn't believe that she had told such elaborate lies to him. But under the anger and shock was a much warmer, fuzzy feeling. With Mimi out of the picture, Henri could ask Molly out properly. He'd been given a second chance with the girl he really cared about and he sure as hell wasn't going to blow it this time.

'I have some other things to show you,' Gabriel continued. 'I didn't deem them suitable for Antoinette to view but I think you need to see exactly what that little girlfriend of yours has been up to.'

'Ah, but she is no longer my girlfriend,' shrugged Henri, the relief washing over him in waves. He was free! 'I do not really care what she has done.'

'Aren't you angry with her?' asked Gabriel incredulously, banging the desk with his fist. 'Don't you want her to be punished?'

Monsieur Gabriel's face glowed an eerie tone of green from the glass shade of the brass table lamp. He looked angrier than Henri felt.

'Her punishment is up to you, Monsieur Gabriel. You are the boss. Me? Me, I am just happy to be rid of her.'

'Well, perhaps this will change your mind,' replied Gabriel, darkly.

The older man picked up a remote control and swung round in his chair. The television behind him crackled into life. Grainy black and white CCTV footage started playing. Henri took a few moments to make out what he was looking at. Aha, it was the beach bar at night. And there were three people there. Two girls and a guy.

'Mimi, Antoinette and ...?' Henri squinted. Who was the man in the suit?

'Sebastian Hunter,' said Gabriel. 'But he is irrelevant, really. He could have been any of our philandering married guests. He is merely Mimi's pawn in her little game. He is not important.'

'When was this?' asked Henri, trying to piece the jigsaw puzzle together.

'Two nights ago, after the party,' he replied. 'Watch. Watch what she does now.'

The video footage had been taken in the early hours of the morning. The bar was all closed up for the night. The shutters were down and locked. Henri had done that himself earlier in the evening. Henri could see Mimi get a key out of her bag. She was grinning, looking very pleased with herself, showing off, flicking her hair, snuggling up to the married man. Hunter looked very pleased with himself too. He had a hot young girl on either side of him, both still dressed in their skimpy burlesque outfits, and now, as Mimi unlocked the shutters, he had a free bar to himself too.

'How does she have a key?' asked Henri, feeling his anger rising. The beach bar was his domain. No one had a key except for him, Jacques and Monsieur Gabriel.

'I expect she had yours copied,' answered Gabriel, a little sternly. 'It is not the first time she has stolen from the resort. She uses that boutique as her own personal wardrobe. She helps herself to whatever she wants – swimwear, dresses, shoes, jewellery – and never pays for a thing. And her family is one of the wealthiest in France! I have been watching her for a while now. I saw all this coming. Now watch, Henri. Watch and learn what type of woman you should be avoiding in future.'

Henri watched as Mimi ran around the circular bar, unlocking the shutters. She jumped over the bar and helped herself to a bottle of champagne that she handed to Sebastian Hunter and then opened another for herself. She offered Antoinette a swig, but Antoinette shook her head. Antoinette was looking a little upset now. She was shaking her head at Mimi and saying something to her. There was a lot of gesticulating and hair tossing. There was no sound to the footage but it didn't matter. It was quite clear what was going on. It looked to Henri as if Antoinette was telling Mimi that it was wrong to break into the bar. She was probably worried about her job. Or maybe she was just a much better person than Henri had given her credit for before. He had thought of Antoinette as nothing more than Mimi's lapdog. But finally here she was standing up to her friend. Mimi was having none of it, though. She had her hands on her hips now, Henri could make out that stubborn, spoilt look on her face and she was mouthing off at her friend. Antoinette looked to Sebastian Hunter for support but he just sneered at her and put his arm around Mimi's waist.

It was then that Henri remembered what he'd seen

earlier that evening. Everyone had seen it! Sebastian Hunter had been all over Antoinette, not Mimi, at the party. The Englishman had been dancing with the waitress like a dog on heat. Henri remembered seeing Lauren Hunter leave early, clearly distressed by her husband's behaviour. It was sad but it was no surprise that the married man and the waitress had ended up down at the beach after everyone else had gone to bed. But how had Mimi ended up with Hunter and Antoinette? Was she so competitive that she couldn't let her friend have anyone? Even if that someone was a vile, despicable married man! Henri remembered with a stab of fury that Mimi had been sobbing on him in the library at the end of the party, telling him that the only solution to their problem was marriage. And he'd fallen for it! He'd bloody well fallen for it! What a complete idiot!

'What time is this?' asked Henri.

'One thirty a.m.,' replied Monsieur Gabriel.

That was only half an hour after Henri had walked a weeping Mimi back to her room. She'd asked him to stay with her, begged him with crocodile tears streaming down her face, but Henri had told her he needed some space to get his head straight and he'd left her at her door. He'd gone home, lain on his bed and actually felt guilty for leaving her alone like that. What a sucker! Because Mimi hadn't gone to bed, had she? And she hadn't really been upset. She'd been scamming him! And then, when he wouldn't stay with her, she'd decided to find someone else to play with. And she stole from his bar! *His* bar! Had he not bought her enough cocktails over the months? Henri watched the footage roll with his blood boiling.

Antoinette left and within moments of her going, Mimi had wrapped her arms around Sebastian Hunter's neck. Henri watched disgusted as the pair feasted on each other's bodies. Neither of them looked at the other and they barely kissed. They just ripped hungrily at each other's clothes and took what they needed. Now Mimi was sitting on the bar with her legs spread wide. She was swigging champagne from the bottle and then licking her lips at the married man. Sebastian Hunter's trousers and boxer shorts were at his ankles. Henri could clearly make out his disgusting bottom, white compared to the rest of his tanned body, as it started pumping in and out of Mimi. The image made Henri feel sick. Not because he felt jealous or hurt by Mimi. It was just all so base. Here were two people who probably didn't even know each other's names, with no feelings for each other, using each other's bodies to fill some nasty, vile, gaping hole in their souls. They were both liars. Both beyond help.

'I think we've seen enough,' said Monsieur Gabriel suddenly and he switched off the television.

'Little bitch!' spat Henri. 'I'm going to—'

Gabriel shook his head firmly. 'No, Henri, you're not going to do anything to Mimi. You're not even going to talk to her. In fact, you never have to see her again in your life. It's all arranged. She's on the first flight to St Martin in the morning. Where she goes from there is not our concern but I expect her father will bail her out as always.'

'Good riddance. And Sebastian Hunter?' asked Henri, appalled that a man with such a lovely, beautiful wife could behave like this. 'Are you going to speak to him about this? He stole from us and he screwed one of your employees on my bar! Are you going to tell his wife?'

'Of course not,' replied Gabriel firmly. 'Sebastian Hunter is a wealthy, important man. I am in the middle of discussing a big business deal with him. It's unfair, but unfortunately in life men like Sebastian Hunter can do pretty much whatever they please. You don't need to worry about him, Henri. Just be thankful that you found out the truth about Mimi before was too late.'

Henri nodded. Gabriel was right. What did it really matter if one more married man had had an affair in Paradise? The sad truth was that it happened every week.

'There is something you have to do though, Henri,' said Gabriel, lowering his head and staring Henri straight in the face. 'Antoinette told me that there's a certain young lady who has been very upset about your "engagement" to Mimi. A young lady who, I believe, from watching your behaviour these last few weeks, you also have feelings for.'

Henri blushed and smiled. Just thinking about her made his heart melt. 'Molly,' he said.

Monsieur Gabriel nodded. 'Molly's a very special girl. You won't find one like her again. Go and get her, Henri. And for God's sake don't mess it up! Once you've got her, promise me you'll never let her go. And don't you dare ever let anything bad happen to her or you'll have me to answer to. Go! Now! Go!'

Henri was up out of his chair already. He'd been given another chance and he was going to grasp it with both hands. This time he was going to get it right. No more fancy cakes from the patisserie for him. He would never be tempted by their bright colours and sickly sweet charms again.

34

The viewpoint, Paradise

Molly made her way right up to the top of Paradise. There was a viewpoint, not far from Henri and Jacques's cottage, that looked over the rooftops of the resort and out over the ocean. By day this view was vibrant and colourful – lush green palms, bright pink flowers and turquoise sea – but at night it was very different, eerie almost. Molly perched on a bench and watched the lights of the fishing boats bob on the black water. Every now and then she heard a faint roar of laughter or squeal of joy float up the hill from the party on the beach. The boom, boom, boom of the music was more of a quiet background track than a theme tune. Molly sat and stared and thought.

Why was Henri marrying Mimi if it wasn't what he wanted? Why was he telling her that she was breathtaking and making her True Love cocktails when he'd just proposed to another girl? Why was he playing with her now he wasn't even free? Was he such a cold-hearted bastard that he would toy with a girl like that? Had Molly got him so wrong? Or was there part of the jigsaw puzzle she was missing? When he'd looked at her tonight there had been something desperate in his eyes. Molly's head hurt. She'd been drinking with Lexi all afternoon and then she'd had more wine at the party. She wasn't used to so much alcohol.

She didn't feel drunk, just exhausted, confused and very, very tired suddenly. Molly got up to walk home. She took off her shoes and started making her way back down the hill barefoot, carrying her beloved Louboutins in her hand.

Molly had only taken a few steps down the path when she thought she heard footsteps following her. She walked faster without looking round. Maybe it was just a turtle in the bushes, or an iguana. But the footsteps got louder and closer and they sounded decidedly human. Molly's little legs went as fast as they could. Her heart was beating so loudly that it thumped in her ears. The gravel path hurt her bare feet but she kept hurrying towards the staff quarters. The footsteps followed her. Molly didn't dare look round. The resort was deserted. Everyone was asleep, apart from the staff, who were all at the party on the beach. Who would be wandering around Paradise at this time of night?

Molly started to run. She tripped on a stone in the dark and dropped one of her shoes. She bent down to find it in the dark, desperately feeling around the stones on the path and the prickles of the bushes to the side. But she couldn't find her shoe anywhere. The footsteps were right behind her now. She stood up to keep running, reluctantly leaving her new shoe behind, but it was too late. Strong hands grabbed her by the shoulders and threw her into the bushes. He was on top of her by the time she saw his face.

'Mitchell!' she screamed.

Mitchell clamped his hand firmly over her mouth.

'Hello, Molly,' he said. 'I think you and I have some unfinished business.'

His breath smelled of stale beer. Molly thought she would faint from the fear. He had her pinned to the ground with his thighs straddling her stomach. He was so heavy that his weight winded her. One hand was thrust so hard against her mouth and nose that she was struggling to breathe; the other held both her arms above her head. She was pinned, with one wrist over the other as he ground his groin against her stomach. There was no way she could escape.

Henri almost skipped out of the Plantation House. Yes, he was angry with Mimi but much more importantly he was pleased with himself and with the hand fate had dealt him. He could hear the music from the party, still in full swing on the beach, and he wondered for a second if he should go back down. But it seemed ridiculous to go to his own engagement party when the engagement was very definitely off. Gabriel had headed down there to collect Mimi and to tell her she was fired. Much as Henri would have loved to witness that event, he thought better of it. Mimi would freak! And to be honest, if he never saw Mimi again in his life it would be too soon.

He wondered how Molly was doing. More than anything he wanted to go straight to her room, to knock on her door and to explain what had happened. But she'd left the party ages ago. She would be asleep by now and he didn't want to disturb her. What he had to tell her could wait until the morning. He hoped she would understand. And he hoped she would tell that American guy that she wouldn't be meeting him for sundowners on the terrace after all. Henri thought about how beautiful she must look when she was asleep and smiled to himself. He decided to head home. A good night's rest and he could wake up a new man with a whole new future ahead of him. He took the hill with a spring in his step.

The screams were muffled at first. Henri wasn't sure exactly what he could hear. There was some sort of rustling going on in the bushes up ahead. He couldn't see anything in the pitch blackness but he could hear something thrashing around in the leaves and, yes, that strange, strangled cry again. Henri wondered if it was an animal hunting or a stray dog attacking one of the resort's cats, maybe? He didn't like it. The hairs on Henri's arms stood on end. He crept closer to the noise until he could see shadows moving in the darkness. The weird muffled noises started to sound almost human. Whatever it was was big. It was huge. Almost as big as a man. Oh Jesus, it *was* a man. And he was attacking someone.

'*Ce que l'enfer se passé ici?*' shouted Henri. What the hell is going on here?

He didn't stop to think about his own safety. Henri piled straight in and pulled the man off his victim. The man was not as big as Henri, though he was thicker set. But Henri was fit and strong and he managed to fight off the thug's blows. They wrestled on the ground. Henri took a couple of punches to the face and several to the ribs but the other guy came off worse. Eventually Henri managed to hit him so hard that he lay unable to move for a second. Henri lunged towards the victim, still lying whimpering in the bushes.

'OK?' he asked, bending down to see who it was.

'It's me,' gasped an unmistakable voice. 'It's Molly.'

The rage in Henri surged like a wild beast. Henri heard a roar coming out of his own mouth as he lunged at the man, still lying on the ground. He grabbed the guy by the shirt collar, dragged him off his feet and held his face right up to his own.

'It's you,' he spat in the American's face, realising it was one of the stag party – Mitchell. 'You disgusting, fucking, perverted scum. I am going to kill you, you bastard!'

'No!' shouted Molly. 'No, Henri, he's not worth it. Really.'

Henri held Mitchell there, an inch from his face. He

tightened his grip on the guy's shirt collar so that he struggled to breathe.

'Did he hurt you, Molly?' he asked, his voice breaking at the thought of what this animal had done to Molly.

'Yes,' she said. 'He hurt me and he scared the living daylights out of me but I'm OK, Henri. I'm OK.'

'Did he ...' Henri stumbled on the words. 'Did he ... touch you?'

'No,' said Molly. 'Not like that. Not how you mean. He tried but I kept fighting and then you came.'

'But you tried to rape her,' Henri snarled in Mitchell's face. He had never hated someone so passionately in his life.

Suddenly Mitchell struggled just enough for Henri to lose his grip slightly and before Henri knew what was happening Mitchell had headbutted him right between the eyes. Henri cried out with the pain, his hands flew involuntarily to his face and Mitchell ran. Henri tried to go after him but Molly grabbed his leg.

'No, Henri,' she said, trying to stand up.

'We need to call the police. He must be arrested for this. He is dangerous,' Henri insisted.

'He goes home tomorrow morning,' said Molly. 'I just want him to disappear. I never want to see that man again. If we call the police this will go on for ever. He didn't get what he wanted, Henri. You saved me. You're here. Just look after me. Please. I was so scared, I was so scared ...'

Molly burst into tears and her body started to shake violently. Henri put his arms around Molly and helped her stand up.

'What do you want to do?' he asked her, pulling her shaking body towards his. 'Do you need to see a doctor?'

'No. I'm not badly hurt. Just take me to bed please, Henri. And don't leave me alone. Not tonight.'

Henri picked up Molly. She felt as light and floppy as a broken doll. He carried her carefully all the way to his cottage. He lay her gently on his bed, kissed her forehead, wiped her cuts and wrapped a blanket around her torn dress. He made her drink a sip of brandy for the shock and then he stroked her hair and watched her drift off to sleep. Her make-up was smudged all over her face, her hair was tangled and she was covered in cuts and bruises but Henri had been right. When Molly Costello slept, she looked like an angel. He curled up beside her, wrapped his arms around her and held her tight all night.

35

Room one, Paradise

Clyde woke up to the sound of someone hammering on his door.

'What?' he called, rubbing his eyes and trying to wake up. 'What the fuck do you want?'

'Clyde, it's me, man. Mal!' came the reply.

Clyde dragged his body out of bed, glanced at the clock (seven a.m., for fuck's sake!) and opened the door. The sunlight hurt his eyes.

'Mal, there's something you need to know about me. I do not wake up until after eight. I can't be held responsible for my behaviour at this time of the goddamn morning,' he muttered, letting his friend in.

Mal handed him a coffee. 'I came prepared. Drink this, wake up and I'll explain. I need your help. I think I've fucked up a bit.'

Clyde flopped back down on the bed and sipped his coffee. Normally he'd have been a lot grumpier about being woken up at this ungodly hour, but luckily for Mal, Clyde was in a good mood today. He was a man with a plan, and a future. He was a man with a new lease of life, thanks entirely to the lovely Lauren Hunter. Or the future Lauren Scott, perhaps? Clyde laughed at himself. What a romantic old fool!

'That's better,' said Mal, pacing the room impatiently. 'At least you're smiling.'

'So what's up?' asked Clyde. 'You look wired. Oh jeez, you're not back on the coke are you, Mal?'

'No!' shouted Mal. 'I am a reformed character. I haven't even had a drink yet today!'

'It's seven a.m.,' Clyde reminded him.

'Oh yeah,' said Mal, scratching at his matted hair. 'I haven't really slept. I'm confused. I've been so busy organising everything and now it's going tits up. I need your help, dude.'

'Help with what?' asked Clyde, half-amused, half-annoyed at the early interruption.

'With my wedding,' replied Mal.

Clyde took a deep breath. 'Mal, are you sure you're not high?' He spoke slowly so that Mal would understand. Just in case. 'You are already married. You have a wife. This is your honeymoon. A fact you seem to have forgotten as you first brought your mother along and then invited your agent. The last time I saw Lexi she was calling you every name under the sun and threatening to divorce you. What the hell are you talking about?'

Mal sat down on the bed beside Clyde and looked at him excitedly. 'I organised a surprise blessing,' he explained. 'On the beach, today. It's what Lexi always wanted, you know, the whole fairytale shebang! Gabriel's closing the entire resort off for us. I've got a fancy frock for Lexi – that's why Blaine's here – he brought the dresses and my suit – and there's an Anglican vicar arriving from Gustavia, and the food and the bubbly are all sorted but I forgot a couple of things. I think I've fucked up. I've got three hours!'

'Wow,' said Clyde, taking it all in. 'I'm impressed, Mal. You're a closet romantic underneath all that hair.'

Mal smiled soppily. 'I really love Lexi,' he said. 'I just want to do the right thing by her. But ...' He got up and started pacing the room again.

'Stop panicking, Riley,' ordered Clyde. 'What do you need? What can I do?'

'I need three things,' explained Mal. 'A photographer, a best man and I need to find the bridesmaid. She's gone AWOL.'

Clyde grinned. Sometimes things worked out just perfectly. 'Well, I know where you can find a shit-hot photographer,' he said.

'Where?' asked Mal. 'He needs to be good and he needs to sign a confidentiality agreement and he needs to be free by ten. Where do I find him?'

'You find *her* right next door,' grinned Clyde. 'Lauren Hunter, room one. She's one of the best in the business.'

'Oh, you fucking star!' shouted Mal, high-fiving Clyde.

'Next?' asked Clyde, enjoying himself now.

There was nothing like someone else's problems to take the focus off your own.

'Um, I erm, I need a best man,' said Mal again, a little bashfully, kicking his feet.

'So ask your agent,' suggested Clyde.

'I can't. Lexi hates him,' replied Mal. 'In fact, I kind of hate him too. It's a love/hate sort of relationship. The guy's an arse but he's my arse, if you know what I mean. I mean, he's not my arse, exactly – my arse is right here behind me but ... Blaine's not best-man material; let's just leave it at that, shall we? I mean, the thought of Blaine doing a speech ...'

'Mal, you're rambling,' laughed Clyde. 'I thought you were in a hurry.'

'I am,' said Mal, blushing. 'What I'm trying to say ...

392

what I'm trying to get at is … Clyde, will you be my best man, please?'

'Malcolm Riley, I would be honoured,' said Clyde, standing up and hugging his friend.

'Now, what was that you said about a missing bridesmaid?'

'Little Molly, you know?' said Mal. 'Lexi really likes her. I've had a dress made for her and everything. But she didn't turn up for her shift this morning and no one can find her anywhere!'

Molly was confused at first. She opened her eyes to an unfamiliar room with a pair of strong arms wound around her waist. She was still wearing her black, slinky dress from the night before. Her body ached and her head thumped and there was a strange feeling in her tummy. She turned round and found Henri, cuddling her and staring down at her with a silly smile on his face.

'Good morning, my angel,' he said. 'I have been waiting for you to wake up. How are you? OK? Do you need a doctor?'

Molly blinked, stretched her legs and yawned. The image of Mitchell's vile face popped into her head for a terrifying instant and she shuddered, but then she banished him to the back of her mind. That bastard wasn't worth thinking about.

'Um … I'm OK,' she replied, truthfully. 'A bit bruised and battered but I've survived worse.'

Molly allowed herself to snuggle into Henri's warm body for a moment longer. It felt so good to finally be in his big, safe arms after all those weeks of dreaming about him. But she knew, with a heavy heart, that this cuddle would be brief. She sighed deeply, took in his warm, musky man smell one more time, and then pushed him gently, and reluctantly, away from her.

'Thank you so much for what you did last night, Henri,' she said politely. 'I will always be grateful to you for saving me from that animal and for letting me sleep here but ...'

Henri was staring at her now, looking a little hurt and confused. 'But what?' he asked, trying to pull her body gently back towards his.

'But Mimi!' said Molly, a little angrily.

How could he forget his own fiancée?

Suddenly Henri's gorgeous face broke into a grin. His hazel eyes sparkled naughtily and his big shoulders began to shake with laughter.

'What?' demanded Molly, starting to feel toyed with again. 'Why do you always laugh at me, Henri? This isn't funny. I don't make a habit of waking up in bed with men who've just got engaged. God, you French are so free and easy!'

'I ... I ... I'm ...' Henri could barely speak for laughing. 'I'm sorry, Molly,' he sniggered. 'Free and easy? You think I am a French tart? My God, you are so funny ...'

'Stop laughing at me, you bastard!' shouted Molly. 'I'm sick of you doing this. I'm not your little plaything.'

Molly tried to get out of bed on wobbly legs but Henri clasped a gentle hand around her arm and pulled her firmly but tenderly back towards him.

'Mimi isn't here,' said Henri, staring at her intently with those heartbreaking eyes of his.

'Of course she's not here,' Molly replied hesitantly. 'You wouldn't have had me in your bed if she was here, would you?'

'It is a long story, Miss Molly, but basically she told me she was pregnant and I thought I had to marry her. Or else! That is why we got engaged. That is why I was acting so strangely with you. I wanted you, not her. But I thought I could never be with you. I thought I was trapped.'

Molly's heart thumped in her chest as her head tried to make sense of what Henri was telling her.

'But if Mimi is pregnant then you mustn't be here with me,' she said, pulling away from him again. 'You have to stand by her even if it's not what you want.'

Henri laughed again. 'You are even more of a Catholic than I am. God, my mother is going to love you!'

His mother? Why would Molly ever get to meet his mother? What the hell was Henri talking about? What sort of girl did he think she was? Molly could never get involved with Henri now: not when Mimi was pregnant.

'You're not right in the head, Henri,' she snapped at him. 'How could you try to seduce me when your girlfriend is pregnant? God, d'you know what? You and Mimi are welcome to each other. You suit each other just perfectly.'

'But ... but Molly, you've got it all wrong ...' Henri stuttered.

Molly stared at him, bewildered. Suddenly somebody started hammering on the door.

'Henri! Henri!' came a female voice. 'Is Molly with you? We can't find her anywhere! She's not in her room!'

'Feck!' shouted Molly, suddenly coming to her senses. 'What time is it? I think I've missed my shift!'

'Mal Riley wants to see her immediately!' shouted Antoinette.

'Mal Riley?' asked Molly, confused. 'Why would he want me?'

Lauren got the blue dress out from the back of the wardrobe. She'd had no idea she'd find a reason to wear it so soon. Mal Riley had just asked her to be the official photographer for his marriage blessing! Once the celebrations were over, the photographs would be published all over the world. She hadn't had a commission in over a decade and now here, suddenly, was the best job offer of her life! Lauren couldn't help jumping up and down and clapping her hands.

'Hmmph,' was all Sebastian said, before slamming the door behind him and disappearing.

Whatever! She'd told him last night that she wanted a divorce. His face had been a picture. He'd actually turned ghostly white, right there at the dinner table in a restaurant full of guests. And for a man as orange as that, turning white was quite a feat. He'd reacted as she'd expected him to do. First he'd been angry. He'd told her she was unhinged and that she needed medical help. And then he'd got bossy: he'd actually tried to forbid her from seeing a lawyer. And then he'd sent her to Coventry. He hadn't said a word since dessert. Which suited Lauren just fine. She had much more important things to do today. She pulled the wisp of blue silk chiffon over her head and grinned at her reflection in the mirror. Lauren looked good. Was it just her, or had she lost ten years overnight?

Lexi woke up to the sound of someone hammering on her door.

'Who the fuck is that?' she muttered to herself, pulling her pillow over her head and trying to ignore the noise.

The hammering continued.

'Fuck off!' she shouted. 'And if that's you, Mal, with that loser Blaine, you can go to hell. Stay away from me!'

'It's me, Lexi!'

Oh. Lexi sat up. It was Molly.

Lexi opened the door and peered out at Molly. Her friend was wearing a man's T-shirt, with bare feet and an exhausted look on her face.

'What happened last night, Mols?' asked Lexi, curiously. 'You look fucked! Isn't that the T-shirt I saw Henri wearing yesterday?'

Molly followed her in. 'Yes, it is Henri's T-shirt but no, it's not what it looks like,' replied Molly, shaking her head. 'And last night was ... Well, it was the worst night of my life. But there's no time for that now. There are more important things to think about. You have to get ready.'

Molly lay two dress bags on the crumpled bed sheets.

'Molly! Get ready for what? I was getting back into that bed,' Lexi complained.

She had no intention of actually getting up yet. It was barely half past eight.

'No, you're not,' insisted Molly, unzipping one of the bags. 'You have to get dressed for your wedding!'

'My what?' asked Lexi, totally confused and disorientated.

She watched as Molly carefully took an exquisite jewel-encrusted ivory silk gown out of the first bag and hung it on the front of the wardrobe.

'Is that Elie Saab?' gasped Lexi. 'Is that for me?'

'It certainly is,' said Molly, smiling now. 'Mal had it commissioned specially. He also sorted out a venue, a vicar, a band, a best man, a photographer and a bridesmaid. Ta da!'

Molly pointed at herself and smiled again.

'Only me, I'm afraid,' she said. 'But I guess he was a bit stuck for choice around here.'

Lexi stood glued to the spot, her head spinning. Mal had organised a proper wedding. And she'd been so cross with him. Oh God, she'd got it all so stupidly wrong. That was why he'd been so busy. Maybe that was why Irene was here and Blaine and ...

'I'm getting married,' said Lexi, the truth finally sinking in. 'O.M.G. I'm getting married, Molly!'

'Again!' added Molly, unzipping her own more simple bridesmaid's gown.

'Yes, but this time I'm going to remember it. And I'm not wearing my jeans!'

Lexi's squeals of excitement must have been heard all the way down at the beach.

'Have you got the bar bill for room eight?' the receptionist asked Henri over the phone. 'They're checking out now.'

Henri took a sharp intake of breath. Room eight, the stag party. That bastard Mitchell was leaving the resort. Henri wanted to storm right up to reception and tear the guy's head off his shoulders. He wanted to call the police and have the animal arrested. He wanted the pervert to pay for what he'd done to Molly. Why should Mitchell walk right out of Paradise scot-free? It wasn't right. But he'd promised Molly that he'd dropped it. She didn't want the pain of a police investigation or a trial and Henri understood that. Mitchell had money and connections. He hadn't succeeded in actually raping her. It was probable that he would get away with it, even if the police charged him. It sucked. Now all poor Molly wanted was for the sick bastard to disappear out of her life for ever. But still, Henri wanted just a little taste of revenge.

'Just one moment,' said Henri, placing the phone down and flicking through the computer on the till.

Suddenly, Henri had an idea. It wasn't the worst revenge he could think of and the punishment certainly wasn't strong enough to pay for the crime. But this would hit Mitchell where it would hurt him the most – in the wallet. Right, who had the biggest bill? Henri scrolled down the tabs and stopped when he got to Clyde's. Jesus! How many bottles of liquor had that man drunk? It was a wonder he was still standing. A slow smile spread across Henri's face. Clyde was broke; he'd told Henri that. This bar bill was going to cripple the poor man. But not if someone accidentally, say, lost his tab. Not if someone, for instance, deleted room one's bill and added it to room eight's instead. Not if a certain bar manager was to make a terrible mistake …

Henri picked up the phone.

'All done,' he told the receptionist. 'I've sent it through to your computer. It is a big bill, though. Do not let them argue about it. They are alcoholics and they are very rude. They have done nothing but drink all week. If there is any problem I am sure Monsieur Gabriel will agree with me.'

'OK,' replied the receptionist. 'No problem, Henri.'

Henri replaced the phone and poured himself a cheeky little champagne cocktail. He gazed across the beach from his beloved bar, watched the waves dance in the sunshine and the pelicans fly overhead. He thought about how deliciously perfect it had felt to wake up with Molly in his arms. And then he remembered that Mimi's flight left the island this morning. He never had to see that bitch's face again. Now all he had to do was explain the whole sorry story to Molly and then everything would be right in Henri's world. He thought about her storming out this morning, looking so sexy and stroppy, in a T-shirt she'd borrowed from him. God, he loved that girl. She was something else. And soon she'd be his. Henri sipped his champagne cocktail and raised his glass in a toast to all he surveyed. Sometimes this place really was Paradise.

'You look very smart, Mr Scott,' nodded Gabriel politely, as Clyde rushed into the reception, hoping that the corsages had arrived from Gustavia.

'Um, erm, thank you,' said Clyde, pulling at his morning

suit self-consciously. 'My mom always said I scrubbed up well but I feel like a penguin in this. Give me a pair of Levi's and a plaid shirt any day of the week.'

'Well, I think you look quite dashing. Every inch the world-famous author that you are! I do hope we'll have time to catch up properly at the reception,' Gabriel continued, passing Clyde a large box from the florist. 'I can see you're very busy now but I have been meaning to pick your brains about your writing. I really am a huge fan.'

'Jeez, thank you, Gabriel,' said Clyde. 'That would be great.'

He didn't mean it for a moment. The last thing Clyde wanted to do today was talk about work. After his chat with Lauren he felt more fired up and focused than he had done in years, but he wasn't ready for polite chit-chat on the subject. And certainly not with Gabriel Abbot. The old guy was charm personified but something about him gave Clyde the creeps. The very fact that he was here, for free, because Gabriel had deemed him an 'interesting' guest left a bad taste in Clyde's mouth. He didn't like being a charity case. And he didn't believe in a free lunch – or a free holiday, come to think of it. Clyde couldn't help wondering if he was a pawn in some game Gabriel was playing. There had to be a reason why he was here. Guys like Gabriel always did things for a reason.

'I am dying to ask you about how blurred the lines are between fact and fiction in your work. When I read your death scenes in particular I'm always convinced that you know what you're talking about. It's almost as if you've had first-hand experience. You really do get into the heads of those psychopaths. It fascinates me, Mr Scott, though, it absolutely intrigues me. Perhaps we are all capable of doing dreadful things if we're pushed hard enough. Don't you think it may be so much easier to kill another person than one might imagine? If the circumstances are right ...'

Clyde opened his mouth to answer but realised that he didn't have a clue how to respond. What the fuck was the old guy going on about? It was almost as if he could read Clyde's mind. Was there some way he could know about Sharona? Was that why he was here? Clyde stood there with his mouth opening and shutting as if he was trying to catch flies.

'Oh, I do apologise,' smiled Gabriel angelically. 'I'm keeping you from your best-man duties. We can continue this little discussion later over a cocktail or two. Ciao for now.'

Clyde nodded as politely as he could, grabbed the box of flowers, and made his way back out into the sweltering morning sunshine. He had far too much to do for Mal's big day to be worrying about what Gabriel Abbot was up to. Maybe tomorrow he'd talk to the old guy some more and try to figure out what was going on in that head of his. But not today. Today was all about celebrating. Today was all about love!

36

Mimi sat on the tiny plane as it took off from St Barts airport and headed towards St Martin and fumed. Monsieur
Gabriel had been so vile. He'd sacked her in front of all the
staff at the party – her own party; how humiliating! And
he'd called her a cheat, a thief and a slut. The hotel security
guard had then frogmarched her to her room and forced
her to pack her bags, and now she was on the first flight off
the island. Mimi had never been so insulted in her life. Just
wait until Papa heard about this. Monsieur Gabriel would
be sorry.

As the plane rose, Mimi could make out Eden Rock, jut-
ting out into the sea, and Nikki Beach, where she'd enjoyed
so many parties, and then, as the plane flew further away,
she glimpsed the colourful cottages of Paradise, nestled in
the palm tress. Mimi laid her forehead against the window
and watched as first the resort, and then the island itself,
became smaller and smaller and finally disappeared into a
speck in the turquoise ocean. Good riddance, she thought.
She was too good for all that anyway. She had been lowering
herself there. How dare Gabriel fire her! How dare Henri
reject her! How dare Antoinette turn on her like that! Who
the hell did they all think they were? Ah well, it was not so
bad. She had become a little bored of Paradise anyway. Papa

would find her a job in Paris. Perhaps at Chanel. Yes, that would be perfect.

Mimi looked down at her flimsy pink beach dress and jewelled sandals. She fingered her long, long hair and stroked her tanned thighs. She was bored of this look now. It was all so casual, so ungroomed. Urgh! What had she been thinking? And Henri? She shuddered. He was nothing but an overgrown beach bum. He was not in her league. What sort of life would she have had as the wife of a lowly barman anyway? Yes, Mimi had had a lucky escape. Suddenly she imagined herself with a sleek, sharp bob, wearing a tight black pencil skirt and high, high heels. In her head she was already strutting down rue Cambon, turning the heads of the beautiful people, eliciting envious glances from the women and lustful stares from the men. Perhaps she would get a small dog. Hmm, but which breed would best suit her new look?

'Hey, Frenchie!' shouted someone, disturbing Mimi from her thoughts.

Mimi looked up and saw one of the American men who had been staying at Paradise. He was leaning over his chair, calling to her, grinning. From the glint in his eye Mimi already knew what he wanted. She summed him up quickly. She took in his Rolex and his Ray-Bans. She noticed the cut of his shirt and jacket. She remembered that these men were from New York and that they all had important jobs in banking. One of them was getting married but it was not this one. This one was called Mitchell. He wasn't the most handsome of the group but he was rich and he was smiling at her. Mimi smiled, provocatively, back at him.

'*Oui?*' she replied in her sweetest, girliest voice. '*C'est moi.*'

Mimi immediately erased the images of Paris from her head. Instead she was now strolling through Central Park in the snow, wearing a full-length cashmere camel coat and tan leather knee-high boots. On her head was a floppy felt hat. She lived in a grand apartment nearby, with a doorman and an elevator. She did not need to work. Not even in a designer clothes store. Her husband was too rich for that. Instead she went shopping and met girlfriends for lunch. She occasionally helped to organise charity balls and in the summer she went to the family house in the Hamptons.

'Come and sit with me, Frenchie,' Mitchell was saying now. 'We didn't get the chance to talk back in St Barts.'

Mimi got up without a second thought and squeezed in beside the American.

'So where are you off to next?' he asked her, his hand already touching her naked thigh.

'New York,' lied Mimi.

In fact it was not a lie, exactly. She already knew she would call Papa from the airport and have him change her flight.

'Ah, what a coincidence,' said Mitchell. 'Me too.'

He grinned at her hungrily. He wanted her. And he was rich enough that perhaps he just might get her. But this was no coincidence. Mimi did not believe in coincidences. She was mistress of her own destiny. She was in control of her life. Mimi knew exactly what she wanted and she knew how to get it too. Mimi snuggled into Mitchell. She was one determined lady. Mimi was going to get what she desired from life if it killed her.

37

The beach, Paradise

Molly stood alone on the edge of the dance floor and watched Lexi and Mal swaying to the music, totally lost in each other's arms. She couldn't help but smile despite the sadness in her heart. The couple looked so happy and blissfully in love. She sighed a little wistfully. So maybe Henri wasn't 'the one' after all. Maybe he was just a French playboy who was far too cocky and good-looking for his own good – or Molly's! But one day she'd get over Monsieur Wrong and find Mr Right. One day she'd wear that same look of sheer joy that Lexi was wearing right now.

A hand touched Molly's bare shoulder suddenly. She jumped, still nervous after the attack the night before, and spun round to find Henri grinning at her – again!

'What?' she snapped, pushing his hand off her skin. She'd been avoiding him all day.

'I believe this belongs to you, Cinderella,' he said, handing Molly her missing Louboutin and bowing. 'I found it in the bushes this morning. I am obviously your Prince Charming!'

'Thanks,' she said, a little ungratefully, taking the shoe. 'But you're no Prince Charming. Goodbye, Henri.'

Molly turned on her heels and headed towards the beach.

'Molly!' shouted Henri, chasing after her. 'Molly wait, please. Hear me out.'

Molly hesitated. What could Henri have to say that she wanted to hear? He was engaged to Mimi. Mimi was pregnant. OK, so he'd admitted he liked her, but he belonged to someone else. It was pointless.

'What?' she demanded, spinning round to face him. 'Haven't you messed with my head enough? Don't you think you should get back to your fiancée?'

'Molly,' said Henri patiently. 'Mimi has gone.'

'Gone?' Molly scratched her head and frowned. 'What do you mean she's gone? Where?'

Henri stepped towards her and took her hand.

'Mimi lied, Molly,' he said slowly and deliberately, letting the words sink in. 'She never was pregnant. And the engagement was a farce. She was trying to trap me. She has been up to all sorts of nonsense. Monsieur Gabriel has sacked her. She's gone, my little angel. I am free. And if you want me, I am yours.'

Molly felt her mouth fall open. 'Wh …? What? When did this happen? I don't understand,' she stammered.

'I tried to tell you this morning but you were too busy shouting at me,' grinned Henri. 'I want you, Molly. Do you want me?'

He stared at her, his huge eyes filled with hope, and Molly felt her heart melt. His beautiful words hung in the warm tropical air. Molly drank them in. For a moment she stood there, just drinking in the delicious sound of those perfect words: I am free, I am yours, do you want me? And then her tummy flipped and her heart pounded and she couldn't contain herself a minute longer. Christ, did she want him! Molly Costello threw her arms around Henri's neck and she kissed him. She kissed him like she'd never kissed a boy before. And he kissed her right back. He kissed her with such warmth and passion and hunger that her whole being tingled, right down to the very tips of her toes. If Molly Costello had died at that very moment, she'd have died the happiest girl in the world.

'I have wanted to do that for the longest time,' admitted Henri, pulling away just a little but still keeping his lips tantalisingly close to hers.

'Me too,' grinned Molly. 'Since the minute I arrived in Paradise!'

'You are my paradise,' murmured Henri.

'And you are a very cheesy Frenchman sometimes,' giggled Molly. 'But I like it!'

Gabriel stood at the edge of the wedding party and surveyed the scene with both sadness and joy. It was such a shame that it all had to come to an end. It was exactly as he had planned. Paradise had been his dream – his and Ben's – and in its heyday it had been so fine. It *was* so fine. But all good things must come to an end and this, tragically, was the final scene. Only Gabriel knew this, of course. The others continued to celebrate with smiles on their faces and champagne in their hands and laughter on their lips. They had no idea how the plot was about to unfold. Blissful ignorance, thought Gabriel, as he watched from the sidelines.

Fittingly, the cast was both glamorous and gorgeous. The women shimmered in their beautiful dresses, the men looked handsome and proud in their sharp suits. The soundtrack was by a quite brilliant local jazz band. The young bride was radiant and glowing in her exquisite gown and the groom looked remarkably austere in his slim-fitting suit. If only Malcolm had brushed his hair. Ah well, some things were beyond even Gabriel's control. The ceremony had been wonderful. Truly wonderful. Gabriel had had to dab tears of joy from his eyes as the vicar had blessed the young couple's marriage. They were so clearly in love. Oh, how Gabriel missed that feeling. But soon. Soon he would walk with Ben again along the sandy shore and all would be peace and calm.

Henri and Molly were safe in each other's arms. He'd seen them kissing on the beach, so obviously smitten that it made Gabriel well up again. Oh how perfect this was. How utterly, wonderfully, heart-warmingly perfect. His favourite disciples, together in love. He couldn't have plotted it better himself. Gabriel thought he may have spotted another fledgling romance too. Clyde Scott and Lauren Hunter had danced together all afternoon and earlier, when she was taking the official photographs, Gabriel had noted that it was the author, rather than the husband, who looked on proudly.

Gabriel felt a little disappointed that he still hadn't managed to talk to Clyde Scott at any length about his work. Psychopaths really did fascinate Gabriel and no one wrote them as well as Clyde did. Why hadn't he invited his favourite author to Paradise sooner, while there was still time for the two of them to sit down together and talk over sundowners? It was a tiny little taste of regret in an otherwise delicious day. Ah well, at least Gabriel seemed to have found love for Clyde Scott. And with love comes inspiration. An artist always needs inspiration. Maybe Gabriel would be partly responsible for a great renaissance in Clyde's work. He did hope so. That would make him very happy.

Gabriel sighed. Yes, everyone was happy. Even Delilah appeared a little better today. She was surrounded by a group of handsome young men, who hung on her every word and admired her grace and elegance. Her dress was stunning, every hair was in place and she held her audience in rapture. Yes, it was just as she would have wanted it.

Gabriel looked out across the bay, saw the blackness on the horizon and nodded. A tropical storm. A great tempest. A crashing crescendo. Of course. It made perfect sense. The last few days had been unusually hot. The sand had scalded the guests' feet and the ice in Henri's cocktails had been melting in seconds. The air had become so humid and oppressive that it had been difficult for Gabriel to catch his breath at times.

The blackness was not far away. These were not the normal rain clouds that swept in, drenched the island and then disappeared. This was a sinister, dark blanket, hovering on the edge of Paradise, waiting to beat and batter her with its stormy wrath. The pelicans had vanished from the sky. They always knew before the humans when a storm was coming and took shelter in advance. Gabriel looked up at the palm trees. The gentle breeze was beginning to turn. The palms whipped against each other. On the beach, the women's dresses began to flap around their legs and the marquee that had been hastily erected for the wedding bent in the wind. Gabriel hoped the guests would be safe, sheltering there when this rogue, unseasonal storm arrived. He searched for Delilah in the crowd. He didn't have long now.

Blaine hid in the toilet cubicle and sent the email. There. Job's a goodun. Well, what did Mal expect? It was his job to get the guy publicity. His clients never really meant it when they said they wanted weddings, or funerals or even their sex lives to be private. What those egomaniacs really wanted was their faces plastered all over the front pages. Column inches were all that mattered. If you weren't in the news, you were yesterday's news. End of!

Anyway, he'd only taken a couple of photos on his mobile

while no one was watching. He'd struck a deal with Lauren Hunter for the official snaps and had been surprised at what a hard bargain the lady had driven. But then he remembered her from the good old days. She'd been one of the best. Her pics were always worth the dough. Next week Mal and Lexi would be on the cover of every celebrity supplement. And for now? Well, Blaine was only leaking his sneaky pics to one TV station. It was no big deal. Just a little taster of what was to come. Besides, he had to recoup the price of his flight somehow, didn't he? What was this – a holiday?

The email was sent, winging its way to London. Blaine did a fat line of coke on the toilet seat, sniffed hard and then rejoined the party. He grabbed a bottle of champagne from a passing waiter and swigged it from the bottle. God, it was a tough job looking after these celebrities. But somebody had to do it!

38

White City, West London

Rebecca was trying her best not to fall to bits about the fact that Sebastian was still ignoring her texts and calls. She understood that he was angry with her. He'd had no idea that Luke had confiscated her phone and she'd been unable to get in touch. He must have thought that she was deliberately ignoring him. And a man like Sebastian did not like to be ignored. But she'd explained it all to him now. She'd sent him several long, apologetic texts and left two messages on his voicemail. God, he was stubborn and pig-headed! She hoped he was just licking his wounds and making her sweat. Every few minutes she'd get her phone out of her bag and check to see whether he'd finally sent that elusive text telling her that all was forgiven. But as yet there had been nothing.

'On air in two minutes, Becky,' the producer's voice came through her earpiece.

Rebecca checked her lipstick and her hair in the compact mirror, glanced at her phone one more time and then reluctantly turned it to silent. She placed her bag neatly under the newsreader's desk and flicked quickly through her notes. Christ, what was she doing? Here she was about to go live on TV and she'd barely even given her stories a thought. Her head was entirely filled with Sebastian Hunter. Her heart raced and she felt a slight panic that she was more unprepared than she had ever been before. There was a brand new breaking story too. One that she hadn't had any time to prepare. Rebecca would have no choice but to just read the autocue with that one. She slapped her own cheeks a couple of times, in a vain attempt to knock some sense into herself, and then took a sip of water.

'Thirty seconds, Becky,' said the producer's voice. 'Is everything OK down there?'

Becky nodded into the camera 'Just feeling a bit lightheaded,' she said. 'Nothing to worry about. I'll be fine.'

'Ten, nine, eight ...' said the producer.

Becky could feel her hands shaking as she tried to put her notes neatly into a pile on the desk.

'Seven, six, five ...'

Her mouth was dry. She took another sip of water and tried desperately to focus on the celebrity news stories she had to report to the nation. For now she absolutely had to banish all thoughts of Sebastian Hunter to the back of her mind.

'Four, three, two, one ...'

'Good afternoon,' said Becky chirpily, beaming into the camera. 'And it's been another busy week for the Glitterati in Celebsville.'

Becky felt her shoulders relax. She was OK. She'd been doing this job for four years now and she could read her autocue on autopilot. Her knees stopped shaking under the desk and she reminded herself that she only had a fifteen-minute slot to fill today. She ran through a story about a rapper who'd been arrested for beating up his pregnant girlfriend in LA, and an ex-*Strictly* star who had started teaching a dance class in Blackpool. She positively whizzed through the story about Paris Hilton's new puppy and she even managed not to laugh as she discussed the merits of Katie Price's latest reality TV show.

'And finally ...' Becky said, hoping the relief in her voice wasn't too obvious to the viewers, 'we can bring you an exclusive, hot off the press. This is the biggest, glitziest, most glamorous story of the week and remember, you heard it here first.'

She waited as the photograph that accompanied the story was flashed up behind her.

'Yes, in a surprise ceremony, finally Mal Riley has given his teenage wife Lexi Crawford the wedding she deserves. After their drunken, quickie marriage in Las Vegas earlier this month, Lexi had been outspoken about the fact that her husband couldn't even remember the ceremony. She told news reporters in New York that she'd had to break the news to Mal that he was a married man the following morning. The singer, who is infamous for his alcohol and drug abuse, and who is a recovering sex addict, apparently had no recollection of the wedding.

'Lexi also complained to *People* magazine that she'd had to get married wearing her jeans rather than in the fairytale dress that she'd always dreamed of. But all that changed today, when the pair enjoyed a lavish blessing on the Caribbean paradise island of St Barts. The bride looked radiant in a diamond-encrusted Elie Saab gown and even the groom scrubbed up pretty well in a slim-fitting navy suit. The private ceremony happened on the beach at the exclusive resort, known fittingly as Paradise, in front of only a handful of guests. No media were invited. Rumour has it that security surrounding the event was so tight that even Lexi herself was unaware of the ceremony until an hour before. The entire event was a surprise, organised by Riley for his wife. So, despite his bad-boy reputation, it looks like

Mal Riley has a romantic side after all. We wish the couple all the very best. They certainly look very happy …'

Becky turned round then, to smile at the picture on the screen behind her, to show the viewers that she too was enthralled by the story. She only had moments of the programme left to get through now. She could do it. She was almost there. Becky's fake smile turned into a real one as she took in the photograph of the bride and groom. Aw, they actually looked genuinely loved-up. Lexi, every bit as beautiful as a young Elizabeth Taylor, was leaning her head against her new husband, with her hands clasped around his arm and her striking blue eyes brimming with tears. Mal's broad mouth was stretched in a huge grin that showed his perfect white teeth, and his eyes were fixed firmly on Lexi. He looked so proud that he might burst at any moment. It looked like the real deal to Becky. She was just about to turn back to camera to say goodbye to the viewers when something made her look back at the photograph.

Jesus, no. It couldn't be. She was going mad. Becky stared at the image as it swam in front of her eyes. But it was. It was him. He was there.

'Becky!' shouted the producer in her earpiece. 'Ten seconds. Wrap this up!'

But Becky couldn't move. Right there, before her very eyes, in all its vivid, lurid, extra-large technicolour glory, was a photograph not only of Lexi Crawford and Mal Riley, but of Sebastian Hunter too. She could see him quite clearly, heartbreakingly handsome in a cream linen suit, his tan deeper than ever, just to the left of the bride's shoulder. *Her* Sebastian Hunter. This didn't make any sense. What the hell was he doing in St Barts at a celebrity wedding? Becky's head felt as if it was going to float right off her shoulders. The studio started to spin.

'Seven seconds!' raged the producer. 'What the hell's going on down there? Rebecca, turn round and say goodbye to the viewers. Now!'

And then Becky spotted Lauren. She'd seen her only once before, when she'd sneakily flicked through the photos on Sebastian's phone. His wife had been hiding a little shyly behind her daughters in the photograph. But there was no denying that this was Lauren Hunter, in a beautiful pale blue dress, standing just behind her husband wearing the same shy expression on her face that she'd worn in the photograph with her children. Becky felt as if someone had punched her in the stomach. Suddenly Luke's words were reverberating around her brain.

'He'll be somewhere with his wife,' he'd said.

Becky let out an audible, 'Oh my God,' and felt her hands reach involuntarily for her cheeks.

'Rebecca!' screamed the producer. 'Pull yourself together! Three seconds!'

Quite how Rebecca managed to drag her eyes away from the screen and mumble, 'Goodbye, see you at the same time tomorrow,' she would never know. But that much she did. And then she ran from her desk, grabbing her bag as she did so. She ripped the earpiece from her ear, ignoring the producer's rant about unprofessional behaviour. She ran out of the studio and along the corridor. She didn't wait for the lift. Rebecca ran down four flights of stairs, two at a time, almost tripping over her heels as she did so. She flew past the security guard on reception and round the revolving door until it spat her out, sobbing and disorientated, onto the cold, damp streets of London. She scrambled for her phone in her bag, found it eventually, fumbled with buttons, paused for a second over the number that said 'SH' and then finally made the first sane decision she had in months.

'Luke,' she cried breathlessly into her phone. 'Luke, I'm outside work. Can you come and get me? Please. That thing, the thing you said would happen ... well, I think it just ... Oh my God, Luke, it just happened ... I think I just got my wake-up call on live TV.'

'I know, babes,' replied Luke, his voice full of concern. 'I was watching. I saw it too. I'm already on my way. Like I said, I'm still here for you.'

Becky stood in the January drizzle with tears pouring down her cheeks and waited for Luke. She had got it all so wrong. Luke had been good as his word – he was still here for her. But Sebastian? Well, Sebastian wasn't here for Rebecca now and she realised, with a shudder, that he never had been. None of it had been real. Not for him, at least.

39

'Where are we going, Gabriel?' asked Delilah, as he accompanied her up the path away from the beach. 'I was enjoying myself.'

'I know, darling,' replied Gabriel, leading her gently towards his front door. 'But the party will go on late into the night. I think you should have a lie down, here, in my house. Get some rest and then later you can have some more fun. Besides, I need to give you your medication.'

'I had my tablets this morning,' said Delilah, frowning at him a little petulantly.

'No, you're confused, darling. I forgot to give you them. You have to have them now. Here, sit on the bed. Take your shoes off. Get yourself comfortable.'

But Delilah wouldn't sit down. She wandered around the room, picking up trinkets and photographs. As always, she picked up the black and white photograph from beside his bed.

'You always looked after me, Gabriel,' she said, fingering the picture of the grubby little street urchins, sitting on the pavement outside their East London slum.

Gabriel stood behind his sister and rested his chin gently on her shoulder.

'Yes,' he said. 'Well, you were too good for all that. We both were. I had to get us away from there.'

'You did such a good job, George,' she whispered. 'Thank you.'

Gabriel's heart filled with love for his baby sister. George and Debbie from Bow. Born into poverty, to a mother who was a prostitute. What chance did they have? Gabriel had known from a young age that it was up to him to save them. He'd sent for Debbie from LA, the minute he had enough money. She had arrived, a stunning seventeen-year-old. She'd changed her name to Delilah and found work as a rather successful model. She'd fallen in love, once or twice, there had been an Italian American actor once who'd almost made her happy, but she was such a free spirit. Men didn't understand that they couldn't put this exotic bird in a cage. They always left her when they realised they could never possess her. She'd been a surprisingly good mother but even that had been snatched away from her far too soon. And so she'd ended up here in Paradise with Gabriel, still watching over her after all those years.

Delilah replaced the photograph and picked up another. This one, taken much later, was of a beautiful young girl, with long auburn hair and startling green eyes.

'I miss her,' was all Delilah said.

'I know, darling,' replied Gabriel. 'We all do. But you'll see her again. I promise. You'll see her very soon.'

Delilah kissed the photograph tenderly and whispered 'Bella' almost inaudibly. And then she lay down on the bed. Gabriel handed her a glass of water. He gave her a tablet which she swallowed down, and then another, and another, and another. She took them obediently, without question, as she always did. It didn't take long before she became drowsy.

'I'm tired, George,' she mumbled. 'I'm going to see Bella now.'

'Yes, my darling Debbie,' whispered Gabriel, stroking her cheek gently. 'Go and find Bella. Tell her I love her and that I'll see her very soon.'

Death came quietly and tenderly to Delilah. She had been tormented all these years and now, finally, her mind was at rest. Her condition had been hereditary. Their mother had suffered terrible mood swings and delusions. She had also suffered from acute depression. She'd taken her own life. As had their maternal grandmother and, of course, Bella. Ah, Bella. That had been the one that hurt the most. Gabriel felt no joy in taking Delilah's life. Of all the lives he had been responsible for, hers was perhaps the most precious to him. But Delilah could never survive without him and he couldn't bear the thought of there being no one to look after her once he was gone. He had no choice.

It was not the first time Gabriel had played God. He remembered with a heavy heart that day in the hospital in LA, when Ben had been in such excruciating pain. Gabriel had simply removed the oxygen tube for a few moments and then, once Ben was at peace, he had replaced it and rung the bell. Gabriel always knew when the time had come. He had always had impeccable timing. It was one of his gifts.

Gabriel closed Delilah's eyes and kissed her tenderly on the forehead. Gabriel felt emotional but not distraught. There was no need for regret. He would see Delilah again soon. Very, very soon. He said goodbye to his little sister for the final time in this world and closed the door behind him.

As he approached the Plantation House Gabriel spotted a lone young man sitting on the terrace, staring out to sea. What was he doing here? The place was supposed to be empty. He realised it was the film-maker from LA, Fred or Frankie or some such name.

'Are you waiting for someone?' called Gabriel, trying to keep the annoyance out of his voice. He needed to be alone now and was not happy about this unwanted guest.

'Yes, for Molly,' replied the man. 'She was supposed to meet me for a drink.'

'Oh dear ...' said Gabriel, patting the younger man's back in as genial a manner as he could muster. 'I'm afraid, my dear boy, that that ship may have sailed. I last saw Molly in the rather muscular arms of my bar manager. But why don't you head down to the beach and join the wedding party? There are lots of nice young girls down there. That's it ...'

Gabriel practically ejected the boy from his seat and started pushing him towards the path that led to the beach.

'But I'm not invited,' said the young man, hesitating.

'You are now,' insisted Gabriel firmly, giving him a shove. 'I own this place. If I say you're invited, you're invited. Now go!'

Sebastian watched as Lauren danced with Clyde, and seethed. Why did he feel jealous? He hadn't wanted Lauren for years. He remembered how he used to feel as a small boy when his younger brother, Tom, played with his toys. There was one battered old train in particular that had caused problems. Sebastian hadn't played with it for ages. He was bored with it and preferred his shiny new bike. Besides, it was a bit battered from where he'd thrown it on the floor all those times. The train lay under his bed for months, dusty and unwanted. And then one day Tom had found it. He'd picked it up, dusted it off and decided it was the best toy ever. When Sebastian saw his younger brother playing so happily with his old train, he'd been consumed with envy.

He'd snatched the train back from Tom and beaten his little brother black and blue. Of course, Sebastian never played with the train again. He hid it at the back of his wardrobe where Tom would never find it. Sebastian didn't really want the train. He just didn't want anyone else to have it either. It was a bit like how he felt about Lauren and Clyde now.

He looked around the party. There was no sign of that filthy French girl from the other night. Mimi. Yes, that was it. The one from the boutique who'd done such a good job as a burlesque dancer. She'd done an even better job on the bar later, Sebastian recalled with a smile. But she wasn't here. The other girl, her friend, Antoinette was here. She'd been flirting with Sebastian all week but today she'd given him a wide berth. He'd even caught her flashing him the odd disgusted look. Girls! They were strange creatures. Sebastian would never understand them. He guessed she was just jealous because he'd screwed her friend rather than her. But there was no need to be jealous. Sebastian would quite happily have screwed Antoinette too if she'd stuck around rather than stropping off when they broke into the bar. Silly girl.

Sebastian sighed. He was bored with no girls to play with and he was angry with Lauren. What the hell did she mean, she wanted a divorce? She couldn't be serious. The sun had obviously gone to her head. It would be Sebastian who would decide if and when their marriage was over. There was no way he was going to let her walk out on him. In a couple of days they would go back to London, to normality, to their routine and Lauren would come to her senses. She would do whatever Sebastian told her to do. He was the boss and when she got home Lauren would remember that.

He wondered if maybe he should give Rebecca a call. He would want to see her when he got home. But that girl needed bringing down a peg or two as well. She'd not only refused to return his calls and texts but she'd also told her stupid friend Luke about their relationship. Luke had sent Sebastian a ridiculous text from Rebecca's phone, warning him to 'stay away from Becks – or else!'. Sebastian wasn't frightened by the likes of Luke but that guy could be a pest. He was a flamboyant queer who worked in the media and knew all sorts of important people. Or so he reckoned. And he had a big mouth! News of their affair would probably be all over London by now. No, Sebastian would not call Rebecca. Not yet. She needed to suffer for a while longer after all the trouble she'd caused.

It had just begun to get dark and a full moon had risen above the sea. An eerie black haze dulled the moon's brightness and cast a strange shadow over the beach. It was windy now too. The bar staff were hurriedly taking down the parasols and ushering everyone towards the marquee.

'Quick,' the bar manager was shouting. 'There's going to be a storm. Get into the marquee. Now!'

Sebastian hovered at the edge of the crowd who were filing into the marquee. The first drops of rain had started to fall and the women were squealing about their hair getting ruined.

'Monsieur Hunter,' said a young girl in a waitress's uniform. 'I have a note for you. Here.'

'Thank you,' said Sebastian, taking the folded-up piece of paper, but the girl had already disappeared into the dry marquee.

It was raining hard now. Sebastian sheltered under a palm tree and read the note.

'Meet me in the library at the Plantation House. Mimi X,' it said.

Sebastian grinned. There. An easy solution to his

boredom and bad mood. Sebastian glanced around him and checked that nobody was watching. But most of the guests had already squeezed into the marquee and the others were so busy trying to escape from the rain that no one was looking in his direction. Sebastian pulled his suit jacket up over his head and ran up the hill towards the Plantation House as quickly as he could.

The big house was eerily empty and dark. The rain and wind lashed on the roof and windows as the shutters rattled in the storm. Sebastian wound his way through the corridors until he came to the library. The door was shut. He pushed it open, his mouth dry with anticipation. Mimi was just the way he liked them – young, beautiful, feisty and filthy as hell! He pushed open the heavy door and found the room in near darkness. A single lamp flickered in the far corner.

'Mimi?' called Sebastian, walking towards the light. 'Mimi? Are you here?'

Sebastian heard the door slam behind him and the sound of a key turning in the lock. He spun round, expecting to find Mimi, dressed provocatively with a dirty smile on that pretty young face, but Sebastian was sorely disappointed.

'What are *you* doing here?' he asked, incredulously. 'I was expecting someone else.'

'I'm sorry to disappoint you, Mr Hunter,' replied Gabriel calmly, walking towards the two leather chairs on either side of the low table and the flickering lamp. 'Please, sit. We have business to discuss.'

Sebastian looked at him warily. The man was obviously confused.

'I thought we'd dealt with all our business. Your people are going to have the papers drawn up for my people next week,' said Sebastian, perching on the edge of a chair.

Gabriel sat down opposite him. 'I must apologise for the

lack of lighting,' he said, jovially. 'We still have problems with electricity when there are storms. Phone lines, too. And also mobile reception. It all fails. Sometimes it's like living in the Dark Ages here. If anything bad was to happen no one would even know about it.'

Gabriel laughed. Sebastian shifted uncomfortably.

'You were expecting Mimi?' Gabriel continued, warming to his role, enjoying himself now.

Sebastian said nothing. His eyes darted nervously around the room as he tried to figure out what was going on.

'I'm afraid I had to let Mimi go,' Gabriel explained. 'She broke into the beach bar and also had sexual relations with a married guest. I saw the CCTV footage. Ah, but then you already know about what Mimi got up to the other night, don't you, Mr Hunter?'

Sebastian's face relaxed a little then. He obviously thought that was why he was here. To have his knuckles rapped for sleeping with a member of staff and drinking some stolen champagne.

'I can pay for the drinks,' said Sebastian. 'And I'm sorry for my behaviour. My marriage is essentially over and Mimi was practically begging me to sleep with her. I'm a red-blooded male. What was I supposed to do?'

'Quite,' replied Gabriel tartly. 'God forbid you would take responsibility for your own actions, Hunter.'

'I don't think there's any need for that tone,' said Sebastian curtly. 'I find that rather offensive, Gabriel. I told you, I'll pay for the champagne and I'll make a generous contribution to a local charity of your choice if that eases your mind.'

'It would take a lot more than that to ease my mind, I'm afraid,' replied Gabriel.

'Look, Abbot, I really don't know what your problem is but I think I would prefer to return to the wedding party than continue this conversation, thank you very much,' said Sebastian, half standing up.

An ear-splitting clap of thunder boomed overhead. The windows lit up with a flash of lightning.

'It would be safer to stay here,' said Gabriel. 'Anything could happen to you if you go out in a storm like that.'

Sebastian sat back down with a reluctant grunt.

'I believe we have someone in common,' piped up Gabriel, changing tack.

Sebastian eyed him warily. 'A mutual acquaintance?' asked Sebastian, obviously relieved to change the subject. 'Who?'

'Bella Romano. Beautiful girl. Eyes the colour of emeralds and the most exquisite auburn hair in the world,' said Gabriel, trying to keep the emotion out of his voice. 'Of course she's long dead, tragically.'

'Bella?' was it Gabriel's imagination or did Sebastian's face actually light up when he said her name? 'Yes, I knew Bella. Lovely girl. *Gorgeous* girl. How did you know her?'

'She was my niece,' replied Gabriel, honestly. 'Delilah's daughter.'

'Your niece? Delilah's daughter?'

Gabriel watched as the cogs of Sebastian's mind turned.

'Delilah's your sister?' he asked finally. 'I had no idea.'

'Yes,' said Gabriel. 'And she was Bella's mother. Bella's father was Italian. He and Delilah split up when Bella was tiny. Bella was all Delilah had in this world. She never did get over her daughter's suicide. Actually, it destroyed her. It destroyed all of us who cared for Bella.'

'I was deeply saddened when I heard too,' said Sebastian.

The frightening thing was that he sounded as if he almost believed his own lies.

'Really?' asked Gabriel. 'I would have thought that

perhaps your overwhelming emotion, when you heard about Bella's death, would have been one of guilt.'

Sebastian looked as if he'd been slapped in the face. 'Guilt?' he said. 'Why would I feel guilty? I barely knew the girl. She was the friend of a girl who worked for me. I met her a handful of times at social events, that's all.'

'Liar,' spat Gabriel, the anger rising in his chest. 'You had an affair with Bella for three long years. You tortured the poor girl. She was deeply, deeply in love with you and she believed all your toxic lies. You told her you were leaving your wife and that she was the love of your life. You played with her heart and with her life and when you got bored you discarded her like a broken toy. She never got over it. Never!'

Gabriel had meant to retain his cool a little longer but it was impossible now. The perpetrator was sitting here, inches away from him. Sebastian tried to stand up again.

'Sit!' demanded Gabriel. 'Sit down and listen to what I have to say. It's the least you can do, you spineless bastard!'

Sebastian sat back down. All the colour had drained from his face.

'What do you want from me?' asked Sebastian, nervously.

'The truth,' replied Gabriel, honestly. 'That's all. Did you love her?'

Sebastian thought carefully for a moment. 'Yes,' he replied finally. 'But there was nothing I could do. My hands were tied. I had a wife and baby. I couldn't leave. I was as much a victim as Bella. We were star-crossed lovers. It was all very sad.'

'Bullshit,' said Gabriel firmly. 'You could have left. You told Bella that you'd stopped sleeping with your wife and then she discovered Lauren was pregnant again.'

'She did?' asked Sebastian, obviously shocked. 'I didn't realise she knew that.'

'No, but then you stopped all contact when Lauren fell pregnant, didn't you? You knew your lies were blown. I expect you went straight on to your next mistress. Someone fresh and new who would buy all your stories.'

'It wasn't like that,' muttered Sebastian, looking genuinely upset for the first time. 'I did love Bella. I loved her very, very much. She was the only one. The only one I ever actually loved. I came so close to leaving Lauren for her, Gabriel. You have to believe me.'

'Why should I believe you?' demanded Gabriel.

'Because it's the truth,' said Sebastian. He had tears streaming down his face now. 'I tried to leave so many times. I even called her, when Lauren was pregnant. I wanted to talk to her and promise her that I would do it when the time was right. But she didn't reply and then her flatmate called me and told me she was dead.'

Sebastian dropped his head into his hands and sobbed like a baby.

'She killed herself because you broke her heart,' said Gabriel, feeling no sympathy for the man in front of him. It was a relief to see that he had some feelings for Bella at least, but mainly he seemed to be suffering from acute self-pity.

'I know, I know,' wept Sebastian.

'Sit up, man,' demanded Gabriel. 'Face what you've done. You didn't even go to the poor girl's funeral, did you? You couldn't even pay Bella your last respects.'

Sebastian sat up, shaking his head.

'Why didn't you leave Lauren?' demanded Gabriel. 'Honestly, Hunter. What was the real reason?'

'I don't know,' replied Sebastian, meekly.

'Oh, I do. It's the same reason that you didn't attend Bella's funeral,' spat Gabriel. 'I'll tell you the reason. It's because you have no balls!'

Gabriel pulled the revolver out from where he'd hidden it under the seat cushion earlier.

Sebastian stared at the gun in disbelief. 'You're not actually going to use that, Gabriel,' he said, a little hysterically. 'Don't be ridiculous. Put it away.'

Gabriel ignored him. 'So, tell me,' he continued, slowly and levelly. 'What's the problem with you, Sebastian Hunter? You've got no ...'

Sebastian sat glued to the spot, his mouth gaping open in terror. He spluttered and blustered but no words came out.

'Say it!' ordered Gabriel, waving the gun at Sebastian.

'I've got no balls,' whispered Sebastian in a weak, terrified voice.

'Louder!' shouted Gabriel, enjoying the power.

'I've got no balls!' Sebastian shouted back.

'That's right,' grinned Gabriel, enjoying himself. 'No balls. I wonder how you'd look with no balls ...'

Gabriel aimed the gun at Sebastian's groin.

'No, Gabriel, please,' pleaded Sebastian, cowering like a frightened child. 'Please!'

Another great rumble of thunder shook the Plantation House and drowned out Sebastian's pathetic cries.

'Your other problem, of course, Hunter,' Gabriel continued calmly, 'is that you have no heart.' He shifted the gun slightly so that it now pointed directly at Sebastian's chest. Hunter looked at him fleetingly, his black eyes filled with fear.

'I'm sorry,' he gasped. 'Don't hurt me, Gabriel, I'm begging you. I have a wife, children ...'

'I'm afraid it's far too late for that now,' replied Gabriel politely. 'Perhaps you should have thought about your wife and your children when you were screwing around.'

Gabriel couldn't quite decide the best course of action.

He shifted the revolver so that it pointed back to Sebastian's groin. 'No balls and no heart,' muttered Gabriel to himself, as much as to Sebastian. 'Deserves everything he gets but what should he get first?' he mused.

Retribution, as always, tasted sweet. This was not the first time. There had been Higgins and Timmy, too. Both had hurt him and both had had to pay. Gabriel had no doubt that he was a good man. A great man! He had known that he was special from a young age. He had never killed anybody who didn't either deserve it – like Higgins and Timmy – or need it – like Ben and Delilah. He had never worried about being caught. He was far too clever and far too good an actor for that.

But this – Sebastian Hunter's downfall – this was Gabriel's finest performance to date. Gabriel knew that above him, angels were applauding this, his last act, but unfortunately there would be no encore this time. His work here was almost done.

'I'm not a bad man,' whimpered Sebastian.

'Really?' was all Gabriel said as he finally pulled the trigger.

Bang! Sebastian Hunter slumped to the floor with a thud. Gabriel held the warm gun in his hands and watched his prey writhe in shock and agony as blood started to pour onto the rug. It made him smile.

'You, you shot me, you bastard,' spluttered Sebastian through his pain. His hands gripped his groin as he stared in disbelief at the blood. 'I think you got my leg. Just my leg …'

'Don't worry, I won't miss next time,' grinned Gabriel, pointing the revolver directly at Sebastian's heart.

Just as he was about to squeeze the trigger, the library door suddenly flew open.

'Stop!' screamed a woman's voice and Lauren Hunter stumbled into the room, dripping wet from the storm, waving her arms frantically. 'Stop, Gabriel. Don't shoot him. Please!'

Lauren's heart was in her mouth. Oh God, she should have done it sooner. She'd been standing there, with her ear pressed to the door, for the last five minutes. She wanted to hear every last, sordid detail of her husband's behaviour. But she didn't think Gabriel would have a gun. How could she have known that? It wasn't until she heard the shot fired that she'd realised what was going on inside.

Oh, she'd known something was wrong all right. She'd had a weird, uneasy feeling in her stomach when Sebastian had disappeared for so long. She'd thought her husband was with another woman again and she'd decided to try to catch him red-handed. Clyde had tried to stop her but she'd insisted on chasing after Sebastian. They'd exchanged cross words and she'd left him fuming and nursing a JD and Coke at the beach bar. But she'd had to do this. Even though it had meant running up the hill in the middle of a tropical storm. She'd thought it would be so much easier to demand a divorce if she'd caught Sebastian cheating. She'd expected to find him with his boxer shorts round his ankles, screwing one of the waitresses. But this? She had never, in her worst nightmares, expected to find *this* going on in the library.

Sebastian lay, clutching his inner thigh, writhing in agony on the floor, in an ever-increasing pool of his own blood. He looked up at her now, his half-glazed eyes pleading with her to make Gabriel stop. She nodded at him to reassure him. She hated her husband for what he'd done to her but he didn't deserve this. Nobody deserved this. Not even Sebastian.

Gabriel Abbot stopped in his tracks. He smiled at Lauren and then offered her the gun.

'You can do it if you like,' he said, nodding, encouraging her to take it. 'You have even more right to finish him off than I do. I expect you'll enjoy it.'

Lauren's legs were shaking and her heart was beating so loudly that she could barely hear herself think. Gabriel Abbot was clearly deranged.

'Put the gun down, Gabriel,' she said, trying to sound much calmer than she felt. 'No one is going to kill Sebastian. We're going to call an ambulance, get him to hospital and he's going to be just fine. Do you hear me, Sebastian? You're going to be OK. We'll get help now.'

'No!' shouted Gabriel angrily. 'He has to die. He killed Bella! He cheated on you, Lauren. Don't be a victim all your life.'

'I know what he did,' replied Lauren, edging towards Gabriel, still holding her shaking hand out for the gun. 'I was listening at the door. I heard it all.'

Gabriel's eyes flashed with rage. He snatched his hand back from her and aimed the gun at Sebastian again. Instinctively Lauren stepped right in front of the gun, blocking Gabriel's shot. She was scared and she was devastated by what she'd heard but she couldn't just stand back and let Gabriel kill Sebastian.

'Don't be stupid, Lauren,' spat Gabriel. 'Why would you protect him? Why are you being so weak? This is your way out. I'm offering you your freedom.'

Lauren shook her head firmly and stood glued to the spot. 'I will get my freedom, Gabriel,' she said. And she meant it. She would. 'But not like this. This is the wrong way. Give me the gun.'

Lauren reached her hand out one more time. Gabriel stared at her with his pale, pale blue eyes. It hit her suddenly that, just like Sebastian, Gabriel's eyes were impenetrable.

She couldn't see his soul. Perhaps neither of them had one. Perhaps these two men had something other than Bella in common after all.

Gabriel stared at Lauren without blinking, and smiled. 'Silly girl,' he said. 'So many silly, silly girls.'

For one terrible moment Lauren felt sure that Gabriel was going to shoot her too. But then he lifted the gun towards his own head, aimed it at his right temple and pulled the trigger without hesitation.

'Christ, no! No!' screamed Lauren, lunging towards the old man. But it was too late. Gabriel Abbot had died with a smirk on his lips. As he lay lifeless on the floor, with blood oozing from his head, his eyes remained firmly open, staring up at Lauren. Gabriel Abbot had taken his final curtain call.

'Did you hear that?' Henri asked Jacques, as they made cocktails behind the bar in the marquee.

The storm raged outside but the party continued. What else were they all supposed to do while they were stuck in here?

'Did I hear what?' asked Jacques, tossing a bottle of absinthe at Henri.

'Those bangs. It sounded like gunfire,' replied Henri, pouring two drinks into shot glasses.

'Don't be silly,' scoffed Jacques. 'It's the thunder.'

'Yeah, you're right. Of course it is,' said Henri, handing his friend one of the shots.

'What are we drinking, boys?' asked Molly, leaning up over the bar with her eyes shining happily.

'Zombies!' replied Henri and Jacques in unison.

'Sounds about right for a night like this,' laughed Molly. 'Cheers!'

*

Clyde heard the bangs too. Something at the back of his mind had told him that the bangs were not claps of thunder. Hell, he knew what a revolver sounded like. But there were no guns in Paradise. Surely? There were guns in New York, and Las Vegas, and Miami, but there were no guns here. The noise made Clyde feel unsettled, fearful even, but he told himself he was being stupid and he did nothing. He sat, and he sulked, and he drank, and he licked his wounds. It was the same old story. Clyde did nothing. Just as he'd done nothing to save Sharona... It wasn't until he heard the faint sound of sirens approaching the resort that a burning panic filled his chest and instinct took over. Clyde was up on his feet and running towards the Plantation House in an instant.

'Lauren!' he hollered from the bottom of the beach track. 'Lauren!'

He yelled her name desperately as he ran, faster and faster, up the steep path towards the Plantation House, but his words were whipped up by the squall and silenced by the lashing rain. Would that bastard actually hurt Lauren? Clyde's mind raced as fast as his feet. Would Sebastian shoot her just to be rid of her? Had she caught him with another woman and things had got out of control? But where would Sebastian get a gun? Why would anybody here, at Paradise, be carrying firearms? It was crazy. None of it made sense. Oh God, please let Lauren be OK. Please God. Please ...

As Clyde finally reached the cliff top he heard the sound of sirens arriving in Paradise, and then cars screeching into the resort. By the time he staggered, exhausted and soaking, round the corner to the front of the Plantation House, the police were already blocking the entrance. An ambulance sat with its doors open, waiting at the foyer.

'No entry, sir,' stated an officer gravely as Clyde tried to get into the building. 'This is a crime scene. Stay back.'

'Who got shot?' demanded Clyde, craning his neck, trying to see what was happening inside. 'Is everyone OK? I need to know if Mrs Lauren Hunter is OK. I need to know. Please.'

But the policeman just shook his head. 'I can't give you any details, sir.'

Clyde saw the stretcher being carried towards the door and a dreadful feeling of déjà vu washed over him. It was just like Sharona all over again. A flashback of the stretcher, and the body bag, and the limp arm swinging over the side, made Clyde's knees buckle. He could barely find the courage to force himself to look. As the paramedics got closer, Clyde realised with a rush of relief that it was a man's body. And he was still alive. Clyde watched, emotionless, as Sebastian Hunter was carried past towards the waiting ambulance. And then he saw her. Lauren. Looking haunted and devastated and tear-stained and distraught, but she was walking. She was walking straight towards him and she was very definitely alive.

He held his arms out to her and she fell into them, gratefully, for a few moments.

'It was Gabriel Abbot,' she said in a tiny, shaky voice. 'He shot Sebastian and then he turned the gun on himself. I was there. It was awful. I can't believe it ... I don't understand ...'

'Shhh,' said Clyde gently, trying to hold her closer.

He desperately wanted to make her feel safe. But she pulled away.

'I have to go,' she said.

'Where?' asked Clyde.

'With Sebastian,' she replied. She looked exhausted.

'No, I'll take you to the hospital,' Clyde offered. 'I'll get you a brandy and some dry clothes and then I'll borrow Henri's car. Stay with me.'

Lauren shook her head firmly. 'No. I'm going with Sebastian. I have to.'

'Why?' asked Clyde.

'Because he's still my husband,' was all Lauren said.

As the ambulance pulled away from Paradise, Lauren glanced back at Clyde from the window. She gave him a weak smile and waved, just once, before turning away. Clyde slumped down onto the kerb and lit a cigarette. The worst of the storm had passed but it was still raining pretty hard. He drew hard on his Marlboro and watched police cars, a coroner's van and a forensic team descend on Paradise. This holiday was definitely over.

Epilogue

One year later ...

Clyde's heart was racing faster than Shiloh's hooves as he galloped her across the plain. He thought his heart would burst with happiness just to have his beloved horse back where she belonged! If anyone could see him now with this ridiculous grin on his face they would think he was a stark raving lunatic. But thankfully, he and Shiloh were alone here, flying through the cold Colorado air so fast that Clyde felt sure they could take off and fly like Pegasus if they wanted to.

The sky was dark grey and oppressively low. An icy drizzle had soaked them both to the bone but neither of them cared. Clyde knew that his horse had been as delighted to see him as he had been to see her. She'd spotted him from across the corral. She'd looked, blinked, looked again and then the crazy mare had reared up on her hind legs and whinnied like a wild stallion. They'd run towards each other like parted lovers reunited, and as Clyde had buried his face in the familiar, musky scent of her muzzle, the tears had come thick and fast.

'I promised you I'd be back, Shiloh,' he'd whispered to her. 'Didn't I, baby? Didn't I? Well, here I am. You're coming home, Shiloh. Where you belong.'

It was dark when they got back to McNabb's place and the old man was pacing the yard impatiently and tapping his watch.

'She's got into a good routine with me, Clyde,' the old

436

man scolded him. 'Don't you go messing around with the poor animal, confusing her and getting her into bad habits. She should've been stabled a half-hour ago now.'

Clyde grinned to himself. He knew that McNabb had grown fond of Shiloh this past year and now that he had to hand her back, he was clucking around the horse like a first-time dad around his newborn baby.

'D'you wanna write me a schedule of her routine?' teased Clyde. 'So that I don't upset the princess?'

McNabb ignored him. 'When you coming for her then, son?' he asked instead, grabbing Shiloh's reins from Clyde. 'You ain't having her back until that money's in my bank. And don't forget the five per cent interest. I ain't running no charity here.'

'Monday, first thing,' smiled Clyde. He couldn't help smiling today. When had it all started to go so damn right all of a sudden? 'The money hits my account tomorrow and I get the keys to the new house too, but it'll all have to wait until Monday. I've got important business this weekend so I gotta go away for a couple of days.'

'You got a decent stable at your new place?' demanded McNabb.

'I sure do,' Clyde reassured him. 'The house isn't big but the paddock and stables are huge. Shiloh'll be living in luxury while I slum it inside!'

McNabb managed a smile. It wasn't true, of course. The new house was nowhere near as big as the ranch house had been but it was a brand new, architect-designed pad, with cedar cladding, huge windows and modern clean lines. It was quite flash if Clyde was honest. A far cry from the shack he'd been living in this time last year. He'd been offered a second chance in life, a clean sheet, and Clyde wanted everything in his life to be new now. Well, everything except for Shiloh of course ...

Clyde kissed the horse's nose softly. 'I'll be back in three days, baby,' he told her. 'And then we'll have all the time in the world together.'

As Clyde turned to go, McNabb grabbed his arm. The old man looked a little moist-eyed.

'Clyde,' he said, awkwardly. 'I just wanted to say well done. You know, for this new book and the deal and all that. I know it's been a tough few years for you and I just wanted to say that, well, your dad would have been proud of you, son. That's all.'

The older man patted him on the shoulder a couple of times and then gave him a gentle shove to help him on his way. This time, as Clyde walked away from Shiloh, he did so with a skip in his step. Yeah, he mused, his old man would have been proud of him. He was kind of proud of himself. And as he jumped in his shiny new truck and headed for the airport, Clyde hoped that someone else might be proud of him too.

The phone beeped and a new message flashed up on the screen. He was outside. Rebecca checked her reflection one more time in the hall mirror and then smiled, satisfied. Yeah, she looked OK. In fact she looked pretty damn hot, even if she did say so herself! She was excited about this date. Really excited. It was the first time she'd felt good about a fledgling relationship since ... Well, since that messy business last year. But, hey, she wasn't going to think about that now. Tonight was about the future.

She pulled on her new leather jacket and slammed the door behind her before skipping down the stairs two at a time. She threw open the door to the street and looked up and down for his car. Ah, there it was, just up the road.

'Hello, Rebecca,' a familiar voice called out in the darkness.

Rebecca jumped. Her heart stopped for a second. The temperature felt as if it had suddenly dropped a few degrees. She turned, horrified, towards the man who had called her name.

'Sebastian,' she said, trying to keep the fear out of her voice. 'What are you doing here?'

Sebastian shrugged nonchalantly. 'I was in the area. I'm just passing. What a coincidence, eh?'

He looked just the same. He sounded just the same. The smug, arrogant expression on his face was exactly the same. Rebecca wasn't sure what she'd been expecting – a cripple? A shadow of the man she'd once known and loved? Somebody broken and belittled who would apologise for what he'd done?

'You look well,' she said. 'I'm glad you're OK. After that terrible business in St Barts.'

Sebastian grinned. 'Takes more than a bullet to kill me,' he boasted.

'Well, erm, um, it was good to see you,' lied Rebecca, backing away from her ex-lover. 'I have to go now. My, erm, my friend is waiting for me, there, in that car.'

'Friend?' asked Sebastian, his eyebrow raising. 'Boyfriend?'

Rebecca shrugged now. 'Maybe, I don't know,' she said, truthfully. 'It's only our third date. But he's nice. I like him.'

She began to walk away.

'Nice is overrated,' called Sebastian, after her. 'You don't want nice.'

Rebecca spun on her heels and faced Sebastian. 'Yes, I do,' she said firmly. 'I had my fill of nasty when I was with you.'

'You don't mean that,' teased Sebastian. 'You still love me. I know you do. I can see it in your eyes. You want me.'

Rebecca laughed then. She threw her head back and laughed so hard that her stomach hurt. 'No, Sebastian. I am so over you that I am actually cringing now at the thought that I ever had any feelings for you at all. I don't know what I was thinking!'

'I suppose I deserve that,' replied Sebastian. 'But I know how you feel, Rebecca. You're not over me. You're not over what we had. It was special. It happens once. You can't walk away from that.'

'Watch me,' was all Rebecca said as she walked calmly away.

And he did watch her. He watched her intently. She could see in his eyes that he wanted to run after her – just like she had wanted to run after him all those times he'd walked away from her – but his pride stopped him. Something had shifted. They both knew that Sebastian couldn't catch her now. She was beyond his reach.

Rebecca glanced back over her shoulder briefly. The man she had once loved, and looked up to, and bowed down to, suddenly looked a little bit older and smaller than before. For a moment she almost felt sorry for him. But the feeling didn't last long. The truth was she didn't feel anything for him any more. She jumped into her date's car, kissed him hard on the lips, and they sped off towards the West End, leaving Sebastian Hunter alone on an empty suburban street.

Lauren checked her emails in her hotel room as she waited for reception to call up and tell her that her cab had arrived. She smiled. There was one from Emily and Poppy telling her how much they missed her but that they'd done all their homework and that they were behaving for Granny and Grandpa. Honest, Mum! They said they hoped she was having a good time in New York and that they loved her very much. There was another from Kitty which simply said, 'I hope you waxed, lady!' and there was one from Molly in St Barts telling her about the work she and Henri had done on the resort and inviting her to come and stay, free of charge, whenever she liked. Molly said that Lexi and Mal were there now, celebrating their first wedding anniversary. Molly said they were all having a ball. She'd attached some pictures of Henri and Mal hanging out at the refurbished beach bar. Lauren laughed out loud when she saw the new sign: Clyde's Bar!

Wow, a whole year had passed since that fateful week in St Barthélemy. In some ways the year had gone very quickly. In other ways it felt like a lifetime ago. Lauren could barely remember what life had felt like before that trip. How could one holiday change so many lives? It had been a tough year.

The girls had been in bits about their father being shot, of course. Well, it had been a shock for everyone. Things like that just didn't happen to people like Sebastian Hunter! But in some ways he'd been lucky. The bullet had lodged in his upper thigh and done serious tissue damage but it had missed the femur, the major arteries and, despite Gabriel Abbot's best efforts, it had also missed his groin by milli metres. And so Sebastian's womanising days were not over. But his life with Lauren was. He was Emily and Poppy's dad, and she was very glad he was still alive, but he was no longer her husband. She had filed for divorce the minute he was well enough to read the papers.

Sebastian now seemed almost untouched by the attack. He still had a very slight limp, but he hadn't really changed at all. He still worked hard. He was still patronising and superior. He still had a flash car. He still wore designer suits and he still had a perma-tan, even in January! He had not taken Lauren's departure well but she was smart enough to know that it was his pride and his bank balance she'd hurt by leaving, rather than his heart. Needless to say she was not at the top of his Christmas card list at present. According to Emily, Lauren's ex-husband was currently dating a twenty-three-year-old dancer. Last month it was a waitress. The month before it was the girls' swimming instructor. And the month before that it was his physiotherapist. He saw his daughters now and again, when he could squeeze them in between dates. Poppy said she had seen him crying once. When he thought she was in bed. She said he was holding a photo of Lauren and the girls and was weeping on the sofa. Lauren thought that Poppy had probably been dreaming. That couldn't possibly be true. Could it?

Lauren had got through the year by throwing herself into work and had been surprised at how quickly the commissions had rolled in. There were work emails too but Lauren ignored them. This was a holiday, not a work trip. She closed her laptop.

Reception rang to say her taxi was waiting. Lauren checked her hair, make-up and dress one more time in the mirror. She felt sick with nerves and her stomach was doing somersaults, but Lauren was excited in a good way. Maybe she was out of her mind. But there was one thing she'd learned this year: you have to grasp life with both hands when you get the chance. She put on her coat, grabbed her handbag and picked up the invitation.

'Aurelia Publications invite you to the book launch of the year. *My Sharona: A New York Tale* a true story by Clyde Scott.'

Lauren shut the hotel room door behind her, went down ten floors in the lift and walked out into the freezing New York night. She jumped in the big yellow taxi that was waiting for her and sped away. Quite where she was headed Lauren had no idea. But she was going there willingly. Wherever she was headed had to be better than the place she'd come from.